Acquired Tastes

• • •

Simone Mondesir was born in London, but spent her childhood on RAF bases in the Far and Middle East. Educated at a convent boarding school in Essex, she read a degree in Middle Eastern History at the School of Oriental and African Studies, London University. After flirting briefly with an academic career, she became a journalist. She has worked for ITV, the BBC and Channel 4, as well as running her own TV production company. Now, as well as writing, she also works as a consultant on television and broadcasting. *Acquired Tastes* is her first novel.

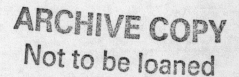

Simone Mondesir

• • •

Acquired
Tastes

Mandarin

A Mandarin Paperback
ACQUIRED TASTES

First published in Great Britain 1996
by Mandarin Paperbacks,
an imprint of Reed International Books Ltd
Michelin House, 81 Fulham Road, London SW3 6RB
and Auckland, Melbourne, Singapore and Toronto

A CIP catalogue record for this title
is available from the British Library
ISBN 0 7493 2251 9

Phototypeset by Intype Ltd, London
Printed and bound in Great Britain
by Cox & Wyman, Reading, Berkshire

For my mother

To all the friends who have topped up my wine glass and kept me laughing as well as sane, my heartfelt thanks. Especially to Corinne de Souza for Brighton which started me writing, to Simi Bedford, Jaci Stephen and Lizzi Becker whose support kept me writing, and to Darley Anderson, my agent, whose enthusiasm got me through the last rewrite!

One
• • •

'Men,' Vanessa announced loudly, her index finger tracing the contours of a large, plump peach, 'should be like summer peaches: firm and hairy to the touch.'

She bit sharply into the ripe flesh and pale sticky juice trickled down her fingers. She licked them clean, the tip of her tongue protruding pinkly cat-like between her lips.

'When bitten they should be sweet and juicy, but when stripped bare . . .' She paused theatrically before pulling the hapless fruit in half, exposing the wrinkled brown stone at its centre, 'they should be very, very hard.'

There was an expectant hush at the surrounding restaurant tables. Vanessa leaned conspiratorially across the table towards her companion as though to whisper, but her final pronouncement could be heard within a radius of ten feet.

'The trouble is most men are like prunes – one taste and you want to run.'

Vanessa dropped the broken fruit on to her plate and raised her wine glass in an ironic toast to her mainly male audience. There was a sudden chorus of deep-throated harrumphs as heads turned away.

'Vanessa . . .' The voice of her companion was hesitant.

Vanessa's day-glo pink mini dress, which clung to

1

her five-foot ten, whippet-thin body by the merest whisper of material, formed a stark contrast to the clothes of her companion who looked small and round and dun-coloured beside her. Even though it was a hot summer's day, Alicia was dressed in a beige wool twin set and a stout tweed skirt.

'I'm sorry . . . perhaps I shouldn't ask, but . . .' Alicia's voice faltered and then trailed off again.

'Why must you always apologise for everything you say or do?' snapped Vanessa. 'For heaven's sake Alicia, spit it out.'

'I'm sorry . . .' Alicia began again and then checked herself. 'What I mean to say is, you never seem to talk much about how you . . . you and Jeremy split up.'

'Jeremy and I are divorced. You know, D-I-V-O-R-C-E-D, like the song said.' Vanessa spelt the word out rather too loudly.

Alicia nervously shredded a paper napkin as heads turned in their direction again.

'You surely don't still believe in all that old crap about divorce and mortal sin, do you?'

Vanessa laughed. 'Christ almighty Alicia, we left the Convent nearly twen . . . well, an awful long time ago, and I gave up believing in all that hell-fire and brimstone stuff well before that.'

'Oh no, I didn't mean it like that,' Alicia said quickly. 'It's just that I thought . . . well . . . it might still be painful to talk about it.'

'Painful?' Vanessa sounded incredulous. 'It's the best thing that I've ever done. God knows I must have loved the little shit once, but for the life of me I can't remember when or why.'

Vanessa poured some more wine into her glass and drank deeply.

Alicia sipped her Perrier water thoughtfully. She was sure Vanessa had been a lot more hurt about the breakup of her marriage than she said, but Vanessa had

2

always found it hard to show her feelings, even when they were at school together.

Vanessa Swift, or Sprunt as she had been then, and Alicia Binns had first met on an unseasonably cold and damp day early in September 1968. Together with thirty other eleven-year-olds, they had stood on the steps of St Aloysius' Boarding School for Young Ladies, surrounded by trunks and sobbing mothers.

Everyone that is, except for Vanessa and Alicia.

Vanessa had planned to arrive in her father's chauffeured Bentley but much to her annoyance, her mother had insisted on taking both the Bentley and the chauffeur on a shopping trip to London, so she was driven to school by her father's elderly secretary in an equally elderly Wolsey. Now she stood slightly apart from the rest of the new girls, clutching an overnight bag in her kid-gloved hands, the rest of her matching luggage piled neatly beside her.

Alicia arrived last, spluttering up to the school steps in the sidecar of her father's motorbike, one hand holding her hat to her head, the other trying to hold on to the assortment of bags and boxes which had been stacked around her. Strapped to the back of the bike was a disintegrating trunk which bore her father's service number and the names of assorted foreign military outposts, testament to the remnants of a post-war Empire much reduced in size, but still in need of a token British presence.

Having hurriedly unloaded Alicia and her possessions, her father had awkwardly shaken her hand and then headed back to married quarters, where Alicia's mother was packing for yet another overseas posting.

A flock of nuns descended on the now weeping girls and herded them into the building, cooing words of comfort as they gently but firmly separated them from their mothers who, with much fluttering of white

3

handkerchiefs, had bid a last bosom-heaving farewell to their dear little ones.

United by their mutual motherlessness, Alicia and Vanessa had given each other cautious, dry-eyed looks and fallen into step at the back.

'How do you do?' Vanessa held out a kid-gloved hand. 'My name's Vanessa Sprunt. My father owns lots of factories.'

The small bare hand that briefly touched hers was still blue with cold from the motorbike ride.

'I'm Alicia, Alicia Binns.'

'And what does your father do?'

'He's in the army, but he's leaving on Sunday. He's been posted to Singapore.'

For the first time Alicia had looked slightly tremulous. Behind the pink plastic frames of her round National Health glasses her eyes grew watery, and a tear slid down her cheek. It was quickly followed by several more.

Vanessa looked Alicia up and down, noting her overlarge and distinctly second-hand uniform. Vanessa's mother Gwenda had impressed upon her that the girls she'd been meeting at her new school were in possession of two things she needed to acquire: class and breeding. Socialising with them would give Vanessa entry into the right circles.

Her mother's new-found obsession with the right circles had coincided with the family's move to a mock-Tudor mansion in one of the leafier areas of Barnet in North London. At the same time Vanessa's father Ted had acquired a new building for the headquarters of his business empire, which was moving away from the manufacture of saucy seaside novelties into quality china and ceramic souvenirs for the growing foreign tourist trade. To go with his new, streamlined business venture, Ted had decided that it was only fit he should have a proper secretary and so

4

Gwenda, who had worked for him since he first set up business in one cramped room off Brick Lane, had become a full time housewife. Since Ted had employed a cook and a housekeeper to go with the mock-Tudor mansion, Gwenda had a lot of time on her hands, which she filled with the voracious consumption of glossy magazines, whose society pages had opened up a whole new world to her – a world she was determined her daughter would enter. Unfortunately Ted, who was otherwise generous with his money, had refused to allow Vanessa to go to one of the more well-known girls' public schools, as he considered money spent on educating a girl was wasted. He believed it was better spent on pretty dresses, since they showed a better return on the investment. St Aloysius had been a compromise, but that had not deterred Gwenda from indulging in a frenzy of preparation so that, as in her constantly repeated mantra, *nobody* could look down on *her* daughter. It was the first time in Vanessa's eleven-year-old existence that she had considered the possibility that anyone might be able to look down on her and it had caused her some trepidation, but it had disappeared the moment she spotted Alicia. Here was someone she could look down on and moreover, someone who appeared to be grateful for it. She smiled solicitously at Alicia.

'Is your father a Colonel or something?' she enquired.

Alicia looked down. 'No, he's a Regimental Sergeant Major.'

Vanessa produced a monogrammed handkerchief which Alicia used loudly.

'Don't worry about a thing. Just follow me,' said Vanessa, taking charge of the situation. An overawed Alicia had been content to do just that – follow Vanessa – and little had changed about their friendship in twenty years.

'Sex was always Jeremy's problem,' Vanessa said,

waving the empty wine bottle at a passing waiter who promptly replaced it. Alicia put her hand over her glass as the waiter attempted to refill it but Vanessa held hers up impatiently.

'He felt it was his duty to perform once a week, in bed and with the lights out. If I blinked my eyes it was all over. God, he was so predictable.' Vanessa drained her glass. 'When I dared to suggest that there were other ways to do it other than with him on top, he couldn't get it up for weeks.' She threw back her head and shrieked with laughter.

Alicia shifted uneasily in her chair, aware that Vanessa had regained her audience at the surrounding tables. She tried to steer the conversation back on to a more congenial subject.

'How's your job going these days? It always sounds so glamorous.'

'Working in television isn't all a bed of roses you know, although everybody thinks it is,' said Vanessa. 'Sometimes I long for the quiet life like you. No pressures, no rat race, no endlessly trying to prove yourself better than the next man.'

'Oh, but university life has its own pressures,' Alicia said eagerly. 'There's always a lot of competition for any available post, particularly with all the cutbacks. Only the other day . . .'

'But of course my life does have its compensations,' Vanessa continued, as though Alicia hadn't spoken. 'The money, the people, the way the adrenalin races when you are about to go on air.'

'But what *exactly* is it that you do?' asked Alicia. 'I always keep a look out for your name at the end of programmes just in case, but I must be watching the wrong sort of programmes.'

'I'm strictly a back-room boy at the moment, but there are big things in the pipeline,' Vanessa said airily. 'PP and I, that's Philip Pryce of Right Pryce Productions, one of the biggest noises in independent production, PP and I have got some really super ideas that will put us right up there among the major players.'

'So you don't work for the BBC any more? Oh dear, I've been telling everyone that you run one of the departments there, documentaries or something. I get a bit muddled, it all seems so awfully technical.'

Alicia never seemed to be able to keep up with Vanessa's career. Academic posts were so hard to get, people tended to hang on to them for life, but Vanessa seemed to change jobs every couple of months. 'The BBC was nothing, merely a stepping stone.' Vanessa waved her hand dismissively, with all the authority that her three-month stint as a temporary secretary in the documentary department had given her.

'The independent sector is where it's all happening these days, not that I'd expect you to know that, tucked away from the real world in your cosy little academic nest up there in the Styx. The BBC is a dinosaur and well on its way to extinction. I wouldn't be caught dead working for it anymore. I'm at the heart of the media revolution these days. We're talking satellite, cable, interactive programming, the demand is insatiable.'

Vanessa leaned across the table, stabbing a long magenta-tipped index finger at Alicia to emphasise her point as she grew more excited. 'It's dog eat dog out there, no room for the faint-hearted.'

She reached over and with the same finger, scooped some cream off the top of the cheesecake Alicia was eating. Vanessa had ordered fruit, but had insisted Alicia order from the dessert trolley. After all, Alicia never seemed bothered about the way she looked and it showed, thought Vanessa. She was beginning to look positively middle-aged. Vanessa caught sight of her own reflection in a mirror opposite and smiled. No one could possibly believe that she was nearly a year older

7

than Alicia. She may be thirty-six, but she looked at least ten years younger.

'Gosh, it all seems an awfully long way from my little concerns over finishing my research paper and preparing tutorials, although Fergus says that I am much too conscientious and work far too hard.' A hint of colour came into Alicia's cheeks.

'Fergus?' Vanessa looked away from the mirror; she could scent sex at twenty paces. 'Who's Fergus?'

'Dr Fergus Archibald,' Alicia said proudly, 'is a lecturer in the Psychology Department at Heartlands University. He should have been departmental head, but there are certain people . . .' Alicia lowered her voice and looked around as though 'they' might be hiding somewhere in the restaurant, 'who are jealous of his brilliant mind.'

Vanessa waved a hand dismissively at what were, to her, matters of little import. 'But do you and him . . .?'

The unspoken word trailed in the air like a blazing comet.

'Vanessa,' Alicia protested, flushing deep red.

'Well, don't you think it's about time you got laid? They don't give prizes for saving it, you know, and Prince Charmings are at the top of the endangered species list. So,' demanded Vanessa scooping another helping of cream, 'is this Fergus person the one . . .?'

Alicia prodded the cheesecake. It was double chocolate cheesecake and well worth its name. 'It's a bit too early to say. I've only known him two semesters.'

'And you haven't been to bed with him! Is he queer or something? You do have a way of picking them, Alicia.'

Vanessa's reference to an earlier disastrous crush that she had formed on a fellow scholar of dubious sexuality, caused Alicia to bridle.

'Fergus is very masculine,' she burst out. It was a rare act of defiance and quickly recanted. She lowered

8

her eyes, 'It's not him, it's me. I'm not like you, Vanessa. You've always been so confident about, well . . . men and things.'

By 'things', Alicia meant sex. Something Vanessa had been aware of from the moment her mother had dressed her in pink satin and lace, strapped her plump little toddler's feet into silver patent leather shoes and urged her to smile and 'ask pappa nicely'.

Vanessa had needed little further bidding and quickly learned that pappa wasn't the only male who, for the price of a smile or a girlish kiss, would press whatever it was she wanted into her outstretched hands. Being sent to St Aloysius had temporarily denied her the requisite males on whom to try out her rapidly maturing charms, but Vanessa had soon found that girlish adoration could be quite as heady.

In the hothouse atmosphere of a girls' boarding school, matters bodily and sexual counted more than academic diligence, which was just as well for Vanessa, for while she was a walking encyclopedia on the former, she came near the bottom on the latter.

While the rest of the Upper Fourth had greeted the changes wrought on their bodies by the sudden rush of hormones like an ancient Greek chorus, plucking helplessly at the unwelcome flesh on their thighs, keening at the eruption of pimples, and hiding their faces with shame as they were forced to deal monthly with a part of their bodies that hitherto they had been taught to pretend didn't exist, Vanessa had watched, untouched by angst as her olive-toned skin remained unfairly clear, and her body grew long and sleek. And with the confidence born of having started her periods first, Vanessa had confidently predicted that she would be the first to wear a bra.

But for once her confidence was not to be rewarded.

No matter how much she thrust out her chest, or how many times she swung her arms backwards and

9

forwards silently chanting, 'I must, I must improve my bust' in the privacy of her cubicle at night, the rosebud-trimmed cups of Vanessa's Modern Miss bra remained resolutely unfilled.

In her cubicle, Alicia sat hugging herself in silent misery, hoping that the pronounced and unwelcome change in her anatomy would miraculously go away. Even attending early morning mass on twenty-seven successive days had failed to have any effect. Her breasts were not so much budding as sprouting.

Up until their unwanted intrusion, Alicia had happily managed to survive largely unnoticed. While consistently in the top three in her year, she had never sought popularity or friendship other than with Vanessa. It had been impressed upon her that as a scholarship girl, great things were expected academically, and she was determined not to disappoint anyone.

Vanessa had lots of other friends but Alicia never felt jealous; in fact she was rather proud that someone who thought of her as a friend should be so popular. Anyway, nobody else in Vanessa's set was able to help her with her schoolwork in the way Alicia could, so why should she feel jealous?

But Vanessa felt more than jealous when Alicia's breasts dared to not just show, but thrust themselves into prominence. She considered them a personal affront, as did their housemistress, Sister Mary, who considered them unbecoming in a young lady in her charge.

Unfortunately, her disapproval had no more effect on the size of the offending breasts than Alicia's prayers, and so it was that one Sunday morning after mass, an embarrassed Alicia found herself standing in front of the thin-lipped triumvirate of Reverend Mother, Sister Mary and Sister Gertrude. They gazed sternly at the buttons on the front of her blouse, which steadfastly refused to stay done up. Tears of shame pricked Alicia's eyes and she had clenched her fists and willed herself not to cry.

Reverend Mother had peered over the top of her half moon glasses. 'Perhaps we ought to leave it in the hands of her mother, a letter . . .?' Her tone was patient although tinged with asperity.

She liked to keep Sunday morning audiences for matters of a moral or a spiritual nature, it seemed only right and fitting. Alicia Binn's breasts were of a distinctly temporal nature and well within the province of a housemistress to resolve.

Sister Mary's nostrils flared, 'Her mother is in Singapore.' She ennunciated the words like an accusation of a dereliction of duty.

Reverend Mother let out a little 'Ah' and sat down behind her desk. She fingered the crucifix around her neck for a few moments and then looked up at Sister Gertrude, whose chief duty was the supervision of habits for the nuns and school uniforms for the girls.

'I think we should pray for guidance,' suggested Sister Gertrude brightly.

Sister Mary had given the older nun a look that was less than charitable, but had joined Reverend Mother in lowering her head.

Alicia had screwed up her eyes and clasped her hands tightly together. She was fast running out of things to offer God, if he would only grant her wish to be flat-chested again. She had added a rosary to her nightly prayers, and had taken to saying them kneeling, bare-kneed on the hard and splinter-ridden dormitory floor, rather than lying in bed, offering up her discomfort as a sacrifice. Her attempt to bathe only in cold water had also not succeeded. The water had been so icy Alicia could not bear to do more than stand shivering in it before she had leapt out. Unfortunately, Sister Mary had been waiting outside the bathroom

11

door, checking that each bather made the requisite amount of splashing and took enough time to thoroughly cleanse their body. Taking *too* much time suggested the sin of vanity and *too* little, the sin of slovenliness, errors of equal magnitude in Sister Mary's eyes. She had marched Alicia back into the bathroom and subjected her to the indignity of a strip wash, which had revealed what Alicia had been trying so hard to conceal.

With a loud, 'Amen', Sister Gertrude finished. 'I always find a little prayer to St Jude, patron saint of hopeless causes, helps,' she beamed.

Sister Mary gestured impatiently at Alicia's still-tumescent chest. 'What we need, Mother Mary Gertrude, is a practical solution. I won't have one of my girls making such a vulgar display of herself.'

Alicia miserably pulled her cardigan across her front and tried unsuccessfully to button it up.

'The Upper Fourth needlework project,' Sister Gertrude announced triumphantly. 'We'll make liberty bodices this term. It's the sort of thing which will be useful for all the girls when their time comes.' She smiled sweetly at Sister Mary, 'There's always a solution if you look in the right place.'

St Jude had been vindicated yet again.

'Praise be to God, Mother Mary, let this be a lesson to us all. The power of prayer succeeds where mere human endeavours fail.' Reverend Mother held up her hands as though in benediction, but it was also a sign that they were all dismissed.

'The Lord sends us trials so that we can overcome them,' intoned Sister Gertrude.

'Amen to that,' Sister Mary added, as she took Alicia by the shoulder and marched her out of the room.

Unfortunately, neither the Lord nor St Jude had allowed for the Upper Fourth's needlework skills. They took up the challenge of making a bodice with considerably more imagination than expertise and the resulting garment bore little resemblance to the portion of Alicia's anatomy that it was meant to confine and minimise.

However, it did restore Vanessa's equanimity and, as she explained to a mortified Alicia, it was a well-known fact that large breasts were distinctly common, and no man from the right sort of background liked them.

Although one of the kindly younger nuns later took Alicia on a shopping expedition, which resulted in the purchase of a suitable, though depressingly ugly bra, Alicia's private opinion of her unattractiveness had been confirmed publicly and humiliatingly.

Since then she had been in full retreat from the world, affecting shapeless clothes and wearing her light brown hair long, so that it fell in a veil across her face in a style she had not changed in twenty years. She always wore glasses, even though her optician told her there was no need to wear them all the time. Lately, however, she had taken to wearing large, brightly-coloured frames, the one splash of colour in an otherwise beige appearance.

'I'd like you to meet Fergus sometime, I'm sure you'd like him.'

Alicia's eyes looked beseechingly from behind her glasses. The habit of seeking approval for her actions was as strong now as it had been when they were eleven-year-olds.

'He's at work on a radical new examination of the meaning of sexual fantasies. He says it will revolutionise thinking about human sexuality.' She lowered her voice. 'Confidentially, Fergus is considering turning his paper into a book. It's already been turned down by the reactionary old academics who edit most of the big psychology journals, but he thinks it's about time he went public, so to speak. If the book is a best-seller, the university hierarchy will be made to look very silly.'

'Sexual fantasies?' Vanessa stopped admiring herself in the mirrored restaurant walls. 'What kind of fantasies?'

'I really couldn't describe them over the dinner table. Some of them are, well, really very odd.' Alicia's voice was so hushed, Vanessa was forced to lean across the table. 'I really can't understand how people can think some of the things they do, but Fergus says we are socialised into being ashamed of our perfectly natural desires, and that we should be able to bring them out into the open and enact them if possible. He says we would all be much healthier if we did, and that many so-called illnesses are just cases of sexual frustration. He intends to call the book *Terminal Diagnosis – A Report on the Nation's Sexual Health*.' Alicia's voice had sunk to a whisper.

Vanessa leaned back in her seat and stared. Either this man was trying the most complicated come-on with Alicia she had ever heard, or . . .

She snapped her fingers at a passing waiter. 'Pen,' she demanded crisply, and when it arrived, began scribbling on her napkin.

Assuming she had once again lost her friend's attention, Alicia was just about to change the subject when Vanessa looked up. 'I'd like to meet this Angus person of yours sometime, maybe read a copy of his research.'

Alicia was about to correct her, but before she could say anything, Vanessa looked pointedly at her watch.

'Is that the time? Must rush. I've got an ideas meeting with PP and the rest of the team. Got to get the old grey matter churning over creatively. My treat this time. Put it on expenses.'

Vanessa slapped down some large notes, picked up the bill and ushered Alicia, still struggling to find her purse, through the restaurant and out on to the pavement.

'Enjoy your afternoon with the corpses. I'll call you soon, lovely to see you.'

Vanessa kissed the air beside Alicia's cheeks while hailing a taxi at the same time. Alicia stood bewildered for a moment, dazzled by the bright sunshine and the noise of traffic on the Old Brompton Road. Then she thought of the cool quiet of the British Museum Reading Room, and tightly clutching her bulging briefcase, headed for the Underground.

Two
. . .

'Beautiful day, isn't it darling?'

Dark eyes flashed at Vanessa in the driving mirror.

A pudgy forefinger casually guided the steering wheel, beefy forearm resting on the open window. As the taxi shuddered to a halt in the traffic yet again, the taxi driver leaned back in his seat and half turned his head.

Vanessa glimpsed a Mediterranean profile.

'Had a good lunch? That place is a bit too expensive for my tastes, but I bet a good-looking woman like you doesn't pick up the tab too often.'

The voice was pure Balls Pond Road.

Vanessa toyed briefly with the idea of deflating his over-active libido, but she had far too much on her mind. She leaned forward and snapped the glass partition firmly shut.

As she did, the large cluster of diamonds on her right hand glittered as it caught the light. The ring had been a little reward to herself for divorcing Jeremy. It was about the only worthwhile thing she had got out of her relationship with him, and even then she had bought it herself. It was the story of her life.

Why Alicia always had to ask about Jeremy when they met, she did not know, although she suspected Alicia might once have had a crush on him. She always blushed and stammered whenever Jeremy spoke to her.

She should have known she was making a mistake with Jeremy right from the start, Vanessa mused. After all, they had met at a cricket match and she simply *hated* cricket.

If she remembered rightly, it was nearly eight years ago. Gavin, Vanessa's then current boyfriend, had been captain of the host team, and had expected her to make tea for all the players, so she had enlisted Alicia to bake sponge cakes and butter mountains of bread. Nobody had been the wiser, not even Gavin who went on and on about Vanessa being 'absolutely spiffing' and 'a jolly good sport' for preparing such splendid tea. Vanessa thought that kind of language had gone out with the ark until she met Gavin, but as his father was rumoured to be in the mega-rich bracket, she had been prepared to tolerate it.

Even so, she was not prepared to sit for hours on a damp, uncomfortable deckchair in a biting wind which Gavin assured her was bracing, while some silly men hit a ball around a field, so she had retired to the relative comfort of the pavilion, where Alicia was doing the washing-up.

Thoroughly bored, she ventured out on to the verandah in time to see a tall, dark-haired man with satisfyingly broad shoulders and a determined look on his handsome face, thundering down the field. His arm had shot up and then his back had arched rather fetchingly as he leapt into the air and bowled a blistering delivery that had scattered the stumps of the opposing batsman, stopping him reaching his threatened half century.

The small crowd of spectators had risen cheering to its feet and Vanessa joined in, even if her appreciation was more for the perfection of the bowler's buttocks than his delivery. It was only then that she noticed that the batsman who had been bowled out was Gavin.

Gavin had trailed back to the pavilion looking

dejected, but if he hoped for any solace from Vanessa it was to be unforthcoming. She hated losers and had already pushed her way through the crowd of admirers around Jeremy to introduce herself.

At the time, Jeremy was engaged to a wraith-like blonde called Chloe who had spent two years designing and making peach and dove grey antique lace-trimmed outfits, based on a Gainsborough painting, for her six bridesmaids and four page boys. But Chloe had not stood a chance against Vanessa. Two months after the cricket match, Vanessa and Jeremy plighted their troth in the very marquee that should have witnessed the sit-down lunch for two hundred, with dove grey table linen and peach rose floral displays lovingly planned by Chloe.

Jeremy had felt guilty about using the same marquee, but Vanessa argued that if it hadn't been for Chloe's last minute cancellation, how else could they have got a marquee in June?

But to Vanessa's disgust, Jeremy's killer instinct on the cricket pitch had not extended to the money markets where he worked. While all around him in the City were getting rich in the get-rich-quick Eighties, he was content to remain in a back-water division of the merchant bank in which several generations of male Swifts had served, safe in the knowledge that a directorship awaited them no matter what their skills, or indeed, their lack of them.

Jeremy proved immune to Vanessa's relentless urging to make more money. For some reason that was beyond her, he claimed to be perfectly happy. When she brought the subject up, he would wait for her to finish and then smile that silly lopsided smile of his and ruffle her hair or kiss her on the end of the nose and say something irritating like 'as long as I have you Vee, I'm the richest man in the world'. It drove her mad that he wouldn't argue with her, no matter what she said.

Forced to accept that Jeremy was not and never would be a financial firebrand, Vanessa had decided that her only hope was Jeremy's father. Before their wedding, she had checked on Swift senior's financial standing, which although not quite in Gavin's father's league, was not inconsiderable. He was also a lot older than Jeremy's mother, and at the time of their wedding had appeared to be close to his demise. But he had proved tougher than he looked, and Vanessa had been forced to wait a further three years before Swift senior met his fate at the age of eighty-three, falling off his horse in pursuit of hunt saboteurs while riding to hounds.

Vanessa had entertained high hopes for the will reading, but they were cruelly dashed. Jeremy's father had left the bulk of his fortune in tax and tamper proof trusts to his grandchildren. The income from the trusts was bequeathed to Jeremy and his older brother James, on the proviso that they, too, produced sons or, failing that, a reduced proportion on the production of daughters.

As Jeremy's older brother James, and his redoubtable wife Lucinda, had already produced four boys, it looked as if they would be the principle beneficiaries.

Jeremy's suggestion that in the circumstances, they too might now consider having children – a long but secretly held ambition on his part – had not met with quite the reception he would have wished.

'*Children*, what on earth do you want children for?' Vanessa had demanded.

'I thought you might like them too. You know, the patter of tiny feet and all that. After all, we could easily move into the country to make room for a litter,' Jeremy said brightly.

Vanessa's lip curled. 'If you wanted a good breeder,

you should have married someone like your brother's wife. I mean, *four* children in *six* years, frankly, I think that's obscene. Have you taken a good look at Lucinda lately, her boobs will reach her knees if she doesn't stop breast-feeding soon.'

Jeremy had looked pained. 'That's a bit strong Vanessa. I mean, fair's fair, Lucinda is a jolly good mother. Those four boys take a lot of looking after.'

'That's exactly it. Who has to walk around looking like a beached whale for nine months? The woman. Who has to clear up all the mess and the puke? The woman. Who has to . . .'

'All right, all right,' Jeremy interrupted, 'I see your point, but I assumed you would have someone to help. I'm still in touch with old Nanny Greig. As a matter of fact, its her birthday next week, and I thought I might pop over with some chocolates or something. I could float the idea by her.'

Vanessa's voice was heavy with sarcasm. 'Wonderful. I do so love your bright ideas, Jeremy. Not only do you want me to ruin my figure bearing assorted little Swifts, but you also want me to turn my house into a geriatric home for senile nannies. Sometimes you astound me.'

Vanessa had waited for Jeremy to get angry. She got the impression that he and his brother James had been largely raised by their beloved Nanny Greig, and Jeremy, who was the baby of the family, had been particularly attached to her. When he spoke of her it was in reverent tones.

For a moment she thought she had succeeded. The colour drained from Jeremy's face and his jaw moved in an agitated way. But he had simply stood up and walked over to the window where he stood with his back to her.

After a moment he had spoken. His voice shook. 'Vanessa, there are times when I think my mother was

20

right. She said you would never understand the duties of being a wife, and although I'm prepared to put up with a lot, insulting Nanny Greig is going too far.'

Vanessa had leapt to her feet and gone to the door. 'Frankly Jeremy, I couldn't give a damn for your mother, your nanny or anyone else connected with the great Swift family. Please read my lips: I do not now, nor will I ever, want children,' and with that, she slammed the door behind her.

Jeremy had never been the same again. The marriage lasted another three years before Vanessa threw him out, and for the last year communication between them had shrunken to words of one syllable and the occasional lawyer's letter, which was why she could not understand the reason for Jeremy calling last night and begging to see her.

Her instinct had been to tell him where to go, but curiosity had got the better of her, so she told him to be at her flat at six that afternoon, which would give her time to change before a hot dinner date that evening.

Vanessa glanced at her watch. The taxi was edging forward, negotiating the traffic around Hyde Park Corner inch by inch. It would take at least another ten minutes to get to the office, which meant she was going to be late for the production meeting. Philip Pryce would not be a happy man.

She snapped open her compact and deftly reapplied her lipstick. In some ways, Philip reminded her of Jeremy. They were both irritatingly diffident when it came to dealing with women. She had been working for Philip for nearly a year now and he still hadn't made a pass at her.

She had dismissed the possibility of Philip being gay – the usual grapevine had yielded no gossip to this effect – and no matter how much they tried, nobody could be that discreet; word always got out.

Anyway, Vanessa decided, as she studied her face in her compact mirror, she had never yet been wrong about a man. No, if the problem was anywhere, it had to be with Philip. It was just a question of discovering his particular taste in sex.

Vanessa and Philip had met at a post-award party she'd gate-crashed. It was an opportune meeting as she had just seen a confidential memo about staff restructuring in the ITV company where she was then working. It had been difficult to read upside down on her boss's desk, but she got the distinct feeling that she would not be considered vital to the new structure.

Vanessa always trusted her instincts. Knowing when to leave was one of her talents, and so far she had managed to do it just before anyone found her out. There was always gossip of course, but she moved so frequently, it barely had time to catch up with her before she moved on to the next job. She had always found parties, rather than offices, happy hunting grounds for advancement, as they allowed her to show off her particular qualifications far better than her curriculum vitae.

Alcohol had the advantage of both lowering critical faculties and inducing indiscretions, which could later be used to her advantage. Vanessa invariably found that once she had seen a man with his trousers around his ankles, he found it difficult to look her in the eye and was only too happy to help her in any way she asked. Vanessa never considered it blackmail, as she never had to threaten anything.

Getting into parties which were by invitation only was another of her skills. It was just a question of looking important and claiming very loudly that you were joining someone suitably impressive inside as you walked through the door. The trick was not to hesitate, even if someone tried to stop you. It never failed to work.

On the evening she met Philip, Vanessa was wondering whether it had been worth taking so much trouble. She had introduced herself to the recipients of the most important awards of the evening, and found herself looking down at the bald pates of a group of portly middle-aged men, still lachrymose after the fulsome and sentimental eulogies they had made about each other at the ceremony earlier.

Only one of them had shown any interest in her, and judging by his lopsided leer, she suspected he was already past his best. Vanessa had just begun to make her excuses when yet another prize-winner joined the group.

'Philip. Congratulations!' The man with the lopsided leer slapped the newcomer on the back, almost causing him to drop the bronze statuette he was carrying. 'If you keep this up you won't have any room left on your mantlepiece.'

General laughter greeted this sally. They could afford to be generous, they were all winners tonight.

Philip had lifted his award aloft. It resembled a globe artichoke. 'Not quite the Golden Rose, but who knows, maybe next year,' he had replied to more laughter.

Vanessa surreptitiously studied the newcomer's appearance which teetered on the edge of flamboyance. Pearl-grey suit, matching shoes, grey and pink paisley waistcoat and grey silk tie, all of which toned perfectly with his grey eyes and grey hair. He was not particularly tall, but unlike the other men in the group, he had not let turning fifty go to his waistline, and his skin was firm and glowed with expensive skin care products.

The man who had first greeted Philip put a conspiratorial hand on his arm. 'I never had you marked as one who would make a go of this independent production lark, but you certainly picked the right moment to get out of the BBC.' He relinquished his hold on Philip's arm and tapped the side of his nose with his forefinger. 'But then, rumour hath it that two years ago there were some nice little sweetheart deals on offer for those in the know.'

Philip looked indignant at this. 'Leaving the Corporation was a choice about artistic freedom. I still felt there were some programmes that I had to make, and if I had stayed I would have had to accept an executive position and unlike some, *I* have never been one to enjoy pushing bits of paper about.'

'Oh, but they say there's money to be made if you know how.' The speaker was not to be deterred. 'Have you heard about Tony, he left at about the same time as you didn't he? Word has it that his company is doing so well, he's traded in his trusty Volvo for a Porsche and has been seen power breakfasting in LA.'

'Well, he would, wouldn't he,' joined in one of the other members of the group. 'Porsches are such vulgar cars, I wouldn't be seen dead in one. They are the yuppy equivalent of a Cortina.'

'I think Tony's a little too old to be described as young and upwardly mobile, don't you?' added another member of the group.

Everybody laughed, united in jealousy against a former friend.

'Some of us want to make quality television, others just want to make money,' Philip added, glad that the uncomfortable probing had stopped.

'And some of us succeed in doing both,' said Philip's inquisitor, slipping an arm around Vanessa's waist and puller her closer. Vanessa could feel his damp palm through her paper thin silk dress. She gave him a saccharine-sweet smile.

'We'd all better watch out for this little lady,' he said looking up at her, 'she'll soon be snapping at our heels. A little bird told me that she was one of the team that came up with LTV's latest success, *Camera Shy*. The format's already been sold to about twenty different countries, including the States.'

The group had all looked at Vanessa with renewed interest. She smiled demurely. She hadn't said she had *actually* come up with the idea, but she *had* been at the meeting where it was proposed, so saying she was part of the team was not strictly a lie. All the same, she didn't want anyone asking awkward questions so she disentangled herself from the sweaty arm encircling her waist with a playful slap, and held out her hand to Philip.

'I'm such a great admirer of your work, Mr Pryce,' she said, trying to remember if she had ever seen any of his programmes. 'I thought your last series was wonderful.'

Philip's chest had visibly swelled and he had cradled his award a little tighter. 'Thank you. The recognition of one's peers as symbolised in this,' he had patted the bulbous artichoke, 'is the greatest award one can achieve.' Not for the first time that evening his eyes grew misty.

The group nodded in agreement.

'Our beloved industry is changing. It's time to make a stand for creative excellence and quality, before the Philistines and the money-men plunder the rich citadel of public service broadcasting and lay waste to our honourable traditions.'

Philip's voice rose. It was his favourite part of his acceptance speech and it had taken so long to write, a little repetition couldn't possibly hurt.

The group signalled its assent with a few 'hear hears' and a general clearing of throats. Small talk exhausted, they drank deeply from their glasses, their eyes sifting the room, assessing new contacts to be made, old acquaintances to be greeted and people to be avoided. The group began to drift away.

Vanessa sipped her wine, conscious that Philip was covertly studying her. He wasn't really her type, but . . .

Philip cleared his throat. 'I hope I'm not speaking out of turn, Miss Swift . . .'

Vanessa waited. It was as good an opening gambit as she could expect on an evening like this.

'But . . . I'm looking for some bright young things to join my company, Right Pryce Productions, and if Elliot says you're good, well, that's recommendation enough for me. I can offer the right kind of package too,' he added hastily.

Vanessa offered a silent prayer to the sweaty-palmed Elliot, whom she had never met before that night, and trying not to look too eager, turned a dazzling smile on Philip.

'Elliot can be a very naughty boy, you shouldn't believe everything he says,' she said, wagging her finger playfully.

'Oh, but I'm sure he wouldn't have said . . . Please tell me if I'm speaking out of turn.' Philip's colour had deepened.

Vanessa put her hand on Philip's arm and dropped her voice to an enticing low.

'As a matter of fact, I might just be open to offers. Without wishing to name names, there are some people in my company who seem to want to stifle creativity and new ideas, so perhaps it is about time I spread my wings.'

Philip had placed his hand over hers and nodded glumly. 'Talent often goes unrewarded.'

Several delightful lunches later, Vanessa had joined Right Pryce Productions and nearly doubled her salary.

At the thought of her salary, Vanessa fished around in her capacious bag for her mobile phone. She had to keep Philip happy. Lately, his normal jaunty demeanour had been replaced by that of a hunted man. Last week she had received a peremptory summons to his office.

Philip had dispensed with his normal preamble of pleasantries: 'It would appear from our accountants that your expenses since joining us have been nearly double your not inconsiderable salary. But you have not as yet generated one viable programme idea, despite being Head of Programme Development. Can you suggest a reason for this sad state of affairs?'

Vanessa had crossed her long legs and pulled her already short skirt higher up her thighs. It was a negotiating ploy she always found effective. It reduced the opposition to either confusion or lust and both achieved the same result: she got her own way. But Philip's eyes had remained resolutely and uncomfortably fixed on her face.

Vanessa had pushed her skirt back down and recrossed her legs before replying. Other tactics were obviously called for. She smiled serenely.

'Philip *darling*. You know how it is. If you want to impress people, you just have to take them to the right kind of place for lunch. How would it look if I invited a Channel 4 Commissioning Editor to lunch at MacDonald's? Think of your credibility rating darling, it would look like Right Pryce couldn't hack it. I mean, we're talking image here.'

'And I'm talking survival.'

Philip had leaned across the desk, his eyes narrowing in a most unbecoming way. 'I'll give you the bottom line, Vanessa. I want a workable idea for a television series, on my desk, one week from today, or else we will have to reconsider your contract. Do I make myself crystal clear?'

Vanessa suppressed a shiver at the memory, and punched the office number on her portable phone.

'Yo?'

'Heather?'

27

'Yo.'

'This is Vanessa.'

The other end of the phone went quiet, but Vanessa was sure she could hear Heather, Right Pryce's typist-come-receptionist, masticating gum.

'What do you want?'

'The correct question is: to whom do you wish to speak? Not whadyawant,' Vanessa snapped.

'Yo. So, to whom do you wish to speak?' Heather irritatingly mimicked Vanessa's voice to perfection.

'I do not wish to speak to anyone. I merely want you to convey to Mr Pryce that I have been unavoidably delayed, but that I and my proposal will be with him in about seven minutes. Is that clear?'

'Yo.'

Heather replaced the receiver, swung one Doc Marten's clad foot on to the desk and continued to paint her fingernails black.

In the back of the taxi, Vanessa rummaged in her bag once again and found an elderly biro and the paper napkin on which she had scribbled in the restaurant. She had to think fast.

Philip was a stickler for memos and ten-point plans. Any meeting was prefaced with a flurry of both. She looked at the crumpled napkin. Philip was hardly going to accept it as a substitute, but if she had an idea or two worked out, it might help.

She chewed the biro for a moment or two and considered what she had written: 'act out sexual fantasies'. What else was there to say? Then a thought struck her – she needed a catchy title. You could sell anything if the packaging was right.

She stared out of the window, desperate for inspiration.

The taxi came to a halt yet again, this time beside a fruit stall in Oxford Street. Its artfully arranged display of mouth-watering-looking fruit was attracting a lot of tourists. Vanessa watched as the stall-holder deftly served his customers from boxes concealed behind the stall, gesticulating angrily at a large sign saying DO NOT TOUCH if anyone had the temerity to try and pick their own fruit.

Vanessa smiled and wrote FORBIDDEN FRUIT in large capitals.

She glanced at her watch and stuffed the napkin back into her bag before leaning forward and rapping sharply on the glass partition.

'Stop here, it will be quicker to walk,' she commanded.

The driver shrugged and pulled in to the pavement. 'It's up to you lady. We're only here to serve the public.'

Vanessa flung the exact fare through his open window and almost ran the rest of the way down Soho Street, across Soho Square to the little alleyway off Charing Cross Road, where Right Pryce had its office above a sex shop and a dubious import-export business which claimed to offer unusual novelties.

She took the three flights of scruffy stairs in twos and then stopped, trying to steady her panting.

Vanessa checked her face in her compact mirror, removing some imaginary shine from her nose with a dusting of powder before recomposing her features into a confident smile, then she swept into the Right Pryce Production offices.

Three
* * *

Philip glanced at his watch. Vanessa was nearly twenty minutes late for the meeting. He sighed. He suddenly felt very old.

A pair of worried brown eyes met his and he manfully summoned a weak smile. Rosie Brandreth smiled encouragingly back, but her round good-natured face betrayed her concern.

For almost twenty years, since joining the BBC as a young trainee, Rosie had been his production assistant and right hand. When Philip left the BBC to set up Right Pryce Productions, Rosie went with him, leaving behind the security of the only job she had ever known.

Philip had felt a little guilty at the time, but Rosie had insisted almost tearfully that she would go wherever he went. By his calculations, she was in her late thirties, but to his knowledge had never had a regular boyfriend. She still lived at home with her mother and a collection of cats whose photographs covered her desk. His friends all joked that Rosie was in love with him, a charge he hotly denied, but she did have this disconcerting way of gazing at him when she thought nobody was looking. Philip had never given Rosie the least cause to imagine that he was interested in her, although even he had to admit that in some ways they were like an old married couple. After twenty years there was little Rosie did not know about him, from his collar size to how many crowns he had on his teeth. Sometimes her dogged devotion was embarrassing, but right now, Philip needed all the sympathy he could get, and he had a feeling that he would not get much from the other members of his present production team.

With the contracts for two documentary series already signed, he had recruited his first team from people he knew at the BBC, and for the first two years of its life, Right Pryce Productions had been a tightly-knit band of like-minded people. They worked together and played together like one big happy family and it had shown in the profits: Philip had sold his comfortable Victorian semi in Kentish Town and bought a large Regency terraced house in one of the better squares in Islington. But the profits had trailed off almost as suddenly as they had started, and Philip had discovered that family loyalties could be as fickle as any other when his team started to drift away to other jobs. Angry at what he considered to be his betrayal by so-called friends, Philip had decided to create a dynamic new production team of young, enthusiastic people with fresh ideas, people to whom he could play a kind of *éminence grise*. Unfortunately, it had not turned out quite as he planned.

As he looked across at Hugo Gordon, his Creative Director, Philip unconsciously smoothed his thinning hair. The mid-afternoon sun streaming through the high arched windows, which were the office's only redeeming architectural feature, provided a perfect back-light for Hugo's slender, ethereal form, suffusing his feathery blond hair with a golden halo. The picture would have been almost angelic had it not been for the dissolute expression which marred Hugo's choirboy features.

Philip felt a sharp pang. He had hoped for so much from Hugo. He reminded him of himself at twenty-five, and he had decided to take a chance on him even

31

though the sum total of his experience was the directing of three pop videos which, while described as inconoclastic by one magazine, had done little to advance the musical careers of the bands involved. Philip hoped he might become Hugo's mentor to help mould and guide his young talent, but Hugo had shown little sign of wanting a mentor. His main communication with Philip since joining the company six months ago had been via his mobile phone. He rarely came into the office, and his body language seemed eloquently to suggest he resented attending the meeting today. Philip made a mental note to have a little chat with him. Perhaps a firmer hand was called for.

A firm hand was most certainly called for with his new researcher, Vijay Seth, who was slumped dejectedly in a chair next to Hugo. Behind his round granny glasses, Vijay's dark eyes stared sightlessly at some far away place; a few wisps of dark hair straying from his ponytail drifted unheeded across his face.

Philip liked to think he payed more than lip service when it came to supporting equal rights for minorities, but Vijay seemed to lack the industriousness and application for which his race was famed. Most of the time he seemed to live in a world of his own. Philip had offered him a job where thousands wouldn't, and yet Vijay walked around looking as though the world was about to come to an end.

Philip checked his watch again and then carefully realigned his blotter and letter tray so that they were at right angles to each other. Vanessa had been his biggest mistake. Once again his liberal principles had betrayed him. He had thought it would be good to have a woman as his second-in-command, and Vanessa had the added bonus of being glamorous, a quality that mattered in an industry where image was so important. She also seemed to know everyone from managing directors to commissioning editors, and while Philip prided himself on his contacts, it was important to have someone who knew her way around the television industry. It was changing more rapidly than Philip liked, and he needed someone whose telephone calls were returned and lunch invitations were taken up.

But while Vanessa had certainly lunched a lot and at great length and expense to his company, not one commission had been forthcoming. However, as he had told her in no uncertain terms last week, lunchtime was over.

Almost on cue, the door to Philip's office swung wide and Vanessa stood poised on the threshold.

'Philip, *darling*. I really am most terribly sorry to be late, but I'm sure you will forgive me when I explain why. I've had *such* a busy morning tying up the last few loose ends on the proposal I have been working on, but please, don't let me hold up the meeting anymore.'

Vanessa swept into the room, her smile beacon-like before her. To Philip's irritation she pulled up a chair so that she was seated on his immediate right, facing the others. She placed her bag on his desk and crossed her legs.

'Now, I'm all ears. What was it you were talking about, Philip darling?'

The meeting was in her hands.

Philip placed his hands palm down on his desk as though to anchor himself. He took a deep breath.

'As you all know, the purpose of this meeting is to discuss programme ideas. By the end of this afternoon, I intend to have targeted at least one idea for development into a fully fledged pilot.'

He looked around. 'I hope I need hardly say that all our futures may depend on it.'

But even as he spoke, he knew it wasn't true. They were all young, their futures were ahead of them, and they had plenty of time to start again, but time was

33

running out for him. He had mortgaged everything, including his pension, to set up Right Pryce Productions and if it went down, so did he.

According to the extremely uncomfortable meeting he'd had that morning with the old Cambridge friend turned financier who had persuaded some City investors to back him, that moment was nigh. And it was not just his house and pension Philip had mortgaged, it was also his pride.

In an undignified manner that even now made his palms go sweaty, Philip had pleaded for mercy. He had been told to wait outside the door like some errant schoolboy, before being summoned back in to be told in most unCambridgelike terms that he had three months to deliver the goods or else.

Nearly thirty years of being a member of what he fondly considered the private gentlemen's club of the BBC, where he had only been expected to produce two arts documentaries a year and an occasional intellectual late-night chat show, had not prepared him for this. If only he had kept to his original plan and taken early retirement from the BBC. He'd had it all worked out: he would buy a suitably rustic villa in the South of France or maybe Tuscany, where he would spend some leisurely years penning the novel which would earn him a paragraph or two in the *Times Literary Supplement*. Now he would be lucky if he could afford a room in a B&B in Brighton.

Philip loudly blew his nose and then carefully folded his handkerchief before placing it in his pocket. He needed time to get this sudden, overwhelming sense of his failure under control, it threatened to make his voice shake. He cleared his throat and then began again. 'Since no written programme proposals have been submitted to me as requested, I suppose I must accept oral submissions. As Head of Development, would you like to take the floor, Vanessa?'

34

'I think we should hear other people's ideas first, don't you, Philip? I really wouldn't like to upstage anyone, that is if anyone else has anything to offer.' Vanessa sat back.

Vijay unhunched his thin shoulders and glumly dug around in his pockets. He didn't know why he was bothering. He was sure someone had put a curse on him, *nothing* he did seemed right.

His mother had warned him that no good would come of his chosen career as a journalist. According to her, no one from a good family would become a journalist in India – where was the respect in it? He tried to point out that he had been born in England and was therefore more English than Indian, and that in England journalism was an honourable profession, it was the Fourth Estate. But she had merely tinkled her many gold bangles at him as she wagged her finger, and told him yet again to mark her words, no good would come of it.

And so far she had been right. He had worked for three publications, all of which had closed down. The first had been a new magazine aimed to bring together the views of anti-racist organisations from all over Europe, but editorial disagreements had descended into a bitter feud with charges of racism on all sides. Not even one issue had reached the news stands and the magazine had folded owing money to everyone.

His second job had been on a men's style magazine. That had lasted for nearly eight months, but an injudicious article about the sexual habits of a politician had resulted in a libel trial which had bankrupted the magazine. From there Vijay had moved to a weekly alternative music paper, but within two weeks of him joining, that, too, had closed down.

He had decided to make a clean break of it and try his hand as a television researcher, but it seemed the curse had followed him. Within the first week of joining Right Pryce Productions, Heather invited him to share a sandwich and a cappuccino in Soho Square, where she had confided that the company was having financial problems, and this morning she had pulled him aside and whispered that Philip had returned ashen-faced from a meeting with his accountants, which could only mean one thing.

Vijay had always dismissed curses as superstitious nonsense of the kind that held countries like India back from fulfilling their true political and economic potential, but he was beginning to change his mind.

He at last found the crumpled piece of paper on which he had written his programme idea and attempted to smooth it out on his thigh.

'Ah, Vijay.' Vanessa's smile glittered. 'Is that your little way of signalling you have something to say?'

Vijay pushed his round granny glasses over the bridge of his nose. His mother said he should get contact lenses, they would make him more attractive to nice Indian girls, but he felt his glasses gave him added intellectual weight.

'I'd like to make a few comments about the criteria you gave us.' His words were pointedly addressed to Philip.

'Ah, a speech.' Vanessa's voice was like candyfloss.

Hugo sat up, sensing entertainment. Vijay was so easy to bait.

Vijay ignored Vanessa and cleared his throat.

'You see, I feel that those of us who have access to the means of mass communication have a moral responsibility to the audiences we serve, and therefore all programming, not just that which is objectively political, should be subject to analysis.'

'And your point is?' Philip asked wearily.

'Well, your criteria for any programme idea was that it should be cheap and that it should have broad-based audience appeal – codewords, if I am not mistaken, for abandoning the principles of public service broadcasting in the interests of profit.' Vijay was warming to his thesis.

Philip held up a hand as Vijay opened his mouth to continue. 'Vijay, I must stop you there. I think we, in this room, are all aware of the dangers of which you speak, but I hardly think that by producing one successful series we are going to precipitate the downfall of Rome.'

Something suspiciously like a snort escaped from Hugo.

Vijay hunched his narrow shoulders. 'Look, what you don't seem to understand is that if we produce opium for the masses, we become a tool of the media barons. Is that what you want, tabloid television? What I'm talking about is television that will make the audience think. The working class may be oppressed, but it does have a mind of its own.'

'I hadn't noticed,' Hugo murmured.

Vijay gave him a malevolent look.

'Perhaps we could move on,' Philip intervened. 'This conversation has ceased to be constructive. From now on could we all please confine our remarks to the issue at hand.'

'But I do have a proposal,' Vijay flushed angrily, stung by Hugo's baiting.

'Then we'd all like to hear it, Vijay. Your contributions to our meetings are always valued, even if they are sometimes a little unorthodox,' Philip said dryly.

'I think we should do a quiz show,' Vijay announced. 'This satisfies both your criteria of cheapness and popularity but it has the merit of being educational. I thought we could go out to the factories and workplaces of the nation and pit assembly-line workers against white-collar office workers, that sort of thing. You could have a good rock band on the show and a comedian too, as long as they were non-sexist and non-racist.'

'By definition that means they wouldn't be a comedian,' Hugo drawled. 'I can see it now.' He held up his hands and gestured quote marks.

' "Tune in to the terminally PC show and win a package holiday for two in Cuba, the only socialist paradise left in the world." '

Philip raised his hand to silence Hugo.

'A quiz show is not such a bad idea, Hugo,' he said mildly. 'They're cheap, they get high ratings if the format and the prizes are right, and the Network is always on the look out for good ones to act as building blocks in the schedule. My real problem is that this feels a bit dated. Factories are not exactly a Nineties image.'

'I think we should consider it.' Vanessa's voice was laced with sarcasm. 'After all, audiences like nostalgia. We could dress the workers in flat caps and clogs as a reminder of the time when they knew their place.'

Vijay looked ready to abandon his pacifist ideals.

Philip held up a calming hand again. 'I'm not dismissing this one out of hand Vijay, but I think we should put it on a back-burner for the time being.' He turned to Vanessa. 'Perhaps you would like to share your proposal with us now, Vanessa.'

Vanessa bathed the meeting with another radiant smile.

'You will all remember the popular children's television series quaintly titled *Jim'll Fix It*, in which little kiddies wrote in with their innocent fantasies, which were then fulfilled to the misty-eyed delight of their parents and large audiences. It had a simple but effective formula, and what might be described as the "aah" factor.' Vanessa held up an admonitory finger, 'We mustn't knock it. The Great British Public likes being sentimental, it is one of the few things it still does well. My idea is equally simple. Instead of well-scrubbed, bright-eyed kiddies captaining an ocean liner, or singing along with some has-been pop group, we will fix it for adults to fulfil their favourite sexual fantasies on screen and in glorious Technicolor.'

Vanessa paused and looked around. She had her audience enthralled: like rabbits mesmerised by car headlights.

'This show has all the ingredients of success: sex, wish-fulfilment, and best of all, people making fools of themselves. Audiences will love it.'

Vanessa sat back and waited for a reaction.

There was silence.

Philip cleared his throat and in an odd voice asked: 'Have you thought of a title yet?'

Vanessa smiled sweetly. '*Forbidden Fruit.*'

Philip straightened his jotter unnecessarily. 'Could you perhaps expand a little more on how you see the show, Vanessa. Sex can be such a sticky subject.' He smiled weakly at his double entendre. 'It's not that I'm against sex on television, everyone knows my record as a campaigner for freedom of artistic expression, but one has to accept that in the present political climate, broadcasters must tread carefully.'

'But that's the beauty of my idea, Philip,' Vanessa said triumphantly. 'It's based on new research that says it's healthy to act out our sexual fantasies, so we can use the research to justify the show and win some brownie points for health education!'

Philip stroked his chin.

'Has this research been published yet?'

Vanessa shook her head.

'Could we get the exclusive rights to it?'

'They're already in the bag,' Vanessa replied quickly.

'And the format?'

'Studio based with an audience,' Vanessa said promptly. 'Audience participation always adds atmosphere. Think of *Blind Date*. We could have video inserts for the more exotic locations and even home videos. No one admits to watching Jeremy Beadle, but he gets the audience figures. We could have a whole section of home videos showing what can go wrong, a kind of fantasy nightmare!'

Philip drummed his fingers on his desk for a moment and then nodded almost to himself, it was so simple it could work. Sex sold, and what he desperately needed now was a series he could sell to the Network. All he had to do was dress it up right.

'I like it. It has definite possibilities. A few problems too, but I definitely like it.'

'But it's exploitative, it's worse than Page Three . . .' protested Vijay.

'Since it's the workers you think so wonderful who gawp at the bare tits on Page Three during their two-hour tea-breaks, I don't see why you should object to it on television,' Vanessa taunted him.

'I like it too,' Hugo announced suddenly. 'It has strong visual potential.'

He leapt up and began to pace up and down, running his hands through his hair. 'Let me run this by you. Imagine a Roman orgy: mounds of writhing bodies, dancing girls, grotesque dwarves, eunuchs, muscular black slaves, naked except for golden chains, their bodies oiled and glistening. I could shoot it in the style of one of those early Hollywood epics – the stuff they used to do before the Hays lot started laying down the law. We could even go all grainy and black and white like Fellini, but using computer graphics. What do you think?'

Philip cleared his throat again. 'I hear what you're saying, Hugo, and I don't want to rule anything out at this point in time, but I suspect we may have to think of economies of scale.'

Hugo shrugged and slumped back into his chair as though exhausted by his effort.

Philip turned to Vanessa. 'Have you given any thought to a presenter yet?'

'I've spent a long time on that one,' Vanessa lied, 'but given the subject matter, I haven't been able to come up with anyone who has the right kind of gravitas combined with the ability to pull in audiences.'

'I think it should be a woman,' Philip said, suddenly resolute. 'If we had a man it could look like it was mere pornography, just another men's locker-room show. A woman presenter would avoid that accusation.'

He had been thinking fast. The series would be easier to sell to the Network with a well-known name fronting it, but household names were expensive and over-protective about their images. They needed someone who was no longer a front-rank celebrity, but still well-known enough to draw audiences as well as willing to take risks with their image. Most of all, they had to be cheap. There was an old friend of his . . .

'It's a bit of a wild card, but how about Gabriella Wolfe?'

'Don't say she's still alive,' drawled Hugo, 'whatever happened to her?'

'Gabriella has her own very successful satellite chat show in Italy,' Philip said primly.

'Ah, so she's gone to the great TV personality grave-yard in the sky,' Hugo grinned.

'But she's so *passé*,' protested Vanessa. 'I think we should go for someone new and fresh.'

'I disagree,' Hugo interrupted. 'If we're going Hollywood Babylon, then Gabriella, with all that cleavage and those eyelashes, fits the image perfectly: kitsch and trashy.'

Philip looked pained.

'Well, I always thought Gabriella was rather nice when she used to read the news,' Rosie ventured, 'and my mother never missed her chat show. She always used to have her supper on a tray so she could watch it.'

'There's our audience for you,' Philip said triumphantly.

'Gabriella it is then. Now, I want a more detailed proposal by . . . where are we now?'

He checked his desk calendar. 'Let's say by the beginning of next week. We've got to move fast on this one.'

Vanessa started to protest again about Gabriella but Philip held up his hand.

'I have taken an executive decision Vanessa, let's just get this show on the road, shall we?'

The meeting was over.

Four
• • •

Jeremy sat hunched up on Vanessa's front door step. He had been waiting for three hours. He knew he was not meant to be there until six o'clock but he had nowhere else to go. Beside him was a suitcase and two plastic carrier bags, which threatened to spew their contents onto the pavement. He stared dully down at them. They contained all the possessions he owned in the world. Not much for a man who would be forty this year.

Why was he sitting here waiting for Vanessa, of all people? If anyone was to blame for his problems it was her. He was unemployed, homeless and broke. He had been disinherited by his father and disowned by his mother, and all because of Vanessa.

If only he'd married Chloe. His mother had said he should. Everyone said he should. She would have been such a suitable wife and would have done all the things that wives are meant to do. Not like Vanessa. But that was the very reason he had wanted to marry Vanessa instead. She was different and dangerous, and his mother hadn't liked her.

He was not a natural rebel. In fact, he rather liked things to be in their place. It made him feel comfortable, and he had been quite willing to choose his wife out of the many suitable girls his mother made sure he met. He had chosen Chloe because she seemed so fragile that it made him want to protect her. He had found a lot of the other girls that moved in his circle a little too hearty for his tastes. They seemed to be able to deliver a foal, cook a five-course dinner for ten and drive a Land Rover all at the same time. Chloe had been the perfect antidote to all that until he met Vanessa.

It had been a particularly good day for him, or so he had thought at the time. It was the first day of the cricket season, and something of a grudge match against the opposing team led by that idiot Gavin Hewitt. Both teams played in a minor league, but competition was fanatical, and Jeremy had sworn revenge on Gavin after his team had won the league trophy the season before, only because the last match was washed out. To win by bowling out Gavin had made victory even sweeter.

He had been walking back to the pavilion when he first saw Vanessa. She strode towards him like some burnished Amazon and took command of both him and the situation.

If only Chloe had been there that day instead of away on some cookery or was it a flower arranging course? If only his mother Henrietta had not been so set against Vanessa, perhaps it would only have been a brief affair, one last mad fling before he settled down to the security of marriage with dear little Chloe. But the moment Henrietta and Vanessa met, it had been war with him as the prize. Both sides had wielded their weapons to inflict maximum damage; Henrietta using filial loyalty and Vanessa sex. Sex had won. Against his mother's strongly worded wishes, he had married Vanessa within two months of meeting her.

He thought that everything would change after the wedding. Henrietta would accept Vanessa as his wife and once babies came along, everyone would live happily ever after. How could he have been so wrong?

Jeremy had assumed that everyone wanted children.

Why else would they get married? It had never crossed his mind to ask Vanessa whether she wanted to have babies, he had taken it for granted, she was a woman after all. Her refusal to have any had been like a physical blow. For the first time in his life, he realised how much he wanted some small being to look up at him and call him Daddy. His mother had made it even worse.

She refused to have any mention of Vanessa made in her presence, but the set of her mouth said it all. She had told him so.

Nanny Greig had been more encouraging, and suggested that he give Vanessa a little more time. According to Nanny Greig, a woman's hormones always took over.

So he had tried to be patient. Nanny Greig's predictions, like her potions for sore tummies, usually worked. They moved out of their flat in Fulham and bought a five-bedroomed, three-receptioned house near Clapham Common. Vanessa had hated the idea at first because she considered south of the river to be foreign territory, but she agreed when she discovered how many media people lived there. Jeremy had wanted to buy it because he thought it would make the perfect family house. He had looked out at the hundred-foot garden and imagined it strewn with children's toys. And while he patiently waited for Vanessa's hormones to do their job, it was to the garden he had turned to fulfill his unspoken need to see things grow.

At first his ambitions had been modest: a nice lawn, neat flower beds and a small patio with a barbecue for the garden parties Vanessa wanted to throw for her neighbours. As his sense of achievement grew, so did his sense of adventure. After watching a Channel 4 programme on organic gardening, he carefully disposed of all his chemical fertilisers and insecticides and made a vow to work hand in hand with Mother Nature.

He bought a rotavator, and his carefully striped lawn disappeared under rows of lettuces, Chinese cabbages, radishes and onions, all of which grew lush and chemical free. He agonised over Big Bud Mites and Mealy Aphids, and harboured murderous intentions towards the neighbourhood cats, whose unsanitary habits showed a total disregard for his prized kohl-rabi.

Being a gardener opened up a whole new world of seed catalogues, garden centres and chats across the fence with fellow enthusiasts. He even joined a local organic gardening club, which was how he met Belle.

She was a guest speaker at the club, and had given a talk on the importance of gardening as an expression of feminist creativity – exemplified by the efforts of Vita Sackville-West. He had not heard much of what she was saying, as he was more intent on studying her.

She was small and slim and very pretty, with dark, lustrous skin. The curve of her cheeks and the perfection of her features reminded him of sculpture, an effect emphasised by her hair which lay flat against her head in an intricate braided design. The faint musical lilt of her voice was a legacy of her Caribbean childhood. After the lecture, Jeremy had made sure he was the first to congratulate her, and they had talked over a glass of organic wine.

Belle lived in a housing estate in Stockwell, but did her gardening on an allotment several streets away from where Jeremy and Vanessa lived. He had taken to dropping by there at weekends to offer her vegetables and flowers from his garden, and they would sit and talk over cups of Celestial Seasonings herb tea. It was Belle's gentle but firm persuasion that had finally decided Jeremy to become a vegetarian. But while giving up flesh was one thing, telling Vanessa had been another.

He had shouted the announcement of his conversion through the bathroom door one evening as Vanessa was getting ready to go to yet another media party.

Vanessa's head wrapped in a towel had appeared round the door.

'This is some kind of a joke, isn't it?'

'No. I've decided that on environmental and ethical grounds I have to take a stand. I wish you'd think about it too Vanessa, I feel so much better, liberated even, since I've taken the decision.'

Under Belle's tutelage, he had acquired some new vocabulary.

Vanessa strode across the room, naked except for the towel on her head, her body pink and glowing from the bath. She rubbed her hair vigorously. 'Whose dumb idea is this? It sounds too idiotic even for those chinless wonders who work at your office. Is it some kind of bet?'

Jeremy perched himself on the end of the bed and tried to be patient. He had wanted Vanessa to understand and perhaps even to join him. They seemed to have so little in common these days.

'I don't think you understand Vee, killing animals for our gratification is wrong. If only you'd seen the documentary about factory farming the other night, you'd never touch another steak. Belle says . . .'

Vanessa had whirled round. 'Belle, who's Belle?'

'She's just someone I met at the gardening club,' Jeremy said defensively.

'Really?' Vanessa had sounded disbelieving. She stood in front of him.

Nakedness made most people look vulnerable, but not Vanessa. Jeremy had tried to avert his eyes but it was difficult.

'Tell me more about this Belle,' demanded Vanessa.

At that time there hadn't been anything to tell, but Vanessa hadn't believed him and began to question him relentlessly, even prodding him awake in the middle of the night. He tried to keep away from Belle at first, but Vanessa's pitiless interrogation had finally driven him to the sanctuary of the allotments and Belle's little shed, where Belle had comforted him while they drank some of her surprisingly strong, home-brewed beer.

Jeremy groaned and put his head in his hands at the memory. He had not intended to commit adultery, it had just happened, and it had been Vanessa's fault. If she hadn't gone on and on at him like that, it never would have happened.

The unmistakeable sound of a black cab stopping made him look through his fingers. A familiar pair of legs got out and strode towards him.

'Well, if it isn't my long lost ex-husband,' Vanessa said mockingly.

Jeremy struggled stiffly to his feet.

Vanessa looked him up and down, shocked by the change in his appearance. He had lost a lot of weight, and his hair which had always been thick and floppy, now straggled long and lifeless almost to his shoulders. The Jeremy she had known always wore Jermyn Street suits and shirts. Even when he was at his most casual he had still worn cavalry twill trousers and a sports jacket. But the man standing awkwardly in front of her wore a scruffy T-shirt, filthy ripped jeans, and a pair of ancient trainers which in some past life, may have been white.

She indicated the bulging carrier bags at Jeremy's feet. 'This is your audition for your new career as a bag-lady, I take it?'

Jeremy made a weak attempt at a smile. 'I'm sort of between homes at the moment.'

Vanessa raised an eyebrow. 'Really. And to what do I owe the pleasure of this touching little reunion?'

'Would it be possible to speak inside?' Jeremy said,

rubbing his buttocks, 'I arrived a bit early and your doorstep is a bit hard.' His jeans bagged about his thighs.

'I'll give you five minutes and that's it, so it had better be good,' Vanessa said crisply, putting her key in the lock.

Jeremy picked up his belongings and followed her in.

'Leave those outside in the hall,' Vanessa commanded, 'I don't want you bringing anything unpleasant into my flat.'

Jeremy meekly put down his suitcase and bags and wiped his hands on his T-shirt, and his feet on the mat, before stepping into Vanessa's flat. He blinked and looked around. Every surface was white.

What had once been a grand ornately decorated drawing room had been stripped of every cornice, fireplace, dado and architectural indulgence leaving flat, featureless walls. Only the floor offered any contrast and that was made of blond beechwood. There were no books, pictures or ornaments, none of the bric-a-brac of life to give a clue to the personality of the occupier.

Vanessa indicated a white leather sofa. Jeremy nervously wiped his hands on his T-shirt again and sat down, gingerly.

'Well?' demanded Vanessa, sitting in a white leather armchair opposite him.

Jeremy took a deep breath.

'I know we're divorced,' he began.

'And whose fault is that?' snapped Vanessa.

Jeremy looked at his hands. His finger nails were filthy. He tried to hide them. 'But I didn't want . . .' he faltered.

'Then you should have thought about it before you slept with that woman.'

'But I didn't, at least I hadn't. Not when you said I had. If you hadn't . . .'

'Are you trying to say *I* was responsible for you committing adultery?' demanded Vanessa.

Jeremy shrugged helplessly. He had never been any good at arguments.

Vanessa relaxed back into her chair; she was enjoying herself. 'Am I to assume from your current homelessness that you are no longer living with the right-on PC little Belle?' Her voice was as light as a soufflé.

Jeremy's jaw twitched as he tried to control his voice. 'She's found someone else,' he said at last.

'Did I hear you right? She's found someone else.' Vanessa's voice rose to a triumphant shrill. 'This calls for a drink.'

She jumped to her feet and went to the kitchen.

Jeremy stared at the ground, misery blurring his vision. He knew he should not have called Vanessa, but he had nowhere else to go. He'd spent the last week living in a cheap hotel near King's Cross, venturing out only to buy an occasional hamburger. But the other rooms in the hotel appeared to be rented by the hour, and the grunts and squeaks coming through the paper thin walls at every hour of the day and night had prevented him from sleeping. Although he would not have thought it possible, the sound effects made him feel even more wretched.

He had been trying to get up enough courage to go home and face his mother, but when he eventually telephoned her from a booth on King's Cross station, a contrite and repentant speech ready, his brother James had answered.

'Jeremy old boy, how are you? We were only talking about you at dinner last night. Mother still seems a trifle upset, but I must say, whatever the old girl thinks, I rather envy you. How's the little coloured gel?'

'She's okay. I was wondering James, is mother there?'

'Not at the moment, old boy, I've been left holding the fort. Mother and Lucinda have taken the boys out on a shopping spree, needed some new shoes or something. Can't keep up with them. Are we going to see you? Lucinda and I are staying here for a few weeks. Lucinda says she's turning into a country bumpkin, so we've come for a dose of the bright lights.'

Jeremy had been silent. If his brother and his family were staying with his mother, there was no way he could face them all. He didn't know which was worse, Henrietta's anger or Lucinda's solicitous little talks.

'You still there, old boy?' James had asked, 'sounds like you're calling from Grand Central Station. Where are you living by the way?'

'Give my regards to everyone, must dash.' Jeremy had put the receiver down; he couldn't cope with explaining about Belle on the telephone.

He looked up as Vanessa came back into the room. She thrust a glass of whisky and soda into his hand before sitting down again. She crossed her legs. 'So tell me, what happened? I thought you and she had found bliss running that silly little sandwich bar.'

Jeremy's chin went up. 'Actually, it was a whole new concept in vegetarian fast food. Belle and I had plans to turn it into a franchise operation with a branch in every high street in the country.'

'But you didn't get further than Peckham, did you?'

Jeremy miserably shook his head.

'And what do you expect *me* to do about it?' Vanessa demanded.

Jeremy drained the whisky in his glass before replying, it burned his empty stomach. 'Well, I was hoping that perhaps, for old times' sake, you might let me stay here just until I get back on my feet again.'

Vanessa snorted. 'I'm not sure we have any old times' sake, Jeremy, and tell me something, why haven't you gone to your darling mother? I'm sure Henrietta would love you to rush to her bosom, or has she seen through you, too? I'd love to have seen her face when you introduced her to that Belle woman. She probably wished you were back with me.'

Jeremy looked at his empty glass; for once Vanessa was right about his mother. When he had announced that he was leaving his job at the bank to live with Belle, she had told him to leave the house. Women had a habit of doing that to him. First Vanessa, then his mother and now Belle. What was he doing wrong?

'All I'm asking . . .' Jeremy fought to control his voice, 'is somewhere to stay just for a few days. That's not too much to ask, is it? I gave you the house and everything else you wanted when we divorced.'

He kept his eyes fixed on the floor. He couldn't look at Vanessa although he could sense her triumph at his humiliation.

Vanessa got up. He could see her feet walking towards him and then her hand took his glass.

'Jeremy dearest, there's an old saying: to the victor the spoils. There ain't no dignity in losing. Now, if you'd let yourself out, I have to get ready for a dinner date.'

Five

• • •

'Under certain circumstances there are few hours in life more agreeable than the hour dedicated to the ceremony known as afternoon tea.'

Alicia sighed.

It was the first line of one of her favourite novels: *The Portrait of a Lady* by Henry James, and a sentence of such elegant simplicity, its sentiments so in accord with her own, it seemed to distil the essence of an age in which, despite all its iniquities, she had always instinctively felt she would have been more at ease.

From the moment she had read the first page of her first Jane Austen novel when she was twelve, Alicia had felt at home, and the novels of Austen and James, Elizabeth Gaskell and Anthony Trollope, had provided a refuge and an escape during her years at St Aloysius. Alicia had found secret corners of the boiler room and the games changing rooms which were largely undisturbed in the evenings and at weekends, and there she could read unhindered. It was a practice frowned upon by the nuns, who considered any activity done in solitude to be suspect, but it was one of Alicia's few acts of disobedience. If they read at all, the other girls in her year read novels by Georgette Heyer, while the more daring, including Vanessa, favoured racy paperbacks which were smuggled in and wrapped in brown paper to disguise their lurid covers, before being passed around.

Alicia's love of books had translated into a degree in English Literature, and now earned her a living as a lecturer at Heartlands University. She had of course specialised in nineteenth-century literature, and in her own quiet way had begun to make a name for herself in academic circles. Quite a few of her papers had been accepted for publication in some of the more prestigious journals, provoking correspondence from interested academics as far afield as Tokyo and Tasmania. Her latest paper was about the significance of food as ritual in the nineteenth century novel. Alicia's favourite meals were breakfast and tea, and it was her thesis that the ritual enshrined in the taking of these two meals had been an essential part of the social cohesion of nineteenth-century life. By contrast, the invention of the instant breakfast cereal and the tea bag symbolised the breakdown of social cohesion in the late twentieth century. Neither product would ever be found in her kitchen.

It was a theme she could normally warm to, but now, as she sat with her fountain poised above her note pad, Alicia could get no further than the first sentence, and that wasn't even hers. The motion of the British Rail Intercity train on which she was travelling did not help. Nor did the thought, as she checked her watch yet again, that she had barely three minutes to change platforms at Birmingham New Street if she was going to catch her connection to Heartlands. Missing it would mean an hour's wait. Even if she made it, it would be a slow journey. Heartlands was at the end of an unprofitable country line which was grudgingly allowed only four fast trains a day. At other times, elderly two-carriage trains, long past their retirement date, chugged slowly round a circuitous route, stopping at every small town. If she had travelled back the following day as she had planned, her journey would have been swifter and altogether less stressful.

Although she would not choose to live there, Alicia liked to visit London occasionally, although her trips were becoming less frequent as she found the traffic and the crowds increasingly disorientating. Quite a few of the other academics at Heartlands kept flats in London, but Alicia did not feel she could justify this expenditure. Anyway, she liked staying at the graduate and professional women's club to which she belonged. Its shabby yet genteel premises were situated in a quiet street in Bloomsbury, and it offered single rooms with basin and shared bathroom, and several comfortable, chintzy club rooms where she could almost disappear into the enormous armchairs and read undisturbed, or pass a comfortable hour or two in conversation with the other women who made the club their base. Like Alicia, most of them were academics.

Unfortunately, the low cost of membership had meant that the club was becoming rather more shabby than genteel, and efforts to cut down on the staff rather than raise the membership fees, had resulted in a down-and-out living in the basement for nearly six weeks before he was discovered. As a result of this unfortunate incident, the members had been offered a choice: a quadrupling of fees or allow the management to let rooms at hotel rates to foreign tourists. The vote had been for foreign tourists, as long as they were female. The idea of men staying in their exclusively feminine preserve was anathema; in fact nobody would probably have minded too much if the unwelcome occupant of the basement had been a woman, but the idea of a man living in the building had been enough to cause at least two of the more elderly members to resign.

Alicia had continued to stay at the club despite the admittance of tourists, who were mainly students anxious to soak up the atmosphere of Bloomsbury. But the atmosphere had changed, the polite murmur of voices being replaced by much louder and brasher accents, and she was not sure how much longer she would keep up her membership.

But the club did have one very great advantage; it was within walking distance of the British Museum. If there was only one reason to live in London, for Alicia it would have been to be able to use the Reading Room in the British Museum every day.

Every time she went there, she felt the serried ranks of the ghosts of great academics and writers who had once worked there, looking over her shoulder, urging her on to academic excellence like celestial cheerleaders. Alicia knew it was just a silly fancy on her part, but somehow she felt that any article or paper that she wrote there had the blessing of the Reading Room ghosts bestowed upon it. So it had been in those hallowed surrounds that she promised herself she would begin, if not complete, her paper on the significance of food in the nineteenth-century novel.

It was a pleasure she had been reserving for the beginning of the summer vacation in four weeks' time. She had intended to combine it with some of the few other treats that London offered like taking tea at Fortnum and Mason's, spending a leisurely afternoon in the Victoria and Albert Museum and the enchantments of Liberty's fabric department. She also hoped to see Vanessa. Their friendship now seemed to consist mainly of her leaving messages on Vanessa's answer machine. Her repeated invitations to Vanessa to come to Heartlands invariably invoked the reply that Vanessa was 'snowed under', so the only way she could get to see her was to come to London.

Anxious to get into Vanessa's busy diary, she had telephoned a week ago and left a message announcing her intention to visit London in a month's time. Much to her surprise, Vanessa had returned the call the next day and suggested lunch the following week. In answer to Alicia's queries about how she was, Vanessa had replied that she was wonderful, but there was something in the tone of her voice that suggested otherwise, so despite the fact that it was a very difficult time of the year to rearrange her timetable, Alicia had managed it. She liked to think that even after all these years, Vanessa could still turn to her if she had a problem.

Nobody had ever been able to understand their friendship. Even Alicia found it difficult to explain. Vanessa could have chosen anyone she wanted as a friend at St Aloysius, but instead of one of the other popular pretty girls who everyone wanted for a friend, she had chosen Alicia and she would always be grateful to her for that.

Alicia could still remember the misery she felt on arriving at St Aloysius that first day. She had wanted to run after her father and beg him to take her home, but her father had always discouraged displays of emotion. According to him they were a sign of character weakness, and Alicia had not dared put his uncertain temper to the test.

Alicia and her mother Eileen had long since learned to avoid provoking her father Bill's temper, but the days leading up to Alicia's departure for boarding school had been very tense, as the regiment was also preparing to leave for Singapore. Her father had made it clear that he had no intention of dealing with indiscipline at home as well as among his men, and so Alicia and her mother had fought to keep their feelings under control, at least when he was around.

But every so often, Alicia entered a room to find her mother looking lost among the chaos of packing cases, her shoulders shaking and tears streaming silently down her face. Alicia had tried to comfort her, but there was something about her mother's mute sorrow that seemed beyond comfort.

Once, Alicia's father had found them clinging to each other, and ordered them not to make an exhibition of themselves. Why were they making such a fuss, he had raged. If it hadn't been for that damned priest with whom her mother spent so much time, Alicia would not be going away to a convent.

Her mother's devout Catholicism had been a constant source of irritation to her father. His religion was the army, and it allowed no time for something he considered to be women's superstitious nonsense. But the angrier he grew, the more Eileen turned to her religion for comfort. It was the only thing that gave her the strength to survive the rigours of married life she told Alicia, and survive them she must, for marriage was the cross women had to bear.

Her parents had not always been unhappy. Alicia could remember a time when she was small, when her father had been as quick to laugh as he had been to lose his temper. She had never known quite what happened to change things, as her mother would not talk about what she called 'those things' even to this day, but just before Alicia's fifth birthday, her mother had gone into hospital for a while. When she came home, she moved into a separate bedroom and never moved back. Her mother and father had become strangers in the same house after that.

Alicia had been a solitary child. She found it difficult to make friends since her father discouraged her from playing with the children of those ranked either below or above him. So when Vanessa had so confidently bade Alicia to follow her on that first day at boarding school, Alicia felt like an orphan who had been adopted, and would have followed Vanessa to the ends of the earth.

If anything, Alicia's hero-worship had grown as the

years passed. Vanessa was everything she secretly longed to be, but never dared, and though it was silly and rather adolescent, Alicia had always felt that just by being Vanessa's friend, a little of Vanessa's glamour rubbed off on her.

And that was one of the strange things about their relationship, Alicia mused, sucking the end of her pen. Even though they were now both mature women, when she was with Vanessa she still felt like an awkward eleven-year-old schoolgirl. She couldn't explain why. After all, she was a respected scholar and had even gained a quiet reputation as a feminist spokesperson among some of the women undergraduates because of her championing of little-known nineteenth-century women novelists, although it was not a reputation with which she was altogether happy. Alicia disliked what she saw as the stridency of some other women scholars who sought to imbue nineteenth-century women novelists with a feminist prescience they could not possibly have possessed, and by doing so, reinterpreted the past in the light of present-day concerns. Alicia liked to view them as creatures of their time.

She glanced out of the window. Another five minutes and the train would be in New Street. She put her unfinished article into her briefcase and retrieved her unused overnight case from the luggage rack.

Perhaps at last she was going to have a chance to show Vanessa a little more of her world. Barely an hour after they had parted company following lunch, a message from Vanessa had managed to find her in the Reading Room. She had immediately called Vanessa back.

'Vanessa, is there something wrong? Your message said it was urgent. I was worried.'

'No sweetie, there's no problem. I just thought I might come and stay with you for a couple of days. I need to get out of town and get a bit of fresh air, so I thought I might also take a look at that Angus fellow's research you were talking about.'

'Fergus,' Alicia had corrected her gently. 'That would be wonderful. When can you come? Next week would be good for me as I've got a busy . . .'

'I'll be there tomorrow. That won't be a problem for you, will it?'

'No, of course not,' Alicia had lied, thinking longingly of Liberty's and Fortnum and Mason's.

'See you then. Oh, and Alicia . . . please don't mention to whatever his name is why I'm coming. Let's keep it between us, okay?'

'Oh, but why? I'm sure Fergus would . . .' Alicia had begun, but Vanessa had already put the receiver down.

The train reached New Street. It was the height of the evening rush-hour, and everybody seemed to be going in the opposite direction to Alicia. She felt like a salmon fighting its way upstream. Buffeted by the flood of humanity, she clutched her bags and fought her way across the concourse, apologising to everyone who cannoned into her.

She breathlessly reached her platform just as they were closing the barriers, but a cheerful black guard winked and let her through and waited until she had scrambled aboard before blowing his whistle.

The carriage was crowded and Alicia was forced to stand for the first part of the journey. Two women were occupying a three-person seat, with their shopping piled proprietorially high between them. Alicia considered asking them to move it, but when she caught one of the women's eyes, the look in it forbade such a request.

Eventually the carriage emptied, and Alicia sank thankfully into a window seat. She abandoned all ideas of doing any more work on her paper, and gazed instead at the passing countryside.

It undulated gently between rivers and dry stone

walls and villages of low honey-coloured stone cottages. It never failed to delight her, and on days like these, calm her mind.

It had been love at first sight, fifteen years before, when she came to Heartlands to be interviewed for a research post. Then it had been late autumn, and the countryside had been cloaked in russet and gold, filtered through a soft October mist.

The first glimpse of the town was heart-stopping. Perched on a hill above the River Hart, the town rose up like a many-tiered wedding cake from the thickly-wooded river banks to its crowning decoration: the university.

The river meandered in a large loop, which surrounded the town on three sides, so that it was almost an island, protected from the urban sprawl that had ruined so many other towns. It remained an almost perfectly-preserved monument to the Victorian age. A town in which Austen or Trollope would still have felt at home.

Its nineteenth-century founders, prosperous from the profits of iron and cotton mills, had prided themselves on their piety as well as their industry. In rendering unto God his due they had endowed the town with an extravagant amount of church spires for a population that, both in size and in outlook, was determinedly moderate. These now reflected the rays of the late afternoon sun back to the heavens.

But perhaps the true nature of its liberal-minded Victorian burghers was displayed by the cathedrals to learning which they had endowed with the profits of Empire in order that their sons and daughters would not have to go to Oxford or Cambridge, and in doing so, acquire the dissolute habits of the upper classes along with an education.

The university was a gothic masterpiece or a monstrosity, according to taste. Embellished with every architectural conceit known to the Victorians, it had been built around a green which was laid out with ornamental paths connecting the different buildings. Only five years before, there had been a fiercely fought battle over whether the nineteenth-century rule that banned anyone from walking on the grass should at last be revoked. It was the only open green space in the town and many of the younger, more radical members of staff, felt that it was elitist that townspeople, students and visitors alike should not be able to enjoy it on warm summer days.

Alicia had supported the group who came in with a late compromise suggesting that benches, designed in keeping with the town's heritage, should be placed at certain points, but that walking, sitting and lying on the green should still be banned.

The Bench Compromise, as it came to be called, was accepted, but the debate about where the benches were to be situated had carried on in sub-committee after sub-committee for two years.

The dispute about the green was not merely arcane. The university lay not only at the geographical, but also the economic heart of the town. The desire of its Victorian benefactors to be seen as men of learning, rather than just trade, had paid off, although perhaps not in the way they had envisioned.

By the mid-1960s, the last of the mills had closed down, and the university had become the mainstay of the town's economy. The rows of two-up, two-down terraced cottages which had once housed the families of overworked and undernourished mill workers who slept ten to a room, bathed in tin baths in the kitchen and shared a line of outside privies, now provided snug, centrally-heated, fully-fitted homes for the lower echelons of the university staff like Alicia. Senior lecturers and professors aspired to semi- and detached villas with front, as well as back gardens.

Alicia loved her tiny cottage. She had lavished care and attention on it in a way she had never lavished on herself, and at its heart was the kitchen, her favourite room.

It was always warm with the fragrance of cooking and the bunches of drying herbs and flowers suspended from the ceiling. The array of gleaming pots and pans and kitchen implements would have gladdened the heart of Mrs Beeton. Food as a pleasure was something Alicia had not discovered until she had left home. Mealtimes had been one of the major battlegrounds between her parents, and she had dreaded them. Her father had demanded that meals were on the table at a precise time, not a minute earlier and not a minute later. Her mother was not a good cook, and the approach of mealtimes would often reduce her to a frenzy of clumsiness – burning, cutting and splashing herself, as she attempted to get everything to cook at exactly the same time, which invariably it didn't.

Alicia was required to be seated at the table when her mother served the food, and she watched in agony as her father inspected the plate that had been placed before him. Overcooked or undercooked, too hot or too cold, too much gravy or not enough, anything could provoke a rebuke. Her father had exacting standards. But perhaps the worse offence was any variation from what he considered to be a proper meal, which for dinner was meat and two vegetables. Her mother's attempt at a curry, after her father had expressed enjoyment at a curry he had eaten at the Sergeants' Mess, had resulted in him hurling his plate across the table where it had smashed against the wall before falling to the floor.

If they got through the inspection, meals were eaten in silence. Her father attacking his as though it were the enemy, and her mother picking at the meagre helpings she gave herself like a wounded bird. Not wishing to cause further offence to her mother, or her father who abhored waste, Alicia ate whatever was put in front of her as silently and swiftly as possible, so she could excuse herself and go to her room where she would lose herself in a novel accompanied by a packet of biscuits.

But where her mother's kitchen had been a place of purgatory, Alicia's was a place of pleasure, and she heaved a sigh of relief as she lifted her bags on to her enormous pine table before reaching for the kettle.

Three cups of Assam tea and two banana and chocolate hazelnut spread sandwiches later, Alicia set to work.

By midnight, she was bleary-eyed with tiredness, but triumphant. The cottage had been cleaned from top to bottom. The spare bedroom had been aired and the bed plumped and spread with crisp, white cotton sheets trimmed with broderie anglaise and scented with lavender from the home-made, cotton muslin sachets of lavender Alicia kept in all her drawers and cupboards.

Downstairs in the kitchen, a dozen spiced wholemeal scones, a sesame seed loaf, a large Dundee fruit cake, some coconut macaroons, a lemon meringue pie and two dozen chocolate brownies lay cooling on the table.

After a cursory wash, Alicia fell exhausted into bed but lay unable to sleep for a long time. She kept repeating in her mind all the things she still had to do to make Vanessa's visit perfect. Vanessa always accused her of being a fusspot, but Alicia could not see what was wrong with trying to please somebody.

She woke with a start just after five the next morning, suddenly aware that she did not know what time Vanessa was planning to arrive. Further sleep was impossible. Driven by the fear that Vanessa might arrive before everything was ready, Alicia rushed down to the kitchen and made an extra batch of dough even before she had brushed her teeth. Still in her dressing-gown, she went into her tiny back garden and cut roses still wet with the morning dew, arranging a large bunch in the sitting room and a smaller one beside Vanessa's bed. Another inspection convinced her that no dust had managed to collect since she had whirled through the cottage armed with spray cleaner and duster a few hours earlier. Only then did she allow herself a bath.

As she surveyed her wardrobe for something to wear, Alicia felt a sense of disappointment. She had devised a uniform of twin-set and tweed skirt for autumn and winter and for formal occasions, and a twin-set and long flowing skirt, sometimes with a small flowery print but nothing too obvious, for warmer days. It was simple and comfortable. But Alicia had felt Vanessa's critical gaze at lunch, and Vanessa was probably right, she did look a bit dowdy, but her only smart clothes were two long, flowing velvet skirts, one black and one wine red with a paisley print, which she wore with white high-necked blouses. Neither were suitable for day wear.

After agonising for a while, Alicia selected a pale lavender skirt and then, with a sudden sense of daring, she put on one of her white evening blouses and added a single strand of pearls.

Now that everything was more or less ready, she wondered whether she should call Vanessa, but even as she gave the early American-style quilt on the spare bed a last unnecessary tweak, Alicia could hear Vanessa's exasperated voice: 'Oh, for heaven's sake Alicia, don't fuss!'

So she wouldn't, Alicia decided, inspecting the contents of her refrigerator. There was some cold pressed tongue, the remains of a joint of honey-roasted ham, some potted shrimp and a dozen free-range eggs — enough to make a snack lunch should Vanessa arrive that morning.

Satisfied that they wouldn't go hungry, Alicia settled down to write her paper. It wasn't easy.

Writing about food made her hungry, and necessitated numerous trips to the fridge and the boiling of copious amounts of water for tea. It was late afternoon, and she was munching yet another chocolate brownie and wrestling with a comparison between Trollope and Austen, when the sound of a car horn and the squeal of tyres in the road outside brought her back to the twentieth-century.

Fearing the worst, Alicia rushed to her front door which opened directly on to the pavement in the narrow street where she lived. Her neighbour's aged, one-eared tabby cat stood in the middle of the street, its back arched and fur standing on end as it hissed at an open-topped, white Golf GTi which had stopped only inches away.

The car door flew open, and a woman wearing a silk scarf and large sunglasses which obscured most of her face, clambered out. Vanessa shook her fist at the outraged animal.

'Bloody thing. I should have run you down!' she yelled.

In reply, the cat spat its defiance once more, and then turned on its heel and walked away, tail whisking nonchalantly.

'Vanessa,' Alicia called, waving her hand, 'I'm over here.'

Vanessa turned in her direction. 'Did you see that bloody animal? It was sleeping in the middle of the road. I was quite within my rights to squash it flat.'

'I am afraid Mrs Walmsley's cat, Marmalade, likes to sunbathe on the warm tarmac. He's getting on a bit, and I think it warms up his joints,' Alicia explained. 'People round here don't drive very fast, so he usually has time to get out of the way.'

Vanessa reached into her car, lifted out a small overnight case, and then slammed the door. 'Well, he bloody well won't get the time if he gets in my way again,' she declared, walking over to Alicia who offered up a cheek. Vanessa kissed the air beside it.

'You're here now, and that's all that matters,' Alicia said soothingly, taking her bag. 'Welcome to Heartlands.' She stood aside, and with a flourish ushered Vanessa into her front room.

'Really, sweetie, you do live a little far from civilisation,' Vanessa declared, collapsing into the largest armchair. 'I always feel I should take malaria tablets before venturing up here.'

Alicia felt a touch of irritation but brushed it away. Heartlands *was* a long way from London and Vanessa was probably shaken up by her near miss with Marmalade. What was needed was a nice reviving cup of tea. 'Why don't I put the kettle on while you put your feet up?'

Vanessa stretched out her feet and placed them on a tapestry foot rest Alicia had lovingly stitched. 'Can I give you a hand?' she called after Alicia.

'Certainly not, you relax and recover from your journey,' Alicia called through the open door. 'I hope you're feeling hungry as I've made some tea. After that we can have a long talk. It'll be just like the old days in the dorm, having you to stay.'

Her reply was an explosive sneeze, quickly followed by several more.

Alicia rushed through to the other room, clutching the warming teapot in her hand.

Vanessa was convulsed with sneezing, but one hand was pointing accusingly at the large vase of roses Alicia had placed on the coffee table.

The sneezes abated for a brief moment.

'Get them out of here,' Vanessa gasped, 'I *hate* flowers.'

Six

• • •

Alicia steadily munched her way through two scones with clotted cream and home-made damson jam, several macaroons and a large slice of fruit cake, her eyes never leaving Vanessa's face.

She had hoped that they would have a little time to chat, but that would have to wait. Fergus was much more important. Luckily, she kept a well-stocked medicine cabinet and had been able to administer a large dose of antihistamine to Vanessa. While this was soothing her irritated membranes, Alicia emptied the cottage of flowers and closed the windows tight against any more marauding pollen. Then she made tea.

But when she brought the loaded tea tray into the sitting room, a red-eyed Vanessa had waved away offers of food, seizing hungrily on a copy of Fergus's research instead. She had been reading it and sipping tea for nearly an hour.

Vanessa wordlessly held out her cup. Alicia refilled it and got up to put the kettle on again. As she waited for it to boil, she popped her head round the door to check if Vanessa was still reading.

'Is it what you were hoping for?' Alicia asked, her anxiety overcoming her timidity at interrupting Vanessa.

Vanessa grunted.

'Terminal Diagnosis – A Report on the Nation's

Sexual Health' by Dr Fergus Bartle Archibald, was more than she had dared hope for. She had only read the chapter summaries, as she hated unnecessary detail, but its message was clear: blame society's sexual ills on what Fergus described as the bourgeois, liberal intelligentsia *aka*, as he put it, the *Guardian*-reading middle classes.

They, rather than the Right, were responsible, because they were the only ones with the leisure to feel guilty, and guilt depended on the possession of a conscience, which by definition according to Fergus, the Right did not have.

This guilt about their sexuality had led them to restrict definitions of normal sexual behaviour within narrow boundaries. In doing so, they had set up a conflict between their natural instincts, expressed in their sexual fantasies, and what was deemed socially acceptable, which had resulted in widespread and corrosive neurosis.

According to Fergus, the only cure was for everyone to fulfil their sexual fantasies.

Vanessa put the manuscript down with a satisfied smile. 'This is pretty hot stuff.'

She looked at the Dundee cake. Alicia had just helped herself to a second slice.

'That looks yummy, I think I'll have some. Marks & Spencer stuff looks so good these days you can't tell it isn't home-made.'

Alicia gave her a large slice and a hurt look.

Vanessa ignored the look and took a bite. 'I was wondering,' she asked through the crumbs, 'about Fergus and you. You *do* have sex don't you?'

Alicia blinked. 'It's not that sort of relationship. We talk a lot and he likes to come round here for dinner. He says I'm the best cook he's ever met, and like most men, he's hopeless at cooking for himself.'

Vanessa popped the last bit of Dundee cake into her

mouth and reached for a chocolate brownie. 'Well, they do say the best way to a man's heart is through his stomach, but it wasn't *that* part of his anatomy I was thinking of you reaching, Alicia. Come on, you can tell me. We've known each other long enough, haven't we?'

Alicia blushed, and twisted a strand of hair around her finger.

She liked Fergus a lot, well, more than that really. He made her feel sort of warm and glowy inside, just like that glass of malt whisky he had talked her into drinking the other evening, even though she never drank spirits. The smell had made her nose wrinkle, but when she drank it, she had felt a tingly sensation which started at the base of her stomach and then spread outwards. She felt quite lightheaded after only a few sips, and had got up enough courage to confide her feelings about her unattractiveness to Fergus; he was the sort of man she felt she could trust. And she had been right.

He had pushed his chair back from her kitchen table, where they had been discussing his research over supper, and he had expansively waved his arms around.

'A man could enter here,' he declared, 'and seeing you, partake in such an epicurean banquet, that he might never desire another meal. Anyone who chooses to eat thin dry bread and water when there is a feast such as you to be had, deserves to be horsewhipped. When you pick a fruit, you don't pick one which is small and hard, you choose one which is round and plump with the promise of sweetness.'

And with that he had kissed her hand.

Just thinking about that evening still made Alicia's cheeks go quite pink. She had giggled at Fergus for his extravagant language but later that night, as she lay in bed by herself and repeated his words, a deep hot blush had enveloped her body and she had eventually been forced to get up and make herself a cup of cocoa.

'There's nothing to tell, really,' Alicia protested to Vanessa. 'We're friends and colleagues, that's as far as it goes.'

Vanessa held out her cup for another refill. 'I'm not criticising you, Alicia, you know I would never do that. I just don't think it's healthy to go without sex. I remember I once went without it for two whole weeks, and I nearly went crazy. I virtually raped the next available man I was so desperate.' She threw back her head and laughed. 'Poor thing. He didn't know what had hit him. So, come on, when am I going to meet the great lover?'

'Oh, but he's not, really he's not . . .' protested Alicia.

'But you'd like him to be.' Vanessa reached over and patted Alicia's arm, 'Don't worry sweetie, leave it to me. I'll have this man eating out of your hand.'

'Please Vanessa, don't say anything. I would be so embarrassed,' pleaded Alicia.

Vanessa shrugged. 'If that's the way you want it. But I wouldn't leave it too long if I was you. If any man is half-way decent, he won't stay lonely for long.'

Alicia glanced at her watch, then scrambled to her feet and began clearing the plates. 'Would you like to freshen up while I clear away the tea things? I hope you don't mind, but I've signed us in to dine tonight at my college as I thought you might like to meet a few of my other colleagues. I know they're longing to meet you. Fergus is going to meet us in the Senior Common Room for a drink before dinner.'

'I do hope you remembered what I said about not mentioning the reason for my visit. People can be so tiresome when they know you work in television. They always think that their opinions are worth a fortune, and start demanding money,' said Vanessa brushing some crumbs off her lap on to the carpet.

'Fergus isn't like that at all,' protested Alicia. 'In fact I don't think you'll find anyone like that here at Heartlands.'

But most of Heartlands academic staff were squeezed into the Senior Common Room at St Ethelred's that evening. Word had quickly spread that a television producer was coming, and St Ethelred's, normally known for its indifferent kitchen, had suddenly found High Table full for dinner.

Alicia was startled by the number of expectant faces which turned towards them as they came through the door. Every chair was occupied, forcing many people to stand or perch uneasily on the arms of chairs. Even though it was a warm June evening, the large arched windows which overlooked the green were firmly shut, and the room was suffocatingly musty. Despite the heat, men and women alike wore tweed or corduroy suits together with academic gowns. An odour of chalk, stale tobacco and perspiration lingered expressively in the air along with the ghosts of thwarted ambition.

Heartlands University was not among the first rank of academic institutions in the country, nor even in the second. While it had been a sanctuary for Alicia, it had been a last resort for many others denied entry into more prestigious universities. In the time before league tables, this lack of academic excellence had not mattered. It was the pursuit, not necessarily the acquisition of learning, that was considered enough. But since the 1980s, when market forces began to hungrily stalk the land, preying on the weak and the ailing, Heartlands had found it difficult to attract grants and several of its more esoteric departments had already closed down, with further cuts threatened. Word that a television producer was coming to dine had spread like a computer virus through the university, and with it the hope for publicity for a cherished department or thesis.

Vanessa hesitated in the doorway. She did not like academics. They always had such a superior air about them, which they did not merit. Degrees were a waste of time and meant absolutely nothing in the real world. She did not have one and it had not held *her* back. All the same, she had chosen her outfit for the evening with care, nothing too outrageous, just a simple black crêpe skirt and cream silk blouse. It made her look elegant but substantive, although glancing round the room, she wondered why she had bothered. She had never seen so many badly dressed people in one room before.

With a confident toss of her head, Vanessa tucked her black clutch bag firmly under her arm and followed Alicia across the room, looking neither to left or right.

A girl of about eighteen or nineteen, her black dress grey with washing, and her straw-like hair unsuccessfully scraped back under a starched white cap, stood to attention behind a table which was serving as a bar.

'What kind of sherry would you like, Miss?' she asked Vanessa.

'We have every type of sherry you can possibly imagine,' Alicia added enthusiastically.

'I'd like a large vodka and tonic with lots of ice,' said Vanessa firmly. She had a feeling she was going to need it to get through the evening.

'Vodka, Miss?' the girl squeaked. She looked hopelessly at Alicia.

'It's all right, Shirley,' Alicia reassured her, and turned to Vanessa.

'I'm afraid its a silly tradition at St Ethelred's, but we have sherry for the women and whisky for the men, although most of the men drink sherry too. We're known for our sherry cellars.' This last was said with pride.

73

'You mean you don't have anything else?' Vanessa glared at Shirley, whose eyes were wide with fright. She managed to shake her head. 'All right. I'll have a large whisky with lots of ice.'

The girl looked ready to burst into tears.

'What's the matter now?' snapped Vanessa, 'Aren't women allowed to drink whisky?'

Shirley leant across the table and whispered in Alicia's ear.

'I am afraid we have no ice,' Alicia said. 'The men drink whisky with water or soda, but Shirley could run down to the kitchen and see if they have any.'

'God forbid! I'll have it with water.'

'And I'll have a drop of that nice Amontillado, if I may,' Alicia added.

Shirley looked gratefully at Alicia and poured the drinks.

'Can we go over by the window? If I don't get some air I shall simply die,' Vanessa said loudly, taking her drink and leading the way. 'Would you mind?' she asked two elderly professors who were standing in front of the windows, deep in conversation. They moved hurriedly away.

Vanessa put her drink down on the windowsill and tried one of the windows. At first it stuck fast, but with a sudden whoosh of air and encrusted dirt, it shot open and fresh air flooded the room.

The surrounding academics backed away as though nervous of this unheard-of intrusion. Alicia and Vanessa were left stand alone, separated from the rest of the room by an invisible no-man's land.

'Dr Binns,' a deep female voice suddenly boomed from the back of the room.

It was so deep, that for a moment Vanessa thought the speaker was a man, but an imperiously-bosomed woman was elbowing her way through the common room towards them. She had dark, mannishly cropped hair and a pronounced Roman nose. Her dark-green, tweed suit looked decidedly military, but instead of the comfortable lace-ups Vanessa expected to see on her feet, she wore feminine, high-heeled court shoes and had slim, shapely calves.

'Alicia, my dear girl,' the woman said as she reached them, putting a beautifully manicured hand on Alicia's arm to emphasise her greeting. 'How nice to see you. We thought you were in London.'

For a moment Vanessa couldn't see the 'we'. Then, peeping round the large woman's elbow, she noticed a thin balding man with watery blue eyes. His mouth constantly twitched, which had an unfortunate effect on his wispy goatee beard.

'Dr Zelda Drake and Professor Ernst Gruber, I'd like you to meet my friend, Vanessa Swift,' said Alicia.

'Ah, you must be the television director we have all heard so much about,' Zelda said, grasping Vanessa's hand firmly. 'I'm afraid you have Ernst and I at quite a disadvantage. We never watch television, do we, Ernst?'

Ernst appeared to both nod and shake his head at the same time.

Vanessa was surprised to find herself looking down at Zelda. Her bearing had given the impression she was much taller, but the eyes looking up at her yielded supremacy to no one.

'You mean a television set won't fit into your ivory tower?' riposted Vanessa.

She hit her mark but Zelda did not flinch. With barely the suggestion of a hesitation, Zelda smiled, although it did not quite reach her eyes. 'No, no my dear. I was saying to Ernst just the other day, that it's time we academics tried to communicate more to the masses. So often they are fed either wishy-washy pap or downright rubbish, don't you think? I am of the opinion that they deserve something a little more challenging, perhaps even provocative and certainly more original than most of the fare that is served up these days on our screens.'

Zelda's thrust was the more effective. Vanessa's eyelashes flickered and then she looked away.

Years of intellectual sword play had sharpened Zelda's ability to find an opponent's vulnerable spots, but she had found few worthy opponents since coming to Heartlands two years ago. Zelda was a psychologist, and before Heartlands had lived in Vienna for twelve years, where she had been pursuing her research into patterns of emotional response and arousal. It was there she had met Professor Ernst Gruber, who was a palaeontologist. Their passion for uncovering the hidden past, in people's unconscious minds on her part, and in the earth's rocks on his, had developed into a passion for each other, according to Zelda. They had felt no need of marriage for they were both well past forty, and were mature enough to have no need of the psychological prop of a sanction for their union from either church or state.

According to one rumour however, Gruber had a formidable wife back in Vienna who refused to divorce him and moreover, had run Zelda out of town. No one at Heartlands had ever dared ask Zelda whether the rumour was true, partly out of fear of her and partly because the idea of anyone daring to run Zelda out of town was inconceivable. Zelda herself, when given to complaining about Heartlands which was often, explained that she would never have accepted a post at such a lowly university if it had not been for her elderly father whose rapidly ailing health had forced her to return to England to care for him. And it was true, as Zelda's friends like Alicia pointed out to her detractors, she and Gruber did share a large and rambling manor house with her ninety-four year-old father, ten miles outside of Heartlands. Much to

Alicia's distress, Zelda's detractors often went on to point out that Zelda was known to have already drawn up blueprints for converting the manor house into a block of luxury timeshare flats, and had only come back to England to wait for her father to die so she could move the builders in.

Alicia liked Zelda, and suspected it was jealousy on other people's parts that caused the unkind gossip. She liked Zelda's elderly father too, and often visited him even when Zelda was not there, taking him home-made steak and kidney pies and bread and butter pudding, which he loved. He was very sprightly for a ninety-four year-old and flirted outrageously. He loved to pinch her bottom if she ever turned her back to him. When Alicia laughingly told him off, he would wickedly protest that he had learned the habit defending king and country in the First World War in France. Nobody could possibly want a sweet old man like that to die, least of all Zelda. Of that, Alicia was certain.

But the expression on Zelda's face as she looked up at Vanessa in the Senior Common Room, made Alicia's certainty waver for a moment. It was the same look she had seen in the eyes of a leopard on a wildlife programme, just before it went in for the kill, but when Alicia looked again, it was gone, and Zelda was sipping her sherry and smiling benevolently.

'Such a good turn out tonight.' Zelda indicated the room with her glass. 'You should come to St Ethelred's more often, Vanessa dear, we do so *adore* having distinguished guests like yourself to dinner.'

Vanessa smiled frostily and drank down half of her whisky.

Alicia chided herself for thinking uncharitable thoughts. Vanessa and Zelda were getting along famously, and if only Fergus would arrive, everything would be perfect. She checked her watch. It was getting awfully late, perhaps she should go and phone him.

She turned to Vanessa, but before she could speak, there was a loud crash and the room fell silent.

'Who the hell put that table there? Damn fool place to put a table, if you ask me. Shirley, a large whisky and none of your short measure nonsense.'

The crowd in front of Alicia and Vanessa parted like the Red Sea as every head craned to see what was going on. Vanessa glimpsed a barrel-chested man with a head of wild, rust-red curls and a beard to match, trying to disentangle himself from a side table he had knocked over. He appeared to be unable to perform the simple task of lifting his leg up and out from between the cross bars, and instead was dragging the table along with him as he walked.

'Drunk again,' Zelda said loudly, so that it would carry. 'I know he's your friend, Alicia dear, but he really is the limit. He ought to be banned from polite society.'

There was a murmur of agreement.

Alicia's cheeks burned. 'I'm sure it was just an accident,' she protested faintly. 'It's so crowded in here, perhaps he didn't see . . .'

Fergus finally managed to get his leg free and gave the table one last kick, which sent it crashing to the other side of the room, causing several people to jump out of the way.

'Goal!' he roared and then drew himself up to his full height, which was about five-feet, eight inches, and hitched his rather shabby corduroy trousers up around his sizeable waist. They immediately slipped down again, so that the crotch was only six inches above his knees.

Winter and summer, Fergus had never been seen wearing anything else but these trousers and a navy blue Aran sweater that was beginning to unravel at the wrists. Together with his weatherbeaten skin, which made it impossible to guess his age – it could have

78

been anything between thirty-five and fifty-five – they gave him the air of the captain of some rusting tramp ship.

That impression was further emphasised by his unsteady rolling gait as he walked across to the drinks table, where Shirley was holding out a tumbler full of neat whisky with a smile that transformed her face.

He grinned at her and downed the glass in one. 'Another one of those, my little darling, and I'll be right as rain.'

His voice was deep and resonant with a slight Scottish burr. Holding his refilled glass, he turned and surveyed the room. 'What are you all looking at? I could sue for industrial injuries caused by that table.'

Heads turned away and conversations started up again.

Fergus spotted Alicia and raised his glass in salute. 'There you are, my pretty. Now where's this poncy media woman you want me to meet?'

Seven

· · ·

Wolfish brown eyes inspected Vanessa with a sharpness that suggested Fergus was not quite as drunk as he wanted his audience to believe.

Vanessa felt an unfamiliar prickle of apprehension. She was used to being admired, but it was not admiration she saw reflected in Fergus's eyes.

'You're a bit of a spindle-shanks. I like my women with some meat on their bones, like Alicia here.'

Fergus put his arm around Alicia's waist and gave her a squeeze. Alicia gave him an embarrassed but adoring smile, but it was lost on Fergus, whose eyes continued to hold Vanessa's.

'Still, you're probably built for speed rather than comfort as my old mum used to say.'

Fergus downed his whisky in one gulp and gave Alicia a resounding kiss on the cheek. Alicia blushed a deep rose-red.

Vanessa drew herself up to her full height, which in heels was nearly five inches taller than Fergus. His provincial cave-man attempts at charm might work on someone as unsophisticated as Alicia, but they were wasted on her.

'It's a pity your old mother didn't teach you manners as well as clichés,' she said caustically. She turned to Alicia, who was rather ineffectually trying to extricate herself from Fergus's grasp.

'Alicia, I thought you had better taste than this . . . *drunk*.'

'Another puritan.' Fergus gave a bark of laughter. 'And I thought it was only universities that were full of small-minded people.'

At this, all the Senior Common Room faces that had been staring in their direction, looked away.

'Fergus . . . Vanessa . . . Please . . .' Alicia looked helplessly from one to the other.

'I did not come all this way to bandy words with an inebriated Scot.' Vanessa managed to make the word 'Scot' sound like an insult. She turned on her heel and stalked out of the room.

Fifty pairs of interested eyes followed her to the door, and then swivelled back to Fergus and Alicia.

Alicia fumbled for a handkerchief and blew her nose. This wasn't what she had planned at all. 'I wasn't really meant to tell you this,' she gulped, 'but Vanessa only came to Heartlands to meet you. I told her about your research and she thought it might make the basis for some sort of television programme. Now she will probably never speak to you again.'

Fergus was instantly alert. He patted Alicia's shoulder. 'There, there my pet. There's no real harm done. Run after her and bring her back. I'll behave myself, I promise.'

Alicia gave him a watery smile. 'You promise?'

'Cross my heart and hope to die,' Fergus squeezed her hand. 'Now, off you go.'

Alicia gave him another grateful smile and trotted off after Vanessa.

Fergus watched her go, shaking his head. How could such innocence be contained inside such a voluptuous body? It was almost too much for a man to bear.

At first, he thought it was a ploy. He had met many a professional virgin among the ranks of academic women, and he had always found that all they needed was a bit of encouragement to shed their inhibitions, but not Alicia. Her innocence was not an artful ploy, it was the innocence of the unawakened, and that was what made stalking her so interesting. It was taking a little longer than he had expected because Alicia scared easily, but there were plenty of gratifying energetic young undergraduates around who were willing to help him with the practical side of his research into sexual fantasies, and keep him amused while he waited.

But once the term had ended and the long summer months stretched ahead, he intended to make his move. He considered Alicia as his vacation project, to be accomplished at his leisure.

Alicia was breathless by the time she caught up with Vanessa's long-legged stride, and plucked at her sleeve to slow her down. 'Vanessa, please . . . I know Fergus can be difficult and he was a little drunk, but . . .'

'A little!' Vanessa stopped and wheeled round to face Alicia. 'How could you have anything to do with such a disgusting man, Alicia? I would have credited you with more sense.'

'But you don't understand. Underneath all that bravado Fergus is really very sensitive. It's just that he's a . . .' Alicia searched for the right words, 'a bit of a free spirit. If only you'd take the time to get to know him . . .'

'Nothing could ever possibly alter my attitude to that man. I think it's best I pack my bags and go back to London.' Vanessa started walking again.

'But what about your programme?' Alicia called after her, 'I thought you had a deadline.'

Vanessa hesitated. Philip would be furious and quite likely fire her on the spot if she didn't come back with something. Fergus was only some third-rate academic. All she had to do was dangle the promise of television exposure in front of him and he would be down on his hands and knees, begging to do her bidding. He was a man after all, and she knew *just* how to handle them.

'At least talk to Fergus. How can that hurt?' Alicia pleaded, spurred on by Vanessa's silence.

Vanessa turned, only to find Fergus standing behind Alicia. 'Have you two girls made it up yet? I've had enough of that lot back there for one evening. Why don't we give High Table a miss and go to that little Ey-tie place on the Green. Is that agreeable to one and all?' He looked from one to the other.

'Why don't just the two of you go?' Alicia suggested eagerly. 'It will give you a chance to get to know each other better.'

Vanessa shrugged her shoulders; she did not want to show too willing. 'If you insist.'

Fergus patted Alicia on her behind. 'Run along with you then. I'll deliver her back to you at the end of the evening safe and sound, Scout's honour.'

He turned to speak to Vanessa but she was already striding ahead, her head held in such a way as to forbid further conversation. Fergus fell into step behind her.

You could tell a lot from the way a woman walked, he had found, far more than from the way she dressed. Some women walked with their breasts thrust in front of them, suggesting a womanly confidence in their sexuality, others walked from the hips, with a pelvic sway that promised a certain athletic sexuality. With Vanessa, the eye was drawn down to her spiky three-inch heels. Some women teetered girlishly on heels, their precariousness a signal they would not run far if chased. But Vanessa's heels struck the ground like weapons, and far from suggesting a quick surrender, they seemed to issue a challenge.

Fergus grinned to himself. There was nothing he liked more.

He was still smiling happily as they reached the

restaurant, and with an exaggerated flourish, held the door open and ushered Vanessa inside.

The *O Sole Mio* Trattoria was an Italian restaurant left over from the Sixties. White stuccoed walls festooned with empty Chianti bottles, a large, yellowing, panoramic view of Naples, photographs of antiquated Italian football teams wearing knee-length baggy shorts, and tinny musak strangling an operatic aria.

Gianni, the owner, greeted them effusively, and showed them to a dimly-lit table at the back of the restaurant. With a knowing wink at Fergus, he lit a candle inside a red glass container. He then picked up a napkin and with a great flourish, shook it out of its folds and tried to arrange it on Vanessa's lap. She pulled it from his hand and shooed him away. He backed off with a little bow.

Fergus reached for a bread stick. 'A carafe of your house red to start, Gianni,' he commanded, and then leaned across the table and pointed the bread stick at Vanessa. 'The wine list is a middle-class rite which serves to keep the working-class in their place, and excludes women from making choices. Ever seen a waiter willingly offer a wine list to a woman?'

'You, on the other hand always offer women a choice, I notice.'

Fergus looked puzzled for a moment and then roared with laughter and slapped the table. 'Quick, aren't you? I like that in a woman.'

Then, to Vanessa's astonishment, he pushed back his chair and went down on one knee. He held his hands clasped together as though in prayer.

'Miss Swift, I hereby beg your forgiveness. The wine cellars are yours to command, just tell me what you desire.'

Gianni rushed over with his arms in the air. 'Dr Archibald, is there something wrong? Have you dropped something?'

He got down on his hands and knees beside Fergus and began looking around.

Fergus grabbed him by the scruff of the neck. 'Just bring the damn wine, Gianni, that is . . .' he looked quizzically at Vanessa, 'if Madam so wishes.'

Vanessa nodded, forcing her lips to form the semblance of a smile. If she had to play along with this embarrassing pantomime she would do it, there was too much at stake.

Breathing heavily, Fergus struggled back into his chair as Gianni arrived back with the wine. He poured a mouthful into Fergus's glass and waited for him to taste it, but Fergus gestured at him impatiently to fill the glasses.

Vanessa raised hers with a gracious incline of her head and then sipped. She winced involuntarily.

'Piss awful, isn't it,' Fergus said cheerfully, downing his glass in one, 'but it's better than paying a fancy price for a pretty label. Now, what are we going to eat?'

Vanessa studied the oversized, gold-embossed, mock-leather menu which had been placed in front of her. The lengthy selection suggested an overstocked deep freeze. Fergus closed his with a decisive snap and waved it at a hovering waiter.

'Spaghetti Carbonara to start, and a proper sized serving mind, then steak and chips. Just show mine to the flame, I need some red blood.'

'And for the Signorina?' the waiter asked.

'Avocado vinaigrette followed by the grilled Spring chicken and a green salad, but no cucumber,' Vanessa ordered.

The waiter bowed again and combined the movement with topping up their glasses.

'Now, let's get down to business,' Fergus put his elbows on the table and leaned forward. 'Alicia tells me you're interested in sex.'

Vanessa sipped her wine before replying. 'I wouldn't

put it quite that way, Dr Archibald. I merely mentioned to Alicia that I thought your theories were quite interesting and could, and I must emphasise it is only a possibility at the moment, *could* form the basis for a programme I am planning.'

'That's a pity. I'm very interested in sex and they're not theories, I've put them to the test.'

His eyes held hers for a moment. Vanessa looked away. She was uncomfortably aware that sex, her own chosen weapon in situations like these, was being turned against her. She drank some more wine, which was beginning to lose its rough edge.

'Your *theories* seem to challenge most accepted teaching, Dr Archibald. How would you answer the charge that they were merely a recipe for sexual libertinism, rather than a serious psychological study?'

Fergus pointed a breadstick at Vanessa. 'The purpose of study should be to increase knowledge, but the purpose of the study of sex has been to limit knowledge by creating sexual zones which are considered abnormal and perverse, and therefore forbidden. People used to believe the earth was flat and prophesied doom and destruction for anyone who tried to sail over the horizon, but look what happened when they did, a whole new world opened up. Well, I believe there's a whole new sexual world out there if we but dare to explore it. You know what they say, Miss Swift.' Vanessa found herself forced to look into his eyes again. 'Travel broadens the mind.'

Fergus grinned evilly and snapped the bread stick in half.

Vanessa toyed with the stem of her wine glass. She felt totally disconcerted and what was worse, he knew it. She was grateful for the arrival of Gianni with her avocado and a large plate of spaghetti for Fergus.

'Would the Signorina like a little pepper?' Gianni

asked, flourishing a wooden pepper mill over a foot long.

Vanessa waved him away.

'Now take that pepper mill,' Fergus said. 'It is an archetypal phallic symbol, but why do they have such large ones in Italian restaurants?'

'It is because it prevents us having to refill them too often, Dr Archibald,' Gianni explained patiently, as he grated pepper over the spaghetti.

'There you have it!' said Fergus slapping the table. 'A collective national fantasy. Not only is the phallus gigantic, but it is also perpetually fecund so it can pump out its seed without pause!'

Gianni put the pepper mill down on the next table as though it had scalded him, and scampered off to the safety of the kitchen.

Vanessa tried to suppress a smile at the little head waiter's discomfiture and dug into her avocado, but her smile turned into a grimace. The pear was under-ripe and the vinaigrette too sharp. She pushed it away and watched Fergus, who was totally absorbed in the task of eating.

He attacked his spaghetti with a speed and lack of inhibition which astonished her. Bending down so that his face nearly touched the plate, he sucked the wriggling strands of pasta through fleshy lips shiny with orange sauce, seeming only to pause for breath when the great mound on his plate had gone. He then mopped up the last traces of sauce with the remains of a bread roll, and popped it into his mouth.

Ignoring Vanessa's glass, he emptied the remnants of the carafe into his own, and then held it aloft and roared: 'Gianni!'

Gianni came running, another carafe already in his hand. He cleared the table.

Fergus unwrapped another bread stick. 'What kind

of programme are you proposing to make. A documentary?'

'Not exactly,' replied Vanessa. 'I was thinking along the lines of an audience participation programme.'

Fergus looked thoughtful.

He pointed the remains of the bread stick at Vanessa. 'And can you give me one good reason why I should help you? You media people are arrogant buggers. Not all of us are prepared to sell our soul to get our arses on the box.'

Vanessa's eyes narrowed, but she kept her voice light. She sensed she had him interested. Everything always came down to a question of price. 'It's difficult to say at this stage of a project how much, if any, remuneration might be entailed. Your involvement in the project would depend to what extent we used your research, if at all.'

'What you mean is, that you hope you can buy my ideas for the price of dinner, as I am assuming you are picking up the bill for this evening, and then you will pass them off as your own. Isn't that how it's done?'

He held up his hand as Vanessa started to protest.

'God didn't grant you a monopoly on wits just because you live in London, even though that's what you metropolitan folk want us to believe out here in the provinces. No, if you want my ideas, you're going to have to pay for them, my girl, but before we discuss that, I like to be able to trust the people I work with, so why don't we get to know each other a little better?' He grinned libidinously, as he refilled her wine glass.

Vanessa lowered her eyes to hide her triumph. He was hooked! All she had to do was play along with his ridiculous little charade and she would have him.

Just at that moment, Gianni rattled over with a trolley and began serving their main course. The bowl of chips he placed in front of Fergus was enough to feed four people.

Claret-coloured blood oozed over Fergus's plate as he cut into his steak. He popped a large chunk of meat into his mouth and munched contentedly, as Vanessa toyed with a limp lettuce leaf.

'You don't appear to have much of an appetite,' Fergus said, pointing his fork which had another large chunk skewered on it, at Vanessa. 'Food is like sex, you should learn to savour the texture as well as the taste.'

He popped the steak in his mouth, reached for his glass, and held it up to his nose. He sniffed, his eyes half-closed.

'And you must never forget the power of smell,' he said, talking with his mouth full. Vanessa looked away. 'It is our most under-rated sense, and yet it can be the most provocative.'

He opened his eyes and Vanessa felt drawn to meet his gaze. He really did have the most strangely compelling eyes.

'Have you ever wondered why the yeasty smell of freshly baked bread sends people into orgasms of desire, and I use the term orgasm deliberately? Champagne has the same effect. They both give off that evocative, yeasty fragrance of our bodily secretions at the height of sexual excitement.'

To her irritation, Vanessa felt a sudden erotic surge. She buttered a roll, trying to regain her composure.

Fergus grinned, sensing her discomfiture. 'Ah, Miss Swift, I see that you, like most of the population of these repressed islands, have never truly explored the outer shores of your senses. We think our eyes tell us all we need to know: that this one has long legs and blonde hair, or that one has broad shoulders and slim hips, ergo we are attracted to them. But if you close your eyes and allow pheromones to do the talking, your sex life would never disappoint you.'

Vanessa bridled. 'Not that it is of any concern of

yours, Dr Archibald, but my sex life has never been disappointing. And as to your absurd theory, any of our senses can be led astray, even our noses, which is why so many people can be led by them.'

Vanessa indicated the scrawny chicken on her plate. 'Rather like this meal, it is my experience that most people promise a damn sight more than they can deliver.'

Fergus speared a large forkful of chips and popped them into his mouth. 'I think your problem, Miss Swift,' he said chewing, 'is that you have been going to the wrong restaurants.'

Vanessa picked up the chicken and with a twist, pulled it apart. She had no intention of discussing her past sex life with this man. Holding a chicken leg in her fingers, she began to tear at its flesh with her small, even white teeth.

Fergus watched approvingly. 'The Greeks have a saying: for fish, chicken and women use your fingers.'

'And do they add: and for steak and men use a sharp knife?' Vanessa retorted.

Fergus threw back his had and laughed. 'Miss Swift, I think we may get along, after all.'

He topped up their glasses. They had nearly finished another carafe of wine.

Vanessa licked her fingers and picked up her glass. She was beginning to feel quite heady. 'I'm curious to know how you carried out your research. For instance, how big was your sample?' she asked.

'Large enough. I conducted most of the interviews myself, especially the women,' replied Fergus.

'And do you think, and I stress this is purely a hypothetical question at this stage, that people would be prepared not only to talk about their intimate sexual fantasies on television, but also take part in some form of enactment?'

Fergus raised a quizzical eyebrow at her and then

crooked his index finger at Gianni who was hovering nearby. 'I'd like a large piece of the Black Forest Gateau you claim is home-made, and don't be stingy with the cream.'

Gianni looked at Vanessa, 'And for the Signorina?'

'Just coffee for me. A large espresso.'

'And two large brandies, Gianni,' Fergus called after the waiter's retreating back.

He turned to Vanessa. 'One of the key elements in sexual fantasy is exhibitionism. Fantasies are largely about that which is forbidden so, by performing a sexual act in a public place thereby risking discovery, or by deliberately performing in public, the sexual fantasy is given added excitement. Most people crave excitement, Miss Swift, but few dare to take risks except in their fantasies. So in answer to your question, yes, I do think you will find people who are willing to perform for you so the rest of us can become voyeurs – it's another popular fantasy.'

Gianni placed a mountainous piece of Black Forest Gateau, barely visible under a layer of thick cream, in front of Fergus, and gave Vanessa her coffee.

Fergus spooned a large piece of cake into his mouth, closing his eyes with pleasure. Then he opened them and looked at Vanessa.

'Tell me, Miss Swift, have you ever made love in a public place?'

The coffee burnt Vanessa's mouth. She coughed, shaking her head.

Fergus swirled the brandy around the bottom of its balloon glass. 'You know, I've often thought of a brandy glass as being rather like the womb,' he said, as his large square hands closed round the glass, caressing its contours. 'It needs warming up to release its true taste and fragrance.'

He ran a stubby finger around the rim of the glass. Vanessa watched, fascinated despite herself.

91

'Its shape is voluptuous but the entrance is smaller than the body of the glass, and it seems to close around your face before you feel that golden liquid trickling down your throat.'

He drank deeply. 'The perfect climax to a good meal.' His eyes caught hers and held them for a long moment.

To Vanessa's intense irritation, she felt a sudden tremor of warmth spreading through her body. She gulped some more coffee. She had to remain in control of the situation, make Fergus think that he was getting what he wanted. She sipped her brandy and watched him.

He turned his attention back to his Black Forest Gateau and noisily scraped his plate as he finished the last few mouthfuls. He used his hand like a cat's paw to wipe his beard, removing traces of the meal. Then sat back and drained his brandy.

The restaurant was now empty of customers even though it was only half-past ten. Gianni and the other waiters were loudly and visibly clearing up.

Fergus placed both his elbows on the table and leaned forward. Vanessa followed suit. Their faces were only inches apart.

'I was thinking, Miss Swift, that you might be interested in a little role-playing to test my theory about exhibitionism. I think you're the kind of woman who needs her palate tempted by more adventurous dishes.'

Vanessa parted her lips slightly, moistening them with her tongue. Reaching across the table she lightly caressed his hand with a long finger.

'So what's on the menu?' she breathed.

'Gianni, the bill!' roared Fergus.

Eight

• • •

'The monstrous regiment indeed,' said Fergus holding up a candelabra which illuminated a row of portraits of determined-looking women, their lips pinched with disapproval and piety.

The past principals and benefactors of St Ethelred's had believed in the virtues of hard work, thrift and Christian charity, and their expressions suggested that they considered immortality in oil to be an unnecessary frivolity.

Vanessa and Fergus were standing on a dais at the end of St Ethelred's long, oak-panelled refectory, from which academics dining at High Table could look down at the serried ranks of undergraduates.

The ceiling of the hall was vaulted like a church, with great oak beams soaring upwards, disappearing into the gloom. By candlelight, the refectory had an eerie magnificence, an effect accentuated by Fergus's vulpine features, which were made grotesque by the flickering light.

Vanessa had followed his shadowy figure in a dream-like journey through St Ethelred's moonlit grounds to a basement door, which had yielded to a kick and a curse. Fergus had seemed to know his way through the dark, labyrinthine corridors even though he was not a member of St Ethelred's, which had clung to its women-only status.

Fergus placed the candelabra on the polished surface of High Table and pulled out the half bottle of brandy he had insisted Gianni sold them before they left the restaurant.

'To fantasy and fornication,' he said, raising the bottle in a defiant toast to the row of disapproving portraits. They represented everything he had learned to hate, growing up in a run-down but respectable part of Edinburgh which had aspirations to be in Morningside, but was forever doomed to tight-lipped disappointment. He had never been able to understand the virtue in moderation and self-denial.

He took a long drink and handed the bottle to Vanessa.

She hesitated. She was beginning to feel, if not quite drunk, at least very heady. She had a feeling the situation was slipping out of her control, an unfamiliar but not altogether unpleasant sensation. She tipped the bottle and drank deeply, her body quivering with anticipation.

Fergus held out an academic gown he had taken from a collection hanging outside the door. College rules dictated that everyone wore a gown to dine at St Ethelred's, and a few hung outside the door for the use of visitors or the forgetful.

'Put it on,' he commanded.

Vanessa's nose wrinkled with disgust, the gown smelt fusty with the odour of many bodies. She held it between the tips of her fingers.

Fergus laughed. 'The smell is part of the fantasy. It is the odour of sanctimoniousness.'

Vanessa gingerly put it on.

Fergus shook his head. 'You've got to strip first.'

Vanessa hesitated for a moment, and then stepped out of her mini-skirt and unbuttoned her silk blouse, letting it slip to the ground. She stood naked except for a black g-string and high-heeled black shoes, the candlelight suggesting contours where there were none on her lean body.

She hooked one finger inside her g-string but Fergus motioned her to stop.

'Leave it,' he said hoarsely and held out the academic gown.

Vanessa turned round so he could slip it over her arms. As he did, he ran his hands fleetingly over her body; they felt rough and calloused. Vanessa shivered.

Then Fergus tore off his clothes, hurling his jumper and trousers into the sepulchral gloom beyond the circle of light created by the candles. He almost fell over in his haste to remove his underwear, hopping around on one leg to remove his grubby blue Y-fronts followed by his socks; one grey, one tartan and both full of holes.

Fergus was powerfully built with a barrel chest and short sinewy legs. His chest was covered with thick, matted hair which curled across his shoulders and down to his buttocks. Vanessa stared, both repulsed and excited by his simian hairiness.

Fergus handed her a mortar board which fitted neatly over her sleek hair.

He stood in front of her grinning. 'And now for the first lesson.'

Cupping his hands under her buttocks, he lifted Vanessa effortlessly on to the richly polished surface of High Table.

Alicia absentmindedly ran a finger along the grain of her scrubbed pine kitchen table top and wondered where Vanessa and Fergus could be. The *O Sole Mio* closed at ten thirty. She yawned and replaced the top on her fountain pen. She was usually in bed by a quarter to eleven with a cup of cocoa, which she drank while listening to *Book at Bedtime* on Radio Four, but it was now nearly midnight. Alicia considered calling Fergus's rooms and then dismissed the idea. He had a dragon of a landlady who did not approve of women calling him, particularly at this time of night. Anyway, if they were there, it was because they were discussing Fergus's research, which was precisely what she had wanted them to do, and they would not thank her for interrupting them.

Alicia allowed herself a little smile of satisfaction. Perhaps after all she had succeeded in bringing her two best friends together. Earlier that evening as she had watched Vanessa stalk across the green ignoring Fergus, her heart sank, wondering if she had done the right thing. Dinner at High Table had not helped either. She had rushed into the refectory just in time to hear four hundred voices murmuring 'Amen' at the end of Grace. Eight hundred curious eyes had watched her as she walked across the platform to High Table.

Punctuality was deemed a virtue at St Ethelred's, and under the antiquated college rules, latecomers to meals could be asked to pay a forfeit like reciting a poem, although this was now usually invoked only on special occasions. However, as Alicia was painfully aware, members of the academic staff were, as a point of honour, meant to set an example to students by never being late and she had not only been late, but also without her guests.

The three empty chairs opposite the college principal, Dame Nora Pike, had loomed large as Alicia edged her way round High Table trying to avoid catching anyone's eye. The Principal was a tall, raw-boned woman with short iron-grey hair. Her tendency to peer over her half-moon rimless spectacles made her look absent-minded, but her sharp brain had served on many government committees. She had greeted Alicia with a benevolent smile.

'Alicia dear, do come and sit down. Ought we to await your guests?'

'I'm terribly sorry, Principal, I must apologise on behalf of my guests, but I am afraid they are unable to dine with us tonight.'

'Never mind, my dear, another time perhaps.' The Principal had given Alicia another kindly smile as though sensing her discomfort.

'Not coming! How awfully disappointing. I was so looking forward to meeting your producer friend, and engaging her in a discussion about the moral responsibilites of the media. It's all very well to discuss these things in theory, but to have a practitioner here in our midst would have been so stimulating.'

The speaker was the college bursar, Dr Joyce Niblett, who was sitting on the Principal's left. She was a tiny plump woman with a doll-like face accentuated by heavily rouged cheeks, and high, pencil-drawn, black arched eyebrows.

'I'm sure Vanessa would have been delighted to discuss the media with you, Joyce. But I am afraid she had some rather pressing business to attend to. You know what the media is like, there's always some last minute problem,' Alicia said, colouring slightly at the untruth.

'I suppose she must lead a frightfully busy life,' Joyce's tiny hands had fluttered as she spoke. 'But one should never be too busy to sit down and consider one's moral obligations, should one?'

The Bursar was fond of telling how she had dedicated her life to St Ethelred's and her girls, as she termed the undergraduates. It was her way of fulfilling her role as a mother. A role denied her by the untimely demise of her fiancé Bertram, who had unfortunately strayed into the path of a number 11A bus just two days before their wedding. Although the event had happened over twenty-five years before, its re-telling never failed to bring a tear to Joyce's eye.

'Speaking of morals. Didn't I see your friend, Miss Swift, go off with Dr Archibald earlier? Was he part of the last minute problem?'

It was Zelda Drake who was sitting on Alicia's right. Alicia's colour had deepened.

'They had some business to discuss, so I suggested they go somewhere quiet to eat,' she said defensively.

'My dear Alicia,' Zelda laughed and slapped Alicia playfully on the arm. 'I wasn't suggesting anything immoral. I was merely referring to Dr Archibald's interesting little treatise. I gather he's having problems getting it published. I was only saying to Ernst the other day . . .' at this point Professor Gruber peered round Zelda's elbow and gave Alicia a wan smile, ' . . . that I should like to see a copy. I'm told it's causing quite a stir.'

'Anything that challenges accepted ideas always does,' said Alicia loyally.

'Oh, how I shudder when I hear those words,' Joyce had intervened, her hands fluttering like trapped birds. 'They usually mean another step down the road to moral decline and degradation.'

'And our friend, Dr Archibald, knows a thing or two about degradation,' Zelda said meaningfully. 'I am constantly surprised that you seem to enjoy his company, Alicia. I can't imagine what you two find in common.'

'Oh, but we . . .' Alicia had begun.

'Mind you, I have to be honest and you know me, I really do believe honesty is the best policy,' Zelda continued, her hand on Alicia's arm. 'I have to be honest and say that my very brief conversation with your friend, Miss Swift, left me with the very distinct impression that she isn't, how should I say this? She isn't quite one of us either.'

'Oh, but she's . . .' Alicia had begun again.

'Are you sure you've been quite wise in suggesting they go off together? I mean, do you know exactly what business they are discussing? The term "business" covers such a wide range of possibilities.' Zelda's tone had sounded concerned, but her eyes were bright with malice.

Alicia yawned and put the papers she had been marking into a file. Zelda was wrong about Fergus, they did have a lot in common. Why else would he come to her cottage so often for dinner? *And* he was a gentleman, in spite of all the rumours about him and his girl students. Zelda of all people should know it was wrong to listen to gossip.

Looking back at her life, she had not had an awful lot of experience with men, Alicia conceded, and she had made a few mistakes, but that did not mean she was wrong about Fergus. She had not been wrong about Roger, she thought, it was just that they had both been much too young.

They had met when they were both students in their second year at university. Roger was tall and mournful looking, and wore old-fashioned and ill-fitting clothes which flapped around his thin body as he dashed everywhere, always late for something, dropping books and papers as he ran. His glasses were in constant danger of falling off the end of his nose, and they sometimes did, causing the other students to laugh. It was this that had led Alicia to take pity on him.

She had taken to sharing a table in the library with him and then her lecture notes, and in their final year she shared the uncomfortably narrow bed in his digs. But while they managed to shyly lose their virginity to each other, the joys of sex had eluded them.

Roger heroically blamed their failure on his inexperience, claiming it was a man's role to give pleasure, but Alicia had never been able to rid herself of the feeling that if she had been attractive enough, he would not have had any problems.

It was a feeling confirmed by her next relationship. She met Marcello on her first foreign holiday in Italy, when she was twenty-four.

After ten days viewing the cultural glories of Venice, Florence and Rome, Alicia had, against her better judgment, allowed the travel agent to talk her into a week's beach holiday in Sorrento. She spent the first two days sitting miserably on the beach with a towel draped around her shoulders and a T-shirt across her legs. By the time she met Marcello on the third day, she had a very odd suntan, but he had reassured her that she was the perfect shape for a woman.

Marcello seemed to imbue the word 'woman' with a dark eroticism that no Englishman could ever achieve, and when he gazed into her eyes over a glass of Chianti, to the strains of a violinist wringing every last emotion from the chords of 'Santa Lucia', Alicia wanted to believe that Marcello was indeed the great love of her life, as he so passionately declared she was of his. And when he swore in the most heart-rending terms that he would die if he did not make love to her, Alicia thought she would be a murderer to refuse.

That night he had romantically climbed up to her first-floor room via the balcony in order to protect her honour, but Alicia's pleasure had been short-lived. Her previously gentle Romeo's rough onslaught on her body left her bruised, but unmoved.

While he dressed, Marcello lectured Alicia on the superiority of Italian lovers, a subject he expounded on for longer than he had taken to make love. According to him, frigidity, like homosexuality, was an English disease. Alicia could only nod wordlessly and bury her tearful and ashamed face in the pillow. She now had irrefutable proof of her failing as a lover and a woman, if proof she needed.

The next morning, a chance enquiry of the other assistant manager at the hotel had revealed why Marcello had chosen the romantic route to her room, and added humiliation to her grief: Marcello had a wife and four children with one more *bambino* on the way.

Alicia had tried to avoid men after that, burying herself in her reading and her life at St Ethelred's.

Then, nearly four years later, she met Donald. Donald was in the history faculty at Heartlands. He lectured in military history and made her laugh. He was also gentle and loved the theatre and cooking. They had so much in common and almost before Alicia realised it, he had become part of her life. A day did not pass without them either seeing each other or talking for at least an hour on the telephone, exchanging gossip about fellow academics or discussing a new book or recipe. Donald had given Alicia the affection she craved, constantly hugging and kissing her and to her delight, he always put his arm through hers when they walked together. They giggled about other people's relationships and he was very sympathetic when she confided her past problems to him. He had reassured her that it was just a question of meeting the right man, and Alicia was sure she had met him. All she had to do was be patient. But then she introduced Donald to Vanessa.

She had known Donald for over a year before Vanessa's diary and a day trip to the theatre in London allowed them to meet.

As lunch progressed, Donald and Vanessa seemed to get on very well. It turned out that they had some mutual acquaintances in the light entertainment department of the ITV company where Vanessa was then working, with whom Donald had been at Cambridge. His undergraduate stories about them made Vanessa scream with laughter.

But Alicia's delight had not lasted long. When

Donald left the table for a moment, Vanessa turned to Alicia with a triumphant look on her face.

'He's a closet queen, I told you so all along.'

Alicia felt as if she had been stabbed in the heart. 'No, he's not. He can't be,' she said faintly.

Vanessa had dropped her napkin on to her plate with a finality that brooked no opposition. 'That man is a fag. I knew it the moment he walked through the door, and when he told me he was at Cambridge with Stuart and his crowd, well, no more need be said.'

But Vanessa as usual had said it.

'They were known as the Fen queens at Cambridge, and they still form a mutual admiration society in Light Ent. None of them will admit to it, of course, and their closets are mink-lined these days but everyone knows about them. God, you're such an innocent, Alicia, didn't you see all that eye contact between him and that little Italian waiter?'

After Donald there had been nobody until Fergus.

Alicia shook her head, trying to clear the memories away. It was so easy to dwell on bad things when you were tired, she thought, stifling another yawn. It would be so thrilling if Vanessa did decide to use Fergus's research; perhaps she could be involved in the programme in some way. She had, after all, typed and annotated all Fergus's research, and it would be so exciting to work with the two people she cared about most in the world.

Alicia cut a large slice of fruit cake and boiled a kettle for tea. She knew she shouldn't be eating at this time of night because it kept her awake, but as she wanted to wait up to hear Vanessa's news, it wouldn't really hurt.

The shrill tone of the telephone almost made her choke, and she had to swallow a mouthful of tea before she could answer.

It was Zelda, her voice high-pitched with

excitement. 'Alicia, I'm dreadfully sorry to call you at this time of the night, I do hope I didn't wake you.'

Without waiting for a reply, she rushed on.

'My dear, the most *extraordinary* thing is happening.' She divided the word extraordinary up into its many syllables. 'Joyce was doing her usual late-night round of the college ... you know how she patrols around like some powder puff vigilante. Anyway, she heard some noises coming from the refectory. Well, she didn't know *what* to do so, she came banging on my door, squawking about thieves stealing the college silver. It took me ages to get some sense out of her, because she was quite hysterical. I was all for calling the local constabulary but she got even more hysterical, babbling on about scandal and the good name of the college.

'So I decided that a little investigation was called for and telephoned Ernst, who bravely volunteered to come over. We decided not to barge in the door just in case it really was burglars, so Ernst and I found a ladder in the basement and we managed to put it up against the outside wall – without any help from Joyce, I might add. She just stood there wailing about death and destruction like some latter-day Cassandra.

'Then Ernst, he's so brave I can't tell you, climbed up and had a look. He was quite pale when he came down. He says the place is lit with candles like some sort of religious service and that there are two people in there and you'll never believe this: one of them is Dr Archibald!'

Alicia felt her throat go dry.

'Well, that made Joyce quite hysterical again, although I pointed out it couldn't be much of a Black Mass with only two people, so short of slapping her face, I left Ernst on guard, and we came back to my rooms so I could get some brandy down her and telephone you. I thought as you are Dr Archibald's friend, you might be able to talk to him, so that we can avoid the terrible scandal Joyce is so frightened of causing if we involve the police. Anyway, Joyce has finally stopped whimpering so we will rendezvous with you in the rose garden in ten minutes.'

Before Alicia could say anything, Zelda hung up.

Alicia stood still for a few moments, the receiver still held to her ear, then she slowly replaced it. What on earth was Fergus doing? And why had he gone back to St Ethelred's, and what was Vanessa, if it was Vanessa, doing with him? A range of possibilities, none of them probable, raced through Alicia's mind as she pulled on a cardigan and searched for a torch.

The walk back to St Ethelred's would have been pleasant in any other circumstances. Beneath a full moon, the warm night air was heady with the scent of flowers, as Alicia threaded her way through St Ethelred's rose garden into the shadow cast by the massive refectory building where, for the first time, she was forced to use her torch.

Whispered voices alerted her to the waiting posse, but Alicia still jumped when the narrow beam of her torch picked out Joyce's ghost-like figure, dressed in a long, white, high-necked dressing-gown and an old-fashioned mob cap, from which wisps of hair escaped over her shoulders. Alicia tried to suppress the thought that she looked like Rochester's mad wife in *Jane Eyre*. Zelda, on the other hand, looked magnificent in a brocade robe and embroidered velvet slippers that looked fit for a sultan's harem while Professor Gruber struck an incongruous note in a powder blue track suit and stout walking shoes.

Alicia switched off the torch as her eyes became accustomed to the dark.

'Are they still in there?' she whispered.

Professor Gruber nodded. 'I slipped back inside and

turned the key in the lock. They are trapped, they cannot escape.'

'Oh, Alicia,' Joyce's voice was a high-pitched squeak. 'What shall we do? Such a scandal . . . the college's good name . . . the Principal will never forgive me.'

Zelda looked ready to carry out her threat to slap Joyce round the face.

Alicia put her arm round Joyce's shoulder. 'Whatever is going on in there is not your fault, Joyce. I'm sure the Principal will understand.'

Joyce appeared mollified and gave a little sniff.

Zelda gripped Alicia's arm, pulling her away from Joyce. 'The ladder's quite steady if you want to go up. Ernst and I will hold it just to make sure.'

Zelda propelled Alicia on to the first rung of the ladder before she could protest. She took a deep breath and handed her torch to Joyce, then grasped the ladder with both hands. The only way was up.

The first six rungs were easy. Alicia paused, breathed out, then started climbing again. She reckoned she was about half way when she stopped to look down. It was a mistake. The earth seemed to heave and her stomach with it. Three ghostly faces, their eyes and mouths dark gashes in the moonlight, looked up at her like demons from some nether world. Alicia shut her eyes and clung to the ladder, which juddered unsteadily.

The enormity of what she was doing suddenly came to her. She didn't like heights, and she certainly didn't like ladders which had probably been lying in a cellar for years, rotting away with damp and woodworm. Alicia felt beads of perspiration forming on her forehead, yet she was icy cold.

'Are you all right?' A disembodied voice came from somewhere far below.

Alicia forced herself to open her eyes. 'Yes. Fine,' she hissed through gritted teeth.

She looked up, knowing she could not look down, and cautiously placed her foot on the next run, testing it for any signs of weakness before she put all weight on it.

The second part of the climb seemed to take an eternity, but finally the window ledge was within her grasp. Ignoring its sticky icing of bird droppings, Alicia clutched at it, her breath now coming in short gasps.

She steadied herself and then leaned forward, trying to see through the window. A small patch of glass had been wiped clean of dirt, probably by Professor Gruber. Alicia made it larger.

At first, all she could see was a flickering golden light which illuminated the faces of the portraits on the wall above High Table. Their eyes appeared to be staring at something below them. Alicia climbed another rung and pressed her face to the window. Twenty feet below, she could see High Table lit by a circle of candles, its polished surface glowing in the light.

Fergus lay stretched out full length on the table. His feet were towards Alicia and he had a broad smile on his face. Alicia caught her breath when she realised he appeared to be almost naked.

She couldn't quite see whether he was completely naked, as someone was kneeling astride him. Whoever it was had their back to Alicia and wore a black cloak and a curiously shaped hat. With a sudden start, Alicia realised that his companion was wearing an academic gown and a mortar board.

Fergus said something and the other person laughed, throwing back the gown with a flick of their hands, revealing white shoulders and unmistakably female legs.

Alicia rubbed the window, trying to see better. Fergus had reached up and placed his hands on the woman's breasts. She began to move up and down, slowly at first and then her movements quickened. She tossed her head back and the mortar board fell to the floor. Alicia saw glossy, deep auburn hair and then glimpsed a familiar profile.

It was unmistakably Vanessa.

Alicia pulled back from the window as though she had been struck hard in the face. The sudden movement almost dislodged the ladder, and down on the ground Zelda and Professor Gruber clung on as it rocked precariously. Joyce squeaked loudly and put her hands over her eyes.

Oblivious to what was going on below, Alicia stared through the window, white-knuckled where she was gripping the window ledge. But all she could see was a bearded face gazing intently at her and a soft voice urging: 'Come on, you can trust me Alicia. Tell me your most secret fantasy.'

Anguished tears rolled down her cheeks as she remembered how she had whispered to Fergus that she would like to make love on High Table and feel the cool polished wood beneath her back, so she could laugh up at the portraits of those disapproving matriarchs.

A strangled sob forced its way out between her lips.

'Alicia. Are you all right? What's happening up there?' Zelda was standing eagerly on the first rung of the ladder. 'Is it a Black Mass?'

Alicia shook her head and wiped away her tears with the back of her grubby hand. She suddenly felt devoid of emotion. She climbed quickly down the ladder, oblivious to its shaking.

Three pairs of eyes looked at her expectantly when she reached the ground.

'Follow me,' she commanded and marched off without waiting to see if they did.

She strode through the side door which Joyce had left open and up the stairs to the refectory entrance. Zelda's long stride only just kept up with hers while Professor Gruber was forced into an awkward jog. Joyce tried to keep up with a combination of jumps and skips, punctuated by nervous squeaks as she trailed in their wake.

At the door of the refectory Alicia turned and waited until they had all caught up with her. She turned an emotionless face to them and placed a finger on her lips, wordlessly holding out her hand to Professor Gruber for the key.

With infinite care, Alicia unlocked the door. Then she silently pushed it ajar and felt along the wall for the light switches.

From within, half-human grunts echoed by urgent sobs had begun to rise to an exultant crescendo.

In one swift movement, Alicia pushed the door open wide and switched on all the lights.

Vanessa was crouched on all fours on the table, naked except for the mortar board which she had replaced. Fergus was kneeling behind her, his thighs locked against hers, his face and upper body flushed and sweating. The veins in his neck bulged in stark relief, as his mouth opened to emit a wild howl which echoed round the rafters.

In the silence that followed, Joyce whimpered and then swayed as though she was going to faint. Professor Gruber placed a steadying arm around her shoulders.

The movement seemed to galvanize Zelda who strode forward, pushing Alicia out of the way. She stood with her hands on her hips.

'What is the meaning of this?' she demanded.

Fergus took one look at her outraged face and sat back on his heels laughing, leaving Vanessa momentarily frozen in her dog-like position.

Alicia picked up an academic gown and held it out to Vanessa, who looked as though she was in a trance.

'Put some clothes on,' Alicia snapped, 'we're going to see the Principal.'

Nine

• • •

An ashen-faced Alicia led the procession from the refectory to the Principal's rooms. She marched stiff-backed, not trusting herself to look back and see if anyone was following her.

Alicia felt numb, but her mind continued to work, replaying the picture of Vanessa and Fergus, their naked writhing bodies locked together on High Table over and over, again and again. When she tried to shut them out by closing her eyes, it was worse. She saw them in close-up and in slow motion.

She felt a hand on her shoulder, and shrugged it off.

'Look, Alicia, let's not be so po-faced about this, shall we? Fergus and I *are* consenting adults.'

Alicia kept going, her eyes fixed on an invisible spot ahead.

Vanessa was forced to lengthen her already long stride to catch up with Alicia. 'You always were an insufferable prig,' she panted angrily. Vanessa was not used to being ignored, particularly by Alicia. 'I sometimes wonder why I ever let you be my friend. You were only a scholarship girl after all.'

Alicia stopped dead, causing a pile-up behind her. Joyce shrieked as Professor Gruber stepped on her foot and Fergus grinned wolfishly as Zelda's ample front pressed up against him. Zelda stepped back with an exclamation of disgust and jabbed Professor Gruber in the chest with her elbow. He spluttered like an outboard motor.

Oblivious to the chaos she had caused, Alicia turned and glared at Vanessa with a look of such hatred that Vanessa stepped hurriedly back.

Alicia turned on her heel and marched off again. The others followed, but a little more slowly this time, with Joyce limping and Professor Gruber clutching his chest and wheezing.

The procession reached the Principal's door. Alicia was about to knock when Joyce suddenly remembered her position and pushed forward. 'I think this had better be me,' she said, and rapped smartly on the door.

It opened almost immediately. The Principal was jacketless and in her stockinged feet, her blouse unbuttoned at the neck. A strong smell of tobacco hovered about her. If she was puzzled by a group of people – some of them dressed in nightclothes – standing outside her door at a quarter to one in the morning, she didn't show it.

'Yes Joyce, what can I do for you?' she inquired with a slight lift of her eyebrows.

The Bursar had begun to recover her normal self-importance. Her chest puffed up like an indignant sparrow. 'I'm afraid I have to report a serious breach of the college rules, Principal,' she replied.

'Can't it wait until the morning, Joyce? I'm in the middle of preparing a speech for tomorrow.' The Principal's tone was mildly impatient.

'I'm afraid not. I really would recommend you deal with it now. I couldn't be held responsible for what would happen if news of this got out.'

'Very well.' The Principal held the door open and motioned them in.

Dame Nora's sitting room was large and spacious with floor to ceiling windows overlooking the town and the river. It was decorated with a dark green lily motif William Morris wallpaper, and furnished with an abundance of well-worn dark brown leather furniture, most of which was invisible under mounds of papers. There were several large, glass-fronted book cases which housed untidy collections of leather-bound books, and against one wall stood a mahogany desk which looked ready to collapse under its weight of books and documents. A small space had been cleared in the middle, on which stood a glass, a half-empty bottle of whisky, and an ashtray overflowing with cigarette butts. The smell of tobacco was overpowering.

Without asking them to sit, the Principal settled herself on the swivel chair which stood in front of the desk. She raised an inquiring eyebrow at Joyce who opened her mouth to speak but was forestalled by Zelda.

'We have just caught these two . . . two . . . people,' she indicated Vanessa and Fergus, 'indulging in the most disgusting acts in the refectory. Never in all my years have I ever seen anything quite so repugnant. It's not that I'm a prude, no one could ever accuse me of being that, I've always believed in live and let live but . . .'

Joyce broke in, anxious not to have her role in the drama upstaged. 'I was the one who actually discovered them, Principal. I was doing my rounds. You know how I like to check the college last thing at night just to make sure the housekeeper has locked all the doors and windows – you really can't be too careful these days and Mrs Roberts is getting on – anyway, I heard these noises.' Her nose wrinkled. 'It sounded like animals at first . . .'

The Principal interrupted. 'Before we go any further – I know Dr Archibald, but could someone tell me who this young woman is?'

Alicia stepped forward. Her voice was low but

111

distinct. 'This is Vanessa Swift. She is . . . was, my oldest and dearest friend.'

The Principal looked from Vanessa, who was staring disdainfully into the distance, to Alicia's stricken features and nodded as though she understood. She turned to Joyce.

'I appreciate that Dr Archibald and Miss Swift are guilty of trespassing, but I am still at a loss to understand what other heinous crime they are accused of committing. Could you be a little more explicit, Joyce?'

'These two – ' Joyce pointed a wavering finger at them as though their identification was in question – 'were committing vile acts of a carnal nature on High Table. They have committed an abomination on the very surface where each night we ask God to bless the food we eat.' She paused dramatically. 'An abomination of the worst kind, transgressing the laws of God and of man, and I have three witnesses who will testify conclusively that . . .'

The Principal held up her hand as Joyce's voice became increasingly Perry Mason-like. She fixed her gaze on Fergus. 'Is this true, Dr Archibald?'

'I wouldn't have put it quite like that,' Fergus blustered. 'Let's just say it was all in the cause of scientific research.'

'Research!' Zelda's voice rose several outraged decibels. 'How dare you call fornication research.'

'We all have our methods, Dr Drake. Mine are empirical rather than theoretical,' Fergus grinned. 'And some of us think that human sexual responses are better tested on human beings than on white mice, or is that how you get your sexual kicks, making white mice twitch?'

Zelda audibly clenched her teeth and a mottled purple flush spread up from her neck. 'That is slander, I shall instruct my lawyer . . .'

'Ladies, gentlemen, please,' the Principal commanded. 'Can we keep to one dispute at a time. I think I have a clear, though thoroughly distasteful picture of what took place tonight. Dr Archibald, I shall request an emergency meeting of the Academic Council tomorrow to discuss your behaviour. You can explain your actions, if there is an explanation then, although in the circumstances, I shall recommend that steps are taken to terminate your tenure immediately. On the evidence I have heard tonight, I feel you are unfit to be in a position of trust.'

She turned to Vanessa and the chill factor in her voice dropped off the bottom of the thermometer.

'I have no jurisdiction over you, Miss Swift, but I can ask you to leave the college immediately and never to return. You probably neither understand nor care about what St Ethelred's represents in terms of the education of women and their fight for equality in all walks of life. A squalid incident like this could sully both our reputation and all we have striven for. I understand from Dr Binns that you are a member of the media. If just one whisper of this incident gets out, I shall see to it that your part in it is fully documented. Do I make myself clear?'

Vanessa flushed and tried to meet her gaze, but was forced to look away.

'But Principal . . .' Joyce objected.

'There is nothing more to be said tonight, Joyce,' the Principal said firmly. 'And it goes without saying that no word of what has happened is repeated outside this room.'

She turned back to her desk, forbidding any further discussion.

They filed silently out of her office where Joyce took command. Clinking her collection of keys like some latter-day chatelaine of the castle, she led the way to the main entrance, locking the massive front doors behind them with the sliding of bolts, which had the finality of a drawbridge being raised. Still silent, the group split into two and went their separate ways through the gardens.

Back at Alicia's cottage, Fergus settled himself comfortably into an armchair, while Vanessa went upstairs.

'Those old biddies worked themselves into quite a lather, didn't they? Old Joycie and stormtrooper Drake have always had it in for me. I think they wanted a lynch party.' His voice was jocular.

Alicia stared accusingly at him; she couldn't trust herself to speak. In the silent walk back from St Ethelred's, she had felt tears welling up, and she ached with misery and the effort of holding them back.

Fergus leaned forward and put his elbows on his knees, composing his features into an expression of concern. 'If you want to yell at me, Alicia, yell. Let your feelings out – it's so much healthier. You have that dispiriting Anglo-Saxon tendency to bottle up your emotions.'

Alicia's look turned to one of outraged incredulity. 'Tell you what I'm feeling,' she burst out, 'after the way you have betrayed me with *her*! You used my private thoughts for your own perverted ends.' She rubbed her hands on her skirt as though trying to clean them. 'I feel dirty, as though it were me on that table. What I told you was private.' Her voice finally broke. 'I *trusted* you.'

'Oh, come now Alicia, I've never tried to hide what I'm like from you,' Fergus protested mildly.

'And that makes it all right to sleep with my best friend, does it?'

'Hardly sleeping, my dear Alicia. Such a passive and misleading term, and such typical English understatement. Try to be more direct: we were fornicating, screwing, fucking, banging, bonking.' He enunciated

114

the words slowly and deliberately. 'There are so many verbs to describe it and they are all active.'

'After all,' interjected Vanessa, who was now standing at the bottom of the stairs with her weekend case in one hand, 'it's not as though you and Fergus were having an affair. You told me so yourself. Honestly Alicia, I really can't understand what all the fuss is about.'

Alicia stood up and advanced on Vanessa, clenching and unclenching her fists. 'You must have had a good laugh at me over dinner.' Her voice was low but charged with anger. She looked back at Fergus. 'Vanessa always did love telling stories about me. The more ridiculous they made me, the better. *Virgo intacta*, the Great White Whale – isn't that what you nicknamed me at school?' She turned back to Vanessa who shrugged and looked away.

'You thought I didn't know, but I did,' Alicia continued, her voice rising. 'Whose idea was it to go to St Ethelred's? Yours? You must have nearly died laughing, acting out the fevered sexual fantasies of a repressed old maid.'

'There you go again,' Fergus said, 'putting yourself down as usual. You really ought to be more positive, Alicia.'

Alicia pointed at the door. 'Get *out*! I hate you both and I never want to see either of you again.'

Vanessa flounced out of the door with a toss of her head but Fergus turned back. 'That was the first positive emotion I've ever heard you express, Alicia.'

Alicia grabbed a vase of dried flowers and hurled it at his departing back, but it smashed harmlessly against the closed door. Outside, Vanessa threw her case into the back of her car and climbed in. Fergus got in beside her. She wrenched the car into gear and accelerated hard.

'After all I've done for her, how dare she treat me

like that,' Vanessa raged. 'And those other shrieking harridans,' she continued, barely braking as the car sped through the narrow streets of Heartlands, 'it was like being attacked by a flock of harpies. I've always thought that there was something deeply unhealthy about all-female institutions.'

She glanced at Fergus, who was silent. 'Where shall I drop you off?'

'London,' he replied, settling down in his seat and closing his eyes.

Ten

• • •

'My dear, I simply *had* to come over and find out what happened after you left us last night. Are you all right? You really don't look at all well.'

Zelda's eyes were greedy with curiosity as she tried to peer round the door which Alicia had only opened a few inches.

Zelda stood on tiptoe and looked over Alicia's head. 'Have they gone?'

Alicia nodded, plucking listlessly at her matted hair. She didn't trust herself to speak.

'You probably feel a little like I do. I couldn't sleep a wink last night, I was so upset. Ernst was so supportive. He made me drink a cup of milky cocoa and take a couple of paracetamols for the shock. I felt positively shattered.'

Alicia tried to focus her thoughts. There were few things she felt sure of any more, but one thing she knew for certain, there was no way Zelda or anyone else could possibly feel the way she did. She desperately wanted to ask Zelda to go away, so she could crawl back into the dark little hole she had inhabited since last night, but her throat still refused to make any sound and Zelda was not easily thwarted. She gently but firmly prised Alicia's fingers from their hold and pushed the door wide. As she stepped into Alicia's sitting room there was a loud crunch. She had stepped on the broken pottery which still littered the floor.

After throwing the vase at Fergus's retreating back, Alicia had blindly lumbered around the room, smashing her entire collection of Clarice Clift pottery, before collapsing at the foot of the stairs where she had finally rocked herself into a grief-sodden sleep.

Zelda's thin-soled, gold ballet pumps afforded her little protection from the shards of broken pottery, but she manfully ignored them as she strode into the middle of the room and stood with her hands on her hips, surveying the destruction. 'Well,' she eventually managed.

Alicia wiped a grubby hand across her face and then waved listlessly at the mess on the floor. 'It was an accident. I . . .' She could get no further, tears threatened to choke her.

Instead, she knelt down heavily and attempted to pick up some pieces.

Zelda crouched next to her and prised the broken pottery from Alicia's hands, dropping it back on the floor as she pulled Alicia to her feet. 'Leave everything to me,' she commanded, shooing Alicia up the stairs. 'What you need is a long hot bath. Go on, I can find my way around,' she urged, as Alicia hesitated.

But Alicia needed no further prompting. Discarding her crumpled clothes on the floor, she poured nearly half a bottle of Camomile and Lavender bath oil into the claw-footed little Victorian bath tub, which she had rescued from a junk shop and which had cost so much to restore. Despite an occasional little hiccup of a sob, she began to revive as scented steam began to swirl around the bathroom. Alicia carefully eased her stiff body into the warm water and lay soaking, listening to the sounds of Zelda bustling around downstairs.

After about twenty minutes, the comforting smell of frying bacon began to waft up from the kitchen. It succeeded in making her mouth water, even though she had sworn to herself that she would never be able to eat again. Five minutes later, her face pink and shining and her hair back to its normal glossy, well-brushed self, Alicia, wrapped in her bathrobe, was sitting in front of a plate of fried eggs, bacon, sausages, tomatoes and mushrooms.

For the first time, she noticed Zelda's outfit: bright purple ski pants and a billowing over-shirt with a start-ling purple, yellow and green pattern, and realised it must be Saturday. Alicia glanced at the wall clock. It was 8.30 in the morning. Only a few hours had passed, yet it felt like a lifetime.

'I've already eaten, so I'll just have some toast and marmalade,' Zelda said, helping herself from the large stack of toast she had put on the table.

Alicia devoured her food as though starved, barely pausing for breath between mouthfuls.

Zelda watched approvingly as she waited for the tea to brew. 'Emotional traumas always make me hungry too. I can't understand these women who say they can't eat when they are unhappy. I'm sure it's the sign of a neurotic personality.'

Alicia nodded, her mouth full of Cumberland sausage.

'I thought it best not to bring Ernst along, as I thought we ought to have a little girls' talk,' Zelda said, sitting down at the table with two mugs of tea. She heaped three teaspoonfuls of sugar into Alicia's mug and stir-red it. 'There, a little bit of sweetness will give you energy. It's good for shock too.'

Alicia gave her a grateful smile and gulped a mouth-ful. She was glad that Zelda had come now. They had never been particularly close, but she was proving a real friend. A lot of people thought Zelda overbearing, but she was really very kind and well-meaning. People might snigger about Zelda and Professor Gruber, but they were obviously happy. It must be nice to have someone considerate enough to make milky cocoa, Alicia thought, and her eyes immediately filled with tears again.

Zelda reached across the table and patted Alicia's hand. 'I'm very sorry my dear, this whole affair must be very trying for you. I know how you felt about Dr Archibald.'

Zelda didn't, but she was determined to find out.

'There was nothing between us, at least . . . not like that,' Alicia said wretchedly. 'But I did, well, I had hoped . . .'

'I think you ought to count your blessings, my dear. I think you had a lucky escape. That man was a pernicious influence on his students and a notorious womaniser,' Zelda said tartly.

'I know he had a bit of a reputation, but he was always a gentleman with me,' Alicia sighed wistfully.

'He was probably just waiting for the right moment to pounce, men are all the same,' Zelda said firmly. 'Look what he did last night and with your best friend, too.'

'It was probably her idea,' Alicia's tone was harsh.

'Oh, surely not,' Zelda protested unconvincingly.

Alicia poured herself some more tea. Zelda waved the pot away, her eyes never leaving Alicia's face.

'I suppose I've always known what she was really like, it was just that I didn't want to admit it,' Alicia said slowly.

'Well, I have to say that I didn't take to her from the start, and neither did Ernst, and he's always a good judge of character,' Zelda said. 'There are certain women . . . how shall I say this, who always let the side down. Men will always be slaves to their libidos, but women should be above such feelings.'

Why? Alicia suddenly thought. What good had it done her trying to be above those feelings? Perhaps if she had been different, Fergus would not have chased after Vanessa. It was all her fault. A tear squeezed its way out of the corner of her eye, trickled down her cheek and plopped into her tea. She sniffed.

'Tell me something,' Zelda asked. 'Why on earth did you allow Dr Archibald and your friend to go off together like that? I should have thought it a trifle unwise.'

Alicia swallowed. 'It was my fault really. Vanessa came to Heartlands to talk to Fergus about his research. She was very excited about it, and thought it might make a good television programme . . . or was it a series? I can't remember. Anyway, it seemed like a good idea to let them talk it over by themselves. I thought it might be a break for Fergus, he's had such a hard time lately with all those academic journals turning him down.'

Zelda's eyes narrowed. It was too much. She had spent months quietly feeding the choicest bits of gossip about Fergus to the right people and now, just when there wasn't an academic journal in the country that was prepared to publish him, his research was going to get national exposure on television.

She tore the piece of toast she was holding in half. Even though it was over a year ago, she could still hear the sound of his bellowing laughter echoing in her mind. She would never understand what grotesque impulse had made her, Dr Zelda Drake, suggest to that buffoon that he come back to her rooms. Nor would she ever forgive him for rejecting her. She thought that he would stay away from her after that, but then he had started to come round to St Ethelred's, openly courting Alicia under her nose. She had tried to warn Alicia, but Alicia wouldn't believe her. Last night had presented the perfect opportunity to prove to Alicia what Fergus was really like, but even she had been shocked by what they had seen when they burst in on

121

Fergus and Vanessa. Although later, when she recalled the scene, she found herself more than a little aroused. Luckily Ernst had been on hand with his soothing milky cocoa.

Zelda offered Alicia some more toast. 'Now, tell me about this Swift woman.'

'She was always the most popular girl in the class, everyone wanted to be in her set. I think it was because she was always first at everything. Not academically, of course,' Alicia said hastily, 'but in the things that matter when you are fourteen. All the other girls tried to look like her. I remember once, she decided she wanted to be blonde, so she dyed her hair and all the girls in her set dyed their hair too.'

'Did you?'

'I didn't have enough pocket money to go to a hairdresser, so Vanessa poured a bottle of peroxide over my hair one night in the dormitory. It looked terrible and started coming out in handfuls. I was given washing-up duty for a month, as it was against the rules to dye your hair.'

'But what about Vanessa?'

'Oh, she said she had been out in the sun. She always seemed to get away with things, even then.'

Zelda sipped her tea thoughtfully. 'I wonder what people would think of her if they knew what she really gets up to.'

Alicia looked worried. 'Oh, but we couldn't. Remember what the Principal said. It would cause such a scandal.'

'I was merely speaking hypothetically, Alicia dear,' Zelda patted her arm. 'I wasn't really suggesting you actually *do* anything. It's just such a pity they will get away scot-free. But, as no doubt our admirable bursar would say: vengeance is mine, saith the Lord.'

'But what about the Academic Council? Surely they

will revoke Fergus's tenure, they are bound to listen to the Principal,' said Alicia.

Zelda buttered another slice of toast and loaded it with marmalade. 'I'm sure they will, Alicia dear, but Fergus will just get a post somewhere else. Given the nature of his offence, the Council are bound to keep their findings secret because of the scandal. And what about your friend? The Academic Council can't do anything about *her*,' she continued between mouthfuls, 'and she has betrayed your trust, humiliated you in front of your friends and stolen your erm . . . boyfriend.'

It wasn't quite the word she was looking for, but it would have to do.

The tears welled up in Alicia's eyes again and she fumbled for a handkerchief. She had never been sure of her feelings towards Fergus before, but now she knew for certain that she must be in love with him. Why else would she feel so awful?

Zelda produced a handkerchief, and Alicia gratefully blew her nose. 'There, there, I didn't mean to upset you,' said Zelda, patting Alicia's free hand. 'I'm sure they will get their comeuppance in the end.'

But they wouldn't, would they? Alicia thought miserably, and blew her nose again.

Heartlands had been a haven of peace – a small, unchanging, predictable world in which she felt secure. Now it had all changed, changed utterly. Whatever the Principal had said, word would be all over the university before the end of the day. She felt exposed, naked. And all because she had trusted Vanessa.

She tried unsuccessfully to refold Zelda's handkerchief and offered it back to her, but Zelda waved it away. Alicia crumpled it up and put it into her pocket, sipping her tea thoughtfully.

'Zelda, could I use your London flat for a while?

Term's nearly over and I really need to get away for a while.'

Zelda looked hard at her. 'Are you sure London is quite the right place?'

Alicia toyed with the pepper pot. 'I just want to go to a few museums and maybe an art gallery or two. You know the sort of thing.'

'Well, if you're sure that's what you want, you're welcome to my little cubby hole. Ernst and I are off to Hungary for the summer. The Blue Danube beckons to our romantic souls. I can hear those gypsy violins already.'

Zelda rose to her feet and, closing her eyes, danced round the room to the strains of a silent waltz. With a final twirl she opened her eyes.

'Ah, how much better the Europeans understand the grand passions of life. When love and honour are betrayed, they cry out for retribution,' she cried dramatically, throwing out her arms.

Alicia hiccuped and put her hand over her mouth.

Mistaking the hiccup for a sob, Zelda enveloped Alicia in a diaphanous embrace. 'My dear, I know how simply wretched you must feel, but believe me, in a little while this will have all blown away like dust in the wind, poof! And then life will return to normal. Trust me.'

Normal, thought Alicia, as she gasped for breath cocooned in Zelda's suffocating embrace. Whatever else life could be, it would never be normal again.

And then just as she thought she was breathing her last, Zelda let go.

'Better?' Zelda beamed.

Alicia could only nod as she drank in fresh air.

'No more tears,' Zelda admonished, 'and Ernst and I will expect you for lunch tomorrow when, if you still insist, I will give you the keys to my flat.'

*

124

Alicia *had* insisted and four days later, she was carefully counting out a ten per cent tip into the outstretched hand of the taxi driver who had driven her from Euston to Zelda's flat in Camden Town.

It was the first time in her life that she had actually been relieved to see the grubby, rubbish-strewn, anonymous streets of London. Even the dull, indifferent eyes of the cab driver, as he watched her struggle to lift her suitcase from the cab, were welcome after the questioning eyes which had followed her everywhere she went on campus those last few days.

An emergency meeting of the Academic Council was enough to rouse intense interest, but when it became known that the meeting and its findings were to be kept confidential, curiosity had fomented into a frenzy of speculation that had engulfed the entire university. The pressures of end of year exams and finals were forgotten, as people clustered in excitable groups all over the campus.

When Alicia had been summoned to attend the Council meeting late on Saturday afternoon, she found her route to the Council room strewn with people who fell suddenly silent as she walked past. The twelve members of the Academic Council listened gravely to her halting account of what had happened, only stopping her once to debate among themselves the correct word to describe what Fergus and Vanessa had been doing on High Table. After a brief altercation, it was decided by an eight to four vote that fornication would be used for the official report. Alicia only got through the ordeal because of the kind urging of Dame Nora, who afterwards assured her that she had done well and must now put the experience behind her.

But she had been left with the feeling that in some way what had happened had been her fault. Vanessa was *her* friend, and if she had not invited her to Heartlands, none of it would have happened. Joyce had hinted as much when she had telephoned later, to tell Alicia that Fergus had not turned up to the Council meeting and that nobody could find him. Alicia had the feeling that Joyce thought she was hiding him. Only Zelda had seemed really sympathetic.

She had turned into a real friend, Alicia thought, as she gazed at the formidably steep flight of stone steps leading up to the front door of the tall house which contained Zelda's flat.

By the time she had dragged, bumped and lifted her suitcase up a further three flights of narrow, dingy stairs inside, Alicia's chest was heaving and her arms felt as though they had been wrenched from their sockets. She leant, gasping against the door to Flat D, trying to remember whether Zelda had said to jiggle the key then pull the door, or push the door and jiggle the key. When she finally got the combination right, she found that Zelda's description of her flat as a cubby hole was accurate. It was the kind of flat estate agents described as compact.

Three doors led off a tiny hall. The first led into a bedroom, in which most of the floor space was occupied by a double bed pushed up against three walls, and a large wardrobe took what little space was left. Next door was a tiny bathroom, which necessitated any occupant to either stand on the toilet or wedge themselves between the toilet and the handbasin in order to open the door to get out. The living room was L-shaped with a tiny galley kitchen at one end, partitioned off by a lacquered screen, decorated with peacocks. One large window opened out on to an unsafe-looking balcony barely two-feet wide, on which stood a window box containing assorted weeds.

The only seating was an ornate but faded *chaise-longue*, draped with multi-coloured, fringed shawls, and a bank of floor cushions covered in an assortment of oriental carpet fabrics which appeared to be the source of a strong, earthy odour, not unlike the sort of smell Alicia would have associated with a camel.

In front of the cushions was a long, low table in dark wood carved with exotic Japanese-looking figures and inlaid with mother-of-pearl.

There was a large shell on the table which looked as though it was used as an ashtray, and which still had some ash in it. Alicia picked it up and sniffed. The ash had a distinctly odd smell. She smiled, thinking it was probably some sort of incense. Zelda liked to think of herself as a bit of a Bohemian.

Having unpacked her clothes and squeezed them in beside Zelda's many flowing, kaftan-style dresses and tops, Alicia made herself a cup of tea with some long-life milk she found in a cupboard, and opened a packet of chocolate biscuits she had brought with her for emergencies. Then she settled herself down on the *chaise-longue* to study her *A-Z of London*.

She had been right. Vanessa's flat was only two streets away. She would take a look at it later, but her first priority was to buy some food, and she had noticed a rather interesting looking patisserie just along the road.

Eleven
• • •

'Magnificent, isn't it?'

Vanessa looked in the mirror. Behind her, stretched out on her bed was Fergus, naked.

His arms were propped behind his head and he was gazing contentedly down at his massive erection which rose pale and taut, out of the dark hairiness of his body.

Vanessa twisted the top off her lipstick. 'Tell me something,' she said flexing her lips. 'Why do all men worship their pricks?'

She began to apply a thick creamy coating of lipstick, skillfully exaggerating the fullness of her lips.

'Because only a divine being could be an instrument of both such agony and ecstasy that it even makes pissing a pleasure. Freud was right about penis envy. From the moment a little girl realises she cannot pee in a beautiful golden arc, like her brother, jealousy is born.'

Vanessa pursed her lips together and blotted them with a tissue. She checked the result in the mirror and then swivelled round on her seat. 'Balls,' she retorted tersely before slipping her feet into a pair of black suede, high-heeled slingbacks. She stood up and checked her appearance in the mirrored wardrobe doors which ran the length of the room.

Fergus groaned loudly. 'It's no good. I can't stand it.

Either you come over here or I'm going to have to take the situation into my own hands.'

Vanessa stood looking at him, her hands on her lycra-smooth hips. She had never met anyone quite like Fergus before.

Driving back to London after the debâcle at St Ethelred's in the early hours of Saturday morning, he had woken up just north of Luton, and to avoid a multiple pile up, she had seen the sun rise spreadeagled on the bonnet of her GTi in the car-park of a motorway service station, with the dawn chorus providing a descant trill to the lorry engines being revved up nearby. Even now, she grew hot at the memory.

They had stopped twice more after that, once in a layby and once in the deserted car-park of a giant DIY superstore. When they eventually got back to her flat just after eight that morning, she hadn't even had time to close the front door before Fergus pulled her on to the floor, forcing her to kick the door shut in the face of her startled neighbour who was setting out for his morning jog.

Five days had passed in much the same way.

There had been no mention of Fergus leaving. In fact, they had hardly spoken at all except to telephone for Chinese takeaways at whatever hour of the day or night one of them, usually Fergus, felt hungry. The pile of discarded foil containers in the kitchen was enough to keep several generations of *Blue Peter* devotees happy.

At first, Vanessa had been a willing partner. Although she felt repelled by Fergus's coarseness, the more he repulsed her, the more excited she became. Each time they had sex, she felt she was striking another blow at those dessicated old women at St Ethelred's. How dare they pass judgement on her and dismiss her like a schoolgirl?

But Fergus's continued presence in her flat was

wearing. Since her split from Jeremy three years ago, she had learned to enjoy living on her own. It wasn't that she didn't want men around, she did, but only for sex. Waking up with a man always complicated things, because it demanded some kind of post-coital conversation in which the man invariably wanted reassurance about his sexual performance, and Vanessa could never be bothered to lie.

But conversation with Fergus wasn't the problem. Far from it. He woke up only to demand food or sex. His sleeping habits were the problem. She had had sex with men who rolled over and immediately fell asleep, but with Fergus, it was as though orgasm triggered narcolepsy. No matter where, or in what uncomfortable or unusual position they had been having sex, he would fall into a deep sleep from which it was impossible to wake him and Vanessa would find herself trapped by the dead weight of his body, or entangled by his limbs which seemed to experience instant rigor mortis. And what made it worse was that Fergus didn't just sleep, he snored in great shuddering bellows that made sleep almost impossible for anyone within a one-mile radius.

As a result, she had barely managed a few hours of uninterrupted sleep since arriving back in London, and was in no fit state to attend the production meeting that morning, especially as she had not written the programme proposal Philip wanted.

She thought that after a day or two Fergus would want to discuss the programme, but she had been wrong, and every time she suggested they talk about it, he replied that business could wait and made a grab for her. She had played along with him because she wanted his co-operation, but her career could wait no longer.

She glanced at her watch. 'Look, Fergus, I really don't have the time. In exactly one hour and thirty-five minutes from now, I have to present a cogently argued proposal for a series based on your research, and I have not as yet committed one word to paper. Now if you would help me . . .'

Fergus waggled his tongue suggestively and grinned.

Vanessa sighed and hitched up her skirt as she walked over to the bed and straddled him.

'You'd better make this quick and no falling asleep,' she warned him as she lowered herself down.

Fergus closed his eyes with pleasure as his back arched up to meet her.

Ten minutes later, Vanessa was perched at the breakfast bar in the kitchen, sipping black coffee. Fergus ambled into the kitchen still wet from the shower, wearing a bed sheet like a toga. Behind him, Vanessa could see a trail of damp footprints and sodden towels. She shuddered at the thought of how the bathroom must look.

Among the many things she had disliked about Jeremy was his sentimental streak. Not only had he refused to throw anything away, but he had also insisted on filling their large, rambling house in Clapham with the decaying clutter of Swift family memorabilia. When he had first suggested bringing a few things from home, she assumed he meant some antique furniture, and she had awaited their arrival with some excitement. But although what had turned up was old, it was most definitely not antique, and completely worthless. When she moved into her own flat after the divorce, she determined to make it a hymn to minimalism, devoid of ornament or any form of clutter. Until Fergus had walked in the door.

Everywhere he walked, sat or lay, he left the imprint of his presence behind him. Discarded clothes, half-eaten food, dirty glasses, and always, everywhere, whorls of hair which clung tenaciously to sheets and towels and blocked plug holes, like some kind of fluffy

131

spoor. Vanessa could not understand why the man leering across the bar at her was not completely bald, given the amount of hair he had shed in her flat.

'What's for breakfast? I need to keep my strength up with you around.' Fergus reached out and tried to grab one of her breasts.

Vanessa slapped his hand away, but tried to sound pleasanter than she felt. She had to regain control of the situation.

'Fergus *darling*, I really do feel we should concentrate on business for a little while.'

'I can't think on an empty stomach. The old grey matter doesn't function without nourishment,' said Fergus noisily rooting around in a kitchen cupboard.

'Oh, for God's sake sit down.' Vanessa's patience snapped, and she began to look for something she could cook.

Her fridge was empty except for a mildewing jar of stuffed olives, the yellowing remains of some green vegetable and a pot of a sinister-looking brown substance which may once have been paté. Her cupboards yielded a tin of artichoke hearts, several tins of anchovies, dried pasta in assorted shapes and a tin of steamed treacle pudding.

Vanessa couldn't imagine why she had treacle pudding in her cupboard, she loathed the stuff. It must have been a leftover from her days with Jeremy, who loved nursery food.

For a moment she felt almost nostalgic for Jeremy. The contrast between him and Fergus could not be greater. Jeremy had his irritating little habits, but he had been so malleable. And his body had been so hairless.

According to the instructions on the tin, the pudding needed only a few minutes in the microwave. After another search for a tin opener, she managed to empty about two-thirds of the pudding into a soggy mound on a plate, pushed it into the microwave, and jabbed the controls.

She perched on a stool opposite him. Inspiration had come not a moment too soon.

'Right. I am, as they say, up shit creek. But you are going to be my paddle. Instead of a proposal, I am going to present *you* to the production meeting. You can tell Philip the broad outlines of your theory, and hopefully dazzle him with science, which will keep him happy for a few days more until I can write something down. What do you think?'

The ping of the microwave pre-empted Fergus's reply.

Vanessa banged the plate in front of him.

'Where's the custard?' he demanded, poking at the pudding with his spoon. 'You can't have treacle pudding without custard.'

'I'm out of milk,' Vanessa said between clenched teeth.

Fergus grunted and began eating.

'So, will you do it?' Vanessa asked.

Fergus ignored her until he had wolfed the last of the pudding. He had been wondering how long it would take Vanessa to get down to business. He'd expected her to insist on it much sooner, but perhaps she had been trying to ensure that he would be in thrall to her charms before she made her move. If so, she was mistaken. Vanessa was an entertaining enough diversion, but only until he had decided what to do next. He yawned and then drank some of Vanessa's coffee, aware that she was impatient for his reply. Fergus stole a glance at her. She was handsome enough in a lean sort of way, but she was not really his sort of woman. She reminded him of the kind of women he had grown up with, hard of body and hard of mind. He liked women to be of a more generous disposition. Now Alicia had breasts in which a man could happily drown, although sadly, that was unlikely to be his fate now, and she could cook too. Still, Vanessa was willing enough, or at least would be while he had something she wanted.

'What's in it for me?'

Vanessa's eyes bulged. 'Absolutely bloody nothing if you don't get a move on and we miss this meeting,' she yelled.

'All right, all right.' Fergus held his hands up in mock surrender. 'Give me two minutes.' He made for the bathroom, trailing the sheet behind him.

Vanessa forced herself to take several deep breaths, and then she began to rehearse what she was going to say to Philip.

A minute later, Fergus reappeared dressed in his jumper and socks. 'Have you seen my underpants?' he asked looking around.

Vanessa stared in horror. She had forgotten. Fergus only had the clothes he was wearing when he left Heartlands.

'Aha,' he declared triumphantly and pointed.

Vanessa followed his finger.

An extremely grubby pair of underpants was dangling from a ceiling light. Fergus scrambled on to a chair and pulled them down. 'Now all I need is my trousers,' he said, cheerfully wandering back into the living room.

Vanessa followed him and sat down heavily on her now grubby white sofa. How could she possibly take him into Right Pryce Productions? He looked positively squalid. She squared her shoulders. She had no choice.

Fergus appeared again, this time fully dressed but with his hair even wilder than usual. He held up the reason.

'I'm afraid your comb isn't up to much.' Half the teeth were missing.

'Keep away from politics,' Vanessa instructed him once they were finally in the taxi. 'All that crap in your thesis about liberal bourgeois conspiracies is passé. All people want to know about is sex.'

'Avoid analysis and stick to people humping donkeys, you mean?' said Fergus sarcastically.

Vanessa took a deep breath. She was not going to lose her temper, at least not yet. 'Look, the academic world might have time for splitting hairs, but television has to grab an audience by the short and curlies in the first few seconds. We don't have time for reasoned argument and anyway,' she shrugged, 'anyone who sits and stares at a box in the corner of a room all day is not exactly going to be a member of Mensa, are they?'

'So you're suggesting I forget my political and intellectual principles and do it for money?' Fergus enquired.

'Exactly. And one more thing . . .'

Vanessa hesitated, as a nightmarish thought had just presented itself to her. Supposing anyone found out that she was sleeping with a man who looked as if he belonged under the arches at Waterloo Station? She would die, simply die.

Fergus put his head on one side and gave her an enquiring look. 'I think it's better that we don't mention that you are staying with me. It would be wrong for me, as the producer, to have anything other than a business-like relationship with someone who might be signing a contract with the production company.'

'So are you saying that you're worried someone might think that you are sleeping with me in order to get me to sign over the rights of my research to you?'

'Well, not exactly . . . I wouldn't, of course, but . . .' blustered Vanessa.

Fergus reached over and squeezed her thigh. 'Then I'd better warn you, I don't come cheap.'

Twelve

• • •

'Nice bum,' Fergus nodded approvingly at Heather's plump buttocks, which were tightly encased in a pair of cut-off jeans.

'Little bitch,' muttered Vanessa under her breath as Heather disappeared.

Heather had uncharacteristically insisted on behaving like a proper receptionist when they arrived, and had leapt up and barred Vanessa's way as she attempted to sweep past into Philip's office. Vanessa was sure it had been an attempt to make her look small.

After a few moments, Heather reappeared with Philip.

'Vanessa, and only . . .' Philip checked his watch with an exaggerated gesture, 'ten minutes late for our meeting. How refreshing!'

He looked at Fergus, taking in the frayed sweater, baggy trousers and scuffed suede shoes, and raised an interrogative eyebrow at Vanessa.

Vanessa mustered a reassuring smile for Philip, while jabbing Fergus sharply in the ribs with her briefcase to stop him ogling Heather. 'This is Dr Fergus Archibald from Heartlands University, Philip. He's a lecturer in experimental psychology, and it's his ground-breaking research which I hope will provide the hard core of the series. I thought it might be useful for him to come along to today's meeting so that the team could meet him.'

'Hard core indeed, I like that,' Philip chuckled mirth-lessly as he shook Fergus's hand. 'Welcome to Right Pryce Productions, Dr Archibald. Why don't we go through to the boardroom, the others are waiting.'

Philip had decided to hold the meeting in what he termed the boardroom, to avoid any repetition of what had happened at the last meeting. Unfortunately it was a rather small room with barely enough space for a large round table and chairs, and it had no windows, which meant it got stuffy, particularly on a warm sum-mer's day.

Philip had learned the art of the meeting at the BBC, and prided himself on being its master. Meetings were the battleground of modern man, and needed careful tactical planning and strategy. He had allowed Vanessa to take him by surprise last time, and to undermine his authority – but not this time.

He had thought carefully about it, and decided that a round table would deter individual precedence and encourage team spirit, while at the same time allowing him to assert his authority by being at the hub of the wheel.

Vanessa's unexpected guest had not been part of his calculations, but if this was her attempt to outflank him, he would not allow it to succeed. He straightened his shoulders and opened the door.

Only Rosie looked up as they walked in. She had been doodling on her note pad, and hastily turned the page over. Hugo was punching the buttons on his personal organiser, and Vijay had his feet on the table and his arms behind his head.

'Good morning, or to be pedantic, good afternoon ladies and gentlemen. Vanessa has kindly brought a surprise guest to our little gathering.' Philip's tone managed to intimate that the surprise was not altogether welcome.

'Let me introduce Dr Fergus Archibald, an eminent psychologist, who has given up his valuable time to come and tell us about sex, a field in which Vanessa tells me he is a great expert.'

Philip looked around the table waiting for someone to laugh. No one did.

He reeled off the names and titles of the three sitting down to Fergus and then motioned him to a chair at the other side of the table.

As Fergus made his way round to his seat, Philip grabbed Vanessa's elbow. 'Why on earth did you bring Archibald along?' he hissed. 'You know I don't like civilians at our production meetings. Everything in its proper place.'

'Without him we don't have a programme,' Vanessa hissed back, and made her way round to sit next to Fergus.

Philip pushed Vijay's feet off the table before sitting down. 'Now, if you can all turn your attention to the business in hand, Vanessa is going to tell us about *Forbidden Fruit*.'

Vanessa took a deep breath, but before she could say anything, Fergus snorted with laughter.

'*Forbidden Fruit*, that's rich!' He snorted again.

Vanessa flashed him a warning frown. 'A fully fleshed out proposal will be on your desks by the end of the week, but in the meantime, I thought it would be useful to summarise progress so far, and then I will hand over the meeting to Dr Archibald, who will familiarise you with the main conclusions of his research.'

She paused and cleared her throat self-importantly. 'My proposal is that we make a series of half-hour programmes called *Forbidden Fruit*. It will be a studio-based, audience participation programme with video inserts, some of which will be provided by viewers, and presented by Gabriella Wolfe.'

She looked across at Philip, who beamed approvingly. 'Each programme will feature punters . . .' she turned to Fergus, 'that is to say members of the public, who will act out their favourite sexual fantasy, aided and abetted by actors and whatever equipment or other accoutrements they may desire.'

Fergus raised his hand like a supplicant school child.

Vanessa swallowed her irritation and nodded graciously at him.

'Might I enquire what qualifications this Wolfe person has to present a programme of this nature?' Fergus asked.

Vijay gave a hollow laugh.

'Miss Gabriella Wolfe is considered to be one of the most experienced and professional television presenters in the business, Dr Archibald,' Philip replied firmly. 'She can handle anything.'

'She may be an excellent television presenter.' Fergus emphasised the word television. 'But what are her qualifications to discuss the psychological ramifications of sexual fantasies?'

Philip raised his eyebrows in an 'I told you so' signal to Vanessa.

'Gabriella will, of course, be fully briefed by me before each show,' Vanessa intervened, giving Fergus a warning look. He ignored it.

'Are you suggesting that years of dedicated research can be reduced to fit on the back of a postcard?' he demanded.

'You obviously do not understand the nature of the medium, Dr Archibald,' Hugo drawled. 'We will not maximise the potential of this idea by presenting some dry old academic thesis. Viewers are interested in sex, not psychology.'

A vein twitched in Fergus's right temple. Even before Hugo had opened his mouth, Fergus had taken a dislike to him. No man should have silky blond curls and baby pink skin beyond the age of three. Hugo ignored his glowering look.

'I hear what you're saying, Dr Archibald, I'm sure we all do,' Philip reassured him with a smile. 'However, I think what Hugo is saying is that television has a duty to entertain as well as to inform.'

He placed his elbows on the table and his fingertips together. 'Just because a subject is serious, does not necessarily mean that by introducing it to a wider audience in a popular format, we are trivialising it. Surely it is beholden on those of us who have been privileged with an education beyond a certain level, to bring subjects that shed light on human behaviour to a popular medium in such a way as to make them accessible to those who have not enjoyed our considerable advantages. However, I am sure I speak for all around this table when I say that while we may be the practitioners, we are all willing to learn from a master. So please, the floor is yours, Dr Archibald.'

Philip sat back, satisfied with himself.

Fergus looked around the table. Only Vanessa and Philip met his eyes. Rosie blushed and looked down at her notebook, pen poised. Hugo appeared to be playing some sort of computer game, while Vijay's eyes were half closed. Fergus grinned. He would make them pay attention.

'As you ladies and gentlemen of the media don't like being bothered with too many facts and figures, I shall endeavour to be brief.'

He pushed his chair back and stood up, scratching his head and gazing into the middle distance. Philip looked enquiringly at Vanessa but she kept her gaze on Fergus. A lot depended on what he was going to say, including her job.

Fergus cleared his throat self-importantly.

'In crude layman's terms, the main thrust of my thesis, "Terminal Diagnosis – a Report on the Nation's Sexual Health", is that we are damaging our physical and psychological health by suppressing our true sexual nature – most of which is revealed in our sexual fantasies.'

As his speech gathered momentum, he began to pace up and down, forcing Hugo and Vijay to twist round uncomfortably in their seats to see him.

'The creed of the so-called liberated Sixties was that sexual fantasies were an amusing and generally harmless pastime. The hors d'oeuvre to the main course – not essential, but stimulating to the taste buds. But all the so-called sexual revolution gave us was the freedom to fuck in a purely mechanical way. Ask yourselves, if there really was a sexual revolution why, thirty years later, is there still so much sexual frustration?'

Fergus looked around, but nobody seemed to be prepared to answer the question. He put both hands on the table and leant forward. 'I believe there is a bourgeois conspiracy to control sexuality,' he said darkly. 'The bourgeoisie had the most to lose from the changing socio-political order and so, with their intelligentsia masquerading as liberals, they have seized upon the sexual revolution and by appearing to sanction it, use it as a means of control. Marx preached that control of the means of production meant controlling power in society, well I believe that control of the means of pleasure gives far greater social and political power.'

At this point Vanessa coughed meaningfully and tapped her pen on the table. Fergus raised an ironic eyebrow at her and then straightened up. 'Have you ever asked yourselves *why* prostitution is the oldest profession? Men very rarely go to prostitutes for straight penetrative sex. What they want is to indulge in their fantasies by being tied up, beaten or humiliated. And why do women suffer most from depression? Because their sexuality is far more powerful than men's and their fantasy life far richer, yet they have even fewer outlets than men to express their true sexuality.

'I contend that we are guilty of suppressing our true sexuality by dismissing it as fantasy and daydreams, and we are condemned to frustration until we learn to liberate it,' Fergus announced in ringing tones, and paused majestically before walking around the table. He stopped behind Rosie and placed his hands on the back of her chair. She smiled nervously. She had tried to concentrate on what had been said, but some of Fergus's arguments had been a bit above her head.

Fergus lowered his voice. 'Take, for instance, the millions of women who buy the kind of romantic novels which are churned out by Mills and Boon.'

Rosie looked desperately around for help. She and her mother devoured at least six romantic novels a week between them.

'An essential part of these novels is that the heroine is unwilling to yield to the hero. The readers are waiting, or should I say, yearning for the moment when the heroine, ostensibly against her will, is swept off her feet and finally surrenders to the passionate embrace of the hero and his throbbing manhood. The heroine cannot appear to be willing but once the man has demonstrated his dominance, she can be just as uninhibited, because she can tell herself that she has no free will in the matter. Romantic love is equated with sexual dominance on the part of the man.

'Twenty years of feminism have not brought about a fall in the sale of these novels – rather the reverse – as well as a demand for increasingly explicit surrender scenes.

'So what does this tell us about female sexuality? That the average woman yearns to be dominated and coerced. Their fantasy lives are full of themselves being tied up, held down and generally being forced to do things they don't want to do. Yet how many woman dare suggest to their partners that this is what they want, for fear of being laughed at or, far worse, abused?'

Rosie's cheeks were flaming. Fergus patted her shoulder reassuringly. Then he walked round and stood behind Vijay, who had straightened up in his chair and was trying to look nonchalant.

'Now the one thing the feminist movement *has* supposedly created, if one is to believe the *Guardian*, is the New Man,' Fergus continued.

Vijay looked relieved and nodded approvingly. He liked to think of himself as a feminist, although he respected the argument of some of his more radical women friends who said that it was impossible for a man to be a feminist.

'This so-called New Man has supposedly got in touch with the feminine side of his nature and sees women as his equal. He does not want to dominate them, which is a pity for all those women romantic novel readers. Nor does he see women as sex objects. He claims to prefer his women free range and organic so to speak, wearing no make-up, shapeless baggy clothes and sensible shoes.'

Vijay stopped nodding.

Fergus bent down and almost whispered in Vijay's ear, 'But deep down, this man craves women dressed in black stockings and suspender belts, crotch-high leather skirts and wet T-shirts.'

The colour drained from Vijay's face, leaving two bright red smudges on his cheek bones.

Hugo sniggered loudly but stopped abruptly as Fergus moved on and stood behind him. He stopped pushing the buttons on his computer game.

'I say, I think we've got the drift . . .' Hugo protested, as all eyes now turned on him.

143

'Education plays a crucial part in the development of sexuality,' Fergus continued relentlessly. 'Particularly for those who go through the great British public school system. Men emerge from these single sex institutions and rush around fornicating like demented stoats, trying to prove they are not homosexual. But underneath it all, they long for the close, sweaty intimacy they have only really experienced in the company of their own sex.

'They mourn the loss of the dewy faced boy who sat next to them in the third grade and with whom they fumbled inexpertly in the locker room as they exchanged whispered endearments. A woman could never understand their feelings about their masculinity in the same way.'

'Now look here . . .' protested Hugo feebly.

It wasn't possible. No one could know what it had been like. He looked at Philip, hoping for rescue, but Philip seemed engrossed in the papers in front of him.

Fergus continued remorselessly. 'And of course one mustn't ignore the importance of pain in sexual fantasy. A lot of boys experience their first sexual arousal when a cane bites into their naked flesh. Pain and humiliation become inextricably linked with sexual gratification.

'Think of the amount of money politicians, judges and senior civil servants would save from not paying blackmailers, if they were only allowed to openly indulge their sexual fantasies,' laughed Fergus.

Philip joined in, but his laugh was just a shade too high-pitched. 'Enough, enough,' he said holding up his hands. 'That was quite a performance, Dr Archibald. I, for one, am convinced we have a winner of a series here. Welcome to the team.'

Hugo stood up, pushed his chair back so violently it fell over, and stalked out of the room.

Thirteen

• • •

Alicia's mouth grew moist with anticipation, as she carefully peeled the silver foil from a half-pound bar of milk chocolate. She snapped off the first row of thick chunks and placed the rest of the bar on to the handkerchief she had spread on her lap. Then she broke the row into separate squares, delaying the moment she popped the first one into her mouth for as long as she could. It was a little ritual left over from her days at the convent, and never failed to increase her pleasure. A little self-denial was good for the soul.

She munched contentedly, her eyes closed so as to concentrate on the sensation of the dark creaminess of the chocolate. After she had eaten eight squares, she unscrewed the top of the flask that she had placed beside her on the bench, and poured herself a cup of tea. Between sips, she looked around.

She was sitting on a bench in a small square just north of Camden Town. It hardly merited the name 'square', as it was no more than a scruffy patch of dusty green, overlooked on all sides by imposing Victorian mansions, which had long since been converted into flats. But it did have three park benches, several tired-looking trees, and a patch of overgrown shrubs – rare commodities in a capital city, and enabling estate agents to add several thousand pounds to the value of the surrounding property.

It was about five thirty on a hot July afternoon. The day would have already begun to cool down if she had been at Heartlands, but as Alicia was discovering to her discomfort, concrete-bound London trapped the heat like a prickly woollen blanket, long after the strength of the sun had faded. She had bought a long, shapeless shift made of crinkly Indian cotton, to try and keep cool, but perspiration was making it cling to her body in all the wrong places.

Alicia would have liked to sit in the miserable shade offered by one of the trees, but had chosen the graffitied park bench because it offered her a clearer view of the block of flats where Vanessa lived.

She ate the last few chunks of chocolate. They were melting in the heat and left her fingers sticky. She rummaged in her bag for some tissues and with the help of a little cologne, cleaned herself up. She then put on the large, floppy straw hat she had found in Zelda's wardrobe. It almost obscured her face, and had the added benefit of providing some welcome shade from the sun. She had also found a pair of opera glasses which she placed on the bench beside her, ready for Vanessa's arrival home.

Alicia had no idea what she was going to do. For four days she had been sitting in Zelda's flat, venturing out only when she needed to buy food. She had felt listless, totally enervated, without even the energy to read. She had found a small portable black and white television in a cupboard, and plugged it in. The picture and sound were terrible, blurred and crackling, but it kept her company, even though she could not remember any of the programmes she had watched. Only Zelda knew where she was, but she had let the phone ring unanswered. She hadn't wanted to speak to anyone, not even Zelda.

She had begun to lose all sense of reality, but that morning, without thinking, she picked up the phone when it rang. It was an excitable Zelda calling from Heathrow Airport.

'Where have you been? I've rung and rung. The university is simply awash with gossip, it's been so exciting. Everyone knows what happened. Not from me, I never gossip, but these things will get out. Anyway, everyone is simply dying to know what has happened to Fergus, nobody has seen him since *that* night. The Academic Council had to deliver its sentence *in absentia*. Of course he's been dismissed or terminated or whatever they like to call it, and good riddance, I say. It's a pity they couldn't order him to be birched or something. People have been asking me about you too, but just as you asked, I denied all knowledge of your whereabouts, although it has added to the gossip, both you *and* Fergus disappearing at more or less the same time. I wish you had let me say something.'

'And no one has seen him?' Alicia asked faintly, when Zelda at last stopped.

'No one,' Zelda replied firmly.

'You don't think he would do anything stupid, do you? Oh Zelda, perhaps he was so ashamed he couldn't face anyone . . .' Alicia's voice rose in panic.

'Ashamed? That one? My dear, I don't think he knows the meaning of the word shame. You really must learn to put the whole nasty business behind you. Enjoy the summer and make full use of my flat. Ernst and I always have such fun in London, and you know what they say: mi casa es su casa. Now I must dash, as it's the last call for our flight to Hungary and Ernst is getting nervous. Flying is not one of his strong points. See you in September.'

Alicia sat holding the receiver, digesting the news about Fergus. Zelda was probably right, he was not the kind of person to do anything silly, but where was he?

Alicia considered the facts. Fergus had claimed to have no living relatives, and had never mentioned any

147

friends or connections outside the university, so logic dictated that her search should begin with the person he had driven off with that fateful night.

It wasn't that she wanted Fergus back; how could she? Whatever her feelings towards him, his behaviour with Vanessa had made it quite clear that he did not feel the same way towards her. But she did want to make sure he was all right. Whatever Zelda had said, Alicia did not believe that Fergus was the guilty party. The more she thought about it, the more she decided that it must have been Vanessa.

Men were easily led astray. Wasn't that what Vanessa always said when she boasted about her sexual conquests? Even married men weren't immune to her wiles, so why should Fergus be? Alicia had always known what Vanessa was really like; she had just been too stupid to admit it.

How many times had Vanessa said, 'don't worry, *trust* me' and she always had, and it had always brought her trouble. Alicia remembered the time at school when Vanessa had got into trouble yet again. As usual, Vanessa had come running to her for help. She always became Vanessa's best friend when things went wrong.

'It's all right for you,' Vanessa had wailed, 'you're such a goody-goody, you're never in trouble, but I've got so many bad marks against me they might even expel me. Reverend Mother said she would last time.'

Alicia had been thoroughly frightened at the thought of losing her best, her *only* friend. 'They *wouldn't*, would they?'

Vanessa nodded. 'I told Sister Cecilia the booby trap was somebody else's idea and I just happened to be in the room when it went off, but she wouldn't believe me. It wasn't *really* dangerous, I just mixed up some stuff from the chemistry lab with a bit of itching powder. I wanted to give Lucy a bit of a fright. She's

148

so stuck up, always going on about her country house and her silly horses,' Vanessa sniffed.

Alicia had put a comforting arm round her shoulders. 'Supposing I said it was my idea, do you think they would expel me?'

Vanessa's tears had dried up instantly. 'Of course not. You've got such a good record, what can they do to you? Trust me, Alicia, you'll walk it.'

But she hadn't.

'We have always considered it our duty to allow girls like you to come to St Aloysius.' Reverend Mother's steel-blue eyes had seemed to pierce Alicia's very soul. 'But knowing the backgrounds many of you scholarship girls come from, we know we are taking a considerable risk. However, it is our sacred duty to help the less fortunate, and I have always been of the opinion that rather than lower our standards, we should seek to raise the standards of the girls placed in our care.'

There were a few moments of silence as Reverend Mother's eyes continued to bore into Alicia. She had looked down at her shoes and realised that they needed cleaning, another black mark.

'What saddens me about this whole affair, Alicia, is that I thought we had succeeded with you. Your schoolwork is excellent, and up until now, your conduct exemplary. According to Sister Cecilia, this was a carefully planned attack which could have led to real physical injury, or at least terrible shock. If it had happened in a moment of high spirits, I would have considered it less reprehensible, although still punishable. But what makes this breach of discipline so much worse is that not only does it make your past record questionable, but you were prepared to let another girl, Vanessa Sprunt, take the blame for it. In some ways, that is worse than the offence itself. What have you to say for yourself?'

149

Alicia had been silent. Her throat felt as though it were in a vice and she couldn't speak.

'Dumb insolence will only make your position worse.' Reverend Mother's voice was relentless. 'If your parents had been in the country, I think I would have asked them to come and take you away, so that we could offer your place to a more deserving girl.'

Silent tears had begun to course down Alicia's burning cheeks.

'Use your handkerchief child!'

Alicia blew her nose noisily and wiped her eyes.

Reverend Mother's voice, revealing an Irish lilt, became softer. 'Is it that your parents are so far away that's made you behave so badly?'

Alicia miserably shook her head and Reverend Mother's sympathy vanished. She stood up and walked round her desk, placing her hands on Alicia's shoulders. Her fingers dug into Alicia's flesh, forcing her to look up into the nun's face.

'You will forego all weekend privileges until the end of term, and I shall ask your house mother to put you on morning and evening cleaning duty in the dormitory for the next month.'

She had relaxed her grip but remained staring down at Alicia. 'It is not part of your punishment, for the Good Lord could never be a punishment, but I hope we will see you at early Mass all next week. It will help you meditate on your sins.'

And with that she had sat down at her desk again and opened a book. Alicia had taken this to mean her ordeal was over, and edged towards the door, but as her hand turned the knob, Reverend Mother had looked up again.

'And I hope, child, that you will go down on your bended knees and beg Vanessa Sprunt's forgiveness for this terrible thing you have done to her.'

Vanessa had never owned up, and it had passed into

school legend that Alicia had tried to blow up one of her fellow students. It was true that to make amends, Vanessa had given Alicia a Marc Bolan T-shirt which she swore he had actually touched when she'd rushed on stage at one of his concerts, but it had been several sizes too small and anyway, Alicia didn't really like Marc Bolan.

She put Zelda's opera glasses to her eyes and studied Vanessa's flat, which was on the ground floor of the terrace opposite. The two large windows overlooking the park revealed no sign of life.

Alicia sipped her tea and studied the rest of the terrace through the glasses. Peoples' taste in curtains was fascinating. She was rather partial to swags and tails and the odd ruffle herself, and a particularly magnificent set of salmon pink Austrian blinds caught her attention. She put her cup down in order to readjust the opera glasses.

As the pink frills sharpened into focus, Alicia realised that someone was standing at the window watching her.

She hastily turned away, only to find herself looking at a man leaning against a tree who was scrutinising her.

Alicia snatched the opera glasses from her eyes and stuffed them into her bag. Then she tossed the remainder of the tea in her cup on to the ground and tried to screw the cap back on to her vacuum flask. Although she didn't dare look, she knew the man was walking towards her. She kept her head down as she hurriedly pushed everything into her bag.

'Good Lord. Alicia, Alicia Binns!'

Alicia reluctantly peered up from beneath the brim of her hat. The good-looking, in a rather gaunt, unshaven way, man who stood in front of her dressed in faded jeans and a T-shirt proclaiming 'Green Power' with a lurid green fist, bore no resemblance to anyone she knew. He ran a thin hand through his unruly dark hair, which immediately flopped back rather becomingly over his forehead.

Alicia felt a glimmer of familiarity at the gesture.

'It is *you* isn't it?' the man asked, his public school tones at variance with his appearance. 'It's me, Jeremy, Jeremy Swift.'

'Jeremy. Vanessa's husband?' Alicia was incredulous.

'Ex-husband,' Jeremy said firmly. 'How are you? I'm surprised to see you in these parts, I thought you were a country girl.' He indicated where Vanessa lived. 'Not staying with Vee by any chance?'

'Oh no. Vanessa and I . . . well we . . . Actually, I'm staying in a friend's flat just around the corner from here.'

Alicia was uncertain. She was finding it difficult to come to terms with the Jeremy standing in front of her. Where was the immaculately-suited, clean-shaven Jeremy of old?

Jeremy was looking hard at her. 'Do I sense you and Vee are not getting on too well?'

Alicia considered her answer. Could she trust him? They had never been close in the past. Jeremy had been so good-looking, she always felt tongue-tied in his presence, and had been sure he thought her an awful bore, or at least Vanessa had intimated he did. But he was Vanessa's ex-husband now, and she did want someone to talk to, someone who would understand, and his eyes which were still that wonderful blue she remembered, looked concerned.

'Oh, Jeremy,' she finally blurted out, 'we've had the most terrible row. She behaved so dreadfully.' Her lower lip trembled.

Jeremy put a hand out as though to comfort her and then thought better of it. He put his hands in his pockets instead. Alicia thought he looked unhealthily thin. The last time she had seen him which must have been at least four years ago, he had been broad-shouldered and muscular. Alicia felt herself beginning to blush, and she looked away.

Jeremy scuffed the toe of his trainer against a brown tuft of grass. 'That's not unusual for Vee. I'm just surprised you put up with her for so long. I learned my lesson the hard way. That woman hasn't got a decent bone in her body.' The bitterness in his voice made Alicia ache.

She looked up into his eyes. There were depths in them she had not seen before.

Alicia had never understood why Vanessa had divorced Jeremy. Vanessa said it was because he had an affair, and Alicia agreed that it was the most awful betrayal, but if he had said he was truly sorry and that he would not do it again, why not forgive him this one indiscretion?

But according to Vanessa, while Jeremy's one infidelity was nothing in comparison to her many, that wasn't the point. Her infidelities meant nothing, that was just the way she was, but Jeremy was a one-woman man so if *he* strayed, it really meant something.

Alicia twisted a strand of her hair round her finger. 'You know, I never really heard the full story of why you and Vanessa broke up. If I made us some tea, would you like to tell me about it?'

Jeremy brightened up. 'I haven't had a proper tea in ages.'

He took Alicia's bag from her hand and they set off across the park together.

Fourteen

• • •

'If only I'd listened to my mother,' Jeremy finished bitterly, emptying the dregs of the wine bottle into his glass.

Alicia put a plate of assorted sandwiches on the low table, and sat down on the cushions opposite Jeremy, tucking her dress round her knees. She reached for a cream cheese and smoked salmon sandwich.

'It really sounds as though you had an awful time. Vanessa always told me she was the one who was badly treated. I should never have believed her, and Belle doesn't sound as though she was much better.'

Jeremy put his glass down. 'It wasn't really Belle's fault. I wasn't much good at running a snack bar. We'd both rather assumed that as I'd worked in a bank I could handle money, but I'm not very good at it, I'm afraid. Poor Belle was doing all the hard work like cooking, and at the end of it we made no profit at all. I could hardly blame her for wanting me out.'

'Oh, but what about your relationship. Didn't you, well . . . *love* each other?' Alicia helped herself to another sandwich.

'We liked each other, but I'm not sure we ever actually loved each other.' He shrugged. 'Anyway, when you're trying to run a business like that, there's little time for sex and all that kind of stuff, which is probably just as well, because Vanessa always said I was hopeless at it like I was hopeless at everything else,' he ended morosely.

Alicia blushed. She found it impossible to believe that anyone as good-looking as Jeremy could possibly be hopeless at making love. Her blush deepened.

'But what happened between you two? I always thought your friendship was indestructible,' asked Jeremy reaching for a ham and pickle sandwich.

Alicia told him, not daring to look at his face, hugging her arms around her body for protection, her face distorted with the effort not to cry. As she reached the end of the story her voice shrank to a tremulous whisper, forcing Jeremy to lean forward to hear her.

When she had finished they both sat in silence. Alicia closed her eyes trying to shut out the terrible visions she had conjured up once again.

Jeremy looked down at his half-eaten sandwich. He felt like an intruder in her grief. But for the first time in ages, he realised that he wasn't the only one with problems. He desperately wanted to reach out and comfort Alicia, to tell her he knew how she felt, but he just didn't know how. He cleared his throat.

'Do cheer up, old thing, things can't get much worse.'

The spell was broken.

Alicia blew her nose loudly. 'Oh, but they can!' the words emerged with surprising force. 'You see, I realise now that Zelda was right, Fergus is a charlatan, a fraud. His theories are dangerous, and if Vanessa promotes them on television it would be terrible. Think what damage it could do to the university to be associated with his research. Someone has to do something about it, so I have decided that it's time to put my own personal feelings about Fergus and Vanessa aside and . . . and . . .'

'Is that why you were sitting outside Vee's flat this afternoon?' encouraged Jeremy.

Alicia nodded and sipped her wine. Then she looked at him.

'Why were *you* there?'

He shrugged his shoulders. 'I don't know really. I suppose I've got nothing else to do apart from signing on, and seeing her again the other day made me think.'

'Do you still love her?' asked Alicia, and immediately wished she hadn't.

Jeremy started on his third ham and pickle sandwich. He munched thoughtfully for a moment or two. 'Perhaps I imagined I did. She's a very powerful woman and difficult to forget, but after the way she treated me, I knew there was nothing left.'

Alicia clambered to her feet trying to hide her relief, and fetched the chocolate gateau she had bought from the local patisserie.

'I'm sorry it's shop bought. I normally bake all my own cakes. I do think that extra bit of effort shows, don't you?'

Jeremy nodded approvingly, his eyes glistening with pleasure as he watched Alicia cut him a large slice. 'I love chocolate cake,' he said with his mouth full.

Alicia smiled at him. There was chocolate around his mouth and he looked just like a little boy. She liked his hair long she decided, it somehow made him look more vulnerable.

'You know, you're awfully easy to talk to. I always feel so awkward with women, under pressure so to speak,' Jeremy said, running a finger round his plate to scrape off the chocolate cream. 'I feel comfortable with you, just like I used to feel with Nanny Greig. She was never too busy to listen, and when I said silly things she never laughed at me. Mother was always telling me to act more like a man.'

He wrinkled his forehead as though trying to recall something. He had drunk nearly a bottle of wine. 'It's funny, but now I come to think of it, that's just what Vee used to say too.'

He lapsed into silence. For a few minutes he and Alicia munched in companionable silence, and Alicia took the opportunity to study him.

She had always thought Jeremy's good looks were spoiled by a certain blandness of expression, a readiness to laughter which belied any real emotion. But now his features had a drawn look about them. Lines had appeared around his mouth, and his eyes looked almost haunted. He was definitely more interesting than she remembered.

Jeremy suddenly looked at her. 'Has anyone ever told you you're really rather pretty. I've always thought so. I used to tell Vee that you hid your light under a bushel, something *she* could never be accused of. I don't understand why some lucky chap hasn't snapped you up.'

Embarrassed, Alicia took off her glasses and polished the lenses with her handkerchief.

'And you look even prettier without your glasses,' he added.

Alicia immediately put them back on.

'Would you like some tea or coffee, or maybe some more wine?' she asked, getting up.

Jeremy followed her into the kitchen area and stood close enough for her to feel his body heat. Alicia tried to move away, but there wasn't much space in Zelda's tiny kitchenette.

'I think some more wine would be nice, don't you?'

Alicia reached for another bottle. Zelda kept her wine cupboard well-stocked, but strictly speaking, Alicia knew she shouldn't really be helping herself, even though Zelda had told her to make the place her own. Her hand wavered. What would Zelda have done if the situation had been reversed? Alicia's hand grasped another bottle of Sainsbury's claret.

As she clumsily attempted to remove the foil from around the neck, Jeremy reached over and took the corkscrew from her. For a brief moment, their hands touched. Alicia snatched hers away as though it had been scalded.

She backed away and watched him opening the wine. It was absolutely ridiculous, she thought, trying to steady her pounding heart, she had probably had too much to drink. After all, this man was her best friend's ex-husband.

Her best friend. Alicia felt a sudden sharp sense of loss that was almost physical. She'd never really *had* a best friend. All these years she had been fooling herself about Vanessa. She had other friends, it was true, but those words 'my best friend' had a special, intimate meaning that was like no other. To discover that the friendship had never really existed was like having to re-edit your life, wiping out all the memories which were no longer true, leaving a large, black hole.

This time Alicia couldn't hold back the tears.

Jeremy led her gently back to the *chaise-longue* and sat with his arm around her, offering her sips of wine between sobs and tissues.

Alicia finally took a deep breath. 'I'm sorry, I'm behaving like an awful idiot,' she sniffed, wiping away the last of the tears.

Jeremy squeezed her arm, 'Not in the least, old thing, best get it out of your system.'

Alicia risked a peep at him and then quickly hung her head so that her hair fell across her face. 'You must think I look an awful wreck.'

Jeremy brushed her hair aside and tucked it behind her ears.

Alicia's nose was indeed a rather unbecoming shade of pink and her eyes were red-rimmed and puffy.

'I think you look absolutely fine,' he said gallantly. 'Like a . . .' he paused. He had never really thought of

Alicia as his sort, but she was really rather nice. She made him feel protective, which was the last thing Vanessa had ever done. '... like a garden after a summer shower: all dewy and fresh,' he finished triumphantly, rather pleased at his turn of phrase.

Alicia flashed him a grateful smile. Her eyes, which Jeremy could have sworn were a kind of nondescript brown, suddenly glinted green and gold, like sunlight in the depths of a wood.

'If you haven't got any other plans, why don't you stay for dinner,' Alicia ventured shyly. 'I do so hate cooking just for myself.'

Jeremy nodded eagerly. 'Vee hated cooking. She always said that if women were meant to cook, God wouldn't have invented microwaves and Marks & Spencer ready meals. I don't think she cooked a meal for us once in all the time we were married.'

Alicia placed a sympathetic hand over his.

'And this is such a nice little flat,' Jeremy continued looking around. 'You ought to see the room where I'm staying in Hackney. Even the cockroaches have packed their bags and left.'

Alicia giggled, 'Surely it can't be that bad.'

'Oh yes it is,' Jeremy said vehemently. 'I can't begin to tell you what that woman has done to me. Look at me, I've lost everything: job, family, friends. She left me with absolutely nothing, not even pride.' Jeremy's voice cracked.

It was Alicia's turn to be the comforter. She slipped her arm around his shoulders. Jeremy buried his head between Alicia's breasts, his shoulders heaving.

Alicia tentatively stroked his hair. It seemed to sooth him, so she continued until his breathing grew even. For the first time in what seemed like years, she felt peaceful.

The warm sounds of a London summer's evening drifted through the window. Somewhere, someone was playing a melodious saxophone, distant traffic providing the base line, and the high clear wail of a police siren the descant. On the rickety balcony outside, two pigeons fluffed out their chests and cocked their heads from side to side as they cooed a beady-eyed serenade of love.

Jeremy's body began to feel heavy, and there was an unpleasantly moist patch between her breasts where he was breathing, although now his deep breaths were beginning to sound like snores.

Alicia gently shook him. 'Jeremy.' He woke with a start.

'Good Lord! Did I fall asleep? How awfully bad mannered of me.' He rubbed his eyes and ran his hand through his hair which was rather attractively ruffled.

'Oh, please don't worry,' Alicia said, surreptitiously trying to straighten her crumpled dress and conceal the damp patch at the same time. 'I think we're both rather sleepy. It's probably the wine.'

Jeremy glanced at his watch; it was after ten. 'It's past my bedtime, I'd better be getting along. Perhaps we could do dinner another night,' he said wistfully.

'Oh, but you don't have to go,' the words came out before Alicia had realised. She blushed. 'What I mean to say is that you could sleep here,' she indicated the room, 'that is, if you don't mind the floor. There are plenty of spare blankets.'

'Anything would be better than the slog back to Hackney.'

Alicia bustled around, finding blankets and sheets and insisting on making a light supper of Welsh Rarebit, followed by more chocolate cake and some milky cocoa to help them both sleep.

But Jeremy did not need any assistance. As she turned at the door to bid him good night, he was already asleep, ensconced on his bed of cushions. With a whispered 'sleep well', Alicia switched off the light and quietly closed the door.

She sat on the edge of the bed and took a deep breath. The day had certainly not turned out the way she'd expected. She put a hand between her breasts where Jeremy's head had lain for that blissful half hour. Poor man, how could Vanessa have treated him so badly?

Alicia reached for the zip at the back of her dress, but she couldn't pull it open past her waist, it was stuck fast. She stood up and twisted the dress round until it was back to front and tried again; the zip refused to budge. Frustrated, Alicia tried to pull the dress down over her hips, but even though she held her breath in, it wouldn't move. She tried pulling it over her head, but it refused to go over her breasts. Holding the zip with both hands, she pulled it down with all her strength. There was a loud rip and it gave way, taking part of the lining with it.

Alicia held the offending article up. It was beyond even her needlewoman's skills to mend. Anyway, she hadn't really liked it. It had made her look even fatter than she was, and she wished she'd been wearing something else today when she met Jeremy. She bundled it up and stuffed it into the bottom of the wardrobe. As she did so, she caught sight of herself in the full-length mirror inside the wardrobe door. It was something she normally avoided, unless she was fully dressed and then only to check that her hair was tidy and that her slip wasn't showing.

Alicia looked despairingly at her body, encased in sensible all-enveloping white cotton pants and her old-fashioned bra, which looked like two armoured breast-plates designed to repel all intruders. She bought her underwear by mail order, as she could no longer face going into a lingerie department. All all those rocks of frothy lace bras and tiny bikini pants, added to the disdainful look on the face of some seventeen-year old, bra-less shop assistant when she asked for her size made her feel wretched. She had once been tempted into buying a corset, which had promised to flatten and streamline all her bulges, but it had merely displaced them to other parts of her anatomy.

Alicia forced herself to look in the mirror. She was beyond any doubt not merely overweight, but disgustingly fat. She had dreaded changing for games at school. While all the other girls flung off their clothes and ran around naked, she had huddled miserably in a corner pretending to untie her laces, waiting for everyone to go before scrambling into her games clothes. All that commotion over her breasts had made it worse. She had felt like a freak and still did. How could any man find her attractive? It was all very well for Jeremy to say she was pretty but he was just trying to be nice to her because she was so upset. He hadn't meant it.

Alicia closed the door so she could no longer see herself, and slowly finished undressing. She pulled on a flannelette nightgown and sat on the edge of the bed to brush her hair one hundred times. She tiptoed to the bathroom, turned off the light, and climbed into bed, where she lay staring up at the ceiling willing herself to fall asleep.

She heard the toilet being flushed, and wondered whether there would be enough hot water for Jeremy to take a bath in the morning. Perhaps she ought to check the immersion heater.

Alicia swung her legs over the side of the bed and tiptoed into the hall. The controls were in the kitchen. She hesitated, and then knocked softly on the sitting room door. There was no answer. She gingerly pushed the door open.

Jeremy lay curled up on the floor, his sleeping face illuminated by a pale beam of moonlight.

Alicia sighed. Jeremy obviously wasn't bothered by her restlessness. She checked the time switch on the wall. The heater was set to come on in the morning just as she had left it. She crept back to bed and lay staring at the ceiling again. Perhaps she should go on a diet starting at breakfast. If she ate only one egg and grilled the bacon and sausages . . .?

Jeremy heard the door close and opened his eyes. He had been thinking about the nights when he was a child, and had crept along to Nanny Greig's room and crawled in beside her. She slept on a high, old-fashioned iron bedstead which had seemed unassailable when he was small, but she always kept a footstool under the bed which he could climb on. She slept, propped nearly upright by four pillows, her hair wound into tight little curls, and pinned flat against her scalp with silver clips covered by a hair net. During the day, her hair was rigidly straight beneath the starched cap she wore, so Jeremy had decided the nightly curls were some kind of mysterious female ritual.

Nanny Greig had never asked questions when he crept into her bed. She just opened her arms and clasped him to her soft, capacious bosom where he fell into a blissfully happy sleep. Next morning he always found himself back in his own bed, and neither he nor Nanny Greig ever mentioned his nocturnal visits.

Jeremy punched a couple of cushions, trying to make them more comfortable. Alicia had smelt powdery and flowery, just like Nanny Greig.

He scrambled to his feet and padded to the bedroom door. He listened for a moment and then slowly turned the handle. There was no sound from the bed. He tiptoed to the bed, slipped carefully beneath the bedclothes, and lay still, holding his breath. A small hand found his and gave it a reassuring squeeze.

Fifteen

• • •

DAY-DREAM YOUR WAY TO STARDOM.
EROTIC FANTASIES? AMOROUS DAY DREAMS?
TELL US AND WE'LL MAKE
YOUR WICKEDEST WISHES COME TRUE.
TV COMPANY SEEKS PARTICIPANTS
FOR NEW ADULT TV SHOW.

Vijay dropped the piece of paper in disgust and looked at Vanessa. 'You can't put this sort of thing out. We'll have every pervert in the country calling us.'

'Calling you, you mean,' said Vanessa sardonically. 'I have already placed this advert in several newspapers and magazines, and dear little Heather has been instructed to put all calls through to you. Anyway, I would have thought it was just your sort of thing, Vijay dear. You're always carrying on about how we ought to be in touch with people on the street, and now I've put you in touch. Now you'll find out what *real* people *really* think about while they make widgets on some assembly line, and I bet it isn't about whether to attend their next union meeting or to campaign for a crêche in their office.'

Vijay thrust his glasses back over the bridge of his nose, as he desperately tried to think of a response that would cut Vanessa down to size.

When he first had heard that his boss was going to be a woman, he had been delighted. He'd always believed that there ought to be more women in positions of power, because they would change the whole culture of the cut-throat, aggressive world of business and make it more co-operative, more nurturing. That was until he met Vanessa. He had never met anyone quite as dictatorial, aggressive and as set on self-promotion. Power had gone to her head. She was just like a man, and the worst sort of man at that.

Vanessa had confused all his feminist principles to the point where he had decided that he hated her, and she knew it, but didn't seem to care. In fact, he had a suspicion she rather liked it, which made him hate her even more.

He fixed what he hoped was his most intimidating glare on her, and opened his mouth to speak. Just at that moment, Philip popped his head round the door.

'I gather we're off and running,' he said cheerfully.

Vijay gave him a baleful look and marched out of the office.

Philip shook his head. 'I am forced to the conclusion that I may have made a terrible mistake hiring that young man. On a delicate project like this, we need all hands to the pump. There can be no place on the team for those who do not pull their full weight. I look to you to make sure everyone does their bit, Vanessa.'

Vanessa smiled reassuringly and shuffled some papers around on her desk.

'Well, of course he wouldn't have been my choice, but I am sure Vijay has some hidden talents, and you know me, PP, I always bring out the best in people. You don't have a thing to worry about.'

Philip turned to go and then hesitated, before turning back. 'I do hope that it goes without saying that it is imperative that no hint of what we are planning slips out to the press, Vanessa. The tabloids would have a field day, and it might scare off the Network. I'm already going out on a financial limb by making a pilot without a commitment from them. This new Committee for Media Morality and all the publicity about cleaning up television, is making even the big players a bit more cautious, so I feel pitching it to them at this stage could be counter-productive. However, I just know that when the Network sees the pilot they're going to go for it in a big way and commission a whole series. But until that happens, I'd like to keep things under wraps. There are a lot of people out there who could get completely the wrong idea, and there's absolutely no point in us making a wonderful series if we can't sell it to the Network.'

Vanessa casually slipped the text of the advertisement into the middle of a sheaf of papers in her in-tray. 'PP, darling. It'll be roses all the way. You know you can trust me.' She flashed him a brilliant smile. 'Now, is there anything else I can do for you?'

'Oh, I forgot to mention it earlier, but Gabriella's arrived in town, so if you have nothing else in your diary, perhaps you would care to join us for lunch. I think it would be an opportunity for you two girls to get to know each other better, since you'll be working so closely together. Heather has booked a table at that new place in Dean Street, the one the *Sunday Times* was praising to the skies last week. We'll expect you at one.'

It was a command, not a request.

Outside the door, Philip decided he had handled the exchange well. Normally, Vanessa seemed to be able to find awkward objections to everything he said. Perhaps it was just a case of him showing who was in command more often. However, nothing could have disturbed his good humour today. By his calculation, it was at least two years since he had last seen

Gabriella, and he was looking forward to seeing her again.

Gabriella had been one of the first women to read the national television news in the Seventies. With the looks of a Fifties film starlet, she had been a publicist's dream, and she soon had her own thrice-weekly chat show on prime-time television. Anyone with a film or a book or a record to sell in the Eighties clamoured to appear. No matter how big the star, if they did not guarantee a first exclusive to the eponymous 'Gabriella!' they were taken off her guest list, Philip recalled with a smile.

For a while, she had been bigger news than some of the stars that appeared on her show, her private life providing the tabloids with endless front pages. Philip had tried to warn her that the public was notoriously fickle and quickly bored but Gabriella by then was past caution. If you've got it, flaunt it, had been her reply to his caution, and her trademark deep, husky voice was heard advertising everything from cat food to Caribbean cruises, while hardly a day passed without a newspaper photograph of her at a party or an opening.

But Philip had been proved right. Like Eighties padded-shoulder glamour, Gabriella went out of fashion in England, although with the growth of satellite channels, she had found new audiences in Europe. It was Philip who had encouraged her to take up a lucrative offer to live and work in Italy, where she'd been for the last six years, just as he had encouraged her to move from bit parts in television soap operas to presenting programmes. It was he who had first spotted that she had a natural feel for an audience, with the kind of presence, as well as looks, which filled a television screen.

When Gabriella first moved to Italy, they had kept in close touch. For the first couple of years she had been offered frequent guest star spots on television shows in England, while he always spent the summer in a rented villa in Tuscany, so they had been able to see a lot of each other. But Gabriella had slipped down the celebrity guest list, and the television appearances had dried up, and Right Pryce Productions, unlike the BBC, could not support him taking two months off in the summer, and they had seen less and less of each other. So Philip's step was decidedly jaunty as he set off from the Right Pryce offices to walk to the restaurant.

He had been even more fastidious than usual that morning in selecting what to wear. He had eventually settled on his new, dark blue suit. His tailor had talked him into the dark blue. He normally chose pale blue or grey, feeling they suggested creativity and a free spirit. But his tailor had been right. The dark blue did give him a certain gravitas, the look of a decision maker. It also made him look a trifle slimmer, he thought. Not that he had let himself go. Twenty minutes each on his rowing machine and treadmill every morning had made sure of that. The finishing touch to his outfit was the engraved gold and diamond studded cuff links that Gabriella had given him ten years before. He smiled at the recollection.

She had presented them to him during a dinner at the Savoy to celebrate her being voted most popular television personality for the third year running. The occasion had been riotous. There must have been twenty people at their table, and they had all insisted on making speeches.

Eventually Gabriella stood and thanked them all for their help and support, but it was to him she raised her glass in a toast to: 'the man without whom none of this would have been possible'.

When she sat down, she had leaned across and pressed a small velvet box into his hand. Inside had been the cuff links with their initials 'PG' intertwined. He had wiped away more than one tear that night.

Of course it was true, Gabriella would have been nothing without him, thought Philip. She really did owe him everything, more than her public would ever know. He paused to look at his reflection in a shop window, surreptitiously patting his hair into place. Would Gabriella notice there was so little of it left?

He had arranged to meet Gabriella half an hour before Vanessa was due. As much as he loved her, Gabriella could be difficult so he intended to do some careful groundwork.

He had told her very little about *Forbidden Fruit* on the telephone. Gabriella would never have agreed to come back to England if she had known the series did not as yet have a guaranteed network slot. He had also judiciously avoided explaining that at this stage, all he had was the finance to make a pilot not a series. Those sorts of details could be dealt with so much better face to face, and he had a feeling that once she had spent some time in her old London haunts, she would want to stay.

Philip took a last look at his reflection, straightened his tie, fluffed up his pocket handkerchief, and then plunged into the cool, dark green interior of the restaurant.

Its discreet entrance, marked only by a small brass plaque, gave no indication that this was a restaurant and this, combined with the formality of the lobby and its ice-cool receptionist, kept casual diners away. It felt like an old-fashioned London men's club, with membership restricted to the chosen few, Philip thought, appreciatively sniffing the air which was scented with expensive cigars.

As he was led through to the bar, or the clubroom as the receptionist called it, Philip decided that it was most definitely a dark blue suit and crisp white shirt

169

sort of place. Decorated in an even deeper shade of green than the reception area, the clubroom was furnished with large, comfortable leather chairs, whose high backs and sides allowed discreet conversation. Unlike similar Soho establishments, full of glossy-haired, slim young media folk in unstructured suits, nobody looked up when someone walked in the door to see if they were famous or useful. This place had been designed for people who were both, and their waistlines were thicker and hairlines thinner as a result. Philip felt at home.

He had only just sat down when Gabriella was ushered through. They would usually have kissed in greeting, but Philip felt this would have been inappropriate in the setting, so he clasped her hand warmly with both of his.

'Gabriella,' he said in an emotional voice.

'Philip,' she replied in the deep, husky voice he remembered so well.

They settled down opposite each other.

'I hope you don't mind, but I have already ordered their best champagne to put on ice,' Philip said. 'I thought we needed something fitting to mark what I hope will be the start of another long and happy association.'

'My darling, you know me. I'd have champagne running from all my taps if I could, it's absolutely my most favourite liquid refreshment.'

As Gabriella spoke, a waiter arrived with the champagne. They watched in silence as he opened the bottle and poured.

Philip held up his glass, 'To the most extraordinary woman I know.'

'To the success of the new series, may it make both of us very rich,' responded Gabriella, holding up her glass so that the pale, straw-coloured liquid sparkled in the light.

Whether it was the soft light or skilful makeup or both, Gabriella looked remarkable, thought Philip. She had to be at least fifty-two or even three, by his reckoning, and yet her skin was still creamy smooth and even her neck, an area which he knew to his cost, usually betrayed the tell-tale creepy signs of age, seemed unlined. Her mane of hair was a shade or two lighter than the raven black it used to be, and styled so that it came forward in becoming little wisps rather than being swept uncompromisingly back the way she used to wear it. But her large, almost coal black eyes were still dramatically outlined with kohl, and her lips were still painted her hallmark crimson.

It was difficult to judge whether her figure had altered as she wore a cleverly-cut, caramel coloured dress, whose swathes of material were draped in such a way as to emphasise her still voluptuous body, but to disguise all but the most serious of figure faults. The dress stopped just short of her knee, not needing to disguise her legs, which were as shapely as ever. Aware that she was under scrutiny, Gabriella took a long gold and jet cigarette holder out of her clutch bag and slotted a Sobranie cigarette into it. A waiter immediately materialised with an ashtray and lighter.

Gabriella leaned forward to light her cigarette. She inhaled deeply and then looked full into Philip's eyes.

'Not bad for an old-aged pensioner, am I?' she laughed throatily.

Philip reddened. He hadn't realised his appraisal was so obvious. In an unconscious gesture, he put his hand up to his thinning hair.

'It's all down to hormones, Philip darling, you really ought to try them. I have this marvellous doctor in Italy who knows exactly how to treat me,' Gabriella said with a theatrical wink.

Philip gave her a tight smile. 'I promised myself I would let Mother Nature take her course gracefully and leave the pursuit of youth to the young, but it gets more difficult every day.'

'Mother Nature sucks,' Gabriella said forcefully. 'Who says the young are the only ones who should have fun, it's wasted on them. I don't want youth, I want beauty.'

'And that my dearest darling, you have in full measure.' Philip raised his glass in salute.

Gabriella exhaled a long stream of smoke which she watched spiral upwards, before turning back to Philip.

'So tell me about this new series,' she said, her expression suddenly business-like. 'Is it going to put me back at the top of the ratings?'

Philip placed his elbows on the arms of his chair and clasped his hands together. Then, with carefully chosen words, he described *Forbidden Fruit*.

Gabriella listened intently, occasionally interrupting him with a question. When he had finished, she sat looking thoughtful.

'It sounds very commercial,' she said at last, 'although this Fergus character worries me. I don't like academics. They always think their research should be treated like a sacred cow, which normally means it gets to sit in the middle of the road, blocking progress and shitting.'

'Leave Fergus to me,' said Philip firmly. 'I'll get rid of him once I own the rights to his research.'

'And what about me?' Gabriella asked. 'I don't like being just the pretty face on the screen. I want control over my role and the content of the programme. I have my image to think about.'

'Now, Gabriella darling,' said Philip soothingly, 'you know I would never do anything that would harm you, so there must be trust on both sides. Vanessa will be your producer for all the little day to day things, but I am the executive producer and so I will have the final say on everything that goes on the screen. I'm sure if there are any problems about presentation, we can sort them out when they happen. I always think that if there are too many hard and fast rules drawn up at the beginning of a project like this, the fluidity of thought and ideas that are essential for the creative process are stultified.'

'You always were the diplomat, darling, you'd have made a great ambassador.' Smiling, Gabriella raised her glass to Philip. Perhaps her agent could get her the right of veto over the script she thought. It was useless trying to push Philip now. She knew him well enough to know when he wasn't going to back down, and she badly needed this series to put her back on the British television map.

Philip sipped his champagne. To his relief Gabriella had not asked him any awkward questions about the Network, but there was no way he was going to give her control over the script. It went with the territory that all presenters thought they were experts on the subject they were presenting, but they were hired for their looks and their ability to read autocue, not their brains. He made a mental note to make sure that clause in the contract was watertight.

Philip glanced at his watch. 'I've asked Vanessa to join us for lunch. I thought it would be a good chance for you two girls to get to know each other.'

Almost on cue, Vanessa walked in. Philip stood up to make the introductions.

'Gabriella, I'd like you to meet Vanessa Swift, the originator of *Forbidden Fruit*'.

Gabriella extended a languid hand from the depths of her chair. She drew deeply on her cigarette and blew the smoke up to the ceiling before drawling, 'How do you do?'

Vanessa gave her a desiccated smile, barely touching Gabriella's hand with the tips of her fingers. 'I'm delighted, Miss Wolfe, I remember your show well. Such a pity you've been off our screens for so long.'

Gabriella's eyes flashed, but before she could reply, Philip intervened.

'Perhaps we should go into lunch,' he said, hastily signalling a waiter.

Sixteen
• • •

Lush green foliage that would not have embarrassed a tropical rain forest filled the restaurant, providing leafy screens between the tables, and climbing upwards towards the vaulted, glass canopy ceiling. A waiter led Philip, Gabriella and Vanessa to a corner table in the shade of a triffid-like Monstera Deliciosa.

As they were seated and handed menus, Gabriella crooked her finger at the waiter. 'I'd like another bottle of that lovely champagne.'

The waiter looked at Philip, who smiled with more grace than he felt. The champagne had been meant to impress; it was too expensive for drinking.

'What an excellent idea, Gabriella. I'm sure Vanessa will join you, but I'd just like some still mineral water, please.'

'And I'd like a dozen oysters followed by Lobster Thermidor,' said Gabriella, handing her menu back to the waiter.

The waiter tapped her order into the tiny computer he held in his hand, and then looked questioningly at Vanessa.

'The asparagus and courgette timbales with the beurre blanc sauce, and then the quail with fresh figs.'

'And the tomato and basil sorbet followed by the venison steak with sage butter for me,' Philip added.

'The vegetables of the day are mange-tout sautéed in

butter with almonds, onion purée with sage, steamed fennel and dill, and our chef's salad today is an English country garden leaf and herb salad, garnished with Nasturtium flowers. Would you like a selection, sir?'

'Please, please,' Philip said waving the waiter away. He turned back to Vanessa and Gabriella.

'Well, isn't this nice,' he announced with a cheerfulness which lacked conviction.

No agreement was forthcoming.

Both women seemed suddenly fascinated by their long manicured nails. Philip knew it was fanciful, but he was forcefully reminded of lions flexing their claws before the kill. But if they were hungry lions, who was their prey? He gave a nervous little laugh.

'Philip, darling,' Gabriella purred, placing a proprietorial hand over his. 'You don't seem quite yourself.'

For a moment, Philip stared at the hand covering his, wrestling with the urge to snatch his hand away to safety. Then he mentally took a deep breath. He was allowing his imagination to run away with him, he needed to take command of the situation. He slipped his hand out from under Gabriella's and picked up his glass.

'Perhaps I find myself overwhelmed at being in the company of the two most beautiful women in the restaurant.' He raised his glass to each of them. But his attempt at rapprochement did not have quite the effect Philip intended. Two mouths smiled in acknowledgement, but two pairs of dark eyes swiftly surveyed the room. Satisfied of the truth of Philip's statement, their eyes momentarily locked. Having eliminated the rest of the competition, there were now only two in contention for the prize, and there could only be one victor.

Vanessa made her bid first.

'PP, *sweetie*.' She leaned across the table and picked an imaginary thread from Philip's shoulder, in a gesture that suggested more than just workplace intimacy. 'You're such a flirt. Sometimes I wonder just how I manage to resist you.'

Gabriella's eyes flashed dangerously, and Philip hastily brushed his jacket where Vanessa had touched him.

'As Gabriella will know from our past association, I like to establish a good working relationship with all my employees.'

A tiny smile danced across Gabriella's lips at Philip's use of the word employees. Vanessa looked discomfited. Philip felt a sense of despair.

He had intended this to be a friendly, relaxed lunch, a time for Gabriella and Vanessa to get to know each other, with good food and wine as the catalyst. It was the way he had always done business. But then, he thought, morosely sipping his mineral water, the good old days seemed to be over. He couldn't even have a glass of wine anymore.

The silence at the table was interrupted by a waiter who arrived with their first course.

Philip's sorbet tasted like sand in his mouth. After two mouthfuls he pushed his plate away.

The waiter hovered anxiously, 'Is there anything wrong, sir?'

'No, nothing at all.' Philip waved him away and forced himself to eat another spoonful.

He watched Gabriella dispatching her oysters with relish. She paused for a moment.

'You should have had the oysters, Philip darling, they're absolutely perfect.' She slid another oyster from its shell on to her waiting tongue and swallowed. Her eyes closed with pleasure. Philip fancied he could see the progress of the oyster along the contours of her smooth white throat.

Gabriella opened her eyes. 'They say that eating oysters is like having angels copulating on your tongue.' She reached over and caressed Philip's hand with her index finger. 'Methinks you could do with a little of that, Philip darling. You have a very bad case of too much work and no play making Philip a dull boy.' Her voice deepened. 'I've always known what makes you feel better.'

Philip put his hand to his mouth and gave a little cough, shooting a warning glance in Vanessa's direction. But the exchange had not escaped her hawklike gaze.

Gabriella pouted at him and then turned ostentatiously towards Vanessa. 'Tell me . . . Vicky, isn't it? What programmes have you produced that I might have seen, bearing in mind that one tends to only get the cream of British productions abroad?'

'Vanessa used to work in the light entertainment department at Capital Daytime before I poached her,' Philip intervened.

'I heard they were letting a lot of people go,' said Gabriella. 'The place has never been the same since Toby Trafford left; he was the real creative force there. I don't think the department has won a single award since he left. All they do now is make tacky, low-budget game shows. Did you know Toby?' she asked Vanessa.

Vanessa glared poisonously at her. 'He left before I arrived. Derek Percival was department head during my time.'

'Old porky Percy?' Gabriella laughed derisively. 'You remember him, don't you Philip? Poor man, he'd burnt out even before he left the BBC. No wonder Capital Daytime has been having problems.'

To Philip's relief, a waiter began to clear the table before another one arrived with their second course.

'This looks absolutely delicious,' he said with an effort, as his plate was put before him. 'This place is certainly living up to its reviews, don't you think?'

He cut into his venison steak. It was thick and moist.

As he munched he tried to think how he could rescue a situation which was fast heading for disaster. The antagonism between Gabriella and Vanessa hung about the table like an uninvited guest. Philip felt a burning sensation in his gut. He had only had one glass of champagne when Gabriella arrived, but it didn't seem to be agreeing with the rich venison steak.

'Are you all right, Philip darling?' Gabriella asked looking solicitous. 'You've gone a little pale. Perhaps we ought to order a tisane, it would act as a *digestif* for your tummy.' She pronounced 'tisane' and '*digestif*' with a French accent.

'I'm fine, really I am,' Philip insisted.

'Are you sure, Philip darling?' Not to be outdone in solicitude, Vanessa put her hand on his arm. 'You do look a little odd.'

A cold sweat broke out on Philip's face. He mopped it with his napkin. 'Will you excuse me for a few minutes?' he said struggling to his feet and heading in the direction of what he hoped were the toilets.

A waiter came forward and guided him around a large clump of ferns.

Philip could feel the acid indigestion closing like a steel band around his chest. He always suffered when he got agitated and that was beginning to happen a lot lately.

The toilets were thankfully empty, and he stood looking in the mirror, holding the edge of the wash-basin as the nausea made his head whirl. His normally healthy, pink skin had an unhealthy green pallor. Philip felt inside his pocket for his tablets, which he carried in a small enamelled box that normally snapped open with just a little pressure.

This time it didn't.

In his frustration, Philip banged it hard on the marble topped washbasin, and it sprang open, spilling all his pills on to the floor.

Clutching his chest with one hand, Philip went down on his knees and felt around with his other hand. It was difficult to see the pills on the elaborately patterned, tiled floor, and Philip was too vain to admit to his shortsightedness and wear the glasses his optician had prescribed.

As he was scrabbling around, the door behind him opened.

'What the dickens . . .?' boomed a loud voice.

With some difficulty, as any movement made the pain worse, Philip swivelled round on his knees and found himself looking at a pair of old-fashioned, highly polished shoes. He looked up past the turn-ups on a black pin-striped suit, worn with stiff-backed bearing to the florid features of Sir Norman Fluck, the newly appointed chairman of the Committee for Media Morality.

The committee's job was to vet television programmes for political balance, taste and decency. Until recently, it had been a little known and innocuous sinecure for retired senior civil servants, failed former politicians or their wives, and other assorted minor luminaries, for whom service on a public committee guaranteed an appearance on the honours list.

But the appointment of Sir Norman had changed all that.

For most of his twenty-five years in parliament, Sir Norman had been a little-known back-bench MP, distinguished only by his rigid adherence to the party line and the fact that nobody, not even most of his constituents, had ever heard of him.

Aside from his maiden speech in which he had called for the Union Jack to be raised and the national anthem to be sung at school assemblies, Hansard had not recorded a single further contribution to parliamentary debate. Even his constituency newspaper had found it hard to find much to say about his political achievements when it announced his retirement, other than to praise his record of solid and sturdy support of the Conservative cause. It was assumed by one and all that in retirement he would disappear into the obscurity from which he had never emerged. But they had been wrong.

One of the requirements for being chairman of the committee was that Sir Norman watch television, something he had never done. According to him, it was bad enough having to leave his estate and go up to damn London in order to occasionally vote, without wasting further time sitting in front of a bloody box.

The shock of what Sir Norman saw when he was forced to sit and watch had fired him with a missionary zeal that on his past record, few would have believed possible. He now saw himself as a man with a mission, not only to cleanse the nation's television screens, but also to purge the television industry itself.

'The television industry is a hot-bed of left-wing sympathisers, alcoholics, fornicators and drug abusers,' he had thundered in his first speech. 'If we are to trust the innocent, unformed minds of our children to these people, we must expect the same moral standards of them off screen as well as on. I intend to root out these malefactors by their toes.'

Philip now found himself gazing into the watery blue eyes of the man who had already earned the tabloid sobriquet – the Sleaze-finder General.

'In . . . indigestion pills,' Philip stuttered lamely, shaking the pill box like a collecting plate. 'I overdid it at lunch.'

Too late he realised that this, too, could be misconstrued and hastily added: 'But only with food.'

Sir Norman's bushy eyebrows nearly touched his receding hairline.

Feeling that he was somewhat at a disadvantage talking into Sir Norman's knees, Philip put a hand on the washbasin and painfully pulled himself to his feet. As he did so, a large ball of wind which had been trapped in his stomach, rose inexorably up and forced itself out of his mouth in a long loud belch.

'Well, really,' Sir Norman declared, now confirmed in his earlier suspicion that he had come face-to-face with a drug-taking drunk. He turned on his heel with military precision, and marched out the door.

Philip put his hand belatedly over his mouth. His indigestion had gone, and along with it the pain, but tears of frustration pricked hotly behind his eyes. Of all the people for this to happen in front of, Sir Norman was probably the worst. He looked in the mirror again and saw a balding, middle-aged man with panic in his eyes looking back at him.

Oh why, oh why, had he left the BBC?

Seventeen

• • •

Jeremy slept clutching the bed covers with the desperation of a small child clutching its security blanket. Alicia lay beside him, her eyes wide open.

She sighed. She had at last got accustomed to the constant night and day rumble of traffic in London, but she still found the murky orange glow which passed for night disturbing. It seemed to insinuate itself around, under and even through the balding pile of Zelda's red velvet curtains, no matter how tightly Alicia drew them across the windows.

Alicia leaned over and squinted at the faint green numbers of the radio clock on the bedside table. It was 2.34 a.m. She lay back on the pillow and screwed her eyes tightly shut. Willing herself to relax, she counted slowly backwards from one hundred. It was usually an infallible way of getting to sleep, but at nineteen, she gave up and opened her eyes.

A sudden, bloodcurdling yowl from the garden made her heart skip a beat. The sound hung throbbing in the air for what felt like an age before it finally died away, only to be replaced by the vicious sounds of two cats locked in close combat. It seemed to Alicia that even if the cats did not disturb Jeremy, the sound of her still-thudding heart must, but when she looked over at him, his eyes remained closed and his breathing deep and regular.

With a loud sigh she turned over on to her side and hugged her knees to her stomach. She had always been such a sound sleeper, but since Jeremy had moved in she found that even when she did eventually fall into a fitful doze, she was troubled by unfamiliar and vaguely disagreeable dreams that made her wake feeling bad-tempered and heavy-headed. Seeing Jeremy's freshly-minted countenance first thing in the morning did not help. With another deep sigh, Alicia turned over on to her stomach.

She hadn't intended they share a bed when she suggested Jeremy come and stay for a while. She had made the suggestion a week ago, after visiting the dingy room he rented in Hackney. The room had been bad enough, but when she saw the squalid state of the kitchen he shared with two others, it had been enough to put anyone off their food.

Jeremy had needed no encouragement. He packed his suitcase there and then and they caught a taxi back to Zelda's flat. Alicia had intended to go out the next day and buy some sort of put-you up for him to sleep on. But when she went into the bedroom, she found his striped pyjamas folded neatly on the pillow next to her winceyette night-dress.

The intimacy of the two sets of nightclothes so close together had brought a blush to her cheeks, but Jeremy had not said anything to suggest he thought of her as other than a friend, or at least she didn't think he had. It was so difficult to tell. She certainly liked him much more than just a friend, but hadn't dared say anything, at least not without first knowing what he felt. Alicia had no intention of making a fool of herself with yet another man. But if she let Jeremy assume he could share her bed, would he think her easy?

Alicia tenderly stroked Jeremy's pyjama jacket. It was bobbly and rough to the touch; he obviously didn't use a fabric conditioner in his laundry. Alicia felt a rush of pity at his helplessness. She would make sure his clothes were properly washed and aired in future.

The decision helped to make up her mind about sharing a bed with Jeremy. He had been having such a hard time lately, it would be churlish for her to suggest he sleep on the floor in the other room when Zelda's king-sized bed was so large and comfortable. She plumped up the pillows and replaced the two sets of nightclothes side by side. If anything happened, she was a mature woman and could deal with it.

But nothing *had* happened.

Alicia raised herself on one elbow and studied Jeremy's sleeping profile. After a week of her cooking, his cheeks were beginning to fill out again and his skin had lost its unhealthy pallor. She stretched over and gently pushed his hair back off his forehead.

Jeremy's long eyelashes fluttered, and she hastily pulled her hand away, but his eyes remained firmly closed, and with a grunt he turned over, pulling most of the bedclothes with him.

Alicia lay back on her pillow, and once again studied the cracks in the plaster ceiling which she had come to know so well. She could have gone to confession without blushing, for all that had passed between her and Jeremy. Almost by telepathy, they had both adopted a morse code of discreet coughs outside doors to avoid the embarrassment of seeing each other undressed, and after a chaste goodnight peck on the cheek, they retreated to opposite sides of the bed, turning their backs to each other. Alicia closed her eyes with shame. She had shared a bed with a man for nearly a week, and all he had done was kiss her goodnight. This time she didn't even have the excuse that he was gay, like Donald. She could almost hear the echo of Vanessa's mocking laughter.

Alicia sat up and rubbed her eyes. It was no good, sleep was impossible when she felt like this. She gazed resentfully down at Jeremy's slumbering form. How could he possibly sleep at a time like this? She eased herself out of the bed and felt for her slippers with her toes. Then she padded into the living room, closing the door softly behind her.

Jeremy heard the door closing and opened his eyes. His heart was thudding against his ribcage, and his forehead still burned from the touch of Alicia's fingers. He let out a long sigh. He couldn't carry on like this for much longer; he was beginning to find it almost unbearable to be near Alicia.

The flowery scent of her body remained in the air like a whisper, even when she wasn't in the room, but when she came so tantalisingly close to him as she had just a moment ago, it threatened to overwhelm him.

He had even taken to waiting until he was alone in the flat so that he could go through the drawers where Alicia kept her underwear. It lay in soft white layers, scented with sweet-smelling sachets of lavender and chastely trimmed with broderie anglais and pink rosebuds. When he buried his face in its folds, it reminded him of being back in the nursery with Nanny Greig. When Vanessa had worn any underwear at all, it had been silly little scraps of black or red silk.

He groaned softly and gathered Alicia's pillow up into his arms, hugging it to his body. Vanessa had been right, he was an abject failure when it came to women. He never knew what he was meant to say or do. It was like trying to speak a foreign language or worse, trying to explain cricket to a foreigner, and he had never succeeded in either.

Still holding Alicia's pillow, he lay on his side and closed his eyes. The jolly thing about Alicia was that she made him feel so secure, he didn't feel under pressure. It was so nice just to be able to *be* with her and not feel that he had to, well . . . perform. She wasn't at all like Vanessa, wanting sex all the time. A happy little smile flitted across Jeremy's lips as he drifted back to sleep. You knew where you were with Alicia, just like Nanny Greig.

In the kitchenette, Alicia whipped the milk for her cocoa with more than her usual vigour. She was determined to put all thoughts of Jeremy out of her head. He had made it quite clear that he was not interested in her, so she had to stop acting like a lovelorn four-teen-year-old adolescent. It was time to be sensible and accept the fact that she was going to be what Fergus had so scathingly called an academic spinster.

He had meant it as an insult, of course. To him a spinster was a woman without sex, and therefore not really a woman at all. But he was wrong, Alicia thought, as she poured the frothy milk into her mug and sprinkled it with nutmeg, being a spinster was an honourable vocation. No matter what Fergus said, sex wasn't everything, and women without it could live rich and fulfilling lives. She had her cottage and her career and much more besides.

Alicia washed and dried the saucepan, then stood in the kitchenette, blowing on her cocoa. She couldn't yet face going back into the bedroom.

A newspaper on the top of the rubbish bin caught her eye, and she spread it out on the worktop, idly turning the pages as she waited for her drink to cool. Why Jeremy should buy a tabloid paper was beyond her. What on earth did he find to read in it?

But then the wording of a small boxed advertisement caught her eye. She read and re-read it. There was no mistake. She almost ran back into the bedroom.

'I just can't believe they will get away with it,' she said loudly, prodding Jeremy with her finger.

'Wha . . .?' he asked, groggily.

'I just can't believe they will get away with it,' declared Alicia again, pushing Jeremy over so she could sit down beside him.

187

Jeremy struggled into a half-sitting position. 'Who can't get away with what?'

'Vanessa and Fergus, of course,' said Alicia impatiently.

'I shouldn't worry about it.' Jeremy yawned again. 'Nothing lasts long with that woman. Take it from me, men are just playthings to her, even this Fergus.' He sleepily rubbed his eyes. 'Anyway, from what you've told me about this fellow, he's a queer sort of cove. Can't see what any sensible woman would see in him.'

Alicia decided to ignore this and instead, slapped the newspaper on to his lap. She turned on the bedside lamp.

'No, look,' she commanded, jabbing her finger at the advertisement.

The headline read: DAYDREAM YOUR WAY TO STARDOM.

Jeremy glanced at it and yawned. 'Newspapers are full of perverts.'

'Jeremy, read it *carefully*. Particularly the bottom part.'

Jeremy picked up the newspaper and studied it. Comprehension slowly dawned on his face.

'Ye gods, that's Vanessa's lot, isn't it?'

Alicia nodded. 'Fergus's research was all about fantasies. I bet this is the programme they're making together.'

'Bit strong, isn't it?' Jeremy said, raising an eyebrow.

'You don't know Fergus,' replied Alicia leaning back against the pillows. Suddenly, she knew *exactly* what she was going to do.

All her life she had tried to do what was right. She had always paid her bills on time, never parked on yellow lines or fed parking meters, always put money in charity collection boxes, and always opened the little doors on her advent calendar on the right day. And yet, while her life was in ruins, Vanessa and Fergus were happily carrying on as though nothing had happened, and were even making a television series together.

'I think we should answer the advert,' she announced.

Jeremy's eyes, which had been closing, snapped open. 'What? Why on earth should we want to do that?' He looked puzzled.

Alicia looked pityingly at him. 'Trust me,' she said.

Jeremy shrugged. Even half-asleep he could tell that she was not to be argued with, especially not at 3.15 in the morning. He settled further down in the bed and unsuccessfully tried to stifle a yawn. 'OK. But let's talk about it in the morning,' he said sleepily.

Alicia looked down at him. His eyes were already closed. She would get nothing more out of him, but now she had decided what to do, sleep was impossible. She turned off the bedside lamp, tucked the newspaper under her arm, and padded back into the sitting room.

Her cocoa had gone cold, so she poured some more milk into the saucepan. As she waited for it to boil, she climbed on to a stool and felt around in the top cupboard where she kept her chocolate store. Her recent sleepless nights had taken a toll on her usually well-stocked cupboard, and she had to feel right to the back before she found a packet of chocolate coated, double chocolate chip cookies. Her questing hand also found some books. She lifted one down. From the title it seemed to be a cookery book she hadn't read before. Next to the novels of Jane Austen and Henry James, Alicia loved reading a good cookery book. She tucked it under her arm, and with the mug of cocoa in one hand and the packet of biscuits in the other, headed back to the bedroom.

Jeremy was fast asleep again and had managed to pull all the pillows on to his side of the bed, as well as the bedclothes.

Alicia turned the bedside lamp back on again, and

tugged a pillow out of Jeremy's embrace. She plumped it up behind her shoulders, and then emptied the biscuits from their packet, stacking them on the bedside table so she could reach them without having to look. Dunking a biscuit in her cocoa, she looked at the book which she had balanced on her knees. It was called *The A to X-to-Zee of Food*.

A biscuit was half-way to Alicia's mouth before she realised it was not a cookery book. The biscuit remained suspended in mid-air as she read the opening sentences.

'To consummately enjoy both food and sex, the ingredients are the same: both should be a feast which employs all the senses, and both should be shared with a partner of exquisite taste and insatiable appetite. But our boil-in-the-bag, oven-ready, fast food, deodorised culture is in danger of losing the essential and sensual link between food and sex.'

A soggy piece of biscuit fell unheeded on to Alicia's nightdress.

'Other cultures have understood it better than us. The ancient Greeks used the same word to mean either "hors d'oeuvre" or "foreplay" while the Tupari Indians of South America express coitus with vivid phrases like Kuma ka meaning "to eat the vagina" and Ang ka, meaning "to eat the penis". Another South American tribe evocatively use the same word to mean "eat like a pig" and to "copulate excessively".

'Starting with 'A' for the apple that Eve offered Adam, this book will take you through the alphabet of the food of love.

'It was not accidental that it was a woman who by offering food, opened man's door to a new world of sex and sensuality.

'And you can be sure that it was no tasteless, chalky textured fruit that Eve offered her mate. No, the apple which tempted man out of the Garden of Eden would have been scented by the spring and summer rains, filling it with sweet juices, and ripened by the warm sun, causing it to blush with pleasure.'

Alicia thoughtfully ate the crumbly mess which was all that was left of the biscuit in her hand. As she licked the chocolate from her fingers, she flicked through the pages, looking for the chapter headed 'C'. There was a long section on chocolate.

Alicia helped herself to another biscuit and munched as she read.

'Chocolate is one of Nature's most neglected aphrodisiacs', the entry began. 'The Aztec Indians prized its qualities and used it in many forms, but the European Conquistadors rigorously suppressed the Aztec civilisation, particularly its religious and sexual manifestations. By the time chocolate reached Europe, it was a soothing drink and a balm for those with a sweet tooth, although Casanova, the Marquis de Sade and Louis XV's Mistress, Madame du Barry, are all said to have used it as an aphrodisiac with great success.

'But, while it has long been a tradition in the West for men to bring their sweethearts a gift of chocolate, few understand the real meaning behind this action.

'Unfortunately, because of chocolate's link with obesity, and the contemporary obsession with slimness, most women equate the eating of chocolate with guilt, rather than pleasure. As many women still equate enjoying sex with guilt, chocolate suffers a two-fold burden. On a more scientific note, chocolate contains phenylethylamine, a chemical the body produces when it falls in love and which, according to at least one authority, is a mood altering substance that can induce the feeling of post-coital bliss, while its amino acid is known to slow the breakdown of one of our "happy" hormones, beta-endorphin.

'But whether based on scientific evidence or not,

advertisers have been quick to exploit the subconscious link between chocolate and sex, hence the phallic shape of some chocolate bars and advertising campaigns, which concentrate on the entry of the bar between a woman's moistened lips.

'Chocolate manufacturers should perhaps take note of a notorious nineteenth-century French courtesan who is said to have made casts of all her lovers' erect penises, which she used as moulds to make dildos of the finest chocolate.'

Alicia's eyes were wide with astonishment. She turned back to 'A' and began to read. By the time she had finished, it was nearly daylight and her limbs were stiff with cramp.

She leaned back against the pillows and picked at the stray crumbs which were all that remained of the packet of biscuits.

Jeremy was curled up in a foetal position beside her. His pyjama jacket had ridden up, exposing the smooth childlike curve of his lower back. In the pale light, he looked completely defenceless. Alicia reached across and gently pulled his jacket down. Her hand brushed his skin, and Jeremy emitted a small mew of pleasure.

Alicia shivered deliciously and reached out to touch Jeremy again but drew her hand back. Vanessa had to come first.

Ignoring her sleepless night, she wrapped her dressing-gown around herself and went back into the sitting room where she found a writing pad and pen and then sat cross-legged in front of the coffee table.

She sucked the end of the pen, frowning with the effort of trying to imagine a fantasy that would guarantee a response from Vanessa. After a few minutes, she began to write in round, babyish handwriting that was quite unlike her usual elegant script.

When she had finished, she read it through with a satisfied smile. What was it the book had said under 'R'?

Revenge is a dish best eaten cold.

Eighteen

• • •

Vanessa closed her eyes and tensed her muscles, waiting for the pain. For one agonizing moment it felt like a strip of flesh was being torn from her leg.

A voice chided from somewhere down near her calves.

'We haven't seen you for quite a while, have we? I can always tell. We've been letting those naughty little follicles have it all their own way, haven't we?'

We, thought Vanessa gritting her teeth, have been doing nothing of the sort, but she had absolutely no intention of engaging in an inane conversation with some silly girl, while she was lying on a table with her legs spread wide apart. But at least this particular girl hadn't asked her if she was going away on holiday this year. Vanessa flinched as more hot wax was applied to her leg.

'That's not too hot, is it?' asked the girl, and applied more without waiting for an answer. 'Now, one more little tug and then we'll start on that naughty bikini line.'

Vanessa clenched her muscles again.

'Is Madam going away on holiday this year?'

Vanessa relaxed her muscles at just the wrong moment.

Her leg was still smarting half an hour later, as the now tight-lipped beautician massaged creamy lotions into her face and neck. Under the soothing motion of the girl's hands, Vanessa began to calm down.

The bikini wax had helped too. As the hairs were being ripped out of her skin by their roots, Vanessa had imagined doing the same to Fergus. All over.

Her desire to inflict pain on Fergus had been growing day by day. He was still refusing to sign over the rights to his research to Right Pryce Productions, and without them, she didn't have a television series.

But it wasn't just that. Fergus had somehow managed to take root in her flat and in her life, and he had created havoc. The only thing he seemed capable of achieving by himself was an erection.

It was like living with some overgrown, precociously hirsute baby, vociferously demanding an almost continuous supply of food, drink and sex. Her instinct was to stay away from the flat as much as possible, but she hardly dared leave it for fear of what new disaster she would find when she returned.

Her once-gleaming, seemingly indestructible chrome and granite kitchen had been reduced to a charred ruin by Fergus's attempts at frying chips, while her white upholstery and carpets were pockmarked with the evidence of his unsavory eating habits. It seemed to Vanessa that Fergus was congenitally incapable of eating or drinking without spilling something which was invariably dark and sticky.

What made it even worse was that her highly-strung but efficient Filipino cleaning lady had resigned, claiming that Fergus had attempted to molest her while she was cleaning the cooker. Fergus had vigorously denied the charge. According to him, it was a linguistic misunderstanding over a rubber glove. Good cleaning women were hard to find, and Vanessa had been forced to go to the woman's house and, surrounded by her many voluble relatives, not only apologise, but offer her two hundred and fifty pounds compensation and the option of returning to work for Vanessa at one pound fifty an hour extra, if she agreed not to report Fergus to the police. Being forced to beg forgiveness of a cleaning woman had been a deeply humiliating experience, and one which Vanessa would not forget or forgive.

But the humiliation was nothing to her fear that someone she knew might find out that Fergus was living with her. She had forbidden him to answer the telephone and refused all invitations to go out. She certainly couldn't take Fergus with her, and she wasn't going to leave him alone at night. Apart from running up a bill for several hundred pound's worth of whisky at the local off-licence, he had already been thrown out of three pubs in the area.

Vanessa had the infuriating suspicion that it was all an act, and that Fergus was trying to see how far he could push her, but she couldn't be sure. At first, it had been rather like playing a cat and mouse game and she had enjoyed it, naturally assuming that she was the hunter. But now she was beginning to wonder whether she might be the mouse after all.

Vanessa shuddered involuntarily. She had even found herself having sexual fantasies about Fergus. As far as she was concerned, fantasies were for old maids and the sexually frustrated, and neither description could possibly be applied to her. Yet no matter how much she told herself that Fergus was physically repulsive, her body responded to his in a way it had never responded to any other man's, and she hated him for it.

As the gooey remains of her face mask were wiped off, Vanessa amused herself by imagining ways of getting Fergus to sign the contract, all of them painful.

'Would Madam like her eyebrows tidied up?' the girl asked rather uncertainly, a pair of tweezers in her hand.

Vanessa glanced at her watch. It was nearly midday.

'No, Madam would not. Have you finished?'

The girl had.

Half an hour later, Vanessa was toiling up the three flights of stairs to the Right Pryce offices. She was so close to success she could almost taste it, and she had no intention of letting anyone, least of all Fergus, stand in her way. The moment he signed that contract, he would be out of her flat and out of her life.

She paused outside the office door to catch her breath and compose her face in a confident smile, but it was a waste on Heather, who sat plugged into her personal stereo, typing slowly with one finger.

Vanessa put her bag down on Heather's desk and waited.

Heather continued to nod in time to the music.

Vanessa leaned forward and yanked one of her earphones out.

'Coffee, black and very strong, and type these notes for me *now*!' she ordered, banging a sheaf of paper down on the desk.

Without looking up, Heather dropped Vanessa's typing into her filing tray. 'Mr Pryce's work has priority.'

Vanessa glowered at her, but was ignored. 'Is Vijay in?' she snapped.

Heather replaced her earphone and pointed wordlessly at the boardroom door.

Vijay had his head in his hands when Vanessa walked in the door. He was surrounded by piles of letters, which covered the table and had spilled on to the floor.

'Replies?' asked Vanessa, rustling as she walked over a carpet of paper.

Vijay looked up, blinking through his round granny glasses. When he saw it was the cause of his misery, the look on his thin face turned from one of despair to intense dislike. His voice was accusing.

197

'I'm trying to divide them into categories, if that's the right word.'

He looked down at the list he had written.

'Sado-masochism and bondage; sex in exotic places; sex with strangers; with more than one partner; with someone famous and/or a character from a soap opera; with inanimate objects including household and other electrical appliances; wearing uniforms; wearing leather, rubber or other fetishistic materials; sex with animals, oh, and we mustn't forget sex with aliens,' he intoned like the case for the prosecution. 'Then there are a whole load which defy specification completely, and most are too disgusting for words, and I haven't even started on the home videos yet.' He indicated a pile of videos in the corner of the room.

Vanessa's eyes lit up at the four-foot high mound of videos. 'I'll take responsibility for viewing them. I have a feeling they could provide one of the high points of the programme. Look what they've done for Jeremy Beadle.'

She picked up a letter and began reading. 'Now I know why donkeys need sanctuaries,' she laughed. 'Are they all like this?'

'The animal section is one of the largest,' Vijay replied, scowling. 'I've broken it down into horses and donkeys, dogs and household pets, farm animals, and gorillas and other wild animals.'

'Sounds like Fergus's research is right on cue,' said Vanessa, and indicated another pile of letters in the animal section.

'What's this one?'

'Miscellaneous animals.'

'This one I've got to see.' She hunted through the pile.

Heather came in with two mugs of coffee. She banged one sloppily down beside Vanessa, and placed the other carefully down in front of Vijay, together with a conspiratorial smile and a chocolate digestive.

Vijay gave her a grateful look in return. They seemed to be getting on really well and had fallen into the habit of spending their lunch hours together, sitting in Soho Square if the weather was fine, or perched on a stool in their favourite Italian sandwich bar drinking café latte at other times.

Although Heather was only nineteen, she had a sophistication Vijay envied. She had had lots of jobs, most of them in the music industry, lived in a flat with five other girls, and went clubbing nearly every night. Vijay had been thinking about asking her out, but had made the mistake of mentioning it to his younger sister, Arundhati, who as usual had run straight to his mother. To his horror, his mother had turned up in the office two days ago, on the pretext that she was shopping in Oxford Street, and thought she would drop by with some of his favourite Indian sweets. He thought he would die of shame. He was twenty-five years old and his mother was still bringing him sweets! He had bundled her, protesting, out of the office, but not before she had taken a good look at Heather. She was waiting for him when he got home and had declared that if he insisted on going out with a girl who not only had shaven hair, but who painted her finger nails black, she would immolate herself. Heather, on the other hand, had thought his mother really cool, walking round in a lime green and gold sari and showing her midriff at her age, so perhaps he still stood a chance.

The friendly looks between Vijay and Heather had not been lost on Vanessa. She held up a letter.

'Does anyone know how snakes breathe?' she asked. 'Because if they can't hold their breath for very long, there could be a lot of dead ones around.'

She looked pointedly at Vijay. 'You should know the

answer to that one, Vijay. Don't you have a lot of snakes in your part of the world?'

Vijay flushed an angry red. 'I don't have to listen to that sort of thing.'

'Are you by any chance offering to resign?' asked Vanessa swiftly, 'Because if you are, I'm sure we'll be more than happy to accommodate you.'

Vijay opened his mouth to reply, but Heather put a restraining hand on his shoulder. 'Don't rise to her bait, Vijay. At the rate we're going, we're all going to be out of a job soon, so why not hang around for the redundancy pay.'

With a toss of her spiky blonde head, Heather marched out of the room, pushing past Hugo, who had just opened the door.

'We are on our high horse today, aren't we?' Hugo drawled, raising an eyebrow at Heather's disappearing back.

'That expression takes on a whole new meaning if you read some of these letters,' Vanessa said, meaningfully.

Hugo pushed a pile of Vijay's carefully sorted letters off the table and put his mobile phone and electronic organiser down. He waved a languid hand. 'Are *all* these letters in answer to the advert?'

Vanessa nodded. Hugo picked one up and began to read.

'I don't believe it. This man's got to be pulling our leg,' he exclaimed after a few moments. 'Nobody would want to do it with a goose. We used to keep them as watchdogs. They're worse than Rottweilers. They can take an arm off with those bloody great beaks of theirs.'

'Some people like big peckers,' Vanessa murmured, and they both started to laugh.

'I hope we have good cause for all this merriment,' said Philip walking in.

'Hugo and I were just discussing changing the name of the show to Old MacDonald Had a Farm,' laughed Vanessa.

Philip looked from one to the other, a smile on his face, hoping to be let in on the joke. Hugo handed him the letter.

Philip read it and paled. 'Are they all like this?' he gasped.

'A lot of them,' said Vanessa dabbing her eyes. 'I think we'll have to have an RSPCA inspector in the studio.'

This set her and Hugo laughing again.

Philip scurried round the table picking up letters from different piles, and scanning them with increasing desperation.

'Oh, my God,' he groaned and sat down, 'this is awful. I'm finished.'

'Oh, come on PP. It isn't awful, it's wonderful. We have enough material here to make a dozen series,' said Vanessa.

'A dozen porno movies, you mean,' Vijay interjected sourly.

'Vijay's right. We can't show people doing these things,' Philip waved a despairing hand at the letters, 'on television. I'm beginning to think I may have made an error of judgement about this whole business. I've already been summoned to a meeting of the Committee for Media Morality. If any of this has reached their ears, I'm in deep trouble.'

Ever since the invitation to meet the new head of the CMM had arrived the day before, Philip had been alternating between blind panic and hot flushes at the thought of coming face to face with Sir Norman Fluck again.

The note claimed that it was merely 'an informal exchange of views and meet the new chairman

201

occasion', but Philip knew a summons when he read one.

'Trust me, Philip,' Vanessa said soothingly, 'there's plenty of material here that we can use without causing riots in the streets.' She fished around among the letters. 'For instance, here's a variant on the old scantily clad girl leaping out of a cake theme. This is from a woman who actually wants to be a cream cake. She wants to be covered in double cream, decorated with fruit and then carried on a silver platter into a room full of men dressed in evening clothes, who then lick her clean. I'm sure Hugo can film that very tastefully, can't you Hugo?' Vanessa's mouth twitched.

Philip looked like a man in a catatonic trance.

'Or how about this. Another woman has written in to say she likes to make love on the back seat of a Morris Minor, because that's where she lost her virginity so she has the back seat of her car in her bedroom. We could have a whole section of a programme asking people which car they first made love in called "Fantasy Cars".'

'I can see a lot of potential in cars,' Hugo added enthusiastically. 'They are a potent sexual symbol. Think of all the television adverts: men controlling sleek, throbbing cars as they power their way along narrow, winding mountain roads, or women abandoning men but keeping the car.'

Philip looked like a man who had been thrown a lifeline. 'I think you may have something there,' he said, the colour beginning to return to his face. 'I'm sure there is some sort of psychological analysis that could be made. Perhaps Dr Archibald could enlighten us. He is fully on board with us now, isn't he, Vanessa?' he asked anxiously. 'The subject matter we are dealing with has enough potential for legal action without someone suing us for infringement of their copyright.'

'Don't worry about a thing, Philip darling,' lied Vanessa. 'You know you can trust me.'

'I like this one,' Hugo announced waving a letter, 'it's full of visual possibilities. Some middle-aged bank manager wants to be dressed up in nappies and frilly baby clothes and sleep in a cot. I can really conceptualize this one,' he continued excitedly. 'We could build a giant nursery but give it a slightly nightmarish quality – more Angela Carter's *Magic Toy Shop* than Disneyland. Check that one out for me.' He threw the letter across the table at Vijay, who picked it up between two fingers as though it were soiled.

Philip nodded slowly. 'There does seem to be a certain amount of potential here, if we are careful in our selection of the subject matter.'

'We could have a section called "Housewives' Choice",' Vanessa laughed. 'A lot of women seem to have intimate relationships with their washing machines and vacuum cleaners. Or even better, how about a consumer advice slot? *Very* Channel 4. I can just see it: how to remove baby oil from black satin sheets; where to buy size 13 stilettos; or how to complain if your vibrator doesn't give you satisfaction. And can you imagine Gabriella giving advice on how to repair punctures in inflatable dolls?'

Philip looked stern. 'I suggest you think about mending bridges with Gabriella rather than inflatable dolls, Vanessa. She was extremely unhappy about working with you after that lunch last week, but I have done my utmost to convince her that you are the best person for the job, so I hope you won't let me down with any lamentable lapses in taste.'

He left the room.

Hugo raised an eyebrow at Vanessa. 'Who's been a naughty girl then?' he asked, following Philip out of the room.

Vanessa turned savagely on Vijay. 'I want this lot sorted out by the end of today.'

She scooped up her handbag and swept out of the room and past Heather's desk.

'I'm out to lunch,' she called over her shoulder, as she exited through the main doors.

Nineteen

• • •

Vijay gazed at the greasy film on his tea. His *Guardian* newspaper lay unread on the ketchup-blobbed, formica-topped table in front of him. Every few seconds, the windows of the café in which he was sitting rattled, as yet another juggernaut thundered past on the A1.

Vijay sighed. Somehow this was not how he had imagined life as a television researcher. He had pictured himself doing a Bernstein and Woodward, revealing corruption in high places, or maybe grabbing his flak jacket as he rushed off to catch the last flight into some war-torn country, where he would sit in the bar of some bomb-blasted hotel, cracking brittle jokes with the other battle-hardened journalists. At the very least, he had hoped to doorstep the odd villain or two.

He sipped his tea and grimaced. It was strong and treacly sweet. The customers of Fred's Place obviously liked their tea ready sugared.

The woman behind the counter had gazed at him a little oddly although not altogether unkindly, when he asked for lemon tea. Pushing her straggly hair back off her forehead, and wiping her large, rough hands on her purple nylon overall, she had considered his request.

'Best I can do is black, ducks. We don't get much call for lemon in these parts,' she said finally.

Vijay had agreed to this, and ordered egg and chips

as well. The woman had slapped two slabs of white bread and margarine on a plate next to his tea.

Vijay had hesitated. 'Er . . . have you any wholemeal?'

The woman's voice had begun to rise, 'Look ducks, if you don't like what we've got, then you can . . .'

Much to Vijay's relief, she had been interrupted when the hatch behind her shot up. Two impressively large, tattooed arms had appeared, and banged two plates down on the counter.

'Two sausages, two eggs, chips, beans, fried slice and black pudding *twice!*' bellowed a voice which matched the arms. The woman took a plate in each hand and began to repeat this litany of cholesterol in an equally loud voice, but before she could finish, a man in paint-splattered overalls scurried to the counter to claim them. Vijay had seized the opportunity to escape to a table. He now looked surreptiously around at his fellow diners. Most were either silently munching or staring fixedly at a newspaper. One was absorbed in excavating the dirt from his nails with the help of a fork.

Where was the glamour and the excitement he craved?

Vijay caught the eye of the woman behind the counter.

She leaned forward and winked at him, her good humour restored. 'Don't look so worried ducks, it may never happen.'

But it had already happened, Vijay wanted to cry out. It was bad enough that he was working on a programme that went against all his political principles, but what made it so much worse was that it was making him so painfully aware of his own inadequacies.

He was twenty-five years old, and his sex-life so far had consisted of a number of fumbling encounters in the dark. To call them one-night stands would be wilful exaggeration. None of them had lasted that long.

Everywhere he looked he seemed to see sex. The

very air throbbed with it. So why was he not getting any?

Sometimes when he walked down the street he found it painful, as he knew that underneath their clothes, every woman he saw was naked. He didn't mind whether they were short, fat, thin or tall – he just wanted them. All of them.

His mother kept arranging parties so that he would meet suitable girls, in the hope that since he had not chosen a sensible career, at least he might marry a sensible girl. Vijay had considered marriage, which at least offered the guarantee of sex. But although he was tempted by the soft-skinned young girls with their glossy, waist-length hair whom his mother thrust at him, he could not marry one, not yet. For the same dark eyes which looked so demurely down when his mother addressed them, slyly flashed their knowledge of his inexperience at him, when his mother wasn't looking.

He had abandoned his idea of asking Heather out. No matter what his mother said about her, Heather was a nice girl, and the last thing he needed at the moment was a nice girl.

Sometimes he felt ready to burst, but dare not do anything to relieve his frustration. His mother and his sister, Arundhati, refused to respect his privacy, and would come into his room at any time of the night or day without knocking. He had once tried putting a lock on his door, but when he came home, his mother had picked it with a hair grip. How could anyone who had sprung from her flesh have any secrets from her? she demanded. When he had remonstrated with her, she had burst into floods of tears and rushed weeping to his aunt's house next door. Within minutes, the house was full of women wailing because of their treatment at the hands of men.

Vijay put his head in his hands. If things carried on

like this for much longer he was in danger of becoming a pervert, just like the people he was interviewing for *Forbidden Fruit*.

He had spent the day before in Leeds, where his first appointment had proved a wasted journey. Mr Randy Mills had turned out to be a twelve-year-old with a colourful imagination, or so his mother said, when an embarrassed Vijay had been forced to explain why he wanted to see her son. Mrs Mills had seemed quite undisturbed by the precocity of her son's imagination, and his unhealthy attachment to his computer. According to her, it was better than him being out on the streets and joyriding and such. Vijay had hastily made his excuses and left, without meeting the pre-pubescent computer and sexual prodigy, but as he glanced back at the house, he was sure he had seen the lace curtains moving at an upstairs window, and a youthful index finger being held up at his departing figure.

His next appointment had been at a small terraced house on a run-down council estate on the outskirts of Leeds. The taxi drivers he had unsuccessfully approached to take him there had seemed unmoved by his threat to take their license numbers and report them to the local council – the possible damage to their vehicles or to themselves, seemingly outweighing both his threats and his offer of a large tip. It had eventually taken him three lengthy bus rides to get there, one of which had taken him ten miles in the wrong direction.

The door of the inappropriately named 23 Greenacres Avenue had been answered by a small, slim woman dressed in tight scruffy jeans and a faded, black T-shirt on which a screaming skull pierced by a dagger announced the 1992 World Tour of a heavy metal band. Her long dark hair framed a pale unmade-up face. She had inhaled deeply on a cigarette held between nicotine-stained fingers, as she wordlessly looked Vijay up and down. With a jerk of her head, she invited him in.

Vijay had followed her down a shabby hallway into a living room bare of furniture, except for a badly beaten up couch and a fridge. The room was dominated by a gigantic sound system with six-foot high speakers. Hundreds of albums lay stacked around the walls.

The woman had indicated the speakers. 'The neighbours love me,' she said laughing, 'and I just love to get them going. They're such a load of old farts. Do you like music?'

'Some,' Vijay replied uncertainly.

She had motioned at the wall behind him. He turned. 'I sold my soul to rock and roll' was daubed across the Sixties orange and green psychedelic wallpaper in two-foot high black letters.

'Sex, drugs and rock and roll, it's the only way to go,' she said. 'Want some coke?'

Vijay hesitated, he didn't want to appear uncool. 'Well, I . . .'

'Diet or straight?' She opened the fridge door which was packed with cans of Coca-Cola.

Vijay blushed. 'Er . . . straight, please.'

She tossed him a can and snapped one open for herself. 'I can offer you some of the hard stuff,' she said, indicating half a dozen bottles of vodka lined up along the bottom shelf, 'but I don't touch it before twelve or after six in the morning. You've got to have some sort of system.'

She settled cross-legged on the floor and took a long drink from her can. 'Shoot,' she commanded Vijay.

Vijay had looked around and then settled himself gingerly on the edge of the couch, trying to avoid a spring that had clawed its way through the threadbare cover. He opened his notebook and sat poised with a biro.

'Mrs McKenna . . .' he began.

'Call me Boots,' she interrupted, 'everyone does, on account I've got so many.'

Vijay noticed the decorative, cuban-heeled cowboy boots that stuck out from under her jeans.

'Boots,' he began again.

'What's your handle?' she asked.

Vijay looked blank.

'Name,' she explained.

'Vijay.'

'VJ,' she repeated slowly, 'nice.'

Vijay had shifted uncomfortably. She had a way of saying 'nice' that wasn't quite . . . well, nice.

'Mrs McK . . . Boots,' he tried again. 'It's about your response to our advertisement. We're interesting in your, er . . . car seat.'

Boots pushed her dark hair back from her face. The movement revealed a tattoo of a writhing green snake on her forearm. 'You mean my passion wagon?' she asked. 'Want to see it?'

She jumped to her feet and led the way upstairs.

The top of the house looked like a building site. Where there had been three rooms, there was now just one, but it had not been decorated since the dividing walls had been demolished, and peeling patches of wallpaper were the only bright splodges of colour on the exposed brick and plaster. A double mattress covered with old fur coats lay on the dusty floorboards in the centre of the room, and lined around the walls were at least fifty pair of boots, from thigh-high patent leather to demure short, laces, granny ones.

Dominating the room like some kind of strange tribal throne was the back seat of a car, which was raised about eight inches off the ground on a wooden plinth. The wall behind it was decorated with car number plates, assorted metal wheel hubs, and a large motorway sign from the M1.

Boots stroked the cracked leather seat, a faraway look on her face. 'I lost my cherry on this seat in 1956. I was fourteen and he was my father's best friend.'

Vijay did some mental arithmetic and looked shocked. She was much older than he had thought.

Boots misinterpreted his looks. 'It wasn't like you think,' she said quickly. 'I really fancied him. It took me a year to seduce him and then it was only because he was off to Suez that he finally did it, just in case he didn't come back. It was just beautiful.'

She reached down beside the seat and flipped a switch. A motor began to purr and the seat vibrated. She stretched out along its length.

'It feels just beautiful under your bare bum. Want to give it a go?'

Vijay shook his head.

'Cars aren't the same anymore. I'm into bikes now. Ever done it on the back of a chopper? It really blows your mind. Me and the old man do it all the time. There ain't nothing better than a 1000cc between your legs, unless it's a 2000cc man.'

Vijay swallowed hard. 'I wonder if you would agree to us filming your, er . . . passion wagon?'

'Only if you'll come for a ride with me. Snake don't mind me playing away from home occasionally, says it does me good to find out there ain't no competition. Want to try and prove him wrong?'

Vijay had backed down the stairs. 'I'm afraid I must rush, I have another appointment.'

Boots stood at the top of the stairs, laughing, as he fumbled with the front door lock.

'You make sure you send a good-looking camera crew, now. I like my men *real* big.'

Vijay had slammed the door shut behind him, just as a black leather-clad figure roared up on a Harley Davidson. His helmet was emblazoned with a golden-eyed snake. The rider lifted one long, leather clad leg over the bike, and stood to remove his helmet at the same time. A mane of blond hair fell over his broad shoulders.

Snake must have been about twenty-one.

Vijay shuddered. Supposing he had said yes? He could see the newspaper headlines: TV RESEARCHER KILLED BY JEALOUS LOVER IN CAR SEAT SEX ORGY. But Mrs McKenna had been rather attractive. Vijay closed his eyes and imagined her wearing only a pair of cowboy boots. He felt a pleasurable glow between his thighs.

'I'll have to have words with Fred again about what he's been putting in the tea.'

Vijay opened his eyes. He was the centre of attention in the café; the other customers were all grinning at him.

The woman behind the counter, who had just spoken, winked at him and held out a plate. 'You're going to need this, ducks, if you're going to keep up your strength.'

Vijay blushed and hurried up to the counter to collect his lunch. Fred, if indeed it was Fred with the tattooed biceps, didn't believe in healthy, low fat cooking. As Vijay carried his plate back to his table, the fried egg slid from side to side on a film of oil. He sat down and squeezed the tomato-shaped, red plastic sauce bottle. Nothing happened. Vijay shook hard, and then in desperation, banged it smartly with the flat of his hand. His chips disappeared under a satisfying stream of ketchup. He speared two with his fork, and poked them into the golden yellow yolk of his fried egg before cramming them into his mouth. They tasted delicious.

Five minutes later, he had finished.

He drank a second cup of sweet tea and then feeling almost cheerful, tucked the *Guardian* under his arm and left a twenty pence tip under his plate. Outside on the pavement, he checked his A-Z again. According to his calculation, his next interviewee lived not far from Fred's Place.

Wellington House proved to be a grim 1960s, twenty-two storey block of council flats on the other side of the A1. The entrance stank of urine and boiled vegetables and was daubed with racist graffiti.

Vijay picked his way uneasily round the rubbish on the floor to the lifts. One had an 'out of order' sign on it, and two whey-faced boys of about fourteen were sitting on the floor of the other. They had wedged the door open, and one held a brown paper bag to his nose.

Vijay hovered, hoping they might move, but they sat gazing hollow-eyed at the ceiling. He began the long climb to the fifteenth floor.

Panting, he knocked on the door of number 153. There was the sound of several bolts being drawn back and then the door still fastened by a safety chain, was opened two inches. A small voice demanded identification.

When he eventually opened the door, Alfred Burton proved to be a small wispy man wearing comically large glasses. He swiftly pulled Vijay inside and bolted the door again.

'Now,' he said with a little giggle, 'you've come to meet my friends. They've been all a-twitter since I told them you were coming. We don't get many visitors up here.'

He wiped his hands on his frilly apron. 'I'm going to get into trouble whoever I take you to meet first, so in for a penny, in for a pound,' and he opened one of the doors which led off the dank hallway.

It led into a bedroom. Perched on the bed, on the floor, and in every available space were life-size, inflatable dolls, staring back at Vijay with dead eyes, their lips forming a chorus of noiseless 'O's.

The collection filled every room of what would otherwise have been a neatly kept, two-bedroom flat.

'When mother was alive, I had to keep them in my room. She said it wasn't proper for a grown man to collect dolls. But since she passed on a year ago last

213

Spring, I've been able to expand,' Alfred explained happily.

Vijay dazedly wondered whether the departed Mrs Burton had known what the dolls were for.

'I hope you don't think me morbid, but Elsie here,' Alfred indicated a doll wedged into a high-backed chair beside the gas fire in the main room, 'reminds me of mother, so I gave her one of my mother's wigs, and dressed her in mother's favourite lilac chiffon. She liked lilac chiffon, same as the Queen Mother. They even had the same birthday. She wouldn't miss a year at Clarence House. It was her birthday treat, too. She would get done up to the nines in chiffon, with matching hat and gloves. Sometimes tourists used to think she *was* the Queen Mother and take pictures. It fair tickled her pink.'

Alfred wiped a little nostalgic tear from the corner of his eye. 'Anyway, I thought it was right she should have pride of place in her throne, so to speak. Mind you, Princess Di is my favourite.'

He crooked his finger at Vijay and led him to a curtained-off alcove.

'Now, I want you to be brutally honest, have I got the hair right?' He drew back the curtain, and sitting as though she were in some sort of shrine papered with pictures of Princess Diana cut from newspapers and magazines, was a doll wearing a blonde wig cut in a fair approximation of Princess Diana's famous peekaboo hairstyle. 'It's, er, very good, very good indeed,' Vijay stuttered.

Alfred beamed radiantly. 'I cut it myself, made the dress too. I copied it from the one she wore to that film première. I couldn't quite get the décolletage right, but I'm working on it.'

It was black, off-the-shoulder dress, but the doll didn't quite have what could be described as shoulders.

Sitting opposite Elsie, her wig askew and her splayed

legs sticking out at right angles from several layers of dusty chiffon, Vijay sipped tea, squeezed between a redhead and a brunette on the couch.

Alfred studied him coyly from his perch on a stool beside Elsie. 'I've got this plan, see, and I thought the telly might be able to help,' he began.

Vijay quailed at what might come next.

Alfred gave a self-important little cough.

'I thought I might do sort of, guided tours. People pay to see all sorts these days, so why not my dolls? I've been thinking I might dress them up in different national costumes, one for every country in the world, so it would be educational.' He reached across and patted Elsie's arm. 'My mother would have liked it, being like a stately home.'

He looked hopefully across at Vijay.

With as much tact as he could muster, Vijay explained the purpose of *Forbidden Fruit*.

Alfred went quiet and replaced a half-eaten bourbon on his plate.

'So you see,' Vijay finished, 'what I really came here to talk about was your, er . . . relationship with your dolls.'

Alfred looked mortified. 'But they're like family! I wouldn't dream of treating them improperly,' he protested indignantly. 'It would be like, well, *incest*.'

Outside the front door, Vijay crossed Alfred off his list. His next visit was to a Mr De Vere who, much to Vijay's relief, lived in a neat 1930s semi-detached villa near Highbury. The door had been answered by his home help, a cheerful black girl with elaborately corn-rowed hair.

'Mr De Vere's really excited about meeting you,' she said over her shoulder, as she led the way. 'He doesn't get many visitors, which is a pity as he's really a nice old man.'

She had made them tea and then left.

Mr De Vere had the air of a faded dandy about him. His three-piece grey suit, though old, was spotless, and a freshly-laundered handkerchief was tucked with a flourish into his breast pocket. His shirt had an old-fashioned, starched collar, and although it was fraying at the cuffs, he wore gold cuff links. His rheumatic hands gripped a silver-topped walking stick.

He leaned eagerly forward as Vijay looked through his collection of erotic Edwardian postcards. Page after page of sepia coloured photographs of buxom young women, their mountainous breasts bursting out of tightly laced corsets, and thighs which now only a body builder would dare show in public, encased in demure black stockings.

When Vijay had finished, Mr De Vere handed him an old penny. 'Drop this in the slot and turn the handle,' he commanded pointing his walking stick at an old machine standing in the corner of the room.

Vijay nervously did as he was told and pressed his eye to a small peep hole. As he cranked the handle, he saw the grainy, jerky figure of a girl being undressed by her maid, and stepping naked into a hip bath. As the maid sponged her body, the girl became playful and splashed her, so that the maid too stripped naked. Suddenly the door to the bathroom was flung open by a butler with an impossibly large, handlebar moustache and eyebrows which could only be described as beetling. The two girls covered their mouths with alarm but no other part of their anatomy, as the butler advanced towards them – at which point the film flickered to a halt.

'Better than any of those new-fangled video games, isn't it?' Mr De Vere asked. 'I rescued it from the end of the pier at Bluehaven twenty years ago. Some woman councillor had got all hot under the collar about it.' He looked mournful. 'You know, I really can't understand women these days. Half of them want to act like men

216

and the other half spend their time getting skinny so they can look like them. A woman should have a bit of flesh on her so's a man can get a good hold. I can't abide skin and bones.'

He pointed his walking stick at Vijay. 'You don't know what you're missing, young man. Women were really women in my younger days. Now if that home help's gone, there's a bottle of whisky in that cupboard over there, so let's forget about tea and biscuits. Women spoonfeed you milk when you're a child and tea when you're old; they think they know what's best, but we know better, don't we?'

Despite Mr De Vere's attitude to women, Vijay rather liked him. He seemed somehow innocent, rather like the seaside postcards he collected. As Vijay walked to the underground station, fortified by two glasses of whisky he decided he would suggest Mr De Vere as a participant for the show. His fantasy was to be the peeping butler in the slot machine, but only if the two girls had, as he had put it, 'real meat on their bones'.

The fantasy had a certain historical relevance to it, Vijay thought, but he had another motive. Mr De Vere could only walk with difficulty, and had a wheelchair, although his vanity rarely let him use it. But if he had to work on a programme about sex, then he would make sure the elderly and the disabled had their say too. At least them he would feel he had struck a blow for two neglected minorities, Vijay thought determinedly. Only he wouldn't mention the wheelchair to Vanessa, at least not yet.

He began to whistle. He still had to visit a Dominatrix in Penge, a checkout girl in Bromley who wanted to work the evening shift at Sainsbury's topless, and a team of naked synchronised swimmers in Orpington. It was going to be a long day.

Twenty

• • •

The now all too familiar sensation of an iron band
tightening around his chest woke Philip before his
alarm clock could. Without opening his eyes he felt
for his pills on the bedside table and gulped down
two ignoring the instructions to chew slowly before
swallowing.

His fingers closed round the pile of newspaper cuttings which lay on the bed beside him. He had fallen
asleep reading them. Philip reluctantly opened his
eyes. Even without his bifocals he could read the
headlines:

FLUCK HITS OUT AT TV MUCK

SLEAZE-FINDER GENERAL IN TV FILTH HUNT

ONE FLUCK TOO MANY – TV COMEDY BANNED

Philip reached for his glasses. There must be a weak
spot in Sir Norman's arguments; all he had to do was
find it.

He scanned one of the articles which recounted ver-
batim yet another of Sir Norman's barnstorming
speeches: 'TV executives sit in self-appointed judgement on the behaviour of politicians and other public
figures, subjecting their every move to close scrutiny
and demanding they answer for their every action. Yet
when someone dares sit in judgment on them, they
yell "censorship"! They lecture us on the freedom of

the press but the freedom they want is to corrupt and to criticise,' Sir Norman had raged. 'How long can we allow these men to consider themselves above the moral codes the rest of us choose to abide by?'

Philip shuddered and picked up another cutting: 'The tide of filth that is sweeping across our TV screens is a canker in the very soul of our great nation. Even if it means the wound is deep we must cut it out. Better the pain of a clean wound than a slow death by gangrene.'

Philip shakily removed his glasses.

The sudden shrill of his alarm clock startled him, but for once it was welcome. He set his computerised rowing and treadmill machines on to higher programmes than usual and for forty minutes, twenty minutes on each – stretched and pulled his muscles to their limits. Panting and dripping with sweat, Philip turned the fierce jets of his specially installed massage shower on to full. Feeling invigorated, he breakfasted on two cups of freshly-ground, decaffeinated coffee, some hi-bran, low sugar muesli and two capsules of extra strength Royal Jelly and Ginseng.

As he carefully knotted his silk tie, he looked in the mirror. There was a time when he had been young and idealistic enough to consider a career in politics, he thought wistfully. He had been quite a rebel in those days. Philip patted some Chanel cologne on his cheeks. It wasn't that he cared any less, it was just that he had matured. His ideals were still intact, but tempered by responsibility and a necessary pragmatism. After all, he had a business to run and employees and investors to consider. It was crucial that he didn't let the situation get out of proportion because of his unfortunate brush with Sir Norman and a few hysterical headlines. The tabloids always distorted the truth, and Sir Norman was probably nothing like the blinkered, right-wing moral crusader he appeared to be.

Philip's pulse was nearly back to normal by the time his taxi arrived, and as it drove through the morning rush hour traffic to the offices of the Committee for Media Morality in Knightsbridge, he chewed two more tablets just to be sure. The last thing he needed was another attack of nervous indigestion.

Sir Norman strode briskly through Green Park, having eschewed an offer of a taxi by the porter at his club in St James. The walk to Knightsbridge would do him good, not that he needed it. Sir Norman felt like a man reborn since he had been appointed head of the Committee for Media Morality.

In his own modest way, Sir Norman liked to feel he had served his sovereign and his country well. His military service during the Second World War had not been quite so distinguished on the battlefield as he had wished, but it was not for want of trying. He had joined up as soon as he could, and had volunteered for dangerous duty at every opportunity. Not that he would have been insubordinate enough to complain, but he privately felt that his superior officers had shown their lack of military competence by confining him to the Pay Corps. When his father retired as an MP after forty years, Sir Norman had stood for Parliament himself. He regarded it as another chance to serve his country, and if once again he was not called upon to be other than a foot soldier, he was still happy to do it.

As he neared Knightsbridge, Sir Norman's pace quickened and he began to whistle. He had not expected to be offered another tour of duty after his retirement from Parliament, but when it was suggested he allow his name to be put forward for the chairmanship of the Committee for Media Morality, he had readily agreed. He suspected that other people had assumed that the chairmanship of the committee was tantamount to putting him out to grass, but he had proved them wrong. He had found a cause that was worthy of a fight to the finish.

He had long been uneasy about the weakening moral fibre of the country, and had put it down to the twin evils of socialism and Europe, but when, as a result of his appointment, he sat down to watch television for the first time in his life, he had realised instantly where the real danger lay.

At first, he had found it disconcerting that his main allies in his crusade were the tabloid newspapers, but a general sometimes had to form strange alliances in order to defeat the enemy. In a war, the end justified the means. But he had recently met a new ally, someone he felt was fired by the same passion to preserve all that was good and right about the English way of life, and he had appointed her as his lieutenant on the committee.

Sir Norman did not normally approve of women in the battlefield. They were bad for military discipline and took a man's mind off his duty. But after years as a dedicated bachelor, he had at last met a woman who could stir him, a woman with the heart of a warrior, a veritable Boadicea.

He pushed his way through the revolving doors into the offices of the committee and was greeted by the receptionist. He glanced down at the visitors' book and what he saw there, written in a large, clear hand made his heart quicken: Mrs Mildred Proudfoot, Chairwoman of the Campaign for Decency and Family Life. With an explosive 'Harrumph' he set off down the corridor to the main meeting room.

A minute later, Philip presented himself at reception. As he waited for the receptionist to announce him, he surreptitiously checked his pulse. It was beginning to rise again. He concentrated on controlling his breathing, it was a technique he had read in a book about stress management.

The receptionist directed him to a couch but almost immediately an efficient looking woman in her early fifties emerged to greet him. The squashy leather sofa on which Philip had been sitting made dignified posture impossible, and he struggled awkwardly to his feet.

'I'm Jenny Haigh, the Committee Secretary. I'm sorry we've kept you waiting, Mr Pryce, Sir Norman has been packing in meetings since his appointment. He's keeping us all on our toes.'

She talked over her shoulder as she led the way down a long corridor and through several sets of swing doors.

'Sir Norman is just trying to get the feel of the job at the moment since he is not over-familiar with the workings of the television industry. I have been arranging a series of meetings with producers selected on an *ad hoc* basis in order to canvass their views about the committee,' Jenny Haig continued. 'The meetings are purely on an informal basis so as to allow a full and frank exchange of views. The full complement of committee members will not be present, so please feel free to raise anything you choose, we have no set agenda.'

Philip felt curiously lightheaded. If he could, he would have hugged Jenny Haigh. The meeting was not after all about *Forbidden Fruit*!

As she opened the committee room door and ushered him in, he felt the unfamiliar sensation of a smile beginning to form, but it was stillborn.

'Sir Norman, this is Philip Pryce of Right Pryce Productions,' announced Jenny Haigh.

Sir Norman was sitting at the head of a long table. On his left sat a large solid looking woman in a severely tailored, powder blue suit and a blouse with a large floppy bow at the neck mirroring her several chins. Her bouffant blonde hair was anchored rigidly in place by a liberal application of hairspray.

On Sir Norman's right sat an elderly, greying man with the mild expression of a country parson. Jenny Haigh sat down next to him and indicated that Philip should sit opposite.

Sir Norman looked gimlet-eyed through thick-lensed glasses at Philip. 'Haven't we met before?' he demanded.

Philip took a deep breath. He had prepared himself for this. With his career at stake, he had decided a little white lie was worth a try.

'At the Golden Screen Television awards,' he began. Sir Norman had been on the table next to his, although they had not been introduced. 'You may remember . . .'

'Yes, yes of course.' Sir Norman interrupted impatiently, before Philip could finish. 'Television spends much too much time patting itself on the back for my tastes.'

Philip stared. Sir Norman obviously hadn't remembered him from the toilets in the restaurant. Then it dawned on him: Sir Norman had not been wearing his glasses in the restaurant and judging by the thickness of the lenses, he would have a hard time seeing without them. He must be even vainer than me, thought Philip with a grim smile. He tried to concentrate as Jenny Haigh continued with the introductions.

'On Sir Norman's left is Mrs Mildred Proudfoot. She is Chairwoman of the Campaign for Decency and Family Life. Sir Norman has recently co-opted her on to the Committee. On my left is Basil Grimshaw who, like me, is a survivor from the old Independent Broadcasting Council. He is our advisor on religious affairs.'

Basil Grimshaw gave Philip a beatific smile. Mrs Proudfoot had barely acknowledged his presence.

Sir Norman cleared his throat and turned to Mrs Proudfoot. 'I'm sure Mrs Proudfoot won't object if I use that old-fashioned term "ladies first", and ask her to open the discussion.'

Yesterday evening over a glass of sherry, Mrs Proudfoot had asked him to call her Mildred, but he didn't think it appropriate in the circumstances. A weaker man might yield to temptation, but he was determined not to sully their relationship with any unseemly improprieties. After all, Mrs Proudfoot was a married woman.

'Gallantry will never be out of fashion in my books, Sir Norman,' Mrs Proudfoot said robustly. 'But sad to say, like moral standards in general, it is fast declining.'

Sir Norman beamed at her. They were two souls in perfect harmony.

Mrs Proudfoot rewarded him with a gracious inclination of her head but when she looked at Philip, her face was implacable.

'Tell me, Mr Pryce, where do you stand on the freedom of the press?'

Philip smiled what he hoped was a reasonable smile, clasped his hands in front of him, and began the speech he had rehearsed in the taxi.

'I must preface my comments by saying that I believe the freedom of the press is one of the cornerstones of our great democracy. However, freedom brings with it responsibilities that broadcasters ignore at their peril.'

Here, he paused portentously and looked around. Mrs Proudfoot still looked stern, but Basil Grimshaw was nodding vigorously. Jenny Haigh was busy taking notes and Sir Norman was studying him intently, a puzzled frown on his face as though he were trying to remember something.

'I believe we have a responsibility not only to inform our audiences, but also to consider what effect that information will have on them. We must always exercise strict editorial judgement,' Philip continued.

'So where do you draw the line on sex and violence?'

There was something about this question that caused Philip to feel a tiny prickle of fear. 'I think the gratuitous portrayal of either is wrong. However, I do believe broadcasters have a duty to deal with difficult issues, if they are placed in their appropriate context.'

Philip glanced around the table. He had prepared the next part of his speech with care; it was intended to take the argument into the heart of the enemy. He took a deep breath. 'And while I would not go so far as to advocate beaming pornography into every home, surely the present government promotes free market principles, which means that television should operate on the basis of what the market place wants.'

His salvo hit home. Sir Norman flinched. Conservatism had been bred in him like an extra chromosome, and disagreement with its policies unthinkable, but there were limits, and all this market place nonsense was one of them. People should be told what was good for them by those born to govern, not allowed to have something just because they wanted it. He looked across at Mrs Proudfoot for support, but she was searching for something in her handbag. When she looked up, her eyes had a purposeful glint in them. She placed some papers carefully on the table and then looked across at Philip.

'If you don't believe in pornography, why are you producing a sex show, Mr Pryce?'

With a triumphant flourish, she placed a newspaper cutting in front of Sir Norman, and then handed photocopies around the rest of the table. Basil Grimshaw produced a pair of pince-nez and began reading.

Mrs Proudfoot sat back and clasped her hands across her ample bosom.

'My association has a media monitoring panel of concerned members, and several of them have sent me this disgusting advertisement which is tantamount to an incitement to immorality and lewdness.'

Rarely had Sir Norman witnessed a trap so skilfully sprung or to such deadly purpose. If Mrs Proudfoot had been a man, she would have been a great general or even a great general's wife, he thought wistfully.

Philip stared at the newspaper cutting in front of him. His first instinct was to say it could not possibly be anything to do with his company – no one who worked for him would place such a crude advert. But as the words burned themselves deep into his consciousness, he knew there was one person. Vanessa.

His hands grew clammy. He wiped them on his trousers.

'That . . . that advertisement was placed by an over-enthusiastic producer who misunderstood the nature of the project,' he said desperately. 'It was an unfortunate error of judgment on her part. She will, of course, be severely reprimanded.'

'An unfortunate error indeed, Mr Pryce.' Mrs Proudfoot leaned forward, an unpleasant smile on her face. 'Pray tell us, what precisely is the nature of this series?'

'It was suggested by some research being conducted at Heartlands University, so it has a sound academic pedigree,' Philip ventured limply.

Mrs Proudfoot snorted dismissively. 'I hardly think *that* recommends it. Universities are the breeding ground for most of the ills of our society.'

'The Prime Minister has an honorary degree from Heartlands.' For the first time Basil Grimshaw joined in the discussion.

Mrs Proudfoot gave him an uncharitable look, but Philip turned towards Grimshaw, sensing that from this quarter at least, he might get a more sympathetic hearing. He knew he could expect no mercy from anyone else at the table.

'I take the view that one of the benefits of television has been that it has allowed millions of viewers to explore the jungles, deserts, mountains and oceans of the world from the comfort of their fireside armchairs.

This series will instead explore the hitherto unexplored landscapes of the mind . . . so to speak.'

Philip held his breath.

Basil Grimshaw nodded vigorously. His head looked in danger of falling off his long, thin, scrawny neck.

'I must concur,' he said. 'Television always seems to concentrate on the literal world to the exclusion of the inner, spiritual worlds we all have within us.'

'I don't think Mr Pryce is planning a series on philosophy begging your pardon, Mr Grimshaw,' Mrs Proudfoot said tartly. 'This advertisement is about sex.'

'But surely you must admit that sex is a powerful motivation for the human animal, Mrs Proudfoot, whether for good or for evil. It is that element of human sexuality we are setting out to explore, in order that we can understand it better.' Philip tried not to remember some of the elements of human sexuality he had read about in the letters that had been arriving.

'Sex is sex,' Mrs Proudfoot said, roundly. 'I don't believe in mincing my words. A nettle should be grasped firmly and pulled out by the roots. I demand we take action to stop this programme, Sir Norman.'

'I think we should avoid doing anything too precipitate,' Basil Grimshaw remonstrated mildly. 'After all, it is possible to throw the baby out with the bath water.'

'Well, I believe in striking while the iron is hot,' retorted Mrs Proudfoot.

This exchange of proverbs was interrupted by Jenny Haigh passing a note along to Sir Norman. He studied it for a few moments and then loudly cleared his throat.

'Mrs Haigh has just reminded me that as this meeting was called informally, and the matter was not officially placed on the agenda, so no ruling can be made at this moment in time.'

He looked across at Jenny Haigh who was nodding her head.

'But Sir Norman ... we can't possibly ... my members ...' Mrs Proudfoot protested angrily.

Sir Norman harrumphed loudly. 'I wholeheartedly agree, Mrs Proudfoot. Something must be done.'

He looked at Jenny Haigh for help, but she was scribbling notes.

Sir Norman harrumphed again. 'Well, if we can't order the withdrawal of this programme here and now, I propose that we, that is the members of the committee here present, come along to the recording of the said programme, after which we will officially make recommendations to place the matter on the agenda at a meeting of the full committee. I think that is a fair decision all round, don't you?'

Philip smiled wanly.

'I would welcome any observations you would care to make, Sir Norman. I'm always happy to co-operate with those seeking to improve the quality of our television service.'

His death sentence had been commuted to one of hard labour.

Twenty-One

• • •

'You did what?' screeched Vanessa.

Philip looked pained. In the old days at the BBC his judgement had never been questioned. He rearranged his blotting pad and pencil holder before looking up.

'I have agreed to allow some members of the committee to attend the recording of the first show. In the current political climate one has to learn to bend with the wind a little, and I believe I have made an astute political move that will stand us in good stead.'

Vanessa leaned on Philip's desk and loomed threateningly over him. 'I come up with the best money-making idea you've ever had and you give those narrow-minded, sanctimonious, self-opinionated kill-joys free rein to destroy it.' Her voice had a serrated edge.

Philip winced. He had the uncomfortable feeling he was in danger of losing control of the situation again. 'Vanessa, may I remind you that if it had not been for your ill-advised and ineptly worded advertisement, this would not be happening.'

Philip saw one of Vanessa's eyelids flutter. She took her hands off his desk. He quickly pressed his advantage home.

'May I also remind you that not only have you antagonised one of the best and most professional presenters in the business, to the point where she may not sign her contract, but you have also signally failed to persuade Dr Archibald to part with the rights to his research. Without them, there will be no series and consequently no job for you.'

Vanessa sat down.

'As it happens,' Philip continued, sensing he was enjoying a rare moment of dominance, 'I think we may now be able to offer Dr Archibald an improved deal, which he will be more than willing to sign.'

Vanessa made a weak attempt to interrupt, but Philip held up a masterful hand. 'I have been giving the question of the presentation of the programme a lot of thought, and I have decided that it will be given added weight and credibility if we have a second presenter with the appropriate academic credentials. Dr Archibald is the obvious candidate.'

Vanessa sat upright. 'But I . . .'

'I will brook no argument on this point, Vanessa. I have made an executive decision.' Philip leant back in his chair with a satisfied air.

Vanessa was silent for a moment. Then she carefully crossed her legs. Philip tensed. He sensed a counter attack.

'Have you told Gabriella about her co-host yet?' enquired Vanessa silkily.

Philip shifted uneasily in his seat; he had been trying not to think about how Gabriella would react.

'Not yet, but I am sure she will understand the wisdom of my decision,' he replied with a confidence he did not feel. 'After all, look at Oprah. She has some sort of expert on most of her shows explaining why people behave the way they do, and it hasn't done her any harm,' he added defensively.

The phone buzzed. Philip gratefully answered.

It was Heather. 'There's a Mr Eddie Spittle on the line, Mr Pryce, he wants to know if the advertisement is for real.'

Philip went pale and closed his eyes.

Eddie Spittle was a journalist on the *World on Sunday* newspaper. He was universally known as the Ferret, a nickname he had earned not only because of his physical resemblance to a small, grey, beady-eyed creature with an unpredictable temper, but also because of his reputation for sniffing into dark secrets and searching for warm bodies into which he could sink his sharp pen.

Spittle's speciality was stories about television personalities.

Philip knew that if he refused to speak to him, Spittle would probably run a story anyway. He opened his eyes. 'Put him through,' he wearily instructed Heather, 'and then if Hugo is around, ask him to join Vanessa and me.'

The voice on the other end of the line was thin and nasal with a hint of Lancashire.

'Philip, we haven't had the pleasure, but I thought we could make up for it over a drink and you could tell me about this new programme of yours. Sounds like a real corker.'

'*Mr* Spittle,' Philip began. He hated people who used first names without a formal introduction. 'An interview at this stage would be a little premature. The series is still on the drawing board and I would hate to pre-empt anything.'

'Oh come now, Philip,' the voice was treacly with enforced bonhomie, 'there's got to be something you can tell me. Rumour has it that Britain's answer to Gina Lollobrigida, Gabriella Wolfe is back in town and she's been lunching with you. Any connection?'

'I really wouldn't like to make any comment on that.' Philip tried to keep the irritation out of his voice.

'I can always call her agent,' Spittle countered. 'She's a bit of a has-been these days, so I bet he wouldn't

231

mind a few column inches to boost her earning potential.'

Philip was outflanked. Gabriella's agent, Lance Cox, would probably offer Spittle anything he wanted. Cox had been very difficult over lunch the other day. Perhaps he knew the newspapers were sniffing around.

'You could say that discussions are under way with Miss Wolfe, but that nothing has been signed, as yet,' he said slowly.

'You mean she's asking more than you're giving?'

'I'm not prepared to comment on the figures involved. That would be tantamount to breaking a confidence,' Philip protested.

'And a big spread about Gabriella, the raven-haired beauty, Queen of the chat show, returning from her European exile would push the price up, eh?' Spittle prodded. 'If you can offer me something more, I'd be prepared to hold fire for the time being.'

Philip thought fast. If Spittle was on to him, the other tabloids wouldn't be far behind. Perhaps he could do a bit of damage limitation.

'Look, Mr Spittle . . .'

'Eddie, please . . .'

'Look, Eddie,' Philip began again, 'this series is going to be very exciting and will break new ground in television. I expect a lot of media interest once we're up and running, but I would only consider a favourable working relationship with one newspaper if we could agree to certain provisos.'

'If they mean I get exclusives on all stories, I'm sure we can agree,' said Spittle.

'Something like that,' hedged Philip. Once he had got a deal with the Network, the kind of publicity Spittle could give the series would guarantee high ratings, but right now, any publicity was likely to bring the full weight of Sir Norman and his committee down on him. Philip blanched at the thought.

'It has to be better than something,' Spittle pressed. 'I would want guarantees of exclusivity.'

'I think that could be arranged,' said Philip guardedly. 'Although I hope you would be prepared to respect the sensitivity of our subject matter at this early stage. I wouldn't like to jump the gun on publicity so to speak.'

'Discretion is my middle name, Philip, and I think I follow your drift. I get the stories but you want a say in when they are published?'

'And of course, you understand this isn't in any way a formal agreement?'

'A gentlemen's agreement you mean?' asked Spittle. 'I could live with that. Contracts aren't worth the paper they're printed on. Anyway, you sound like a man I could trust Philip, and I'm sure you know what would happen if you broke the agreement.'

The threat hung large and visibly in the air.

Spittle replaced the telephone, a satisfied look on his face. Ignoring his intercom, he bawled through his office door at one of his researchers.

'Tebbit! I want absolutely everything we've got on Gabriella Wolfe, that's with an "e", and anything you can find on some wanker called Philip Pryce. That's P-R-Y-C-E. From the sound of his voice I bet he's an ex-BBC leftie poofter. And get your bloody skates on.'

Back on the other side of London, Philip slowly replaced the receiver. There was a low whistle and he looked up to see Hugo standing in the doorway, his arms folded.

'Was that *the* Eddie Spittle?'

Philip nodded.

'Bit dangerous doing deals with him, isn't it? They say it's safer to sell your soul to the devil.' He came into the room and draped a long leg over the edge of Philip's desk.

'I can handle him,' Philip said, with an attempt at bravado that was unconvincing even to his ears. 'This way he'll keep the other tabloids off our back and all I need to do is to drop him the occasional little titbit. He might think we have a gentleman's agreement, but he can hardly be classed as a gentleman, so I consider any agreement null and void.'

Hugo raised a questioning eyebrow at Vanessa, who just shrugged. 'Anyway, apart from the Ferret, what's up?'

Philip made a visible effort to pull himself together. 'I have decided to give Dr Archibald a try-out as a second presenter. I think he will give us the intellectual weight we need.'

Hugo's eyebrow shot up again. 'Does Gabriella know about this added intellectual weight yet?'

Vanessa ostentatiously examined her nails.

'No. But as I've already told Vanessa, I can handle Gabriella,' snapped Philip peevishly. 'What I want to know from you is how this will effect the studio set. We ought to get the designer working on it immediately.'

'Well another presenter rather puts the kybosh on the design Jasper and I have been talking about,' Hugo said, running his hands through his hair. He began to pace up and down. 'I find it difficult to get my head around the concept of a second body. No strong visual images spring to mind when I think of a psychiatrist.'

'He's a psychologist,' Vanessa interrupted.

'Whatever,' Hugo continued. 'But my real problem is Archibald. The visual statement he makes is that he should be living underneath the arches at Waterloo Station.'

He stopped pacing and closed his eyes for a moment, pressing his hand to his forehead. Then he snapped his fingers.

'I've got it: Freud is our key. We can use that awful beard and crumpled corduroy to our advantage with a kind of mad scientist look. I know this stylist who can work wonders with the roughest material. I'll give him a bell. We could also have this kind of post-modernist version of a psychiatrist's couch. There's this little place in Covent Garden which makes amazing furniture, it's run by a friend of mine.'

He excitedly punched some keys on his electronic organiser. 'I like it, I really like it, although we'll have to revise the budget for the set. This wasn't included in the original costings.'

Before Philip could remonstrate, Hugo strode out of the room. He looked at Vanessa. She got up to leave.

'Have we got any participants we can actually use without a raid from the vice squad?' he asked in a small voice.

Vanessa gave him a superior smile. 'Philip, *trust* me. Little Vijay is beavering away out their in fantasy land even as we speak, and the letters are still pouring in. I've just read this great one from some frustrated woman wittering on about defrocked nuns, you'll just love it. I'm sending Vijay to see her tomorrow. I promise you, we *can't* lose.'

She blew him a kiss and swept out of the room.

Twenty-Two

• • •

Jeremy dug his hands deep into his pockets and disconsolately kicked one of Zelda's large oriental floor cushions. It emitted a little puff of dust, but otherwise failed to satisfy his urge to hurt something. He tried kicking an ugly brass urn which contained a disintegrating display of dried grasses. It made a more satisfying sound but also hurt his big toe. He limped over to the window and stood, staring sightlessly out.

He had thought he and Alicia were getting on so well. They had established such a nice, comfortable daily routine. Getting up late, eating a cooked breakfast on a scale he had thought long since dead, followed by a gentle walk to Camden High Street for a little shopping and to buy the newspapers which they read over a cappuchino and a plate of freshly baked croissants, before coming back to the flat where Alicia prepared lunch.

Most afternoons Alicia would go to the British Museum Reading Room for a few hours, while he finished reading the newspapers or watched an old film on the large colour television Alicia had rented when he complained he had nothing to do when she was out. In the evenings, Alicia seemed happy in the kitchen, preparing some mouthwatering concoction which they would eat watching television. It was bliss. Or it had been.

About a week ago a change had come over Alicia. One afternoon when he assumed she had gone to the British Museum as usual, she had arrived home in a taxi with a camp bed contraption which she set up in the front room, and to which he had been banished that night.

When he had said he would make love to her if that was what she wanted, she got upset and demanded to know whether it was what *he* wanted. He tried to explain that he wanted whatever she wanted, but that seemed to make her even more upset. Either way he couldn't win. He just didn't understand women.

And then there was this ridiculous plan she had cooked up to try and find out what Vanessa and Fergus were doing. It was all very well to wish something horrible would happen to someone who had hurt you, but you couldn't actually go around *doing* things to people. It could get you into trouble.

Jeremy took his hands out of his pockets and squared his shoulders. He would make one more attempt to dissuade Alicia. He strode into the hall and knocked on the closed bathroom door.

'Alicia, I really think we should talk some more about this. I thought we had agreed to put all that business with Vanessa behind us.'

'*We* agreed to nothing, Jeremy. That was your suggestion, not mine.'

Alicia leaned over the washbasin as she tried to get a better view of her face in the bathroom mirror. She never wore make-up apart from a little face powder to stop her nose getting shiny, and she was finding the intricacies of foundation, blusher, highlighter, eyeshadow, eyeliner, lipliners, lipstick and mascara, a little hard to master.

The girl at the cosmetics counter at Boots had made it all sound so simple, as she painted Alicia's hands with a bewitching array of powders and creams. Alicia

237

had only wanted some pink lipstick and maybe a little pale blue eyeshadow, but the girl had been so kind and had taken such trouble, Alicia felt honour bound to buy all the products the girl had recommended. The memory of the final bill made Alicia blush two shades deeper than the Savannah Rose blusher the girl had promised would provide the perfect definition for her face. Alicia sucked in her cheeks and peered in the mirror. Finding her cheekbones was not as easy as the girl in Boots had claimed.

'Alicia, please . . .' Jeremy scratched at the door.

Since she suggested he sleep in the other room, Jeremy had been behaving like a puppy who had been punished for making a nasty mess. He had taken to trailing her everywhere, his brown eyes full of reproach, eager to help but clumsily causing chaos.

She had tried to talk to him, but every time she broached the subject of their relationship, he managed to find some urgent task that needed doing, so she had decided on unilateral action. Sleeping separately had been her first move. If they were going to share a bed, it would not be just for sleeping in.

'How do you know Vanessa won't turn up in person?' Jeremy called through the keyhole.

Alicia didn't reply for a few moments. She was concentrating on applying mascara to her bottom lashes. She had discovered that the best way to do this was to bury her chin in her neck and stretch her facial muscles downwards, which made meaningful conversation impossible.

She replaced the mascara wand in its tube and opened her eyes wide to study her handiwork. 'Because I didn't sign my own name on the letter, silly. Anyway, Vanessa's much too grand to do her own research. There's some man coming. I couldn't quite catch his name.'

Her make-up wasn't quite in the same league as that

238

worn by the exquisitely maquillaged girl in Boots, Alicia decided, but it was still quite a transformation. She had also bought some hair colourant which had promised subtle highlights and some hair gel. Not being conversant with substances like colourants and gels, Alicia had been a little heavy-handed, and the result was a startling honey-blonde, pre-Raphaelite mass of tendrils.

Alicia turned her head from side to side. It was definitely not her, she decided, but it certainly suited her alter ego for the evening.

The door handle rattled impatiently.

'If a man is coming I really think I ought to stay around. You never know what he may be like.'

Jeremy had noticed a bottle of wine and two glasses, together with bowls of savoury nibbles on the coffee table.

Alicia tweaked one of the ringlets which curled rather fetchingly over her forehead.

'I'll be perfectly safe, Jeremy. He's hardly likely to jump on me. After all, he's just coming to conduct a perfectly normal interview.'

'Normal, my foot!' Jeremy snorted. 'I hardly call the subject matter normal.'

Alicia had shown him the letter she had written in reply to Vanessa's advertisement. It had been a mistake.

'For heaven's sake, Jeremy, *stop* fussing! You're going to your club and that's that.'

There was a grunt from outside the door which seemed to suggest Jeremy had conceded defeat. Alicia gave her hair one more pat and then began to get dressed.

She had decided none of her clothes were suitable for the occasion. It wasn't just that she wanted to look like a woman who had exciting sexual fantasies, she wanted to feel like one too, and even when she put on her prettiest white evening blouse and Laura Ashley print skirt, she still felt like Dr Alicia Binns, over-weight spinster and university lecturer.

After offering up a silent prayer for forgiveness to Zelda in faraway Budapest, Alicia had searched through the wardrobe. Zelda had a penchant for the theatrical in what she described as her off-duty clothes. Alicia had counted at least a dozen flowing kaftans, two richly embroidered silk kimonos, and several pairs of wide-trousered, satin pyjama-style suits.

She had eagerly tried some of them on, but Zelda was a good four inches taller, and the sleeves had drooped over her hands and the hems trailed on the ground. She had looked like a child dressed in adult clothes.

As the pile of clothes on the bed grew, Alicia's inhibitions diminished. She had rummaged through all of Zelda's drawers and even picked the lock on a trunk which had revealed a collection of underwear that made a burning-cheeked Alicia wonder whether she could ever look Zelda in the face again.

The top of the wardrobe disclosed even more delights. It was piled high with shoe boxes containing a collection of stiletto-heeled shoes in every imaginable hue, except black or brown. With intricate straps, delicate lacing, bejewelled, beribboned and with paper-thin soles, none could be described as sensible – the hallmark of all Alicia's shoe purchases.

Alicia had sat on the floor entranced. The revelation that shoes could be a thing of beauty and desirability made her feel quite giddy.

She had eventually chosen a pair of perspex heeled, gold leather sandals, embellished with a large mock ruby, and had painted her toenails to match. From Zelda's wardrobe she selected a pair of black velvet leggings which had the advantage of stretching to fit almost any size, and a sheer black organza blouse.

The blouse had posed an embarrassing problem:

Alicia could not possibly wear one of her white cotton bras underneath it. So quelling her blushes, she had picked the lock on Zelda's trunk again and borrowed a black satin bustier. Although Zelda was much taller, they seemed to have the same ample breast measurement, although doing the bustier up was proving more awkward than Alicia had anticipated, because of the hundreds of tiny hooks and eyes. She considered asking Jeremy to help and decided against it. She had a feeling he was not going approve of her outfit.

Red-faced with exertion, she finally fastened the last hook and slipped the blouse over the top, then stepped into Zelda's gold sandals. With a last look in the mirror, which she found much easier now as she was nearly three inches taller, she opened the bathroom door.

Jeremy took a step back, his mouth open.

Alicia tried to walk casually past him, but unused to heels, she found this a little difficult. Keeping her balance demanded throwing the weight of her body backwards to counter the height of the heels, while at the same time taking short little steps to hold the sandals on her feet as the thin straps served no practical purpose. Her slow, swaying progression down the hall and into the centre of the main room gave Jeremy time to collect his senses.

Alicia was pouring herself a glass of wine as he came in the door.

'What on earth have you done to yourself?' he demanded.

'Don't you like it?' Alicia held out her arms and very carefully executed a full circle.

Jeremy stood as though transfixed.

He did like it, he liked it very much. That was the problem.

His jaw began to work before his vocal chords. 'You can't see anyone looking like that,' he said at last.

'Why not?' Alicia asked, and lifted up an arm as

241

though to admire the floaty material of her blouse, but her heart was thumping. She hoped she hadn't gone too far.

'Because . . . well . . . because . . . It's not proper. You can see all your . . .' he gestured at her breasts. 'You could give a man the wrong idea dressed like that.'

Alicia smiled. 'Perhaps that is just what I want to do.'

Jeremy stared at her for what seemed like a very long time and angrily left the room. He slammed the front door behind him and ran down the stairs two at a time.

Half-way down he almost knocked over a young Asian man who was coming up the stairs. He carried on without an apology.

Vijay rubbed his bruised shoulder. 'Well, pardon me for breathing,' he yelled after Jeremy's disappearing back.

He paused on the stairs, out of breath. He felt thoroughly dejected, and being knocked aside as though he didn't exist was just about the perfect end to the perfect day.

It had begun with Vanessa spending nearly an hour telling him loudly, and with the use of many Anglo-Saxon expletives, just how incompetent she considered him to be. Then he had spent the rest of the morning listening to callers describing their fantasies in graphic and unnecessary detail, including one man who had wanted unpleasant sounding instruments inserted into the various orifices of his body.

The afternoon had not proved much better. He had gone all the way to Gerrards Cross to interview a woman who met him at the front door brandishing a cat-of-nine tails, and wearing nothing but a pair of knee-length, black leather biker boots. Without waiting to make his excuses, he turned and fled.

When he had eventually arrived back at the office, Vanessa was waiting for him. The woman with the cat-of-nine-tails had rung up to complain. With Vanessa's voice echoing in his ears, he had made for the nearest pub and downed four pints of beer in quick succession, and even though he was a bit unsteady on his feet, there was no need for anyone to knock him down.

He climbed the last few stairs to Flat D and stood outside, trying not to think of what might be waiting on the other side.

He swallowed hard and knocked gently. Perhaps nobody would be in? He stepped back, just in case he had to make another swift getaway.

As he waited for the door to open, Vijay checked the name in his notepad. It had a faintly familiar ring but he could not place it. He heard the door opening.

'Elizabeth Gaskell?' he enquired, before looking up.

Alicia stood framed in the doorway, her hair softly lit by the hall light. 'Yes?'

'I'm, um, Vijay, Vijay Seth,' he stuttered. 'From Right Pryce productions?'

'Do come in,' Alicia said, and led the way through to the main room.

Vijay followed, mesmerised by Alicia's voluptuously swaying gait. His heart thudded against his chest. This was the woman he had been looking for, he could feel it. She was like an oasis of loveliness in his desert of despair. She was a vision of soft womanliness. He licked his lips, which had suddenly gone dry. She was very, very sexy.

He perched awkwardly on the end of the *chaise-longue*, gripping his knees tightly together. He must try and concentrate on the programme. He could not face another session with Vanessa like the one earlier. Vijay pushed his glasses firmly back into place and attempted to formulate his first question. He looked at Alicia and opened his mouth to speak, but just at that moment she leaned over the low table to pour him a glass of wine, and Vijay glimpsed a creamy expanse of breast. The question died in his throat.

But it was when Alicia sat down on the other end of the *chaise-longue* and carefully crossed her legs that Vijay's heart really began to race, for he suddenly caught sight of her tiny, plump feet encased in gold sandals, each dainty little toe crowned by a perfect half moon of lacquered nail. They were the most exquisite feet he had ever seen.

Unaware of the effect she was having on him, Alicia sipped her wine and studied Vijay from under her lashes. He was not what she had been expecting. He was rather good-looking, in a serious sort of way, with lovely caramel coloured skin and soulful, bitter chocolate eyes, but Alicia found it quite disconcerting that they were fixated on her feet. Perhaps the sandals were a little vulgar, after all. Alicia tucked her feet under the *chaise-longue*.

With her glass poised, she waited for Vijay to speak, but he continued staring at the spot where her feet had been.

'You must have an awfully exciting job,' she began.

Vijay reluctantly looked up. 'Not really,' he said, trying not to think about Alicia's feet, which had so tantalisingly disappeared from view.

'Well, you must meet some awfully interesting people then?' Alicia tried again.

Vijay seemed to be having a problem holding his wine glass and his notebook at the same time. After some deliberation, he gulped down the wine, stood his glass on the table, and then opened his notebook. Alicia gave him an encouraging smile and leant forward to refill his glass. Vijay averted his eyes.

'That's what everyone thinks,' Vijay replied bitterly. 'But it's not like that at all.'

He looked back at Alicia, and suddenly he was overwhelmed with the desire to make this woman, above all people, understand him. 'Once I had dreams, ambitions, ideas,' he waved his arms about expansively. 'I wanted to be a foreign correspondent, or to produce documentaries which would change the world, but instead I end up working for a tin-pot outfit run by a woman with the soul of Margaret Thatcher, who would put Genghis Khan to shame.'

He stopped. Perhaps he had gone too far. The woman sitting beside him must want to come on the programme, or why would she have answered the advertisement?

Alicia picked up Vijay's wine glass and pressed it into his hand. 'Tell me about this woman,' she said sympathetically, 'she sounds absolutely frightful.'

Vijay needed no further bidding. Emboldened by a mixture of beer and wine and Alicia's occasional 'gosh, how awfuls', he related the whole story of his difficult childhood, misunderstood adolescence, unsuccessful university career, even more unsuccessful journalistic career, and now his problems with Right Price Productions, *Forbidden Fruit* and most of all, Vanessa.

'And you ought to see the bills for the lunches *she* has, and yet if I so much as try to claim for a cheese sandwich, I'm accused of trying to fiddle my expenses,' he ended with an aggrieved air.

Alicia sat up. She had found the ally she needed, or at least she thought she had.

'Actually, I have a bit of a confession to make to you,' Alicia began. 'You see I never really wanted to take part in the programme, I just wanted to find out what was going on as ...'

'I was right,' Vijay interrupted her triumphantly. 'I just knew you couldn't be that sort of woman.'

He leaned towards her. The alcohol that had made him garrulous now made him emotional. 'I sensed from the very first moment I saw you that you were a woman I could relate to. You looked like a goddess standing in the doorway, your hair like ... and your ...' he made undulating shapes with his hands.

He took another gulp of wine. 'Oh, I know it's all wrong,' he rushed on, 'because it sounds as if I'm treating you like a sex object, which goes against everything I believe in. But it's a bit difficult not to when a woman looks like you. But I wouldn't want you to think I was making a pass or anything ...' he said quickly.

'Vijay,' Alicia said firmly, 'there is something I really must tell you ...'

Before she could finish, Vijay tried to put his arm along the back of the *chaise-longue*. Unfortunately, he was sitting on the end where there was no back, and he fell drunkenly sideways. With some difficulty, he hauled himself back upright.

'Elizabeth ...' he pleaded and lunged along the *chaise-longue*.

'Actually, my name's Alicia, Alicia Binns,' Alicia said briskly, standing up. 'Would you like some coffee?'

Vijay lay sideways looking up at her. 'Aleesia?' he slurred. 'So it wasn't you who sent the letter about the nuns and things?'

Alicia put several spoonfuls of coffee in a mug and waited for the kettle to boil. Vijay had managed to struggle upright again and now sat with his head in his hands. She took the coffee over to him. He nursed it for a few moments in silence.

'I'm sorry,' he mumbled without looking at Alicia, 'I've made a bit of a fool of myself, haven't I?'

'You've probably been working too hard,' Alicia said generously.

Vijay gave her a grateful smile and sipped his coffee.

'Look,' said Alicia, 'I think I'd better explain. I did write that letter but I'm not Elizabeth Gaskell. There's no such person. Well, actually there was, she's one of my favourite . . .' Alicia stopped. She had never been very good at explanations.

She took a deep breath. 'Anyway, I used her name as a sort of *nom de plume* because I didn't want Vanessa to know it was me.'

Vijay went a decidedly odd colour and coffee slopped over the rim of his mug on to his hands. He ignored it. 'You know Vanessa?' he asked hoarsely.

'I've known her since I was eleven. We went to school together. We were best friends,' Alicia explained.

'Best friends . . .' Vijay repeated almost soundlessly.

Alicia suddenly noticed the effect her words were having on him. 'But we're not friends any more,' she said hastily. 'In fact, we're quite the opposite.'

'So why did you write the letter?' Vijay asked, the colour beginning to return to his face.

'Well, I thought I was in love with Fergus and I intro . . .'

'You mean, Dr Archibald?' Vijay interrupted. It was profane, the thought of that uncouth man with this fragrant goddess. If Archibald had so much as touched one of her beautiful little toes, he would . . . would . . .

Alicia misinterpreted Vijay's incredulous look. 'It's silly, I know. Why should Fergus want me when he could have Vanessa? But she was my friend, and . . .'

The words caught in her throat. She felt a sudden rush of pain, and humiliation.

'And I *hate her*,' she said slowly, as though for the first time.

'I know exactly how you feel,' Vijay said glumly.

'Oh no, you don't. You can't possibly,' Alicia said, leaning towards him.

He backed nervously away. Alicia's eyes were burning.

'Nobody can feel the way I do. When I think of all the times she's humiliated me. The poor little scholarship girl in the hand-me-down uniform – but now I'm going to do it to her,' she said vehemently, and pointed at Vijay, 'and you're going to help me.'

'Me?' asked Vijay. He was in danger of falling off the end of the *chaise-longue*.

'Yes, you,' Alicia said firmly and gripped his arm. 'You're going to keep me informed about everything Vanessa does, every move she makes, every person she sees. I'll do the rest.'

She released his arm. Vijay sat rubbing it.

'But supposing Vanessa finds out?' he asked nervously.

'Who's going to tell her?'

'Look, I really don't think this is a very good idea,' Vijay said getting to his feet. He was sobering up fast.

Alicia reached out for his hand, but this time her touch was a caress. She smiled up into his eyes. 'I need your help, Vijay, I really do.'

She pulled him gently down beside her.

'I'm asking you because I feel I can trust you.' Alicia's voice was husky. 'Will you help me, Vijay?'

Vijay felt intoxicated again. He gazed into her eyes. 'I'll do anything for you,' he replied earnestly, 'anything . . .'

Twenty-Three

• • •

Jeremy unlocked the front door and stood in the hallway listening, his head on one side. There was silence. With a satisfied nod, he closed the door and tiptoed unsteadily past the bedroom. But as he fumbled in the dark to open the living room door, the plastic carrier bag full of Indian take-away he was carrying, fell to the floor with a dull thud.

'Damn,' Jeremy swore loudly, and then giggled.

He dropped clumsily on his hands and knees and felt around in the dark to see if anything had been spilt. His fingers came into contact with something warm and unpleasantly glutinous. Jeremy sniffed his fingers, it was probably the beef biryani. He wiped his hands on his trousers and picked up the containers that were still intact. The clearing up could wait until morning. Still giggling softly to himself, he crept into the living room.

'Hello,' Alicia said, looking up from the book she was reading. She was curled up on a pile of cushions beside the window, a small reading lamp for light.

Jeremy looked startled, and then held up the dripping carrier bag. 'I've got an Indian take-away,' he announced.

'So I can see by your trousers.'

Still holding the bag in mid-air, Jeremy looked down.

There were golden brown streaks all over his trouser legs. 'Damn,' he said again.

'Stay there,' Alicia ordered, scrambling to her feet. She tore off some paper kitchen towels and thrust them into his hand. He held them under the bag and made for the kitchenette.

Alicia retrieved her book and sat down again. Jeremy turned on a light and heaped the contents of the silver foil boxes on to a large plate until they formed a pungent mound. He then crowned the heap with a stuffed paratha, and stood back to admire his handiwork, a drunken grin on his face.

Alicia watched him over the top of her book. The grin was replaced by a wrinkled brow as Jeremy seemed to be having a problem remembering something. Muttering impatiently to himself, he began rummaging through the kitchen cupboards.

With a sigh, Alicia got to her feet again and opened the fridge. She wordlessly held up a jar of mango chutney.

Jeremy took it from her and spooned half its contents on to the side of his plate, then licked the spoon clean. 'I didn't bring enough for two. I thought you'd be asleep by now.'

'I'm not hungry,' said Alicia, although the aroma of cumin and coriander was making her nostrils twitch.

Jeremy carried his overfilled plate to the coffee table and sat down with a bump, spilling more sauce down his trousers and on to the table.

'Damn,' he said, angrily mopping himself. 'Why can't you get a decent sized table and chairs so that I can sit and eat like a civilised human being? This infernal thing gives me indigestion.'

'I like it,' Alicia said firmly.

Jeremy began to eat quickly. Alicia stood in front of the table watching him.

'I had a very interesting talk with Vanessa's researcher,' she said after his first few mouthfuls.

Jeremy grunted and continued to spoon food into his mouth.

'Did you have a good evening?' she inquired.

Jeremy nodded. 'Went to my club, caught up with some old faces. I thought it was about time I showed I was still in the land of the living, drop the odd word in the right ear and all that, just to show willing. I might be tempted back to the City if the offer was good enough.' His voice was full of drunken self-importance.

Alicia crossed her arms. Jeremy had obviously forgotten that it was her idea that he go to his club. 'I'm pleased you're doing *something* positive.'

Jeremy paused between mouthfuls and wiped a dribble of sauce from his chin. There was something about the way Alicia had said 'something' that rang a warning bell, but he decided it was safer to ignore it and ate another mouthful.

'Jolly good stuff, this, for mopping up a bottle or two of claret,' he said cheerfully.

'Jeremy . . .' Alicia said slowly.

The warning bell went off even louder.

Alicia sat down next to him on the *chaise-longue*. 'I think it's about time we discussed our relationship.'

'Relationship?' repeated Jeremy looking blank.

'Yes, *relationship*,' said Alicia firmly. 'If we are going to have a relationship, and I presume that is what we are doing, I think we ought to discuss it properly.'

Jeremy reluctantly put his spoon down. 'Now steady on old girl, let's not rush things. Look what a cock-up I made the first time around.' He smiled weakly.

'I'm not talking about marriage,' said Alicia.

Jeremy looked relieved and speared an onion bhajee.

'I'm talking about sex,' said Alicia.

Jeremy choked and pushed his plate away. 'Couldn't

you have waited until after I'd finished eating?' he said peevishly. 'After all, it's not quite the done thing to bring it up while one's eating one's dinner. It's taking unfair advantage of a chap to surprise him like this.'

Alicia pushed his plate to the other end of the table and then took both his hands in hers.

After she had gently but firmly pushed an adoring Vijay out of the door, she had felt giddy with the sense of her own power and had eaten the best part of a carton of pecan nut-crunch and toffee ice-cream while planning what she intended to say to Jeremy when he came home. She had decided to be firm with him. Whatever his good points, she had to accept that Jeremy's way of dealing with problems was to avoid them in the hope that they would go away, so she would have to take the lead if she wanted things to change. Alicia took a deep breath to steady her racing heart.

'Look Jeremy, I'm sorry if I've ruined your dinner, but the longer we put off talking about our relationship, the harder it becomes.'

Jeremy refused to meet her gaze. 'I really can't understand this vogue for endlessly talking about relationships. I'm sure the mater and pater never talked about such things and they jogged along quite happily. Least said soonest mended, that's what my old nanny used to say.'

Along with the tweed jacket and calvary twill trousers he had put on to go back to his club, Jeremy seemed to have put back on the attitudes that went with them.

Alicia tightened her grip on his hands, willing him to return to the present. For all his weaknesses, she wanted the new Jeremy, the one she had met a couple of weeks ago, not the one who had married Vanessa. She looked into his eyes. 'Would you like to make love to me?'

Jeremy stared at her. He opened his mouth to speak

but nothing came out. He did want Alicia. Very much. How many times had he imagined touching the curve of her ample buttocks? Lying between the softness of her plump thighs? Kissing her creamy, swelling breasts? But they were only fantasies, and his dreams had a habit of turning into nightmares. Why couldn't he find the right words?

'You're very pretty, and I like your . . . erm,' he nodded at Alicia's breasts. 'But it's just that, well, I've never been too hot on the sex thing and I, well . . .'

He trailed off. He could see by the expression on Alicia's face that he wasn't doing very well. Why was it so difficult to say what he meant? He looked down at Alicia's hands which were still holding his.

'Yes please, yes I would, very much, but . . .'

Alicia gently placed a finger on his lips. 'I want you to go to the bedroom and wait for me there.'

Jeremy nodded his head still down.

Alicia leaned forward and kissed him lightly on the lips.

Instead of returning her kiss, Jeremy gently pulled his hands free and ran his fingers slowly through her hair. Alicia held her breath, waiting for his kiss. But, Jeremy suddenly grasped her tightly and buried his head between her breasts, like a child seeking comfort. Then he leapt to his feet and almost ran from the room.

From the bathroom came the sound of teeth being vigorously brushed, then a loud gargle. After a moment's silence, there was a second gargle. Jeremy was taking no chances with the Indian takeaway. There was the sound of water being frantically splashed about in the wash basin, and then Alicia heard the bathroom door opening and Jeremy crossing the hall into the bedroom. She sat quite motionless for a moment or two more and then stood up and slowly undressed, dropping Zelda's clothes in a heap on the floor.

One of the fantasies that Vijay had recounted at her urging had given her an idea.

She padded naked across to the kitchenette and took an aerosol can of whipped double cream out of the fridge. Then she stood on tiptoe and reached up for a bottle of dark chocolate syrup and a jar of Morello cherries. After a moment's indecision, she reached for a bottle of butterscotch sauce and squirted a stream of satisfyingly sweet sauce into her mouth. She added it to her assembly of ingredients. Then she searched around for a tray which she placed on the edge of the work top. Alicia reached for the whipped cream. It was perfect.

In the bedroom, Jeremy sat irresolutely on the edge of the bed. He had twice put his pyjamas on and twice removed them, and was now wondering whether he should have taken a shower. He sniffed under one arm. Perhaps a shower would have been a good idea. He stood up, but his resolve wavered and then collapsed. What was the point? It was all wrong, he'd drunk far too much claret, he just wouldn't be able to do a thing.

Jeremy gave a despairing groan and fell back on the bed, covering his face with his hands, trying to block out the memory of all those times Vanessa had taunted him with his impotence, gloating over him as he had shrivelled away to nothing.

'Happy Birthday, Jeremy.' It was Alicia's voice.

He opened one eye and peered through his fingers. Alicia was standing beside the bed, her face lit by the soft glow of a candle which stood on the tray she held in front of her.

'But it's not my birthday.' Jeremy's voice was muffled by his hands.

'We can celebrate anything you want, only you have to blow out the candle and make a wish.'

There was something in Alicia's voice which made

Jeremy take his hands away from his face. She appeared to be carrying some sort of cake. He levered himself on to one elbow and then sat up. On the tray were two mounds of whipped cream laced with whorls of chocolate and butterscotch sauce, glistening in the candlelight. At the tip of each creamy mound was a large plump cherry.

Momentarily dazzled by the candle, Jeremy blinked, then he suddenly realised Alicia was naked. Almost scared, he reached out to touch her. Her skin felt soft and acquiescent.

Jeremy's eyes held Alicia's for a moment, then he blew out the candle. He leaned forward and gently took a cherry between his teeth. He swallowed hard and then did the same thing again, this time licking and sucking until his face was covered with cream.

Grinning like a small boy at a birthday party, Jeremy wiped his hand across his face before slowly smearing cream down his body to his already hardening erection.

Twenty-Four

• • •

'Come on,' murmured Fergus, his hot breath on Vanessa's cheek and his hand on her thigh, 'just a little grope.'

'No.' Vanessa slapped his hand away and retreated to the other side of the lift.

'What happened to the woman who claimed she wanted to explore the outer boundaries of sexuality with me?' Fergus grumbled, as the lift doors opened and a man stepped in.

Vanessa gave Fergus a warning look as the man pushed the lift button to go up four floors. The doors closed and the man stood staring fixedly ahead.

'Last night you couldn't get enough of me. You were begging me to do anything I wanted, anywhere, anytime any place,' Fergus continued relentlessly.

The man whistled silently and pretended to look at something on the mirrored steel walls so that he could steal a glance at Vanessa. She glared at him, and he turned hastily back to his study of the lift doors.

Vanessa felt herself growing hot. The thought of anyone, even this horrible little stranger, knowing that she slept with Fergus, made her shudder. She had only been doing it so that he would sign the contract and now that he had, she could stop.

'Women are all the same, don't you think?' said

Fergus companionably, enjoying Vanessa's obvious embarrassment.

The man turned and looked at Fergus, sensing the remark was directed at him. He started to nod, but it turned into a contorted twitch as he caught Vanessa's eye again. He clutched his briefcase close to his chest and looked down at the floor.

'Sex is okay as long as it's kept in its place: in the bed and in the dark,' continued Fergus blithely.

Vanessa looked murderously at him. Bed was the one place in which they had not had sex the night before, and her body had the bruises to prove it. Her back was raw from the tiled bathroom floor where they had started, before careening into the kitchen where Fergus had inadvertently turned on the hot tap in the kitchen sink as he had reached the heights of orgasmic passion, scalding her left buttock. But it had been worth it, because much to her surprise, when she had performed her now normal morning ritual of putting the contract in front of Fergus, he had signed it.

The lift reached their fellow passenger's floor and the doors opened. He hesitated and reached for the 'close' button but Vanessa's long finger reached the 'open' button first, and she kept her finger on it. With a sheepish look at Fergus, the man stepped out. Vanessa stabbed the button marked 'close' and then put her finger on the top floor button and kept it there.

Unfortunately, it left her vulnerable to Fergus, who now had her trapped in a corner. He moved in, sliding his hand under her short skirt and between her thighs, using his knee to force her legs apart.

Vanessa made an ineffectual effort to push him away. 'Don't, not here,' she panted.

Fergus grinned evilly as he thrust himself up against her. 'Go on, admit it, you like it.'

Vanessa shook her head, closing her eyes as the now familiar musty animal smell of his body filled her nostrils. She would rather die than admit she wanted Fergus. She buried both her hands into his hair, pulling and twisting as her body arched.

'Christ woman, you don't have to scalp me,' protested Fergus. 'Those talons of yours can do a man lethal damage when you get carried away like that.'

Vanessa opened her eyes and pulled her hands away, hastily smoothing her dress down.

The lift jerked to a halt and the door slid open. Vanessa stepped out and marched swiftly ahead of Fergus. There was only one door at the end of the corridor. Vanessa stopped outside and fished in her handbag for her compact, flipping it open to check her make-up and hair.

Her tone was business-like when she spoke, but she avoided catching Fergus's eye.

'Promise me you'll behave this afternoon. This friend of Hugo's is one of the hottest stylists around. Most people would kill to have a session with him.'

'It's all appearances with you media lot, isn't it? Substance just doesn't count,' Fergus snorted contemptuously.

Having retouched her lipstick, Vanessa turned to face him. 'Since you signed that contract this morning you are now one of the media lot you feign to despise, so you'd better get used to it.' She pressed the door bell. A buzzer sounded and the door clicked open.

Inside, a slender young black girl in a wispy short summer dress and four-inch high platform soled boots greeted them.

'Damien is expecting you, Miss Swift,' she said crisply, and pressed a button on her desk.

Double doors on the other side of the room clicked to reveal a large, open-plan room, one corner of which was set up as a photographic studio with lights and screens. In another corner was a work station, complete with a computer terminal and several drawing boards covered with sketches and photographs and draped with swatches of material. The centre of the room was lit from above by large skylights, beneath which three chrome and black leather sofas were grouped around a giant television screen. In front of the television was a glass-topped table whose base was the sculpture of a kneeling man, naked except for a bow tie. The table was littered with videos and glossy magazines. To one side was another naked man sculpture, this time standing and holding a tray that served as a mini-bar. Someone had tied a large pink bow around his erect penis.

Hugo and a bald-headed man were sitting on one of the sofas with their backs to the door, as Vanessa and Fergus walked in. Hugo glanced around and then leant towards his companion.

'Looks like our little problem has arrived,' he said in a theatrical whisper.

They both stood and turned to face the newcomers.

Vanessa was surprised to see that the bald man was only about twenty-four or five. He had pale, coffee-coloured skin and features that looked as though they had been sculpted by a latter-day Michelangelo. The body under his black Levi's and sleeveless white T-shirt was tightly muscled and he moved with a dancer's poise.

'Damien, I'd like you to meet Vanessa Swift and Dr Fergus Archibald,' Hugo said.

Vanessa put on her most seductive of smiles and held out a hand.

Damien gave her a cursory nod, his dark gaze fixed on Fergus. He crossed his arms and walked over, looking Fergus up and down. Then he walked slowly around him, all the while making little 'tsk tsk' sounds and shaking his head.

'Oh dear, you were right as always. We do have a

teensy-weensy bit of a problem, don't we?' he said, looking at Hugo.

Hugo shrugged and perched on the back of one of the sofas.

Damien took a tuft of Fergus's beard between his thumb and forefinger and pulled a face. 'Do you want to keep this?' he inquired, completely ignoring Fergus's glare and looked across at Hugo. 'I personally think beards are a hygiene risk.' He turned Fergus's face into profile. 'The problem is, they so often hide a multitude of sins. A weak chin or possibly no chin at all.' He prodded Fergus's face where his chin ought to be. 'Perhaps we can trim this one down and give it a more sculpted shape so that it makes a stronger statement. At the moment it just says woolly wild man to me.'

Damien stepped back.

'The hair will have to be thinned out, and I would recommend it being relaxed just a tad, with maybe a little highlight here and there? This boy looks as though he ate all the crusts on his bread when he was little.'

Hugo snickered.

An angry dark flush crept up Fergus's neck. 'Now look, you little . . .'

Damien held up an imperious hand. To Vanessa's astonishment, Fergus lapsed into a bad-tempered silence.

'You're going to have a bit of a problem with his complexion under the lights, Hugo,' Damien continued. 'He has the dreaded beetroot tendency. I suggest a little green in his make-up base to tone down the red. I would also suggest a good facial and liberal use of a toner on that skin; he's got a real problem with his nose.' Damien sighed, 'If only men would look after their pores better. You could drive a juggernaut through the potholes on the average Englishman's face!'

'I'm a Scotsman, you ignorant son-of . . .' snarled

Fergus but stopped as Vanessa's long nails bit into his arm.

Damien gave Fergus's beard a little tweak. 'I should have known. That northern climate does nothing for the complexion and less than nothing for the figure.'

He turned to Hugo. 'Did you know that the Scots have the most unhealthy diet in Europe, if not the world, and that's *your* biggest problem,' he said, pointing to Fergus's large stomach. 'I can paint and I can primp, but you can only disguise so much, and I'm no miracle worker. I can recommend a super personal trainer, but we're still talking months, if not years.'

Fergus's throat began to emit noises that sounded like a volcano ready to erupt. Vanessa decided it was time to intervene.

'I think we should be practical. We've got a tight budget and an even tighter schedule. We're in the studio in one week's time, so I think we should concentrate on the things we can actually change, like clothes.'

Damien looked at Hugo, who nodded agreement.

Damien shrugged and draped an arm around Hugo's shoulders. 'For this little love bunny, anything.' Then he walked across to his drawing board and started sorting through swatches of different coloured material.

'Much more of this and I'm going to do something one of us is going to regret,' Fergus growled to Vanessa.

'You are going to do no such thing,' Vanessa hissed. 'We have an agreement and I'm going to hold you to it.'

Their eyes locked for a long moment and then they were interrupted by Damien.

He draped swatches of material in shades of gold, green and brown over Fergus's right shoulder.

'There, I was right, he is most definitely an autumn person.'

Damien wagged his finger at Fergus. 'You really shouldn't wear blue, it isn't your colour, far too cold.'

Fergus brushed the pieces of material off his shoulder and dug his hands into his pockets. A vein on his right temple began to throb.

Damien linked his arm through Hugo's and they both considered Fergus. 'When you said Freud to me, Hugo, I immediately saw high collars. But now I've seen his neck, I think the casual college campus look. You know, chinos, button-downs and loafers would be better. Such a pity as I found this darling Edwardian-style bottle green suit, so *very* Freudian, but one can't make a silk purse out of a sow's ear. What do you think?'

Hugo shrugged. 'Anything you can do will be much appreciated, but I have a problem with greens or browns as I want the dominant theme of the set to be a sort of Fuschia pink. I talked it over with Gabriella at lunch yesterday and she simply adores the idea, but I just can't see how he will blend in. There's something so very *un*pink about him.'

Vanessa gave Hugo a sharp look. She did not like the idea of Gabriella and Hugo getting on well; it edged the balance of power further away from her. She wondered what else they had discussed over lunch.

'Now there's a woman who's a star down to her toenails. Since you had lunch with Gabriella yesterday, she's called me three times to discuss designers, and we're having a little tête-à–tête tonight in her hotel suite with a few samples.' Damien walked over and patted Fergus on the shoulder. 'However, in the meantime, I will try to do my best with this chunk of unreconstructed northern man here.' Damien indicated one of the sofas to Vanessa. 'If Madam would like to make herself comfortable, I shall now wave my magic wand and see if I can turn a pumpkin into a gilded carriage so that Cinderella here *can* go to the ball, but I must warn you, it may take a moment.'

Vanessa settled herself on to one of the sofas. Hugo sat down beside her.

Damien pulled a dust sheet off a rail of clothes and pushed it into the centre of the room. 'You said large Hugo, so I asked for everything in extra large just to be sure.' He selected a mustard yellow velvet jacket and turned to Fergus. 'Right, strip off, and God forbid, let's take a look at the bare canvas.'

Fergus glared at him. The tic on his temple was now executing a pulsating duet with a vein on the side of his neck.

'Fuck off.'

'Oh, come now,' Damien said, impatiently advancing on Fergus with the jacket in one hand and a shirt and a pair of trousers in the other. 'We're all friends here, and I don't suppose you've got anything the rest of us haven't seen before. Even if you have, I'm sure we'd all enjoy seeing it.'

Damien addressed this last remark to Hugo, so he didn't see the large fist which hit him on the side of his face, lifting him off his feet and landing him flat on his back on the floor.

He lay still for a moment, a surprised look on his face. Then he shakily raised himself on one elbow and put his other hand to his nose. When he took it away he saw blood.

Damien gave a low moan and fainted.

Twenty-Five

• • •

'Gabriella, *please*. I thought this was something we could settle like old friends over a drink,' pleaded Philip, and then hesitated as his chest started to constrict.

He searched hurriedly for his pills and popped two into his mouth. His face involuntarily screwed up with disgust at the unpleasant taste. He drank a mouthful of mineral water, but it didn't help much. What he really needed was some good malt whisky but his doctor had ordered him to avoid rich foods, alcohol and stress. So much for his doctor understanding a television executive's life, Philip thought bitterly.

Gabriella sipped her champagne cocktail, avoiding Philip's hurt look. A waiter delivered their main course. Gabriella's was a large pinky-brown crab artfully arranged on a sea of feathery endive, surrounded by carrot starfish, radish sea anemones and pasta shells in a creamy sauce. Philip looked morosely at his undressed green salad and steamed, unseasoned fish.

Gabriella gazed around the restaurant as she thoughtfully munched a carrot starfish. They had come here at her insistence, Philip had suggested a quieter and less expensive place, but she wanted it known she was back in town. People were nodding in her direction. She raised her glass at a table occupied by a group of men she had known as junior production staff, and who were now the heads of their respective companies. They smiled and nodded back.

Gabriella noted their receding and in one case vanished, hairlines with pleasure. At least two of them were younger than her. Her choice of restaurant had been perfect.

She turned back to Philip.

'People still admire and respect me. What do you think it would do to my credibility rating if it got around that I had agreed to share the billing with an amateur quack, on some cut-price show?'

Before Philip could reply, Gabriella switched on a gracious smile for two more suited men walking by their table. They stopped to shake her hand and murmur greetings, barely acknowledging Philip's existence.

'Did you see that?' Gabriella asked triumphantly. 'I'm still a name in this town. I'm sure I could get a better deal elsewhere.'

Philip massaged his chest with one hand. Had Gabriella been away so long that she had forgotten what a smile in a place like this meant? Gabriella might no longer be on the celebrity 'A' list, but she was still a celebrity nonetheless, and by acknowledging her in public, grey suited businessmen could later claim her intimate acquaintance in private.

Philip watched Gabriella graciously acknowledge several other people. Not one of them would take a chance and employ her at the moment, he thought, but if she was a success on his show, they would come swarming round her like sharks at a feeding frenzy, all wanting a piece of her.

'Gabriella.' Philip tried to recapture her attention. 'Gabriella, *please*. I just can't offer you a better deal at the moment because my budget is very restricted. But if we get the ratings and I promise you we will, then we can renegotiate.'

Gabriella's voice was business-like, even as she smiled radiantly at someone walking through the door. 'Will you put that in writing? I want an agreed rise for every percentage point I push up the ratings after the first show.'

'I wouldn't like to be quite as specific as that,' Philip said hastily, 'but I'm sure we can come up with a form of words that we will both find agreeable.'

Gabriella picked up a crab claw and with the silver pincers provided, expertly cracked it open, exposing its soft white flesh. Deftly hooking out a morsel, she dipped it into some mayonnaise and with a little mew of satisfaction popped it into her mouth.

Philip listlessly prodded his fish with his fork, and then reached for the salt cellar. Gabriella wagged an admonitory finger at him. Philip sighed and put his fork down. He had lost his appetite.

Gabriella examined the claw to see if there was any meat left and then dropped it on her plate. She looked across at Philip. 'And what about this other presenter? I don't like working with amateurs. They are worse than animals. At least you know there's a good chance an animal is going to bite or shit, but you can never tell with an amateur.'

'Let's just try him out on the pilot, and if it doesn't work out then we can lose him. Anyway, I would like you to think of Dr Archibald as our resident expert, someone for you to occasionally address questions to, not your co-presenter. He will also be the perfect foil for your great beauty. A case of beauty and the beast – rather apt imagery for a series about sexual fantasy, don't you think?' Philip chuckled, but there was no answering warmth in the look on Gabriella's face.

'My dearest girl . . .' Philip entreated and reached across the table for Gabriella's hand.

She picked up her glass.

Philip felt a stab in his chest that wasn't anything to

do with his indigestion. In a world in which the old certainties seemed to have gone, he had thought that Gabriella at least would remain constant to their past. But perhaps she was right, sentiment had to take second place to business. He straightened up.

'I have complete faith in your abilities, Gabriella,' he said crisply. 'But Archibald is a psychologist with expertise in these matters, and I anticipate we are going to have a lot of detractors in the current political climate. Having him on the show gives us academic credibility. However, you have my assurance he will not be allowed to interfere in any way.'

Even as he said the words, the vision of Fergus punching Damien on the nose rose up before him. He tried to swallow it along with a little water.

Gabriella looked unconvinced and toyed with a radish. Philip had always been so malleable in the past One smile from her and he would agree to almost anything. But there was an air of determination tinged with something akin to desperation about him now, and it was not a combination that boded well. She would just have to change Philip's mind for him once they got into the studio, Gabriella decided, as she snapped another claw in half. She could easily make this Archibald man look a complete fool without damaging herself. She smiled. After she had finished with this Archibald person, Philip wouldn't be able to get rid of him fast enough.

Philip mistook her smile for agreement and smiled back. Gabriella scooped out a forkload of dark flesh from the crab's body and offered it to him. He waved it away. His digestive system was in no condition to accommodate shellfish.

With a final sigh of pleasure, Gabriella pushed her plate away. It was piled high with the shattered remnants of the dismembered corpse. Philip held out a napkin as she dabbled her fingers in the finger bowl. Gabriella smiled at him.

'Philip darling, I trust you. Haven't I always? I'll do my best with this psychiatrist fellow if you will agree to just one or two teeny little things for me.'

Philip crunched on another pill.

'First of all, I'd like my own make-up artist. Most of the girls these days think they're house painters, but I know this absolute sweetie of a little man – Joan and Britt and Gina all swear by him, and secondly, I'd like all my outfits to come from Cesare's. I simply adore his designs, they're so me.'

Philip choked. Gabriella handed him a glass of water. Philip drained it in one gulp.

'Cesare's.' Philip's voice was little more than a hoarse croak. The flamboyance of Cesare's clothes was only matched by the extravagance of his prices.

'Cesare's,' Gabriella repeated firmly, 'and now if you don't mind darling, I must fly. I have another appointment.'

Two waiters rushed forward to hold Gabriella's chair as she prepared to leave. She pecked Philip lightly on the cheek before sweeping out of the restaurant, waving regally to the other tables as she went.

Philip sat motionless for a few moments. The crab's lifeless eyes stared back at him from Gabriella's plate. He signalled to a waiter.

'A large whisky,' he demanded hoarsely.

Outside the restaurant, Gabriella started to hail a taxi and then changed her mind and decided to walk to her hotel. Today she wanted to feel the warmth of the sun on her face and the pavements of London beneath her feet again. As she walked, she felt like singing aloud. London was going to be her town again. She had seen it on the faces of those men in the restaurant. She was on her way back, and she was going to do it on her terms. She had been forced to leave England when her debts escalated and nobody returned her calls. When she was back on top, she would remember all those people.

Her hotel was just off Piccadilly. It was small, discreet and very smart. She smiled at the thought of what Philip's face would look like when he received the bill. He really had become such an old stick in the mud. He had never been a good looker, but he'd had a certain style in the old days, with his long blond hair, dark glasses and battered MG sports car, which he drove open-topped, winter and summer. He had been such fun then.

She hurried up to her suite to change out of the tailored, charcoal grey suit she had worn for lunch. She wanted to create just the right impression for this interview. Most of the new school of female television presenters looked as though they had been cloned out of the same shop window dummy mould, and a chain store shop window, at that. They were plastic and colourless and so anxious to be taken seriously, they didn't dare be sexy. She'd never been scared of being a woman, and woe betide the man who hadn't taken her seriously.

After some deliberation, she decided on a black, figure-hugging polo-necked dress with a clever cut-out at the front which artfully revealed a large expanse of cleavage which she dusted with a little blusher. The dress was trimmed at the neck and cuffs with fake leopard skin, and the stole she draped casually over one shoulder, and the cossack-style hat she perched cheekily on one side of her head to complete her outfit were of matching fur. In the old days the leopard skin would have been real, she thought regretfully, but a girl had to move with the times.

From her jewellery cask, she selected large diamanté earrings in the shape of snarling leopards' heads, and slipped several real diamond rings on her fingers.

She was just retouching her scarlet lipstick when a quiet purr from the phone alerted her to the arrival of her visitors. Gabriella instructed the receptionist to keep them waiting for nine minutes exactly, no less and no more, and then opened a bottle of pink champagne and settled down to wait.

Ten minutes later the doorbell rang. Gabriella checked her smile in the mirror before opening the door.

'Mr Spittle, I'm delighted to meet you.' She held out her hand to a tall thin man. He looked uncomfortable.

'I'm Eddie,' said a tiny ferret-faced man whom Gabriella hadn't noticed because he barely came up to the other man's elbow. 'This is Sid, my photographer.'

The tall man apologetically held up one of the several cameras he had draped around his neck.

Spittle was through the door before Gabriella had recovered enough to invite him in.

'Very nice, very nice,' he said approvingly his small eyes sliding over everything. 'This hotel's got real class. You don't find too many pop stars staying here. It costs a few spandulies too so you can't be doing all that badly.' He raised an interrogative eyebrow.

'Just because one is not appearing on British television does not mean one is no longer a star, Mr Spittle,' Gabriella said frostily.

'Oh I know, I know,' said Spittle, and without waiting for an invitation, he settled down in an armchair and opened his notebook. Gabriella posed beside the marble fireplace, her head held imperiously high.

'You've been voted top female television personality in Norway, Belgium and Luxembourg according to my research.'

'*And* my show regularly tops the ratings in Italy, where I have been voted sexiest woman on television twice in the last five years and been runner-up in the other three,' Gabriella added, her voice now registering a sub-zero temperature.

'That's your show with Cicci, the performing penguin, and the boob of the week spot, where men send in photographs of their wives' and girlfriends' boobs and the audience gets to vote on size and shape, isn't it?' said Spittle, consulting his notebook again. 'Not quite the kind of programme for a woman of your great talent, is it Miss Wolfe, or may I call you Gabriella?'

Spittle's eyes were fixed on her face, greedy for every reaction.

Two bright spots showed on Gabriella's carefully made-up cheeks. Spittle nodded imperceptibly; his carefully aimed barb had hit its target. His voice changed.

'Our television screens have been a much duller place without you, Miss Wolfe, we sorely need what a star like you has to offer.'

Gabriella looked mollified. With a gracious sweep of her stole, she artfully arranged herself on the sofa opposite Spittle so that the light was behind her.

Spittle watched, noting where and how she sat and the high neck and long sleeves of her dress. He was sure she wouldn't see fifty again, whatever the newspaper cuttings said. He made a mental note to get his researcher to dig harder for her real date and place of birth.

He always began his interviews by playing the hard man; it invariably provoked his interviewees to anger, which in turn made them less cautious. Then, when he made the sudden switch into the 'only wanting to set the record straight' mode, he caught them off guard. For some reason he had never been able to understand, most celebrities clung to the childlike belief that inside each of them was a fairy-tale character called 'the real me' who was misunderstood by everyone. But if they thought the public was interested in paying to read how they really led quite ordinary lives, they were mistaken. The public wanted to be entertained, and it was his job to make sure they were.

Gabriella crossed her black-stockinged legs. 'And what *exactly* do you think I have to offer to British television, Mr Spittle?'

'Eddie, please. In three words I would say: class, glamour and sex. I'm not saying that the girls on our screens these days aren't pretty, but they aren't in your league.'

Gabriella graciously inclined her head.

'The angle I want to take in this article is that the glamour has gone out of television in the same way it has gone out of Hollywood. A good analogy don't you think?' Spittle asked.

Gabriella leaned forward and picked up a gold cigarette box from the onyx coffee table. The movement allowed Spittle a full view of her deep cleavage. He ran his tongue over his lips. She might be pushing fifty, but at least that part of her anatomy was in good shape. Not too many wrinkles either, but he'd hold judgement on whether Mother Nature had been kind until he had seen a copy of her medical records. Plastic surgeons were getting too clever by half. They went in for injections these days, rather than the knife, and the results were so much harder to detect.

Gabriella placed a cigarette in her cigarette holder and waited.

Spittle snapped his fingers at Sid, who fumbled for some matches before lumbering shyly forward with a proffered light.

They were a great team, Spittle thought. Sid's painfully shy exterior hid a killer instinct to get the right shot. He would wait any length of time, climb over or under any obstacle, subject himself to excruciatingly uncomfortable positions, anything to get a picture of his subject off-guard and defenceless. And in situations like this when they were invited in by their quarry, Sid's seemingly harmless presence helped to make the subject feel more secure.

'Why don't we talk, while Sid here does his bit?' Spittle said, as Gabriella exhaled a long stream of smoke. 'I always find we get more relaxed shots that way.'

Gabriella's hand involuntarily went to her hair. 'I want to know when he's going to take a shot. I don't like being caught off-guard.'

'Leave it to Sid, he's an artist. He's never caught a wrong side yet, have you Sid?'

Sid gave Gabriella a shy smile and then concentrated on assembling his battery of cameras.

Spittle placed a small tape recorder on the onyx table. 'Now tell me about Gabriella the woman,' he began. 'Rumour has it that you've had some of the world's most eligible men at your feet, and yet you've not married. Why not?'

Gabriella blew a languorous smoke ring. 'I like to think of myself in the same mould as that doyenne of Hollywood glamour, Mae West, who said: "It's not the men in my life but the life in my men I care about",' Gabriella replied in a Mae West drawl.

Spittle dutifully smiled.

'So you see,' Gabriella continued, 'when I was a young girl, I liked older men who could teach me about life. Now I'm a mature women, I like to teach young men about life. It has a perfect symmetry. Marriage would only have got in the way.'

'So you mean you're into toy boys?' asked Spittle, eagerly leaning forward.

Gabriella exhaled another long stream of smoke before replying, 'Toys need winding up. I like my men to be self-starters.'

Spittle smiled. He could see the headlines already.

Twenty-Six

• • •

'Yes?' enquired a sleepy female voice.

Vanessa stiffened. 'I'm sorry, but I understood this was Dr Archibald's number.'

'It is,' the voice replied.

'Is he there?' Vanessa demanded.

There was a muffled exchange and then Fergus came on the line. His voice sounded sleepy too.

'Archibald,' he yawned.

'What the hell are you up to?' Vanessa yelled.

There was a long silence on the other end of the line.

'Don't you *dare* hang up on me!' Vanessa's voice went up an octave. 'Where in hell's name have you been these last two days, and who is that woman? Answer me, damn you.'

'Are you trying to wake the dead, woman? There's no need to shout,' Fergus remonstrated mildly.

'Shout! I'm not shouting,' yelled Vanessa, 'If you're not back here by first thing tomorrow, the whole deal is off. And just in case you've forgotten, I have your signature on the bottom of a contract.'

'Without me that contract is worth nothing, so if you want me back, my price has just doubled,' retorted Fergus.

'You have the nerve to ask for more money after your performance the other day?' Vanessa's voice was incandescent with rage. 'You nearly killed that man.

We've had to agree to pay for some extremely expensive, reconstructive surgery on his nose, as well as a large amount in damages to stop him suing you for assault and battery. That wouldn't do what little you have left of an academic career much good, would it?'

'It wouldn't do your company much good either, would it?' Fergus replied with merciless logic. 'If you want me to look like some ponce as well as emasculate my research because your boss is lily-livered about some committee of virgin vigilantes, then you're going to have to pay more for it.'

'I just love the way you left-wing academics rediscover your principles when you want more money,' sneered Vanessa.

'At least we have some left to rediscover,' snarled Fergus. 'Call me tomorrow with a better offer or say goodbye to your meal ticket.'

He slammed the telephone down and rolled over on to his back, where he lay gazing up at the ceiling. On the other side of the rumpled bed lay the naked, sleeping body of one of his research students, or rather, ex-students, Fergus thought. She had been one of the few people to greet his arrival back at Heartlands with any enthusiasm. There weren't many university people about, as it was the summer vacation, but the few members of staff who had seen him had ostentatiously avoided meeting him. Mrs Peploe, his landlady, had been equally frosty. She had presented him with a bill for his rent arrears and a letter of dismissal from the university for grossly immoral conduct. It had taken all his charm to talk her into letting him stay for a couple of days.

Fergus had fully intended to go back to London. He really had no choice. Academic posts were hard to find, and after what had happened at St Ethelreds, he doubted any academic institution in the country would hire him. But he had wanted to give Vanessa a bit of a scare, and judging by her voice on the telephone, he'd succeeded. Fergus grinned and stretched out a questing hand. It met pliant warm flesh. He still had until tomorrow.

Vanessa stared at the receiver. Everything in her rebelled against getting Fergus to come back to London, but she had no choice, and she didn't have until tomorrow either. Time was fast running out; it was already two days since Fergus had punched Damien.

In the confusion, she had not at first noticed that Fergus was missing. Hugo had been almost as hysterical as Damien, and had insisted on rushing Damien to the emergency department of the nearest hospital, where he recovered his senses in time to refuse treatment from an NHS doctor. He insisted on yet another taxi dash to a private clinic where the plastic surgeon, who had only recently given him the profile denied him by Mother Nature, had pronounced a year's worth of expensive surgery ruined.

Despite Vanessa's protestations, Hugo had promptly agreed to Right Pryce Productions paying all Damien's medical bills, plus compensation for pain and distress. When an ashen-faced Philip was told this, he swallowed nearly a whole box of his indigestion pills. In the ensuing argument, Philip yelled at Hugo and then they both turned on Vanessa, but when she turned to vent her spleen on the cause of the problem, she discovered that Fergus had gone.

Reasoning that he would turn up on her doorstep sooner or later, she had waited, carefully honing the words she intended to shout at him. But after thirty-six hours her confidence had begun to wane, and by that morning it had disappeared altogether.

Not knowing where else to begin, she called the university.

Given the manner of his departure, not many people would have dared to return, but Fergus was not most people, and he obviously still had at least one admirer there. The problem was, now she had found him, how was she going to get him to come back to London? There was no way that Philip would agree to paying him more money after the incident with Damien.

Just at that moment, Philip put his head round the door. 'Is everything under control again with Fergus?' he enquired coming into the room. 'I've just had lunch with Gabriella, and like the true professional she is, she immediately agreed with me that having Fergus as our resident expert was an excellent idea.'

'Everything is just fine, Philip darling,' Vanessa lied. 'Fergus has gone up to Heartlands to collect some of his background material from the university, and he'll be back tomorrow or the day after.'

'So we're back on course after all that unpleasantness with Hugo's friend?' asked Philip.

'Absolutely. Between you and me, I think Hugo got a little hysterical. I would have demanded a second opinion. It was only a playful blow. I'm sure Fergus didn't mean to cause any damage.'

'Be that as it may, Vanessa, I want no more problems. I like to think I run a tight ship,' Philip said sternly.

'Philip sweetie, you can depend on me. Now if only Hugo and Vijay would get their skates on, we will be ready to go into studio on Sunday week.'

Philip hovered uncertainly beside Vanessa's desk, fingering the papers piled in her in tray.

'Was there anything else, PP darling? I really am pushed for time.'

Philip shook his head. 'No. But you will make sure that there are no more loose cannons, won't you? Sir Norman and the Committee don't need much of an excuse to prevent us ever getting on air.'

Vanessa blew him a kiss and with a last anxious nod, he left the room.

Vanessa slotted one of the pile of home videos sent

in response to her advertisement, into her VHS recorder, and began to spin through it on fast forward. She hadn't had much time to do anything else but chase Fergus for the last few days, but she still had a programme to produce.

With one eye on the screen, she pushed the button on her intercom.

'In here. *Now*,' she barked.

A couple of moments later there was a hesitant knock on her door and Vijay sidled in. He stood with his back to the wall.

'I thought I told you to have a list of all the possible programme participants on my desk first thing this morning,' snapped Vanessa. 'I seem to be the only person working round here.' She ostentatiously lifted up the remote control and turned the video off.

Vijay held some papers in front of him as though they would shield him from the evil eye.

'It's all here. I've put the original letters together with my notes and suggestions.' He hurriedly dropped them on Vanessa's desk before retreating out of reach.

Vanessa eyed them distastefully. 'All I asked for was a couple of brief sentences on each participant, not a dissertation. I don't have time to read all this. How was the woman who wanted to be a defrocked nun? I liked that one.'

Vijay reddened. 'Not much good. She was a bit too . . . too old.'

'I thought you wanted to fill our screens with the old and the lame and the underprivileged, Vijay. What's happened to all your good intentions?' mocked Vanessa.

Vijay reddened even more. 'She just wouldn't have worked, that's all,' he insisted stubbornly.

'Well find some more who will,' Vanessa yelled, sweeping his notes off her desk.

Vijay was out of the door before they hit the floor.

Heather looked up from the magazine she was reading. 'The old cow on the warpath again? Fancy a free drink? A group of us are planning to crash the opening of that new bar in Frith Street, it should be a gas.'

Vijay ruefully shook his head. 'I'd better make a few more phone-calls, just to show willing.'

Heather nodded at a winking light on her small switchboard. 'You're not the only one hitting the phone. If that cow isn't out to lunch, she's on the phone. Does she ever do any work?'

'Not if she can help it, why should she? She's the boss and I'm the worker,' Vijay said bitterly, heading for his office.

The term 'office' was misleading. Vijay worked from a store room which he shared with some large filing cupboards, several thousand tapes and reels of film, and an elderly Steenbeck.

He sat down at his small desk and consulted his list of possible interviewees. Wedging the receiver between his chin and shoulder, and without looking, he pressed a button for an outside line. Instead of a dialling tone he heard a voice. He had pressed the line Vanessa was using, by mistake.

Vanessa sounded unusually conciliatory.

'Fergus, can I put my cards on the table with you?'

There was a grunt on the other end of the line.

'I really can't ask Philip to put more money up front at the moment. Right Pryce Productions is not a large company and we will sink or swim depending on the success of *Forbidden Fruit*. But you and I know we have a mega success on our hands. Think of it: the newspapers will be queuing up to serialise your research, and publishers will be throwing money at you, and we mustn't forget the American market. Your kind of stuff tops the bestseller lists over there.'

There was silence on the other end of the line as Fergus appeared to be digesting this.

Vijay started to put the receiver down; it was morally wrong to eavesdrop on other people's conversations. He hesitated. Nobody ever told him anything around the office. He put the receiver back to his ear and listened, holding his breath.

'You might even be offered a post at an American university,' Vanessa continued, her voice now positively honeyed. 'Imagine UCLA with all those long-legged, Californian blondes, or Harvard and those bright-eyed, bushy-tailed preppies? You could put two fingers up to Heartlands and all those repressed old biddies.'

Fergus cleared his throat. 'Just out of curiosity, what kind of money are we talking about for newspaper serialisation?'

Vanessa knew she had him hooked. All she had to do was play out the line a little more before giving it a final tug and reeling him in. 'I couldn't say for sure, but I think you could safely think in terms of a five-figure sum,' she said, and then tugged the line. 'Of course, I do have quite a few good contacts in Wapping. If you were really interested, I could float the idea with them.'

There was another silence as Fergus considered this. It was true, popular psychology was a growth area in publishing. All it needed was either love or sex somewhere in the title.

Switching the phone on to loudspeaker, Vanessa walked round her desk and put another home video into the machine. They were really quite amusing, if a bit amateurish. She perched on the edge of her desk and watched. Unfortunately the best ones were too explicit to broadcast, although they looked like fun to make.

'And what do I have to do to have all these riches thrust at me?' asked Fergus noncommittally.

Vanessa suddenly smiled. The solution to her

problem was in front of her. She leaned towards the telephone. 'Come back to London and appear on the show as agreed next week, and I might just be able to offer you a small personal incentive by way of making the deal even more attractive,' she said huskily.

Vijay thought he heard Fergus swallowing. 'And just what might that be?' he asked.

Vanessa laughed. The sound made Vijay jump.

'I think it's about time you were familiarised with the workings of the studio. Hugo has had this delightful little set built and it's all ready for the first fantasies. I think it's my job as producer to make sure all the equipment works, don't you? So I thought we might give it a little test run when no one is around...' Vanessa paused. 'We could even make our own little home video. You always said you could have earned a fortune making porn movies, now's your chance.'

Fergus made one last attempt to resist. 'I have some unfinished business here,' he parried, 'I don't think I can come down to London until after the weekend.'

'If that unfinished business is that little bitch I spoke to this morning, you can forget it,' snapped Vanessa.

'I didn't know you cared,' said Fergus mockingly.

'I'm warning you,' said Vanessa, her voice beginning to rise again, 'get back here today or the whole deal's off.'

'Okay, okay, don't go ruffling your feathers again. Today it is,' Fergus said, looking at his watch. The next train was not for another hour, which gave him plenty of time.

This time he left the phone dangling on its cord to prevent further interruptions.

Back in the Right Pryce offices Vanessa allowed herself a tight satisfied smile, then a glance at her watch told her she was late. She picked up her bag and raced out of the door and down the stairs. Ten minutes later she was pushing her way through a crowded bar.

She had insisted on meeting in a dark little pub near the British Museum, as no one she knew ever went there. It was the haunt of university students and foreign tourists, although what tourists made of traditional British pub food like pizza and chicken curry, she failed to understand.

But the pub still had one old fashioned virtue: glass panelled partitions which allowed some tables to be used for discreet conversations.

Sitting at the table in the darkest corner was Eddie Spittle.

He got up to kiss her, but she swerved out of reach and sat down opposite, strategically placing her bag on the seat beside her so that he could not move too close.

Spittle pushed a glass containing a double vodka and a bottle of tonic towards her.

'I always remember what a lady drinks.'

Vanessa nodded and splashed some tonic into the glass, and then raised it to her lips. But before she could drink, Spittle raised his glass of whisky in a toast.

'To the destruction of our enemies.' He held her eyes for a moment.

Vanessa gave him an acidic smile and drank deeply. Spittle had been a useful way of supplementing her income for nearly fifteen years. He had always been willing to pay well for any juicy bits of gossip she passed on to him and the source of the information had never been traced back to her, but she always had the uncomfortable feeling that one day it might be her own indiscretions splashed across the front of his newspaper.

Spittle reached across her bag and put his hand on her knee. 'You are going to owe me one really big favour, Vanessa dearie, and one of these days I'm going to collect.' He fondled her knee.

Vanessa made an unsuccessful attempt to pull her skirt over her knees. 'So what are you going to do for me, Eddie? Big favours are not your usual *modus operandi*.'

'I'm going to do a really big spread on Gabriella Wolfe, which will send the ratings of your show through the roof.'

'I wouldn't have thought there was anything new to say about an ageing and outdated chat show host,' Vanessa said offhandedly.

'She said she loved you too,' Spittle laughed.

'Exactly what *did* she say about me?' Vanessa demanded, instantly alert.

'Let's just say you two won't be forming a mutual admiration society,' Spittle replied, 'that's why I called you. I thought you might be able to help me with the article. There are a few things about Miss Wolfe I can't quite pin down.'

'Like what?' asked Vanessa.

'Like what she did before the age of twenty-one,' Spittle replied.

Vanessa considered this for a few moments. 'No trace?' she asked.

'Nothing. Zilch. Nada,' Spittle replied, 'and I've had my researchers hard at it for days. The first mention of her is as a young actress, aged twenty-two, playing a good-time girl in a BBC cop series.'

'She must have changed her name. Actresses do, you know.'

'Maybe. We're pursuing that one, but my instincts tell me there's more to it than that. I think we may have some dirty washing that needs to be hung out to dry. You know the sort of thing: "Shameful Secret of Glamorous TV Star".' He drew large headlines with his hands. 'I've got plenty of stuff for recent years. Our Miss Wolfe has kept a stable of young Italian studs to amuse her while she's been living in Rome. Two of them were barely sixteen when she picked them up. But I want to know what she was doing when *she* was sixteen. Will you see what you can do to help?'

'Anything to help, Eddie, you know that,' Vanessa said. 'But I trust you will keep my name out of it, should I come up with anything.'

Spittle tapped the side of his nose. 'You know me, Vanessa sweetheart, the soul of discretion. And of course, there will be something in it for you.'

Vanessa stood up. 'I can't make any promises, Eddie, but I'll keep you posted on any developments, and I'd be grateful if you would do the same for me.'

Spittle grabbed her hand. 'Perhaps we could make the next meeting dinner? I could do your career a lot of good.'

Vanessa gave him a good imitation of fluttering eye-lashes. 'Give me a call sometime and perhaps we can arrange it.'

Outside in the street, Vanessa had to control her urge to do a little dance of triumph. Fergus was coming to heel, and now that little weasel Spittle was hot on Gabriella's scent. If he put Gabriella on the front page, *Forbidden Fruit* would be right there with her guaranteeing the ratings. A girl couldn't ask for better news!

Twenty-Seven

• • •

The warmth of the late afternoon sun on his face made Jeremy reluctantly open his eyes. The window was wide open, and bees were humming around the flowers which Alicia had planted in the window boxes out on the flat's tiny balcony.

Jeremy's left arm was stiff, but he dared not move for fear of waking Alicia. She lay with her head on his shoulder, her body moulded against his.

They had started to make love on the *chaise-longue*, but had toppled on to the floor where they now lay sprawled among Zelda's oriental floor cushions. With infinite care, Jeremy tugged a cushion from under his buttocks and tucked it behind his head.

Sex, Jeremy was discovering with delight, was not just about sex. It was about a whole combination of sensations and feelings and moments like this, just being able to lie beside Alicia, looking at her wonderfully plump, pearlescent pink body.

With the tip of his forefinger, Jeremy almost imperceptibly began to caress one of her nipples. After a moment or two it began to harden, and Alicia's eyelashes fluttered. With a small whimper of pleasure, she opened her eyes, and yawning, stretched her arms and legs wide. His arm free, Jeremy wriggled down, his mouth seeking and claiming her other breast.

Alicia thoughtfully stroked his hair. 'It's nearly six o'clock, we must get dressed,' she murmured softly.

Jeremy kept his mouth clamped to her ample breast.

Alicia stopped stroking his hair.

'Jeremy darling, we've got to meet Vijay at seven. It's all planned, the recording is tomorrow.'

An unfamiliar note of firmness had crept into Alicia's voice of late. Jeremy had found it was not to be disobeyed. With a last regretful lick, he sat up. 'Are you sure you want to go through with this? This cockeyed plan you and this researcher fellow have dreamt up could be construed as breaking and entering, which is illegal.'

Alicia began gathering her hastily discarded clothes. 'Actually, it was all my idea. Vijay merely told me what Vanessa and Fergus were planning this evening. If you don't want to come, you don't have to, Vijay and I are quite capable of managing by ourselves. He doesn't even know about you.'

In their many telephone conversations since the evening Vijay had come to interview her, Alicia had not mentioned that she happened to be living with Vanessa's ex-husband. Vijay assumed she was single, and Alicia had not disabused him. In order to get him to co-operate with her plan, she had vaguely intimated that she might be prepared to spend some time with him afterwards. It had not exactly been a promise so Alicia did not feel that she was being dishonest, but she hadn't mentioned it to Jeremy either. She had a feeling he would get possessive, something he had become prone to recently.

Jeremy leapt to his feet and squared his shoulders. 'I have absolutely no intention of letting you and this . . . this person run around London like a couple of cat burglars without my protection. You could get into all kinds of trouble.'

Alicia tried very hard not to smile. Jeremy's attempt

to be masterful was completely undermined by his
nakedness. It had come as a surprise to her to find that
a man could look vulnerable when he was naked, but
she was learning a lot of new things lately.

'Well, we'd better hurry up then, or else we'll be late
and Vijay will be a bundle of nerves.'

Alicia's prophecy proved accurate. They were fifteen
minutes late reaching the narrow alleyway behind the
converted warehouse in Covent Garden, which housed
the television studios where *Forbidden Fruit* was to
be recorded. An extremely tense Vijay was crouched
waiting behind a large industrial rubbish bin, whose
malodorous contents filled the hot evening air with the
dank odour of putrefaction.

Jeremy put his hand to his nose.

'Who's this?' Vijay demanded in an angry whisper,
as Alicia pulled Jeremy down to crouching position
beside her.

'Oh, I'm sorry, you two haven't met have you?' Alicia
whispered ingenuously. 'This is Vanessa's ex-husband,
Jeremy Swift. Jeremy, meet Vijay Seth.'

She looked from one to the other. They reached
across her and awkwardly shook hands.

'You should have told me this was going to be a
works outing, I would have hired a charabanc,' Vijay
whispered sarcastically to Alicia.

'Don't be silly, Vijay, Jeremy is part of this too.
Vanessa treated him very badly. Why, she very nearly
made him impot . . .' Alicia began but was interrupted
by Jeremy.

'Could we stand up?' he said huffily. All this amateur
James Bond stuff was bad enough without Alicia
broadcasting his past sexual shortcomings to the
world. 'I'm getting very uncomfortable.'

He hauled himself to his feet, using the rubbish bin
for support but it was not as solid as it looked and

he sent it lurching noisily down the alleyway. Jeremy crouched down again.

'Idiot,' Vijay hissed loudly.

Alicia grabbed his arm and put her finger to her lips. They waited motionless for a few minutes, but nobody came to investigate. Vijay mopped his face. It had been a long and very hot day. Philip had negotiated a cut-price deal from Silver Screen Studios to use their facilities for the weekend, but it had meant only one day for the erection of the complicated and expensive set conceived by Hugo and his designer. Unfortunately, the set was of Cecil B. de Mille epic proportions and much of it had to be abandoned, provoking lengthy and acrimonious exchanges between Hugo, Philip and Vanessa, and constant rewrites of the script.

Vijay had been caught in the middle. All that had kept him going was the thought of spending some time alone with Alicia that evening.

He watched Jeremy out of the corner of his eye. He had not reckoned on another man, particularly one who had such an obviously proprietorial air towards her. He would just have to show her who was the better man.

Jeremy caught his look and put a protective arm around Alicia's shoulders.

Vijay reached into his pocket and pulled out a red cotton bandana which he tied round his forehead. He thought he looked rather dashing, dressed in black jeans and a black polo-neck, but he was very hot and sweat kept trickling uncomfortably into his eyes.

'Who does he think he is, Che Guevara?' murmured Jeremy.

Alicia gave him a warning look. She thought Vijay looked rather glamorous in black with his long dark hair in a ponytail.

Jeremy noticed her appreciative gaze and glared fiercely at Vijay, but the look was lost on him as he rose to a half-crouching, half-walking position and began to edge along the wall. Alicia followed suit, forcing Jeremy to adopt the same uncomfortable stance and follow them.

After a few yards, Vijay motioned them to stop and listened. The only sound was the distant drone of traffic along Holborn Kingsway. The centre of Covent Garden, with its tourist-trap piazza and cheek by jowl wine bars, restaurants and pubs, was packed with Saturday night revellers, but the studios were surrounded by deserted office blocks.

Alicia tapped him on the shoulder. Vijay jumped.

'How do we get in?' she whispered.

'I left a window open this afternoon. I think it's at the back somewhere,' Vijay replied, and set off again.

His knowledge of the geography of the building was extremely hazy. He thought the window he was looking for opened on to the alleyway, but he had obviously been wrong – not that he was going to admit his mistake to Alicia and Jeremy. He reached the corner of the building and signalled to them to stop again. He peered cautiously round the corner.

Alicia stifled a giggle as Jeremy rolled his eyes.

Vijay turned round and scowled at them. Alicia struggled to keep a straight face.

Having ascertained it was all clear, Vijay led them down yet another alleyway where, to his relief, he saw the window he had left open.

He pointed triumphantly, 'That's it.'

Alicia and Jeremy gazed upwards. The window was barely two foot square and nearly eight feet off the ground.

'This is ridiculous,' Jeremy declared, 'none of us can get through that.'

'It is a bit high and a bit small,' Alicia said dubiously.

'Well, I could hardly leave the front door open, could

I?' Vijay said angrily. He had expected a little more appreciation from Alicia.

He'd taken a big risk slipping away from the main studio, and had been stopped and questioned several times when he had blundered into technical areas which were out of bounds to him. He eventually found the window in a little-used corridor at the back of the building, and it had taken him nearly ten heart-stopping minutes to prise it open, because fifty years or more of accumulated grime had glued the frame shut. It had not crossed his mind to check whether it was accessible from the outside. He was too worried about getting caught.

Alicia tugged at his sleeve. 'If you and Jeremy fetch the rubbish bin, we could put some of those on top of it.' She pointed at some wooden pallets.

Keeping their heads turned away from the stench of whatever was rotting inside, Vijay and Jeremy dragged the bin over and stationed it against the wall. They then placed a pallet on top and one beside it to act as a step.

They stood back and surveyed their handiwork.

'Are you sure you want to do this?' Jeremy anxiously asked Alicia, 'It could be dangerous.'

Vijay gave him a contemptuous look. 'I'll go first.'

He scrambled up on to the bin and pulled the window open. A shower of grime powdered his hair. He shook his head and studied the window; it was difficult to decide which portion of his anatomy should go first. He lifted a leg. It wouldn't work. There was nothing for it, it would have to be head first.

He placed his hands on the window ledge, but pulled them hastily away. It was thick with pigeon droppings. Vijay looked uncertainly around.

'Something wrong?' Jeremy enquired in a mocking voice.

Vijay wiped his hands on his jeans and placed them

firmly on the ledge. This was no time to be squeamish. With a loud grunt hauled himself up, thrusting his head and shoulders through the window. Alicia and Jeremy watched as the top of Vijay's body disappeared, but then he appeared to get stuck, his buttocks up in the air and his legs dangling down. With a wild kick he launched his body through the window, slithering out of sight. There was a loud bump, a muffled yell and then silence.

Alicia and Jeremy looked at each other.

'Supposing he's knocked himself out?' Alicia said anxiously, 'We'd better go and look.'

She stretched up to pull herself on to the bin but it was too high. She looked at Jeremy. He bent down and clasped his hands together. Alicia placed a foot into Jeremy's hands and hopped. Jeremy heaved but nothing happened. With not altogether good grace he got down on to his hands and knees. Alicia stepped on to his back and pulled herself up.

She balanced unsteadily on the bin and peered through the window. As she did, Vijay popped his head out. She gave a little scream.

'Oh my goodness,' she squeaked clutching her breast, 'we thought you were dead or something.'

'Not quite,' said Vijay, bitterly rubbing his head.

He reached through the window and taking Alicia's arms, unceremoniously pulled her inside. She fell into his arms and stood panting on the small landing.

'You can let go now,' Alicia giggled. Vijay's arms were still held tightly around her.

Vijay reluctantly took his hands away, and Alicia straightened her sweatshirt.

'You promised you would come alone,' Vijay hissed. 'I only agreed to do this for you, not for him,' he jerked his head at the window.

'I do believe you're jealous,' teased Alicia.

Vijay flushed.

Alicia brushed some dirt off his shoulder and straightened his bandana. 'We'll talk about you and me when this is all over, I promise.'

Vijay's eyes lit up.

'But for now I want you to be nice to Jeremy, just for me,' Alicia smiled flirtatiously up at him.

Vijay nodded.

'Alicia?' It was Jeremy's voice from the alleyway. 'What's going on up there?'

Alicia looked out of the window. 'Aren't you going to join us?'

'I think someone ought to stay here and act as look-out,' Jeremy stalled.

'Coward,' teased Alicia.

Jeremy almost knocked the bin over in his haste to climb up. He put his arms through the window and waited for Vijay and Alicia to help him, but they had already set off up the stairs. Cursing under his breath, Jeremy hauled himself through the window and hurried after them.

Vijay led them through a maze of dark passages. Alicia had thought to bring a torch, but it gave no more than a pencil-thin shaft of light. Jeremy stumbled and cursed behind her until she finally turned on him, shining the torch up into his face.

'For heaven's sake, Jeremy, shut up! You're making enough noise to wake the dead.'

He gave her a pained look and then continued in a sulky silence.

After another ten minutes, Alicia began to get the feeling that they were going round in circles, but Vijay's hunched shoulders did not invite questions. Finally, he signalled to them to stop.

'The studio is through there,' he whispered pointing at some large double doors, 'and down there are the galleries where the director and producer sit during the recording and where the lighting and sound are controlled, but we're heading for the Video Transfer room, where everything is recorded on tape.'

He led them down yet another set of stairs praying that he had got it right this time. He heaved a huge sigh of relief as he saw a sign saying VT, and pushed open the door.

VT was a cavernous room with small glass partitioned cubicles housing banks of monitors and large control panels along one side. Dark, brooding machinery covered with switches and dials took up the central floor space, while at the back of the room were shelves stacked high with tapes.

Alicia was overawed with the technology, and even Jeremy could not stop himself looking impressed.

'How on earth do you know what to do?' asked Alicia.

Vijay looked self important. 'Oh, it's easy,' he said airily, leading them into one of the cubicles. '*Forbidden Fruit* will be recorded tomorrow morning in the main studio, which is controlled from here. You can watch what is going on in the studio on the monitors up there.' He pointed to a bank of television screens. 'Vanessa and Fergus are planning to record their own private version of the programme starring themselves, tonight. But what Vanessa doesn't realise is that we can watch what they're doing in the studio from down here without them knowing, and we can record a second tape.'

Alicia gave Vijay a delighted kiss on the cheek. 'You're so clever, Vijay. Isn't he clever, Jeremy?'

Jeremy did not look as though he thought so.

Vijay shrugged nonchalantly and sat down in front of the control panel. He did not feel as confident as he sounded. He had plied a VT engineer with drink in order to get the information he needed but he had also drank rather a lot himself, and some of the later details were a little hazy. He glanced up at the clock on the wall.

'I think we'd better make ourselves scarce. Vanessa will be arriving soon.'

Vijay shepherded them to the back of the main room, where they crouched in the darkness behind a shelf stacked with tapes.

Although Vijay had said Vanessa was arriving soon, it seemed like hours to Alicia. As the minutes ticked by, she began to feel her determination ebbing away. What on earth were they doing there? Supposing they were caught? If she got arrested it could mean the end of her academic career. Was Vanessa worth it?

A shaft of light suddenly illuminated the gloom as the door was pushed open. Alicia crouched down almost to the floor, her heart thumping as though it would burst. She could feel, rather than see Jeremy and Vijay tensing on either side of her. Then she heard a familiar curt voice.

'Wait outside.'

There was the click of a light being switched on. Ignoring Jeremy's restraining grip, Alicia cautiously lifted her head and peered through a gap in the shelves, holding her breath. There was a figure bent over the control desk in the cubicle they had been in earlier. Alicia heard an exclamation of satisfaction and then the figure turned, and for one brief moment, she saw Vanessa's smiling face. It was enough.

As the room was plunged back into darkness and the door closed behind Vanessa, Alicia was filled by a cold sense of purpose. She pulled Vijay and Jeremy to their feet.

'Right,' she ordered. 'Let's get this show on the road.'

Twenty-Eight

• • •

'You promise there'll be no damage?' the security guard asked, as Vanessa came out of VT. 'It'd be more than my life's worth. The guv'nor would have my balls for breakfast.' He followed Vanessa down the corridor.

'I've already told you, there'll be no problems. Dr Archibald just needs some extra rehearsal time,' Vanessa snapped impatiently over her shoulder. 'Now isn't it about time you got back to the front desk?'

She stopped outside the dressing room where she had left Fergus. The guard hovered.

'We'll be about an hour. Just make sure no one, and I do mean no one, comes near the studio, or I'll be the one to have your balls, got it?' Vanessa held up a ten pound note.

The guard hesitated. His tongue flickered nervously over his lips as he balanced the possibility of discovery and dismissal against the certainty of the ten pound note. He reached for the money.

Vanessa waited for him to pocket it, and then watched until he had disappeared from sight at the end of the corridor. She had no idea what awaited her inside the dressing-room, but her instincts told her it would not be for the eyes of a security guard.

She had seen very little of Fergus since he had returned to London. She decided that she wanted her life back to normal, so she had booked him into a hotel and charged it to Right Pryce Productions. Philip had objected to the extra expense, but she avoided awkward questions by saying that the friend Fergus had been staying with had gone to Peru on a research trip.

Somewhat to her chagrin. Fergus had agreed to the arrangement without an argument, and had been quite content to sit in his hotel room drinking whisky and watching blue movies on cable television. The bill for the movies was mounting up, but as she pointed out to an increasingly irate Philip, this was one occasion when dirty movies could legitimately be put down on expenses as research.

She had delegated Rosie, the production assistant, to look after Fergus, and much to Vanessa's surprise, they were getting on rather well. Rosie clucked around him like a mother hen, declaring that all Fergus needed was a bit of what she insisted on calling 'TLC'. Fergus had meekly agreed to go with her to a hairdresser, and even for wardrobe fittings, although not with Damien.

When Fergus had turned up at the studios earlier, he looked almost presentable with his hair and beard cropped short, and wearing a tan sports jacket and trousers which actually fastened up somewhere approximating his waist.

He had also been carrying a large hold-all, which contained what he mysteriously described as his props for the evening. He insisted on going to a dressing room to get ready, and Vanessa decided to humour him.

Vanessa had been anticipating the evening more than she would admit. Since Fergus's departure, almost two weeks ago, she had not had much sex. A good looking cameraman had provided a momentary diversion while out on a shoot for the show, but while he had been willing, it had proved as predictable as it had been unsatisfying. If nothing else, Fergus could always be guaranteed to deliver satisfaction.

She knocked on the door and without waiting for an answer, went in.

Fergus was standing in front of a full-length mirror admiring himself. He was dressed in a scarlet corset, trimmed with black lace, black stockings and high-heeled shoes.

He twirled round. 'Well, what do you think?' he asked.

Vanessa wanted to laugh, but she couldn't. Most men would have looked ridiculous, but not Fergus. He looked brutish. The tightly-laced corset emphasised the massiveness of his chest and shoulders, the shiny red satin contrasting with the thick matted hair that covered his body. Even the high heels served to stress the sinewy strength of his legs.

'How . . . how did you find anything to fit you?' she asked faintly.

Fergus snapped one of his suspenders. 'There's a whole industry out there catering for transsexuals, transvestites and just plain little old cross-dressers. Look behind the lace curtains of one in three suburban semis and you will find a man itching to get into his wife's underwear – but not while she's wearing it. Marks & Spencer could make a killing selling men's lingerie instead of just plain underwear. Just think what a difference it would make at Christmas – no more socks.' Fergus grinned, but Vanessa didn't respond. He fluffed up the lace across his chest. 'It's rather fetching, don't you think? The only problem is the choice of colours, it's either basic black or red. I was looking for something a little more in the way of an autumnal shade.'

Vanessa managed a weak smile and sank down on to the narrow bed which was the only other furniture in the room, other than a dressing table and stool.

'You're not a . . .?' she asked uncertainly.

'Vanessa, Vanessa,' Fergus shook his head with mock

sorrow. 'You're just like all the rest, trapped in the narrow Victorian confines of what passes for sexuality in the late twentieth century. Look at nature. The male of the species is always the flamboyant sensualist, and in the past, fashion reflected this. Cod pieces, tights, wigs, face powder, lace, high heels, corsets; they were all part of a man's wardrobe, but now women see this as their sacred territory and feel threatened by men who want to explore the female side of their sexuality. It has always been thus. Do you know the story of Teiresias?'

Vanessa shook her head.

'Ah, the shortcomings of the modern education system. We have computers, but the ancient Greeks had wisdom. Teiresias was a prophet who struck two serpents in the act of sex. He killed the female and was instantly transformed into a woman. He remained a woman for seven years until he killed a male serpent, whereupon he became a man again. When called upon by Zeus to settle one of his many arguments with his wife, the goddess Hera, Teiresias declared that from his unique experience as both a man and a woman, women got far greater pleasure from sex than men. Zeus used this to justify his philandering, as he claimed that since he got less pleasure, he ought to get more sex. Hera, who was to say the least not amused, struck Teiresias blind.'

Vanessa shrugged. 'I thought we were just going to have a bit of sex.

Fergus snorted. 'And that about says it all. No, my dear Vanessa, we are not going to just have a bit of sex. We are each going to explore new sexual territories. I have already chosen mine, and I have taken the liberty of choosing one for you.'

He picked up his hold-all. Something inside clinked ominously. 'Lead the way, dear lady. I'm ready for action.'

Vanessa recovered herself. 'You're not walking round dressed like that. We might bump into a security guard. Cover yourself up,' she ordered, holding out a thin cotton robe that had been hanging behind the door.

Fergus shrugged and slipped it on. It didn't meet around his front and barely came to his knees. If anything, it made him look worse.

Vanessa looked around for something else but there was nothing. The room was bare. She would just have to pray that the security guard remained at his desk. She opened the door and looked up and down the corridor. It was empty. She tried to hurry Fergus through the building but his high heeled shoes made haste impossible. She heaved a sigh of relief when they reached the comparative safety of the studio.

'Wait here and don't move until I turn the lights on,' she ordered, leaving Fergus standing in the gloom.

As the studio was flooded with light, Fergus blinked and then began to roar with laughter.

The *Forbidden Fruit* set looked like a 1930s Hollywood version of heaven. Swathes of soft pink gauze were draped from ceiling to floor and rosy-cheeked cherubs cavorted among pink fluffy clouds, their chubby limbs entwined in what, on closer examination proved to be less than cherubic positions. On one side of the set a mock marble staircase curved upwards to nowhere and on the other stood a huge phallus-like tree around which was entwined a green serpent, a shiny red apple in its jaws.

In the middle of the set was a low couch, whose upholstered pink cushions were in the unmistakable shape of female genitalia.

'That's meant to be your consulting couch,' Vanessa called from the back of the studio, as she walked down between the rows of chairs.

'Freud couldn't have done it better,' he guffawed.

Vanessa waved her hand at the set. 'Hugo claims

it's a post-modernist, *faux-naïf* interpretation of sex, whatever that is.'

'It says a lot about the British psyche. It's sex dressed up and disinfected so that it doesn't look like sex,' snorted Fergus. 'The visual equivalent of a vaginal deodorant.'

He sat down on the couch and stroked the labia shaped cushions. 'But this sums up the cosy television chat show exactly. It's just perfect for a spot of mutual masturbation, don't you think?'

Vanessa began unbuttoning her blouse. 'Let's get on with it, shall we,' she said, briskly, stepping out of her skirt. 'Where do you want me, on the couch?' She stood naked in front of Fergus, her hands on her hips.

'My dear girl, haven't you been listening to me? Sex is not just some minor bodily function you can satisfy with a quick scratch. Nor is there just one simple physical route to satisfaction, or haven't you been reading the letters that have been coming in, either?'

Vanessa crossed her arms. 'Okay, if that's the way you want me to play it. What do you want me to do, dress up as a French maid?'

'Tsk tsk.' Fergus wagged his finger. 'Oh ye of little imagination. Fetch me my bag.'

Vanessa tossed her head impatiently and walked over to where Fergus had left his hold-all. She started to open it.

'Bring it here.' Fergus barked the command so sharply, Vanessa obeyed automatically.

'Good,' Fergus said approvingly, 'that was your first lesson. Tonight you must do anything and everything I tell you without question or you will be punished.'

He dug around in his hold-all and produced a leather mask and a large, metal-studded dog collar with a lead attached to it. 'Put these on,' he commanded.

Vanessa swallowed hard. The mask looked like

something from a medieval torture chamber. It had no hole for the eyes and a metal bit across the mouth.

'Look Fergus, we agreed to have a little fun, maybe a few games but there's no way I'm going to . . .'

'Scared?' Fergus challenged her, holding her gaze in his.

Vanessa looked away. 'No, of course not. Don't be ridiculous. I just don't think we have time for a Halloween party, that's all.'

Before Vanessa could protest, Fergus fastened the collar around her neck. He gave the lead a sharp tug. 'This time I won't punish you for disobeying me, but next time . . .' He pulled a cane out of the bag and swished it through the air.

Vanessa's eyes widened. 'You wouldn't dare!'

'The question, my dear Vanessa is, would you? I fear you have a jaded palate from too much tasteless, fast food sex, so I thought I might spice things up a little bit. Haven't you ever thought about inflicting pain on someone?'

Vanessa's eyelashes flickered.

'And what did that thought engender in you?' Fergus pulled the lead so that Vanessa was forced to look into his eyes. He smiled. 'Ah, just as I thought, pleasure. But the most exquisite pleasure comes after denial, so your second lesson is going to be submission. It will be a new experience for you, as will humiliation. You see, my dear Vanessa, you have nothing *I* desire, but I have the means to *your* pleasure here in my hand,' he swished the cane again, 'and here,' he indicated his crotch, 'and *you* are going to have to beg for them.'

He pointed at the floor. 'Get down on your hands and knees.'

Vanessa looked down. The floor hadn't yet been cleaned and painted for the recording and was thick with dust.

'But it's . . .'

'Down!' The cane whistled through the air.

Vanessa sank to her hands and knees.

Fergus held out the mask. Vanessa pulled it on and then tried to speak. Fergus bent down and pushed the bit between her teeth, silencing her. With a satisfied grin, he teetered off across the studio, tugging Vanessa along on all fours behind him.

Twenty-Nine
• • •

Alicia thoughtfully sipped her mug of tea and gazed out of the window. She was already dressed, though it was not even six-thirty in the morning. The garden below Zelda's flat was largely occupied by a huge oak tree, and what little of the rest of the garden Alicia could see, looked very overgrown, but she didn't suppose anybody in a building divided into flats like this would care about gardens. She wondered how her little garden back in Heartlands was looking. The roses were at their glorious best at this time of the year. There had been no rain for weeks, and she really should have been there to water them.

Alicia had not given much thought to Heartlands and her cottage, but seeing Vanessa and Fergus last night had reminded her of the home she had fled so unhappily almost two months ago.

She turned away from the window and looked at the video tape lying on Zelda's coffee table. It would have been much easier to have let Vijay hide it somewhere at the studios in readiness for today, but she had not wanted to let it out of her sight, at least not until absolutely necessary. Now she had the instrument of Vanessa and Fergus's downfall, she did not intend to let anything go wrong.

She thought she would be upset watching them having sex in the studio last night, but she had felt quite calm. Jeremy and Vijay, on the other hand, had very peculiar expressions on their faces until she produced a bag of popcorn. They relaxed after that, putting their feet up on the desk and munching handfuls of the stuff like children at a Saturday morning cinema show, laughing at Vanessa and Fergus's ridiculous antics. They had waited until Vanessa and Fergus left and then, emboldened by what they had seen, walked out of the front entrance past an open-mouthed security guard. Outside in the street they had linked arms and walked laughing to the nearest pub.

She had originally intended to send the tape to Vanessa's boss, but a remark by Vijay in the pub had given her another idea. For once, Jeremy had promptly agreed to her new plan. The sight of Vanessa and Fergus together had made him forget his earlier caution, but Vijay had taken a lot of persuading because it meant him taking more risks, although he eventually agreed. She just hoped that when he sobered up this morning, he would not change his mind.

Alicia finished her tea. She and Jeremy did not have to rendezvous with Vijay back at the studios for several hours, so they had time enough for a good fried breakfast. She intended to enjoy today and she couldn't do that if she was feeling hungry.

Gabriella swallowed the last of the handful of vitamin pills which she took in lieu of breakfast, and placed her satellite dish-sized sunglasses firmly on her nose. Mornings were not her best time.

'Darling! You look absolutely wonderful, fresh as a daisy,' Philip cooed, as she stepped from her taxi outside the Silver Screen Studios.

Gabriella avoided his embrace and proffered a single smooth cheek, which Philip meekly kissed. 'You look wonderful too, darling.'

Gabriella thought she had never seen Philip looking

so tired. There were bruise-like purple shadows under his eyes and his skin looked puffy and grey. Her skin, on the other hand, looked as near to a twenty-year-old's as two hours at the hands of a skilled make-up artist could render it.

The taxi driver, who had been holding the door for her, reached into his cab and picked up her black crocodile case.

'Can I carry this in for you, Miss Wolfe?' he asked eagerly.

'Philip will take it, won't you darling, and make sure you give him a nice large tip, I like to keep my fans happy.'

Gabriella swept her voluminous serape over her shoulder and left Philip to pay the disappointed taxi driver. By the time he had counted out the correct notes, Gabriella was already in reception. He scurried after her.

'I thought we'd have a read through of the script over coffee first. It will give you and Dr Archibald a chance to get acquainted, and then I thought we'd ...' he began.

'Philip darling, please,' Gabriella interrupted him. 'My biological time clock says I should still be asleep, so please don't rush me. First, I want to go to my dressing-room, then I'd like a few moments alone to compose myself and then, and only then, will I discuss the changes I want in the script.'

'Changes? But I thought we'd agreed ...'

'*Philip*, my dressing-room please.' It was a command that brooked no disagreement.

Philip led the way down the corridor and opened a door. 'I'm afraid this is the best we can offer,' he said.

Inside was a small room dominated by a large, brightly lit mirror and a dressing table, on which stood a vase containing a dozen red roses and an ice bucket with a bottle of champagne. A single bed, a chair, and a clothes rail with a few wire hangers dangling from it, completed the furnishing. Another door led to a bathroom.

Philip anxiously watched Gabriella's face as she looked around.

'Well, it isn't exactly Hollywood, is it darling, but the flowers are wonderful,' said Gabriella, picking up the gold embossed card which had been placed beside the vase. She smiled. 'From you, how sweet.'

She snapped a bloom off and tucked it into Philip's buttonhole and kissed him. 'For you, for luck. Now be a darling and wait outside just for a few minutes. There are times when a girl needs her privacy.'

She ushered him out of the door and locked it behind him before sitting down at the dressing table and opening her case. She took a silver flask out, unscrewed the top and took a long drink. Then she found a small silver pill box and placed two tiny pills on her tongue. Frankie, her hairdresser, had said they worked wonders for him, kept him bright-eyed and bushy-tailed all day long. She toasted herself in the mirror with the flask and drank some more brandy, before spraying her mouth with breath freshner. Then she checked her nose for shine and locked her case. After giving her hair one last pat, she opened the door.

'There, all better. Now, where were those people you wanted me to meet?' She gave Philip a radiant smile.

Philip straightened up. 'About those changes, I really do think . . .'

'You mentioned refreshment?'

Philip gave in and led the way to a large room on the next floor which was serving as the Right Pryce production office for the day of the recording. Rosie was sitting at a computer, playing with the keys, when they walked in. She jumped up and rushed forward.

'Oh, Miss Wolfe, how nice to see you again, it's so nice to have you back. Is there anything I can get you?

I've got tea or coffee and some Danish pastries or some jam doughnuts.'

'Thank you . . . er, dear.' Gabriella could never remember the name of Philip's production assistant. 'I'd just like a glass of mineral water with a slice of lemon. I don't like stimulants at this time of the morning.'

Rosie bustled out.

Gabriella dropped her script on to the table. 'Now, about this script, Philip darling. I can't possibly work with it, it simply *has* to go.'

Philip sank into a chair. He didn't trust himself standing up. 'Gabriella, darling. At this stage it would . . .'

But he was interrupted as the door swung open and Vanessa walked in smiling. She waved a cheery hand in their direction and made for the coffee pot. Philip wondered whether he was hallucinating, Vanessa never smiled. At least, not the way she had smiled just then. She looked almost *happy*.

Mug in hand, Vanessa turned. 'Have you read the script?' she asked.

'Yes, I have,' Gabriella replied, 'and as I was just saying to Philip, rarely have I been presented with such an incompet . . .'

'What Gabriella would like to say,' Philip hastily interrupted, 'is that she likes it, but thinks there should be a few small changes here and there. Purely stylistic, you understand.'

Any semblance of contentment melted from Vanessa's face. Her eyes narrowed and her lips became a thin red line.

Recognising the familiar danger signs, Philip intervened again. 'Perhaps we had better delay further discussion until Dr Archibald arrives. He will be here soon, won't he Vanessa? It's after nine.'

'I sent your little treasure, Heather, to collect him from his hotel. I'm sure she'll get him here on time.'

As Vanessa spoke, the door opened and Fergus, followed by a flustered Heather, came in.

'Top of the morning to ye all,' Fergus announced in a false Irish accent.

'Ah, Dr Archibald,' Philip said, getting up. 'I think it's about time you met our star, Miss Gabriella Wolfe. I'm sure you and she will work well together.'

Fergus made a sweeping bow before Gabriella and pressed the hand she held out, to his lips. 'How could I not work well with such a ravishingly beautiful woman? No, forgive me, a Venus. No mere mortal woman could be possessed of such incandescent beauty.' Fergus straightened up but held on to Gabriella's hand.

Gabriella looked coquettishly up at Fergus. 'My dear Dr Archibald, although I hope I may call you Fergus,' her deep husky voice lingered over his name. 'I'm sure our coupling will be one to remember.'

'Shall we get on with the read-through, the mutual fan club can wait until later,' said Vanessa savagely.

Fergus had not even glanced at her. After what had happened between them last night, she had been expecting some kind of reaction from him, but it was as though she did not exist. She glared at Gabriella, who ignored her, and pulled Fergus down to sit on the chair beside hers. She kept her hand on his arm.

'We really ought to know each other better if we are going to be working together.'

Rosie placed a glass of mineral water beside Gabriella, and a cup of coffee and two doughnuts beside Fergus. She dimpled at him. 'The coffee's got three sugars and lots of cream in it, just as you like it.'

Fergus gave her a friendly pat on her behind as she walked away. Rosie giggled.

Vanessa slammed her script down on the table. 'Shall we begin?'

'I think we had better wait for a moment, Vanessa,' Philip said, looking round. 'We're still missing two of our number.'

'Hugo and Vijay are in the building,' said Rosie, looking up from her computer. 'Hugo's down in the studio and I think Vijay's checking something in VT.'

'I think we should begin. They are both aware of our tight schedule today,' said Vanessa, impatiently opening her script. She looked at Gabriella. 'Would you like to begin?'

Gabriella carefully pushed an imaginary stray hair back into place and with another smile at Fergus, looked down at her script.

'Good evening,' she began, 'and welcome to *Forbidden Fruit*. A new show that is going to lift the lid off Britain's sexual fantasies.'

She stopped and looked up. 'Lift the lid off,' she repeated, 'hardly Shakespeare, is it?'

'And this is not the Globe theatre,' Vanessa retorted. 'So could we please forego the literary criticism until we reach the end of the script?'

Gabriella looked indignantly at Philip for support. He looked from one to the other, caught between them. 'Vanessa, I think perhaps you are being a little too abrasive,' he said placatingly. 'Gabriella is, after all, a very experienced presenter, and I'm sure we welcome her criticism.'

Gabriella smiled triumphantly at Vanessa.

'However, Vanessa does have a point, Gabriella,' Philip continued, 'so perhaps we should press on for the time being. I'm sure there will be plenty of time for adjustments later on.'

Gabriella sniffed loudly and began again, 'Good evening . . .'

'Good morning,' announced Hugo walking into the room.

'Aren't we just a little late?' said Vanessa caustically.

'Actually, *we* have been here since eight o'clock this morning, if we're counting,' Hugo replied tartly. 'There were a few problems with the set. Some idiots have been mucking around with the props, but I've sorted it out.'

Vanessa shuffled the pages of her script.

Hugo sat down and put one leg up on the table. 'It was a devil of a problem to get the crew to abandon their tea and tabloids this morning. I presume you've all seen this?' He casually tossed a newspaper across the table.

Philip reached over and picked it up. It was the *World on Sunday*.

The front page headline read: TV STAR IN SEX CHANGE SHOCKER! WOLFE IN SHEEP'S CLOTHING!

Underneath was a huge picture of Gabriella.

'Oh my God,' groaned Philip. The colour drained from his face and he slumped back in his chair.

Vanessa grabbed the paper. She burst into laughter. 'Is there some little thing you forgot to tell us, Gabriella?'

Gabriella glared at her. 'Give me that,' she demanded.

Vanessa held it away from her and began to read out loud:

'Glamorous TV chat show host, Gabriella Wolfe, who filled the gossip columns with her string of famous and infamous lovers in the 1980s, started off life as plain George Fox. When her British TV career took a nose-dive, she headed for the Continent where she became one of the first of the Euro satellite TV stars. Although she has recently returned to these shores to host a new late-night porn show, her home is now in Italy, where she keeps a whole stable of young Italian stallions, some of them as young as sixteen, to keep her regularly serviced.

'Turn to pages two and three for Gabriella's guide to the juiciest Italian meat-balls and to our middle pages for an exclusive interview with her ex-lover rock star, Wayne Warlock, who spills the beans on their steamy nights of passion. Wayne claims: she really foxed me! We also list twenty ways to spot a sex-change.'

Vanessa was jubilant. This was even better than she had hoped for.

'Shall I go on?' she asked.

Gabriella had turned white. 'The bastard,' she hissed, 'the dirty no-good, rotten little bastard.'

'I assume you're referring to the TV star's best friend Eddie Spittle,' Vanessa said. 'I thought you said you had him under control, Philip?'

Gabriella turned on Philip. 'Have you been speaking to him?' she demanded.

'No, of course not,' Philip protested indignantly. 'I merely agreed to give him the occasional little titbit about contestants on the show. I thought the publicity might help.'

'Then who's been talking to him?' Gabriella screeched.

'Well, it says here that *you* revealed all about your Italian toy boys in an exclusive interview with the said Eddie Spittle,' Vanessa said.

Gabriella nearly threw herself across the table and tore the newspaper from Vanessa's hands. 'But I never said anything about . . .' she frantically scanned the pages.

'You mean you agreed to an interview without consulting me?' Philip gasped.

'It was my agent's idea, he thinks I need a higher profile,' Gabriella said as she read. She dropped the newspaper on the table. 'As I thought, I didn't say

311

anything to him about my operation. I'll sue him and his newspaper until they beg for mercy.'

'But you can't,' wailed Philip. 'It will all come out about you and me and . . .' his voice tailed off.

'*You* and Gabriella . . .' exclaimed Vanessa. It was getting better by the minute.

'Philip was very kind to me when I was a young boy. He helped me to pay for the operation,' Gabriella said defiantly.

'So you knew Gabriella when she was a man?' Hugo asked incredulously.

'I was a mere boy at the time,' Gabriella interjected, 'and a very beautiful one at that.'

'Not nearly as beautiful as you are a woman,' said Fergus, patting her arm. Gabriella was beginning to interest him even more.

Vanessa looked across at Philip. He had suddenly aged. His hands trembled as he put some pills into his mouth.

'What about the show?' Rosie asked in a quavering voice, 'Surely we can't go ahead now?'

'Nonsense,' Vanessa said briskly. 'The publicity will make everyone in the country switch on. People love watching freaks.'

Gabriella stood up, her eyes glittering. 'I am not a freak. I am a woman and more of a woman than you'll ever be,' she said, her voice breaking. She swept out of the room.

'Rosie, get after her and make sure she doesn't leave the building,' snapped Vanessa.

Philip made a strangled noise and clutched his chest. Rosie and Heather rushed over to help him.

'It's nothing, it'll pass,' he gasped feebly waving a hand. 'Do as Vanessa says, Rosie, get after Gabriella and don't leave her alone.'

The telephone shrilled. Vanessa grabbed it. 'Yes?'

It was the receptionist. 'I have about thirty

journalists and photographers down here. They want to see Miss Wolfe.'

Vanessa thought quickly. 'Tell them no interviews before the show, but if they'd like to come to the recording, they're welcome. I'll send someone down with some tickets.' She put down the receiver. 'The vultures are gathering. They smell freshly killed meat, so let's give them something to gorge on. Heather, take about thirty tickets down to reception and then show them to the hospitality room.'

Heather was holding a glass of water to Philip's bloodless lips.

She looked indignantly at Vanessa. 'I think Philip needs a doctor.'

Philip motioned her away.

'I'll make sure he's all right, just get down to reception,' ordered Vanessa.

'But if I give them thirty tickets, that'll mean one of the coach parties won't be able to get in,' Heather protested.

'Refund their petrol or something. For heaven's sake woman, use your brain, but get rid of them,' yelled Vanessa shrilly.

Heather scowled at Vanessa but hurried out of the room.

'Well, what *are* we going to do about the show?' Hugo asked. 'We're rehearsing in fifteen minutes.'

'I'll go and talk to Gabriella,' croaked Philip, and with a superhuman effort, pulled himself to his feet. 'She knows what she has to do, she won't let the side down.'

'I'll go with you,' Hugo said, as Philip walked unsteadily out of the door.

Vanessa looked at Fergus. He was reading the article about Gabriella and chuckling to himself.

'What a remarkable woman, quite remarkable.'

Thirty
• • •

Philip knocked softly on Gabriella's dressing room. Rosie peered warily round the door, her eyes red-rimmed.

'Will she see me?' Philip asked in a low voice.

Rosie nodded and opened the door a fraction more to let him in but shook her head as Hugo tried to follow. Hugo shrugged and wandered off down the corridor, his electronic organiser in his hand.

'She's in the bathroom,' whispered Rosie, closing the door. 'I think it's just dreadful. What right have they to pry into somebody's private life, like that? Mother always thought Gabriella, Miss Wolfe, was wonderful. This will break her heart.' She checked her watch. 'Do you want me to stay? I should be in the studio preparing for the rehearsal.'

Philip shook his head. With a last sorrowful sniff, Rosie hurried out.

Gabriella emerged from the bathroom. Seeing Philip, she held out her arms and enveloped him.

'Philip darling, I knew you'd come to me in my time of trouble. You've always been there for me,' she said dramatically.

Philip freed himself from her embrace. 'Gabriella, I'm so sorry about all this, but whatever happens, you know you have my full and unconditional support.'

Gabriella sat down in front of the mirror and began retouching her make-up.

Philip sat on the edge of the bed and watched her, seeing her as he had first seen her all those years ago: a slim, pretty boy nursing the dregs of a shandy at the bar, a mixture of fear and daring in his large, black eyes. His hair had been long before it was fashionable, curling over his shoulders. Nineteen-year-old George Fox had been fresh down from Nottingham where the only escape from the mines was to work in a shoe factory.

Philip had been with two friends from Cambridge. They had all just passed their finals and were out to celebrate. Philip had wanted to go somewhere smart and drink champagne, but Gerald and Mark had wanted to go slumming, as they put it, so they headed for the wrong end of Notting Hill. They had been in four pubs already and had more than enough to drink by the time they stumbled into the one where George was drinking. Gerald and Mark were very raucous, and seemed unconcerned about the angry looks that their Cambridge accents and loud comments about the working classes were causing. Philip had matched them drink for drink, but he was not too drunk to sense that their presence in the pub was not welcome. When Mark had insisted on yet another round, he had been glad to escape their company for a moment and go to the less-crowded end of the bar to order some more drinks. It was there that George was sitting, apart from the other drinkers.

They had made eye contact, but both looked quickly away. Not daring to believe what he had seen, Philip looked back. This time they held each other's gaze for what seemed like a long time.

When he returned to the table with the drinks, Gerald looked across at him. 'Fancy a bit of rough, do you?' he asked in a voice that could be heard all over the bar. 'Well, he's certainly pretty enough, although I'd keep my socks on if I was you. You never know what you could catch in a dump like this.'

Philip had tried to leave, but found his way suddenly barred by two men. He was no fighter and backed away, but Gerald and Mark had been too drunk or maybe too arrogant, and had lashed out at the men now surrounding them.

As the fight spilled across the bar, Philip had felt a hand on his arm guiding him to a back exit. He had not stopped to think what might be out there, but when he stepped into a narrow side street, he was face to face with George.

Without speaking, they had raced down the street together, and kept running until they had put enough distance between themselves and the pub. Panting, Philip had tried to thank his rescuer.

'It was nothing. If you grew up where I did, you had to be either very good at fighting or very good at ducking trouble, and I have no intention of getting my nose broken for the sake of a pint of beer.'

George had smiled at him and Philip felt his heart lurch.

He had not wanted George to have the operation, but when he realised that the boy was prepared to go to a cut-price, back street butcher, he had paid for the best surgeon money could buy.

There had never been anyone else for him, and Gabriella knew that, but Philip could never love a woman in the way he could love a man.

It was George's dark eyes that looked questioningly at Philip in the mirror.

'Are you going to go ahead with the recording?'

'Well, you know what they say about show business,' Philip said, summoning up a wan smile. 'And as long as this is my show, I say it must go on.'

Gabriella looked concerned. 'You mean there's a chance you may no longer be in charge?'

'No, of course not, this is my company.'

'But what about your backers and that awful moral majority lot, the committee for whatever?'

'They don't have legal sanction over who appears on television, at least not yet,' Philip said, 'and my backers will keep backing me as long as I earn them profits. The awful irony is, although I don't sanction Vanessa's terminology, she's right you know. People will now turn on in their millions to see you.'

Gabriella turned to look directly at Philip. 'Then I'll give them a show to remember. I'm not ashamed of who I am. The only freak was that boy George, a woman trapped inside a man's body. But he's gone and I'm who I really should be. How many people can say they've been to hell and back and survived? And I've done more than just survive, I've become a successful and beautiful woman, desired by some of the richest and most powerful men in the world and a role model for other women. Not bad for little old George from Nottingham, eh?'

She turned back to the mirror.

'Run along now, Philip darling, I want to make sure I look my best, even if it is only for the rehearsal.'

Philip stood behind Gabriella, his hand on her shoulder. Their eyes locked for a moment, and then he kissed her lightly on the cheek.

'I know what you're going to say, darling,' Gabriella said, 'you still love me. I know. Off you go and tell Rosie to make sure wardrobe and make-up are ready for me directly after the rehearsal. I intend to knock everyone's little cotton socks off, now shoo.'

Outside the door, Philip hastily wiped away a tear, as Heather walked past clutching an armful of wine bottles.

'What are those for?'

317

'Miss High and Mighty is having an impromptu press conference in hospitality. She sent me out to buy some more wine. The gentlemen of the press have already drunk what was there. Can't you stop her?' Heather appealed.

Philip considered this. Yes, he could, but what good would it do? The situation couldn't get any worse.

'Tell Vanessa to keep it short as we have to rehearse,' he said wearily. 'I'll see her in the gallery.'

Heather watched Philip walk away. His shoulders were stooped and he looked as though he had lead weights in his shoes. As bosses went, he wasn't so bad, she thought, gripping the wine bottles tightly and kicking open the door to the hospitality room with her Doc Martens. Inside, Vanessa was trying to speak.

'Ladies and gentlemen, please.'

The noise slowly subsided.

'Ladies and gentlemen,' Vanessa began again. 'I would like to introduce myself. I am Vanessa Swift, producer and originator of *Forbidden Fruit*, the new television series which will break every television taboo, give Disgusted of Tunbridge Wells a heart attack and make your hair, and a lot more besides, stand on end.'

There were hoots of loud laughter.

'For a start, how many TV programmes are presented by glamorous transsexuals, or at least, how many are presented by people who admit they are?'

The laughter was even louder at this.

'Now, I know you have all come to meet Gabriella Wolfe, but she will not be giving any interviews until after the show. However, there are seats available for all of you if you would like to watch the recording, although I must insist that no-one takes any photos while they are in the studio. I promise you, anyone doing so will be forcibly ejected.'

'By gorgeous George?' someone shouted.

There was general laughter again.

'Now before I go, are there any questions?'

'When will the series be broadcast?' asked someone.

'In the very near future. We are in negotiation with all the major networks at the moment.' Or at least we will be after this, Vanessa thought, looking around the room.

'Did you know about Gabriella before you hired her as a presenter?' someone called.

'Of course,' Vanessa lied smoothly. 'Her past in no way detracts from her professionalism. If the entertainment industry started discriminating on the grounds of who had submitted themselves to the surgeon's knife in search of beauty, we'd have to get rid of an awful lot of people.'

'Did you plant the story to get publicity for your show?' a voice called from the back.

'Absolutely not. Gabriella's gender has never been an issue. Since I first conceived and developed the idea for *Forbidden Fruit*, I have always known that the show would generate more than enough publicity on its own merits, as I am sure you will see in approximately an hour's time. So if you will excuse me, I must go and prepare for the rehearsal. In the meantime, please avail yourselves of our hospitality.'

Vanessa pushed her way to the drinks table, where a harassed Heather was trying to open bottles of wine and pour drinks at the same time.

'Keep them drinking,' Vanessa hissed. 'I want them happy as little skylarks when they write their reviews.'

Outside the door she saw Vijay's back disappearing down the corridor. Vanessa yelled after him.

He reluctantly turned round.

'Where have you been all morning?' Vanessa demanded. 'You certainly know how to make yourself scarce when there's work to be done.'

319

'I've been looking after our guests,' Vijay protested indignantly.

'Guests?' Vanessa said blankly.

'You know, the little people without whom we would have no show. The postman from Sheen who wants to do a banana split, the couple from Dartford who want to play master and pupil, and then there's . . .'

'All right, all right, you've made your point,' Vanessa interrupted irritably. Vijay seemed less cowed than usual, and if she was not mistaken, there had been a touch of sarcasm in his voice. 'Are they all here and ready to rehearse?'

'Oh, they're all here, it's Fergus we're missing.'

'But I told Heather to look after him,' Vanessa said angrily.

'You also told her to look after thirty tabloid journalists.'

Vanessa glared at Vijay. She was right, there was something openly defiant about his manner.

She jabbed a finger at him. 'Now look here . . .'

Just at that moment, Rosie rushed past, a clipboard in one hand and a stopwatch in the other.

'Have you seen Fergus?' Vanessa called after her.

'No, sorry,' she called over her shoulder. 'And Hugo says can everyone get to the studio immediately, we're running very late.'

Vijay plunged his hands in his pockets and strolled off.

'You could try the pub over the road. I think I heard him muttering something about having a quick one before the rehearsal,' he said, before disappearing round the corner.

'Shit,' said Vanessa, and tore off after Rosie.

In the gallery, Hugo and Rosie were busy checking the monitors and giving instructions to the studio floor.

320

Philip was sitting behind them. He tapped his watch as Vanessa came in. She shrugged.

'Someone had to do some damage limitation with the press,' she said, sitting next to him.

'Is everything under control now?' Philip asked anxiously.

'No problem,' Vanessa said firmly. 'I've left Heather oiling the wheels of publicity, so to speak, and then we'll just roll them into the studio for the recording. I've promised them Gabriella afterwards, so I hope she'll be able to hack it.'

Philip bridled. 'Gabriella is a trooper, she'll deliver the goods.'

'Can we get everyone on the studio floor, ready to rehearse pronto,' Hugo barked into his microphone. 'And please remember, the guests keep their clothes on this time, this is just a run-through for autocue and positions.'

Rosie looked across at him. 'The floor manager says they can't find Dr Archibald.'

'Then get a bloody search party out,' snapped Hugo angrily. 'If he's not here in two minutes then we'll go without him. Gabriella will just have to cover for him. We do know where *she* is, don't we?'

There was the sound of applause from the studio and one of the monitors showed Gabriella smiling graciously. As she walked across the set, studio technicians patted her on the back or shook her hand.

'Bloody marvellous,' snorted Hugo, 'they love her.'

The phone chirruped softly and Rosie picked it up. She listened for a moment and then turned to Vanessa, one hand over the mouthpiece. 'Reception says there's a drunk making a fuss down there. Claim's he's part of the show. Should they get security to throw him out?'

'Why bother me with stupid details, of course they should throw him out,' snapped Vanessa. Then an unpleasant thought struck her. 'No wait, I think I'd better go down.'

'I'm going to begin this rehearsal in two minutes, whether or not you're here,' warned Hugo, as Vanessa went out.

Swearing under her breath, Vanessa stopped at the doors leading into the reception area and peered through the glass panel. A dishevelled-looking Fergus was standing like a prisoner between two nervous security guards. She pushed open the doors. 'It's all right, you can let him go. I'll vouch for him,' she ordered.

The immaculate blonde receptionist wrinkled her nose. 'He was extremely rude when I asked him for his security pass, and I have orders not to let anyone in unless . . .'

'I'll take full responsibility for him,' Vanessa interrupted impatiently. 'He does have a pass, he's already been through here once today.'

'That doesn't make any difference. I can't be expected to remember every face that comes through those doors, and I have my orders,' the receptionist said primly. 'I'm not to let anyone . . .'

Vanessa ignored her and went over to Fergus who was swaying from side to side.

'Bloody gestapo,' he muttered, looking up at one of the guards who had the pimply skin of late adolescence, and whose skinny frame looked as though it would blow over in a sudden gust of wind. 'It's a bloody police state, that's what it is.'

He saw Vanessa and tried to straighten up. 'Tell these stormtroopers I'm all right. That wine young Heather was serving was piss awful, so I just popped out for a decent dram of whisky.'

Vanessa stood in front of him, hands on her hips. Fergus had drunk more than one dram of whisky by the look in his eyes. 'You no good son-of-a-bitch. If you ruin my big chance, I'll . . .'

But before she could continue, a large middle-aged woman in a loud black and white check suit marched up to reception. Obediently following her sensible court heels were a heavy-footed man in a pin-striped suit, and a tall, thin man with an apologetic smile.

The woman planted her large handbag down on the reception desk as though claiming it for some imperial power. '*I* am Mrs Mildred Proudfoot, and this is Sir Norman Fluck and the Reverend Basil Grimshaw. We are here to see Philip Pryce,' she announced in a voice born to command.

'Look at the behind on that one,' said Fergus loudly. 'Have you ever seen such a magnificent pair of buttocks?'

Before Vanessa could stop him, Fergus had lurched forward and grasped a handful of outraged female flesh.

Thirty-One
• • •

Vijay slunk round the corner of the building and into the alleyway where he had arranged to meet Alicia and Jeremy. It was the same alley in which they had met the evening before. He was late for the rendezvous because his way out through reception had been barred by the irate figures of Vanessa, Sir Norman Fluck and a man and woman he had not recognised. An unusually subdued Fergus had not been part of the altercation. He was standing to one side nursing what appeared to be an injured eye.

Peering through the glass-panelled door which led into reception, Vijay had not been able to catch everything that was going on, but it had become clear that Fergus's wounded eye had been inflicted by the handbag which the woman in the loudly checked suit was clutching to her formidable bosom, and not by the rather large fist Sir Norman kept flourishing.

Vijay had been forced to retreat into the ladies toilet when the still vociferous Sir Norman and his party had been shepherded past by a harrassed looking Heather, closely followed by stony-faced Vanessa and a moaning Fergus. He had waited several more minutes before putting his head round the door to check that everyone had gone. He was meant to be looking after the guests during the rehearsal, but as they were already running nearly half an hour late, he was hoping that in the confusion, no one would notice he was missing for a few minutes.

It was with an almost overwhelming sense of relief that Vijay looked up and down the alley and saw that there was no-one there. They had all had too much to drink last night and had made some crazy plans. Like him, Alicia and Jeremy must have woken up this morning and realised they had been foolish, but at least he had kept his side of the bargain and turned up, so they could not accuse him of letting the side down. Vijay turned to go back into the studios, but he found the end of the alley barred by two figures. His heart did not so much sink, as go into freefall without a parachute.

The two figures advanced towards him. Vijay backed against a wall.

'You came then,' he said lamely, as they stood in front of him.

Alicia held out the videotape. Vijay stared at it for a moment, his hands still in his pockets, then he looked up, a mute appeal in his eyes. But he saw no mercy in the hazel green eyes that gazed back into his, only implacable determination. He held out his hand unwillingly.

'Have you got us tickets for the show?' demanded Alicia, as Vijay tucked the tape inside his shirt.

Vijay nodded. 'It was very difficult, all the spare tickets and even some of the allotted ones have been given to some journalists who've turned up, something to do with Gabriella.'

If he had hoped that this might deter Alicia, he was wrong. A look almost bordering on ecstasy crossed her face.

'*Journalists!*' She grabbed Vijay's arm, her fingers digging into his flesh. 'You will do it, won't you? You promise?'

He nodded reluctantly, rubbing his arm. Then he

dug into his pocket and took out the two tickets he had begged from Heather.

'The audience will be allowed in after the rehearsal at about 12.15. You will be careful, won't you? If Vanessa sees you she might guess something is up.'

In answer, Alicia and Jeremy donned wrap-around sunglasses and baseball caps. Vijay grinned despite himself, and then turned their caps around so that the peaks faced backwards.

'That's the way to wear them,' he said.

Jeremy grasped Vijay's hand. 'Good luck, old man,' he said warmly, 'we're depending on you.'

Then Alicia hugged Vijay and kissed him on the lips. 'I think you're being very brave. Thank you.'

With a last wave, Vijay sprinted back into the building as bravely as he could. He had a dangerous mission, but he didn't intend to let them down. He would make his move after the rehearsal was over, which should be in about half an hour.

Philip mopped his face with his handkerchief and straightened his tie, then took several deep breaths to steady himself. There was no need to panic, the rehearsal could have been worse.

Fergus had fallen over twice, but anyone unfamiliar with a studio could trip over camera cables. And lots of people got so nervous before a performance that they threw up. When he had been producing arts programmes for the BBC, he had interviewed several leading actors who said it happened to them all the time. At least Fergus had thrown up in a corner where nobody could see and not over a vital part of the set. The assistant floor manager had been a bit upset, but luckily she had a spare pair of shoes.

Anyway, it wasn't like the old days, they weren't going out live, just in front of an audience which now consisted mainly of tabloid journalists.

Philip's heart did a funny little somersault. He took another tablet.

'You can come in now, darling,' Gabriella's voice bade him.

He smoothed his hair and opened her dressing-room door.

'What do you think?' she asked, holding out her arms and executing a stately twirl.

Gabriella had changed from her black rehearsal clothes into a peacock blue, shot silk tunic and voluminous harem pants. Her hair had been swept up into a turban of embroidered blue and gold silk, and around her neck she wore a many layered oriental gold necklace.

Philip stared. He had never seen her looking so beautiful.

'Well, say something, darling. I thought a touch of the Kama Sutra would be appropriate. You don't think I've gone over the top, do you?' Gabriella asked, slipping an egg-sized lapis lazuli ring on to her finger.

'You look absolutely ravishing,' Philip managed at last.

Gabriella rewarded him with a radiant smile. 'Let's go and face the vultures who want to pick over my bones. I intend to show them there's plenty of life in me yet.'

Philip held out his arm, and Gabriella slipped her hand through, giving him a reassuring squeeze.

'Lead on, dear friend, I'm as ready as I'll ever be.'

Philip brushed away another tear and attempted to compose his face in the semblance of an answering smile, but it curdled on his lips as an anguished bellow came from the next dressing room. It sounded like the death agonies of a large animal, but the string of curses which followed were distinctly human.

Philip gripped Gabriella's arm tightly and propelled her along the corridor like a man possessed. Whatever was happening in the other dressing room, he didn't want to know.

Behind them, Fergus gasped for breath as Vanessa let him up from the basin of cold water in which she had been holding him face-down.

'Damn it, woman, you could drown a man like that,' he said, trying to catch his breath.

'Don't tempt me,' warned Vanessa, and twisted her fingers in his hair.

Fergus winced. 'I'm sober, I promise you, there's no need for any more water.'

Vanessa reluctantly released her hold and let Fergus straighten up. She thrust a towel at him and he slumped into a chair and dried his face. He winced again as he touched the large purple bruise that was beginning to form near his eye.

'What is it with you women? *You* try to drown me and that other harridan nearly took out my eye. I think I need to see a doctor.'

Vanessa unsympathetically twisted his face towards her so she could take a look at him.

'You need nothing of the sort. It's only a little bruise. I'll go and get the make-up girl, she'll cover it with a bit of foundation.'

Vanessa turned to go. Fergus reached out and caught her arm.

'Don't take this the wrong way but I need a drink.'

Vanessa peeled his fingers from her arm. 'No way,' she said firmly.

'I need a whisky or I can't go on,' pleaded Fergus hoarsely.

Vanessa looked at him. His eyes were like two black holes and his normally florid complexion was white. One small whisky would either kill or cure him. Either way, she'd won.

'All right,' she relented, 'I'll see if there is anything

left in hospitality. But don't move from here. I'm going to send the make-up girl in, you look bloody awful.'

Fergus winced again as Vanessa slammed the door behind her. He mopped his face with the towel, but this time he was damp with cold sweat rather than cold water. Someone should have warned him about the studio lights. How was he to know they would have that effect on half a bottle of wine and a few double whiskies? And that wallop from that woman had probably given him concussion, which was why he had double vision and had tripped over. He could probably sue her for assault with a deadly weapon. He groaned and closed his eyes. The room had started to do an Irish jig.

Mrs Proudfoot hooked her deadly weapon firmly over her arm and looked around. 'Well, Sir Norman, what are we going to do?'

They were standing in the centre of the hospitality room which was now empty of journalists. It was littered with bottles, plastic cups and half-eaten sandwiches studded with stubbed out cigarettes.

But Sir Norman was oblivious to the debris around him; he had eyes only for Mrs Proudfoot. Never had he seen such a magnificent woman. She was indeed an Amazon warrior.

'Mrs Proudfoot . . . Mildred. I just feel I ought to say how much I admired the way you handled the situation out there, it was truly splendid. I would of course have been happy to defend your honour, but I realise that you are a woman with true British fighting spirit.'

Mrs Proudfoot inclined her head and smiled graciously. But Basil Grimshaw, whose movements had been becoming increasingly more agitated, suddenly spoke. 'Although I recognise the grievous nature of the provocation, I do feel that it behoves those of us in a position of influence to act in a less precipitous manner. After all, the Good Book says that we should turn the other cheek . . .' He stopped as the door burst open and Vanessa rushed into the room.

'Look here,' protested Sir Norman, angrily advancing towards her. 'This just isn't good enough, young woman. Some flibbertigibbet of a young secretary abandoned us here hours ago. I want to know what's going on. I'll have you know that neither I nor my colleagues appreciate being treated in this off-hand manner.'

'It doesn't surprise me in the least, Sir Norman,' said Mrs Proudfoot primly. 'Not after that display of lewd drunkenness we experienced downstairs in reception. Just look at this place,' she made a sweeping gesture, 'it looks as if an orgy has taken place.'

'I'm afraid we had some tabloid journalists in here, and they're not house-trained yet,' said Vanessa, hastily checking discarded whisky bottles to see if any remained. Fergus was her priority. Philip would have to deal with these people. It had been his idea to invite them.

'Desperate are you, my dear?' asked Mrs Proudfoot witheringly.

'One of our guests needs a drink for medicinal purposes,' Vanessa said, holding another bottle up to the light. It had a few mouthfuls left. She checked a plastic cup for cigarette butts and poured the remaining whisky into it:

'I'll send someone down to sort you out in a moment,' she said as she left the room. When she got back to his dressing room, Fergus was staring belligerently into the mirror as a make-up girl dusted his face with a large powder puff. He cheered up at the sight of the whisky.

'Like water to a dying man,' he said, gulping it down.

'More like water to a drowning man,' Vanessa retorted and glanced at her watch. It was nearly time

330

for the recording to begin. She pointed a long menacing finger at Fergus.

'Don't move from this room until the floor manager comes to collect you.' She hurried out.

Minutes later, Vanessa pushed her way through the heavy doors into the gallery, which had now taken on the hushed tense atmosphere of a recording. Hugo and Rosie were looking at the bank of monitors and checking the last minute preparations on the studio floor, occasionally murmuring instructions into the microphones which connected them to the studio and to all the other control centres in the building. Beside them, a vision mixer was making amendments to her script.

Vanessa sat down beside Philip and watched the monitors for a moment or two. Then she touched his arm.

'By the way, Philip darling, what were you planning to do with those dreadful committee people?'

Philip clapped his hand to his head, 'Oh my god, I forgot all about them. Where are they?'

'In hospitality, and not in a very congenial mood.'

Philip leaned forward. 'Rosie dear, can you organise someone to bring them up here at once, please?'

Rosie issued the request through her microphone.

Philip cleared his throat. 'Before they arrive, I'd like to say something to you all.' He stood and straightened his jacket.

Hugo looked irritated at this interruption, but sat back and crossed his arms. Rosie turned around in her chair.

Philip clasped his hands together. 'I like to think of my production team as a family, and that like a family, we work together, laugh together and sometimes cry together. If we argue, it is only because we want the best for the show. I'd like to say that I think you have all done a wonderful job so far, and that as a family, we must pull together this afternoon. Gabriella has given me her assurance that she will go out there and give them hell, and I know we will all be rooting for her.' His voice shook and he paused.

Rosie reached out and squeezed his hand. Philip gave her a wan smile.

'It's at times like this I know I work in the best industry in the world, because I know we all care about each other. We're a team, so let's show those people out there what we can do.'

Philip sat down and loudly blew his nose.

Moments later, Sir Norman Fluck, Mrs Proudfoot and Basil Grimshaw were ushered in.

Philip tucked his handkerchief into his pocket and leaped to his feet again.

'Welcome, welcome,' he said with enforced cheerfulness. 'Let me introduce you to my production team: this is Hugo, my immensely talented director, Rosie my right hand and indispensable production assistant, Caroline our vision mixer for today, and the driving force behind the show, Miss Vanessa Swift.'

With a curt nod of acknowledgement, Sir Norman advanced on Philip, a thunderous look on his face, but with a surprisingly nimble manoeuvre, Mrs Proudfoot stepped in front of him.

'Mr Pryce, I'd like to say that never, in all my life have I been so insulted as I was . . .'

Hugo leant back in his seat and interrupted her. 'I'm sorry, but I'm going to have to ask you to take your seats and not to speak from now on, we're ready to record.'

'We'll have plenty of time to talk afterwards,' whispered Philip as they all sat down. 'But I am afraid that rather like the captain of a ship, Hugo has the power of life and death over us in here and if we speak once the recording begins, he'll make us walk the plank.'

'As far as I'm concerned, this is a *sinking* ship, Mr Pryce,' Mrs Proudfoot hissed. 'Not only was I attacked

332

by some bearded sex maniac in your lobby, but while I was waiting in your so-called hospitality room, I discovered that your programme is to be presented by a pervert.'

She brandished a copy of the *World on Sunday* at Philip. 'It's an absolute disgrace, an affront to all right-minded people. You can't possibly go ahead with that . . . that *woman* on the show.'

'Live and let live, Mrs Proudfoot,' whispered Grimshaw, leaning forward. 'The good Lord taught us to be tolerant of sinners. This poor woman is obviously a tormented soul.'

'Rubbish,' snapped Sir Norman loudly, and then remembered himself. 'It isn't a question of tolerance, Reverend Grimshaw, but a question of public morals. The church must take a stand on such issues.'

'Sir Norman is right. This isn't a question of sin but of perversion and unnatural practices. I demand you put a halt to this travesty right now, Mr Pryce,' Mrs Proudfoot demanded her voice rising.

Hugo leant back in his chair. 'If you must have an ecclesiastical debate, can you please leave the room until after the recording.'

Mrs Proudfoot flushed angrily and lapsed into a festering silence.

Hugo spoke into his microphone, 'Places everyone and good luck.'

Rosie held up her stopwatch and began the countdown.

Thirty-Two
• • •

'Good evening and welcome to *Forbidden Fruit*, the show that will be taking you, the audience, into hitherto forbidden territory,' Gabriella announced smilingly into the camera. 'The territory that all our minds inhabit when we allow them to wander off into the realms of sexual fantasy.'

The camera pulled back into long shot to reveal her sitting on the couch beside Fergus, who looked suitably solemn.

Vanessa stared hard at the monitor. Fergus looked surprisingly good on screen. The camera seemed to like his dark, demonic features. Even his barely concealed bruise looked part of his character.

'I'm Gabriella Wolfe, and together with psychologist Dr Fergus Archibald, I will be guiding you through the uncharted territory of your minds. What you might call the final frontier.'

The audience clapped wildly, urged on by the floor manager.

'They both look terrific, don't they?' Philip whispered to Vanessa. 'I think we're on our way.' The knuckles of Philip's hands were white where he was gripping the arms of his chair.

Gabriella turned to Fergus, languidly crossing her legs. 'You're an expert on these matters, Dr Archibald. Tell me, are sexual fantasies important or are they just a harmless way of passing the time as we wash the dishes, work on the assembly line or ride on top of a bus?'

Vanessa held her breath. This bit was unscripted. Fergus could ruin the whole show if he got it wrong. He had adamantly refused to use the autocue after stumbling over it in rehearsal.

He bestowed an authoritative smile at the camera.

'Well Gabriella, I think it's about time we took our fantasies more seriously. My exhaustive research has shown that our fantasies reveal more about our true desires than we would like to admit.'

'You mean, if we fantasise about, say, wanting to run naked through the supermarket and make love on the check-out counter while other shoppers look on, this really does say something about our sexual preferences, rather than we've just discovered Sainsbury's are doing a special offer on our favourite chocolate biscuits?'

The audience laughed loudly.

'Absolutely,' said Fergus. 'The animal world struts its stuff openly for all to see. Look at the sexual displays of even the most common garden bird. They understand exhibitionism is an essential part of sexual interaction, but human beings consider it taboo and suppress it, yet we have a deep need to flaunt ourselves in public; that's why so many fantasies have the common element of exhibitionism in them. We are, after all, only animals ourselves. However high tech our society becomes, we still have the same basic needs as other animals, like food and f . . .' Fergus winked theatrically at the camera, '. . . er, sex.'

There was a chuckle from the audience.

Philip leaned across to Vanessa. 'See how right I was about Dr Archibald? He's a natural.'

Gabriella stood up and walked to centre stage. 'For

the time being at least, thank you very much, Dr Archibald.'

The audience dutifully applauded, urged on by the floor manager.

'Please hurry, Mr Beasley, you're on first,' Vijay urged through the dressing room door. 'And please keep your underpants on until we get to the studio.'

'All I was told I had to do was powder a few noses,' grumbled the make-up girl, who was waiting with Vijay in the corridor. 'I've just seen to one of your guests who wanted me to help him put body make-up all over and I do mean *all* over.' She rolled her eyes. 'I'm going to ask for danger money next time.'

Vijay looked at his watch and then raised his hand to knock again, but the door opened to reveal a small skinny man in his late forties, wearing an oversized pair of bright yellow boxer shorts patterned with red hearts.

The make-up girl suppressed a giggle.

'From an admirer,' Beasley announced with injured pride. 'I promised to wear them for luck.'

The make-up girl produced her powder puff. 'I need to eliminate shine on all parts of your body which are going to be exposed, Mr Beasley.'

Beasley clapped his hands together delightedly. 'With that? Oh, bliss!'

'Perhaps you should just stick to his nose or something,' Vijay said hurriedly, 'he's due in the studio any minute now.'

Beasley looked crestfallen. He put his hand up to his head.

'Could you at least do something about my bald patch? I'd hate anyone to notice it.'

The make-up girl rolled her eyes at Vijay again and then followed Beasley back into the dressing-room. Vijay waited outside. He had managed to slip down into VT just after the rehearsal was over. Luckily, the

VT engineers were taking a tea break and complaining about the way Hugo kept changing his instructions, so no-one had noticed him. He had managed to switch the tapes, but there was still a chance that someone might notice. It was too late to do anything about it now. He stuck his head round the dressing room door.

'Mr Beasley, you're on next.'

'And now for our first guest who, as Dr Archibald so aptly pointed out, wants to make an exhibition of himself,' Gabriella announced. 'Leonard Beasley is a postman from Petts Wood in Kent, and his fantasy . . . well, I think I'll let you see for yourselves. All I will say is that it's the perfect way to begin this very first edition of *Forbidden Fruit*.'

The cameras mixed through to a giant banana standing upright against a tropical green background. Four girls clad only in tiny bikinis shaped like banana leaves stood posed around it. The audience tittered with anticipation as the stage began to revolve, and the girls each slowly peeled a portion of the banana skin to reveal a beatifically smiling Leonard Beasley. His hands were in front of him, but from the way they were moving, it was not to protect his modesty.

Philip stared in horror at the monitor, beads of sweat breaking out on his forehead. He leaned forward. 'Can't you do something?' he whispered desperately to Hugo.

'Any suggestions?' Hugo retorted.

Philip sat back and mopped his face. Perhaps no one else had noticed. But as one of the cameras panned round for audience reactions, it was clear they had. He looked at the committee members. They at least seemed oblivious. Philip crossed his fingers. It would soon be over, as long as none of the cameras went into close-up.

But as the music swelled to a tumescent climax, Mrs Proudfoot suddenly sat bolt upright and pointed at one of the monitors.

'Sir Norman, that man is . . . is . . .' she spluttered.

Hugo held up his hand to silence her. 'Get ready everyone,' he said into the microphone, 'I want no cock-ups with this one. Wait for it . . . wait for it . . .'

The stage revolved to bring Beasley back full frontal to the audience.

'Now!' barked Hugo, and the lights dimmed except for one illuminating Beasley's face and chest, which were now streaked with sweat, his face contorted. He uttered a strange guttural sound, and then the spotlight went off.

'Hold it . . . hold it . . . and . . . camera one!' ordered Hugo.

The cameras switched back to a smiling Gabriella.

'Why a banana, Dr Archibald?'

'The banana is perhaps the most priapic of fruits,' replied Fergus. 'Its shape is unashamedly phallic and, when a bunch, it resembles a hand, all the better to touch and feel with.'

The audience tittered.

'And it reveals its nakedness so easily. It has no inhibitions. Unlike other fruits, which cling to their skins like born-again virgins, a banana is made for peeling.'

The audience laughed appreciatively.

An assistant floor manager rushed over to Vijay who was waiting off-stage. She grabbed him by the arm.

'You've got to get that man off the studio floor, he's just sitting there staring into space,' she hissed.

'But that's your job,' Vijay protested. He had been craning his neck trying to see where Alicia and Jeremy were sitting in the audience, but he couldn't see either of them.

'Not likely,' the floor manager said pulling him across the studio floor. 'Keep the applause going,' she muttered into her talkback, 'the floor isn't clear yet.'

Vijay looked down at Beasley who was sitting in the

centre of the banana skin in a dreamlike trance, smiling happily to himself. Vijay tapped him on the shoulder.

'That was wonderful,' sighed Beasley and looked up. 'How was it for you?'

As Vijay hurried the beaming postman away, Gabriella was introducing the next part of the show.

'And now for a short film about a woman who is sent into a frenzy of desire by this.' She held up a can of whipped cream and pressed the button.

As rehearsed, the camera went into close-up on the can, but instead of spurting cream, a drop of watery liquid trickled out.

The audience laughed.

'Will someone get that bloody cream sorted out,' Hugo yelled into the microphone, 'and tell Gabriella we'll take that introduction again from the top.'

An assistant floor manager appeared with half a dozen cans of cream, which Gabriella and Fergus proceeded to shake and press.

Seizing the opportunity, Mrs Proudfoot stood up and placed her hands on her formidable hips.

'I think we have seen enough. This is monstrous. It must stop at once.'

Sir Norman nodded vigorously. 'I heartily concur. I could not countenance this ever being broadcast.'

Basil Grimshaw delicately cleared his throat, 'Without wishing to sow further dissension in the ranks, I think we should consider seeing the whole programme. I feel it is the only way we can make an informed judgement. Presumably it will be edited at a later stage, allowing for any unfortunate errors to be excised?'

They all looked at Philip, but he seemed to be gazing at something very far away, an unhealthy sheen on his face.

'Is he quite all right?' enquired Mrs Proudfoot.

'Of course he is,' Vanessa snapped, wishing Philip

339

didn't look quite so vacant. 'If you want to leave, you had better go now, or else you must stay for the rest of the recording.'

Mrs Proudfoot looked uncertainly at Sir Norman, but he showed no signs of moving so she sat down again, placing her handbag firmly on her knees.

'Are we ready to go?' Hugo demanded impatiently into his microphone.

On one of the monitors, the floor manager gave the thumbs up sign and then addressed the audience.

'Thank you for your patience, ladies and gentlemen. Now if you look up at the monitors above your heads, you will be able to see the short film which Miss Wolfe is going to introduce.'

The audience craned their necks upwards as Gabriella began the introduction. This time the cream spurted and oozed to Hugo's satisfaction.

'Run insert A,' Rosie instructed, and looking at her stop watch counted, 'five, four, three, two, run VT . . .'

Gabriella and Fergus settled back on their couch to watch.

In the back row of the audience, Alicia gripped Jeremy's arm tightly and closed her eyes for a moment. When she opened them, two out-of-focus figures had appeared on the screen. They both appeared to be female, even if the portly one with her back to the camera and dressed in a tight red corset, was remarkably hirsute and bow-legged for a woman. The second, much slimmer woman, who was completely naked and all fours, was being led around on a leash like a dog.

Up in the gallery, Vanessa had leapt to her feet and was standing beside Hugo. 'What on earth's going on?' she demanded. 'The quality of this film is terrible, I thought it was meant to be about . . .' her voice trailed away as she watched the screen.

The women were now facing the camera and one

was bearded. The second one was wearing a mask, but looked ominously familiar.

'One of those women looks just like Dr Archibald,' Philip said in a strange, singsong voice. He looked over at Vanessa and then back at the screen, screwing up his face as though he was trying to concentrate. 'And isn't that . . .?' He pointed to the screen. The masked figure was now doing a fair imitation of a dog begging.

Vanessa's eyes bulged as she stared transfixed at the screen with her mouth open.

'It's her.' Mrs Proudfoot leapt to her feet and pointed at Vanessa. 'And that drunk.' She grabbed Vanessa's arm. 'Filth, obscenity, Sodom and Gomorrah,' she screeched hysterically.

Vanessa tried to shake her off but Mrs Proudfoot clung to her, shrieking loudly. Vanessa struck her hard across the mouth.

Mrs Proudfoot staggered back in amazement, and then collapsed on to Sir Norman before sliding slowly to the floor.

Down in the studio, pandemonium had broken out. All the journalists were on their feet, yelling questions at Fergus.

He was staring at the screen in astonishment, but then a smile began to spread across his face. He threw back his head and began to roar with laughter.

'Stop it. For God's sake, somebody stop it!' Vanessa yelled, recovering her voice. But nobody moved.

She lunged at the controls, punching switches and buttons. For a few seconds a naked image of her was frozen on the screen, and then everything went black.

At the back of the audience, Alicia smiled serenely and put down the bar of chocolate she had been eating. The taste in her mouth was even sweeter.

One Week Later

• • •

Alicia and Jeremy were sitting up in bed munching cinnamon and raisin Danish pastries, avidly engrossed in the Sunday newspapers.

Alicia suddenly squealed loudly, her mouth full of warm pastry. She gestured at the front page of the *World on Sunday*.

The headline read: TV FANTASY FILM IS REAL SEX SCORCHER.

'A horrified audience watched last Sunday as glamorous 36-year-old brunette divorcee, TV producer Vanessa Swift, and sex doctor Fergus Archibald indulged in torrid full-frontal, sado-masochistic sex games when a home video got muddled up with tapes destined to be part of TV's first sex fantasy show, *Forbidden Fruit*.

'The show's executive producer, Philip Pryce, was rushed to hospital with a suspected heart attack, while members of the TV watchdog committee who had come along to monitor proceedings had to be treated for shock.

'Mrs Mildred Proudfoot, the battling blonde granny who heads a viewers' clean-up campaign, says she will be considering taking legal action on the grounds of obscenity and mental cruelty. But the newly-appointed producer of the show, Vijay Seth, says he intends to carry on with the series, although he may take a new approach to the subject.

'The show's presenter, glamorous transsexual Gabriella Wolfe, whose other life was revealed exclusively to *World on Sunday* readers last week, declined to say if she would remain as the show's star. However, in yet another twist to the story, Gabriella was photographed leaving one of London's most exclusive restaurants with randy doctor Fergus, after an intimate *tête-à-tête* this week.

'There was no comment either from long-legged, lovely Vanessa, the producer with a penchant for dog collars of the canine variety. Our chief showbiz reporter, Eddie Spittle, tracked her down to a luxury hotel in an exclusive resort in the Caribbean, where her personal publicist said she is considering substantial offers from several glamour magazines to do a centrefold spread, complete with dog collar.

'But until sexy Vanessa reveals all once again, we bring *World on Sunday* readers exclusive pictures from the hottest video on town. Turn to pages 2, 3 and 4.'

The pictures were blurred and had been extensively retouched, but they were unmistakably from Vanessa and Fergus's video.

Jeremy looked at Alicia. Her eyes were closed.

'Are you all right?' he asked anxiously. 'You shouldn't let this silly business upset you again.'

Alicia opened her eyes. 'It doesn't. I just caught the smell of someone frying bacon. I'm starving.'

Jeremy inhaled deeply. The smell of tendersweet, sizzling bacon wafted in through the window. His mouth watered.

Alicia swept the newspapers off the bed and rolled over. She kissed him full on the lips.

'How about some eggs . . .' she murmured, nuzzling his neck. Then she began to rain soufflé-light butterfly kisses over his chest, '. . . and some bacon . . .' She worked her way lower, down over his now satisfyingly round stomach, '. . . and maybe some mushrooms . . .'

Jeremy closed his eyes.

A Selected List of Fiction Available from Mandarin

While every effort is made to keep prices low, it is sometimes necessary to increase prices at short notice. Mandarin Paperbacks reserves the right to show new retail prices on covers which may differ from those previously advertised in the text or elsewhere.

The prices shown below were correct at the time of going to press.

All these books are available at your bookshop or newsagent, or can be ordered direct from the address below. Just tick the titles you want and fill in the form below.

Cash Sales Department, PO Box 5, Rushden, Northants NN10 6YX.
Fax: 01933 414047 : Phone: 01933 414000.

Please send cheque, payable to 'Reed Book Services Ltd.', or postal order for purchase price quoted and allow the following for postage and packing:

£1.00 for the first book, 50p for the second; **FREE POSTAGE AND PACKING FOR THREE BOOKS OR MORE PER ORDER.**

NAME (Block letters) ....

ADDRESS ....

....

☐ I enclose my remittance for ....

☐ I wish to pay by Access/Visa Card Number ☐☐☐☐☐☐☐☐☐☐☐☐☐☐☐☐

Expiry Date ☐☐☐☐

Signature ....

Please quote our reference: MAND